A Note on the Author

CELIA IMRIE is an Olivier Award-winning and ~~~~ ~~~~ ~~~~ ~~~ ~~~ ~~~ ~~~~ s best known for her film roles in *The Best Exotic Marigold Hotel*, *The Second Best Exotic Marigold Hotel*, *Calendar Girls* and *Nanny McPhee*. On stage, she won Best Actress in a Musical for *Acorn Antiques: The Musical* and was nominated for Best Actress in *Noises Off*. Celia Imrie's most recent films are *A Cure for Wellness*, *Year by the Sea*, *Bridget Jones's Baby* and *Absolutely Fabulous: The Movie*. Her autobiography, *The Happy Hoofer*, was published in 2011, and her acclaimed *Sunday Times* bestselling first novel, *Not Quite Nice*, was published by Bloomsbury in 2015.

celiaimrie.info   @CeliaImrie

Nice Work
(If You Can Get It)

Celia Imrie

BLOOMSBURY

LONDON · OXFORD · NEW YORK · NEW DELHI · SYDNEY

Bloomsbury Paperbacks
An imprint of Bloomsbury Publishing Plc

50 Bedford Square   1385 Broadway
London   New York
WC1B 3DP   NY 10018
UK   USA

www.bloomsbury.com

BLOOMSBURY and the Diana logo are trademarks of Bloomsbury Publishing Plc

First published in Great Britain 2016
This paperback edition first published in 2017

British Library Cataloguing-in-Publication Data
A catalogue record for this book is available from the British Library.

ISBN: HB: 978-1-4088-7690-9
       TPB: 978-1-4088-7691-6
       PB: 978-1-4088-7694-7
       ePub: 978-1-4088-7692-3

2 4 6 8 10 9 7 5 3 1

Typeset by Integra Software Services Pvt. Ltd.
Printed and bound in Great Britain by CPI Group (UK) Ltd, Croydon CR0 4YY

To find out more about our authors and books visit www.bloomsbury.com.
Here you will find extracts, author interviews, details of forthcoming events
and the option to sign up for our newsletters.

Dedicated to all my friends in the South of France

Part One

RATATOUILLE

Traditionally, a ratatouille has six ingredients:

tomatoes
courgettes
onions
aubergines
garlic
red peppers

These are chopped and dropped into a pan with some hot olive oil, then stirred, covered with a lid and left to simmer until everything joins into one tasty, thick dish.

I

THE SMALL TOWN OF Bellevue-Sur-Mer nestles in a neat inlet on the Mediterranean, in that south-east corner of France known to the British as the French Riviera and to the natives as the Côte d'Azur. A few miles from Nice, these days Bellevue-Sur-Mer is quite self-sufficient, although it was once, and not so long ago, a sleepy fishing village. There are cafés galore, little art galleries, a small casino, beaches, both private and public, chic clothing boutiques and many mini-marts, open all hours and selling everything from fresh fruit to chocolate bars and fishing rods. There is also a *port de plaisance*, where small fishing boats moor alongside pleasure boats. The pleasure boats come in all sizes, from tiny canoes to the gigantic white gin palaces so popular in Mediterranean holiday towns.

The picturesque old houses of the town, mainly small, have little windows protected by colourful shutters that serve two purposes: to keep out the glaring light of the sun in summer and to keep the inside warm in winter. These houses perch along the steep roads and lanes that wind their way, zigzagging up from the sea to the foothills of the Alpes-Maritimes.

Behind everything, mountains, snow-capped for many months of the year, provide a shelter against the north wind and contribute to the wonderful microclimate of the French Riviera.

The major roads above the town – the Highway of the Sun and the Corniche – have been carved through the hills and span the valleys on tall bridges. Branching from the main thoroughfares, smaller roads, busy with shops, lead down to dark alleyways, and vertiginous flights of stone steps take visitors and locals from the bus stops, high in the town, to the bustling shoreline, with its railway station, souvenir shops, brasseries and small pebbly beach.

In winter Bellevue-Sur-Mer is a quiet sort of place.

In summer it buzzes.

And during those times in between ... well, that all depends ...

Festivals and conferences bring people into the area, cruise ships regularly dump thousands of tourists on the shore for the daylight hours of a single day, filling the lanes with dawdling gawpers. Occasionally a huge celebrity visits here, and with them come their entourage, the paparazzi and the fans. Madonna is known to have hired a villa once for the summer vacation, and a single member of One Direction is believed to have briefly rented a place at the top of the town for some weeks after Christmas.

But celebrities are not the only English-speaking inhabitants of Bellevue-Sur-Mer. Like all the beautiful places of the world, from Spain, Italy and France to Australia and Canada, Bellevue-Sur-Mer is home to British and American expatriates: retirees, people on the run from their families or their past, and those who have simply come to escape the dreary, rainy winters. Many are attracted to the warm weather or the food and continental way of life, or seek to follow in the famed footsteps of so many painters, writers and members of royalty, from the Russian tsars to the kings of the Belgians, Henri Matisse to Pablo Picasso and Anton Chekhov to Somerset Maugham.

The South of France has always been very kind to the Anglophone invader. After all, the British, led by Queen Victoria, invented the Riviera as a holiday destination. As a result, there are English newspapers and local radio stations that broadcast in English, telling of cinema screenings, coffee mornings and evening dances.

Wherever they live, many English-speaking residents have satellite dishes beaming in regular doses of *Coronation Street* and *EastEnders*, keeping the roots attaching them to home. There are even a few shops devoted to all things British – these establishments have paintings of Coldstream Guards, Union Jacks and red phone boxes on their doors. One even has a genuine red double-decker bus parked on the fore-court. In these jolly little shops, chino-wearing men, and women in potter's smocks stock up on teabags and marmalade, Marmite and baked beans.

Like expats the world over, the English speakers of Bellevue-Sur-Mer tend to gather.

Straddling the expat community, our particular small band of friends eschew the English way of life, but still spend time with each other.

* * *

Beside the Gare Maritime, right down on the seafront, Theresa Simmonds, a relative newcomer to the town, lives in a small ground-floor apartment; William and his younger partner Benjamin occupy a house up a bit from her. Zoe, an eccentric ex-1960s King's Road dolly-bird, now in her late seventies (or is it more?), has a place a few doors away. Sally Connor, once a celebrity herself, lives in a little house not far from Zoe. And their American friend Carol is staying, for the moment, in the home she had shared with her soon-to-be-ex-husband, who had recently returned to live in the States.

Their French-speaking skills are varied. William, Zoe and Sally, having lived here for many years, are fluent. The others are trying hard to get better, attending classes or avidly watching French TV and listening to local radio.

The sun was out that morning and Theresa slumped into her armchair with a cup of coffee.

She sighed with happiness. Theresa had moved from London to Bellevue-Sur-Mer five months ago. It may have been a short while, but it had certainly been an eventful one, and Theresa was still nursing the remnants of a black eye from an encounter with a burglar a few days ago. Her eye was now an unseemly shade of ochre.

But things were looking up.

Theresa was living here in the South of France after an unwelcome blow from her London boss had put her into early retirement. Although she had received the news of her dismissal only a few months away from her sixtieth birthday, Theresa felt short-changed. These days, didn't people go on working much longer? Old-age pensions didn't start being doled out till you were older, so why were you expected to give it all up? Nonetheless Theresa had found herself out of work and out of luck. She had sold her Highgate house, cashed in her savings and moved to the Côte d'Azur. But now that she was here, just because Theresa was entering her sixtieth year, she didn't want to turn into a couch potato. She wanted to keep active, to be busy. She wanted a purpose, something to strive for, something to keep her stimulated in mind and body. Her vision of moving into old age had never consisted of sitting in a deckchair, sleeping, going on cruises or pottering around in the garden. She wanted to look forward and, as the song goes, 'Open a new window . . . every day'. Just because you were over sixty didn't mean you couldn't still have ambitions.

Three of Theresa's neighbours had big schemes for the future. The whole idea had hatched at a recent party, where she'd got talking to them, and they had discussed starting work on a project together, based here in Bellevue-Sur-Mer.

The plan was to open a small bistro-style restaurant, with Theresa volunteering herself, naturally, as head chef.

On the bus home from the party three of the five had shaken hands on it.

Theresa loved food and cooking and even sitting reading old cookery books, but, she wondered, was this project the right one for her?

For a start it was a hell of a risk and would take up all of her money, including the better part of her recent windfall, and all of her time. If she signed up, there would be no more mornings sitting here, gazing out of the window, sipping coffee. She would be committed to working a six-day week, with late hours, for the foreseeable future.

Theresa was in a quandary – to join or not to join?

She was not alone. Sally, their mutual friend, was also sitting on the fence.

So far, it was suggested that William would supervise the wine, the business affairs and the welcome, and, with his boyfriend Benjamin, he would also oversee the fetching and carrying. Benjamin would work on advertising with Carol. Carol meanwhile would manage the internal ambience – the décor, music, lighting, tableware, etcetera – as well as being in charge of public relations.

Once they opened, William, Carol and Benjamin would run the front of house, acting as maître d' and waiters.

If she did join them, Theresa would be expected to be the obvious chef-in-residence, as she had offered at the outset. If Sally came in with them she had a choice: she could work in the kitchen or be the chief welcoming party and reservations manager, freeing up William to concentrate fully on his favoured duties as a sommelier and bookkeeper.

Benjamin would be jack of all trades, assisting Theresa in the kitchen or William and Carol in the dining room – wherever he was most needed.

If Theresa and Sally decided against joining the project, or it proved too much work for the little band of friends to manage, they planned to hire others to help out. But Theresa worried that it would be a huge task to find someone else to take on the cooking, and secretly she wouldn't want that anyway. It was a conundrum.

This morning they had arranged to meet at her place for breakfast to hear her decision and to share their information.

To get things rolling, the gang still had to find the perfect premises. Somewhere small, preferably with a previous licence and a decent aspect.

The meeting was due to start in ten minutes, but meanwhile Theresa was enjoying sharpening up her French-language skills by reading the local paper, a dictionary at her side.

The headlines and many pages today were full of one thing only – the preparations for the upcoming film festival at nearby Cannes. There were detailed articles about the stars who were going to make up the panels and the jury and more about the films that had been chosen to compete for the prestigious Palme d'Or. Quite a glamorous array of Hollywood faces covered the front page. Theresa was a particular fan of the American actress Marina Martel, who was topping the array of A-listers due to be at the festival.

On an inside page Theresa found an article about a man who owned a tiny bistro in a hillside village not far from Bellevue-Sur-Mer (and many miles away from Cannes) who had found fame last year when George Clooney and Leonardo DiCaprio arrived unannounced late one evening, after attending some screening at the film festival, wanting dinner. The ensuing brouhaha had made the man's restaurant so popular that during the following months the owner had had to squeeze in extra tables and lay on additional staff to cope with the long list of reservations. Now local people and tourists were booking tables there six months in advance and a Michelin star was predicted.

This all seemed rather odd to Theresa, rather like shutting the stable door after the horse had bolted. Surely the would-be diners had missed their chance of seeing the famous stars? Or was it a case of: if it's good enough for George and Leo, it's good enough for me?

If only they could guarantee something like that happening, it would take a bit of the risk out of it.

Still, even if she didn't join them, there was no harm in helping the others – in an advisory capacity, maybe.

Theresa grabbed a pencil and wrote the word 'publicity', rather than just 'advertising'. Word needed to be spread, and nowadays celebrities were the easiest way to get newspaper coverage. Someone would have to be in charge of ideas about that kind of thing. Carol, perhaps, as she had a sense of flair and fashion and an enviable way of charming the birds from the trees.

Publicity was a strange beast. No one seemed to be able to control it, and it caused misery for many, but sometimes it worked in your favour, as in the case of that hillside bistro.

Now Theresa was already wishing that some similarly serendipitous event might bring this projected 'dream' restaurant success.

A sharp rapping on the door jolted Theresa out of her reverie. She looked at her watch.

As usual, William and Benjamin had arrived on the dot.

Theresa welcomed them in and they took their places around her wrought-iron and glass table while she fixed a fresh pot of coffee.

William pulled out paper, pads and pencils and happily arranged them in front of him, while Benjamin went to the kitchen to help Theresa, fetching cups and saucers. Theresa brought to the table a tray of rolls she had baked early that morning.

'Carol phoned yesterday to say that the owner of that filthy café behind the station is thinking of selling.'

William took a large pot of jam from his bag and plonked it in the centre of the table.

'I thought we were only looking for classy locations?'

'The station is busy, William,' said Benjamin. 'Lots of passing trade.'

'Is that the kind of trade we're after?' said William. 'Lazy tourists who're looking for a bag of chips or an ice cream for the beach?'

Theresa's guests started buttering their rolls and she sat.

'I suppose somewhere is better than nowhere.'

'Don't be daft, Theresa. You only get one chance at a first impression. It's do or die; we'd be better on the seafront, or in one of those high-up streets, somewhere with a terrace and a view.' William popped the jam jar open, letting the *framboise* fragrance escape, and started spreading the jam thickly on to his roll.

'Beggars can't be choosers, William,' said Benjamin. 'You know how hard it is to get any property round here, especially at this time of year.'

'Anyhow, where is Carol?' William sounded vaguely annoyed. 'Always, always late.'

Theresa listened to the two men bickering and her mind was made up.

She would not join them.

She would wait a few weeks and hopefully something else would come along to keep her busy.

Before she spoke up, the phone rang. It was Sally.

'I know you're having the meeting around now,' said Sally. 'I've thought long and deep and I've decided not to be part of it.'

William was up and standing at Theresa's shoulder, listening in. He grabbed the receiver. 'What do you mean, you don't want to be part of it?'

'It's just not my kind of thing, I'm afraid, William. But seriously, if you need help further down the line, I'd be glad to be of assistance if I can. Good luck.'

She ended the call.

Theresa returned to the table. She didn't dare mention her doubts now and leave them in the lurch without a chef.

'Oh God!' Benjamin put his face into his hands. 'How bloody disappointing. I was sure she'd join us.'

'I wouldn't touch that place by the station. Frankly, I think you'd do better converting this place into a restaurant,' said Theresa, sitting.

'And where would you sleep? A caravan at Le Camping?'

'Do we want to catch some of this summer's trade or not?' Benjamin stood and poured coffee for everyone. 'We'd be mad to hang about till we find the right place and open in the winter when there isn't the influx of tourists to give us good write-ups on TripAdvisor.'

'Or bad ones,' said William.

'I see your point, William,' shrugged Theresa. 'It is already May. You've got a lot to do very quickly.'

'If we go for the station place, you can count me out,' said William, deliberately smoothing back his hair. 'I'm not running a burger bar.'

'If you *don't* go for the station place, you can count *me* out,' said Benjamin, pursing his lips into a tight knot. 'I want to get on with it, *now*. I will not miss the tourism boat.'

Theresa shut her eyes for a second. Was this what it was going to be like for the next year and beyond? The more they went on, the more convinced she was not to join them. She certainly did not want to be in the middle of endless spats between William and Benjamin for the rest of her life.

She picked up her pen. 'You haven't got anywhere yet,' she said. 'For the moment why don't you concentrate on the facts, figures and legal stuff?'

'Fine with me,' said William. 'Let's get on with it.'

Benjamin looked markedly at his watch and said, 'What on earth is keeping Carol? Too busy touching up her lipstick, or maybe she lost a false eyelash?'

Theresa took a deep breath.

Tall, elegant and blonde, Carol was a very snappy dresser. In the style stakes she was unbeatable. Only a few months ago Carol had appeared to be the perfect wife, in a perfect couple, but a minor dalliance had led her husband to employ a private investigator. What the detective uncovered was more than her husband was bargaining for – for Carol had, in fact, been born a boy. After writing to all

Carol's friends to spill the beans, her husband had packed up and left.

But her friends let the news wash over them without a qualm. To them all, Carol was still the most beautiful, stylish and dashing gal in town, and that was that.

So well did they take the news that they had never mentioned the letter since, and Carol still had no idea that her secret had been rumbled.

'Forget Carol for the moment,' said William. 'The legal stuff is hell. The French are very formal and ever so fond of red tape.'

'They can't be worse than the English,' said Benjamin.

'They can,' said William.

'Oh, sure.' Benjamin laid down his pen. 'I'm certain it would be easier to get a late-night drinks licence in Newton Poppleford . . . not.'

'I've done the research,' said William. 'I know what I'm talking about.'

'I've done the research,' mimicked Benjamin in a childish voice. 'Blah-blah-blah!'

Theresa felt her stomach go into knots. This domestic squabbling was extremely embarrassing and not a good sign for the future.

'More coffee?' she asked, hoping to break up the marital spat. 'We can't really make any decisions while she's not here, can we?'

For all her style and glamour, Carol was not quite the queen of etiquette. She was now over twenty minutes late for the meeting and Theresa wished she would hurry up and arrive, if only to balance things out a little.

'It's all pie in the sky, anyhow,' said William. 'Because until we get an address we can't even start on any of the legal stuff.'

There was a loud rapping on the front door.

'This'll be her,' said Benjamin.

Theresa opened up.

It was the postman, who handed over a packet too large for the letterbox and scooted off.

Theresa took the packet and dropped it on the sofa before returning to the table

'That's it!' William stood, sweeping all his pens and papers into his folder. 'What's the point?'

'I'll call her.' Benjamin whipped out his mobile phone and started stabbing at the screen.

'So, Theresa, are you in or out?' William was making a thing of drumming his fingers theatrically on the glass tabletop in front of him, demanding a reply.

She had made up her mind. She was out.

She opened her mouth to speak, glanced out of the window and did a double-take. Carol was there, sitting on the harbour wall, chatting gaily with a debonair well-dressed stranger who must have been all of twenty years old.

Theresa dared not tell William and Benjamin. Instead she moved back towards the front door, opened it and took a step outside, using the palm of her hand to shield her eyes from the sun's glare.

It really was Carol. A woman came and joined her and the young boy. She couldn't be sure, but it looked like the estate agent who had sold Theresa this flat. The woman shook hands with Carol, handed her some papers and a pen. Carol signed, handed the papers back and the estate agent walked away.

Oh Lord! thought Theresa. Please don't let Carol have just locked them in to the ropy place by the station.

As Theresa watched, Carol stood up and held out a gloved hand to the young man. She still had not seen Theresa. She shook hands now with the man and gave him a coy smile, then she strode across the road towards Theresa's front door, tossing her hand into the air to give him a backward wave.

Theresa could hear Carol's mobile phone ringing, but Carol was ignoring it – just walking right on. Behind her, in the front room, she heard Benjamin say, 'She's not answering. I hope she's all right.'

When Carol saw Theresa she quickly put her finger to her lips and made a face of 'don't say anything'.

'Theresa, darling!' Carol called. 'I hope the coffee is brewing.'

William lurched into position behind Theresa. Theresa could feel his hot breath on the back of her neck.

'You're fired!' he snapped. 'That's it. Enough! No more amateurs. Too late.'

Theresa removed herself from buffer position and went back inside her apartment.

Carol kept walking till she met the solid wall of William's chest, then, like a showgirl, raised a hand and pushed him back into the flat, shushing all the while.

When the door was firmly closed behind her she spoke.

'I've done it. All signed and sealed. I know I should have consulted you, but there wasn't time, I had to grab the chance ...'

William threw his file into the air, and a shower of pieces of paper, clips, pencils and pens rained down on them as he said: 'Well, while you weren't here we all decided against the place by the station. So if you've signed for it you'll have to buy it all on your lil' ol' ownsome.'

'Oh Lord!' said Carol, flopping down on to the sofa. 'How foolish do you think I am?'

'We were meant to be meeting today to decide strategy.' Benjamin sidled up behind William, putting on a show of solidarity with his partner now that they shared a common enemy – Carol.

Theresa nodded. What could she say? This was not the moment to drop another bombshell on them.

'Does anyone remember the old widow Magenta?' asked Carol.

They all remained silent.

'Exactly!' said Carol after a significant pause. 'No one remembers her, because she's dead and before that she was in a retirement home for an absolute age.'

'What's she to do with anything?' asked Benjamin.

'No one remembers her little restaurant, which shut a few years ago?'

'What restaurant?' William blinked carefully, awaiting enlightenment.

'It's a nice place, but it hasn't been a restaurant for eight years, or more,' said Carol. 'Today it's that vile little giftshop, selling buckets and postcards and "I heart Côte d'Azur" fridge magnets.'

'I see! So we're moving into the tourist giftshop business are we, dear?'

'Darling!' Carol sighed. 'For such a clever man, William, you really are being remarkably slow.' She pulled a piece of paper out of her bag. 'Everything is still there in the kitchen. It's only the dining room that's currently full of spinning postcard racks. Backstage, so to speak, there's a pizza oven, a large griddle, an eight-ring stove, an industrial-size fridge-freezer, pots, pans, ladles . . . Need I go on?'

'And how long have you tied us into this "dream location"?'

'That's the joy,' said Carol. 'I've just been speaking to the old lady's grandson, Costanzo, a very personable young man. He inherited the place when he was still a child. Now he's of age he can't wait to get it off his hands. He realises property matters take a few months, so we have a lease to rent the place for six months. At some moment during that time he's going to put it on the market and we have first refusal to buy at the asking price.'

'What's the catch?' said Benjamin.

'No catch,' said Carol. 'I have the contract here.' She waved the paper and flourished it in the air. William whipped it from her hand.

'Nothing can be as perfect as this sounds,' he said, peering down at the paperwork.

'Do you know what I think?' Theresa spoke as firmly as she could. 'I think we should stop talking about it and go to see.' She reached for her door-keys. 'As I remember, in French law there's always a cooling-off period, so, while we still have the chance to change our minds, let's go and decide whether or not we need to make use of it or plunge straight in.'

2

S ALLY CONNOR PUT DOWN the phone and cursed Facebook.

How many years had she lived in Bellevue-Sur-Mer, happy as a lark, almost forgotten by old enemies back in England? Nine, that's how many, and by now she really thought she had made a new life for herself, and had totally left the old one behind.

Although she'd once been a well-known face on English TV, even the hundreds of English tourists who rolled off the cruise ships in the nearby port and trudged past her in the street no longer recognised her.

Sally had given up her acting life and now lived happily in Bellevue-Sur-Mer. She was a fluent French speaker, although she knew her accent gave her away.

Sally lived alone in a small salmon-pink house with pale-green shutters, which opened to reveal a wide panorama of ultramarine blue sea. Her cobbled street was a narrow cul-de-sac to vehicular traffic, so that the only cars that came past were looking for a parking space. But Sally loved to walk everywhere. Her front door was only minutes away from many friends.

In Bellevue-Sur-Mer, Sally was surrounded by real-life flesh-and-blood friends, not the virtual 'click-here-to-like' variety.

Bellevue-Sur-Mer was her safe haven.

In Bellevue-Sur-Mer she was free.

She was only on Facebook under orders of her children – to instant-message her daughter Marianne, or to click 'Like' every time her son Tom uploaded one of his paintings or talked about some exhibition he was showing in. But now, thanks to putting herself online, she had been tracked down, and, worse than that, discovered by the one person she would most like to have left behind.

Jackie Westwood had always called herself Sally's 'best friend'. Ever since they first worked together at Salisbury Playhouse, where they had both appeared in the musical *Cabaret*, Jackie had owned Sally in a way that was inescapable. But, far from being supportive and kind, Jackie never had a good word to say about anything Sally ever did. She gleefully wrote to her offering sympathy for Sally's bad reviews in a play. When Sally won a small but coveted role in a television soap, Jackie phoned to ask why, when she had such potential, had she 'sold out', and after she played a well-received interpretation of Natasha in Chekhov's *Three Sisters*, Jackie came round to the dressing room and gave her 'helpful' notes on how she could tweak her performance into better shape.

At the time Sally had believed that Jackie meant well; after all, she was very much more successful than Sally was. Or at least it felt that way.

When they first met in rep at Salisbury, Jackie was playing the lead role, Sally Bowles, while Sally was a Kit-Kat girl – or, essentially, chorus.

That relationship, star and chorus girl, had stayed with them through the years, even when Sally achieved great fame, enough to get her face plastered over every women's magazine on the bookstand. But as Jackie pointed out, this was only because Sally had rejected her classical training and was 'wasting' her talents in pursuit of the wicked TV god, Mammon, while Jackie maintained her 'important' highbrow career playing Hedda Gabler at the Byre Theatre, St Andrews and following that up with a 'controversial' interpretation of Rosalind in *As You Like It* at an open-air theatre outside Chester.

At the time all those arguments seemed very plausible but, for Sally, the effect of Jackie's comments was always pain.

Giving up the business to be a wife and mother had been one level of escape, but Sally had still been plagued by phone calls in which Jackie told her in great detail about the work she had, always adding, 'I bet you wish it was you, don't you, Sal?'

For Sally, one of the biggest delights of moving to France after her husband died had been losing all contact with people like Jackie.

Now Jackie had not only made contact for the first time in twenty years but was asking Sally if she could come and visit. She needed somewhere 'supportive' to stay, Jackie said, as she had a heavy fortnight ahead attending the première of 'a little film' she had starred in which was to be a feature of this year's Cannes Film Festival.

Another thing weighing on Sally's mind was the restaurant project. It had all seemed such a good idea when they were at the party and drunk. But today she knew she should not join the others. It was their kind of thing, but it really was not hers.

She made the call.

Afterwards the relief was palpable.

Sally opened the front door and let in a blast of sun-drenched air. The sea was like an azure silk throw, sparkling with diamonds. It was time for a walk to clear her head.

She grabbed her purse and keys and started running down the narrow alleyway that led to the old port.

As she skidded round a corner she bumped into Zoe.

'Jog! Jog! Jog!' Zoe was coming up the hill in full evening dress. Sally's watch read 9 a.m. 'But for all that exertion *sportif*, Sally, you never seem to get any slimmer.'

Sally bit her lip. She was usually amused by Zoe's acerbic barbs, but today she wasn't in the mood.

'Where are you coming home from now, Zoe?'

'I attended the May Masquerade Ball last night in Cap Ferrat,' said Zoe.

'A ball that went on till nine a.m.?'

'Don't be ridiculous!' said Zoe. 'I sat on the beach and watched the sun come up with two lovely young men from Brazil. They taught me to samba,' she added, putting a wrinkled hand on her hip and wiggling her pelvis.

'Watch out, Zoe, you'll dislocate something.'

'Oh dear! What's bitten you this morning?'

'Nothing, actually, Zoe. I'm just late. Got to get on.'

'Me too,' cried Zoe. 'Off to the hairdresser's this morning.'

Sally pushed on and bowled down the alley, running all the way till she hit the open air and blazing sun at the seafront. She then strolled across the road to the sea wall and sat with her legs dangling in the water, breathing in the salt air.

Her mobile phone buzzed in her jeans pocket. She inspected it before answering. It was her daughter Marianne, so she picked up.

'Ted's got a writ from Sian, Mum. Could you have a word with her and get her off our backs?'

Sally took a deep breath. So her daughter had run off with her friend's Australian husband and Sally was somehow to sort it out? She felt bad enough being caught in the middle of this mess by being mother of the scarlet woman – Marianne – and had no intention of stirring things up any further with her friend, Sian. It was well known that Ted's wife was a termagant, but Sally felt rather sorry for her and also slightly cross with Marianne. After all, it was also well known that Ted was an incorrigible womaniser. Sally knew that Marianne was not the first of his extramarital dalliances, and she felt sure that she would not be the last.

'What does the writ say?' she asked.

'We have to get out of the house by the weekend and Ted has to take all his things, and Sian's cutting off his allowance.'

Allowance! The man was over fifty years old. He declared himself to be a poet – did that mean that the world (in the form of a wife he was cheating on) owed him a living?

Sally gritted her teeth.

'I think you should do as the writ tells you,' she said. 'It's Sian's home. I don't know why you're there. Aren't you supposed to be a high-powered businesswoman yourself?'

'She sacked me.'

'Naturally!' Cruel as it might be, Sally was glad to have hit the mark. 'You cannot run off with your boss's husband and expect anything else. Unless it's a kick up the backside. If it was me I'd have given you worse.'

She ended the call and turned the phone off. It was going to be one of those days.

What was worse than getting caught up in other people's sordid sex lives? Sally felt happy that she was through all that stuff herself, and no longer interested in romance.

'Madame Connor?'

What now?

Sally turned towards the shadow cast by a tanned man standing on the pavement in tight shorts, trainers and nothing else.

'Jean-Philippe Delacourt. I was your sea-school trainer.' He spoke in French.

Sally stood up. She had indeed taken lessons with Jean-Philippe to get her nautical seaworthiness certificate. But, while wrestling with knots, compasses and charts, she had never really noticed how handsome he was.

They shook hands – here in France the obligatory degree of formality reserved for acquaintances.

'I need someone to be my mate.'

Sally looked at his tanned, muscle-bound, tattooed arms and gulped.

'I am putting a little boat through some tests and the wretched boy who does these things for me has let me down again. I need a qualified person to take the helm. I know you are qualified, having signed your certificate myself. Might you perhaps be free?'

'When?'

'Now!'

Well! That would certainly be one way of getting out of town at the same time as getting a little wind in her hair.

'There's money in it too,' said Jean-Philippe. 'A modest fee.'

Sally smiled. This was more like it, she thought.

'I'm not properly dressed.'

Jean-Philippe laughed, revealing a perfect row of pearly teeth. 'You never were. But don't worry, I have life jackets and wet-weather gear on board. I will need to wear a jacket myself.'

Sally felt excited and relieved that her fluency in the French language enabled her to enjoy his tease.

It seemed a pity to cover up that torso, she thought to herself. But his offer of a few hours out at sea was exactly what she needed today.

'*Allons!*' she said. 'Let's go.'

3

THERESA COULDN'T HELP FEELING disappointed at the first sight of the property Carol had roped everyone into. She could see that the front room of the late Madame Magenta's ex-restaurant, for all its garish displays of novelty beach towels and cheap jewellery, had potential. Clear this stuff out, whitewash the walls and replace the fluorescent-tube lighting with some decent adjustable lamps, and the dining room would be fine.

The kitchen, though, was horrible. The room itself was sizable enough, but the black cookers were ancient, filthy and caked in congealed ten-year-old grease topped with layers of dust. The prehistoric fridge looked as though it had come out of the murderer John Christie's cellar and the pots and pans were thin aluminium rubbish, grubby and full of mouse-droppings.

Unless the whole place was totally stripped and re-fitted with modern cookers, it would never pass even the most superficial inspection.

'Carol,' Theresa asked, trying to sound as polite as she could, 'I thought you said the equipment was good?'

Carol was doing a very bad job of looking cheerful, but even her face betrayed the disillusion she felt. She was realising the absolute folly of having signed before checking. 'He told me it was all new.'

'Then he was a total liar,' said William, holding his hands tight to his chest, as though frightened that if he touched anything he would get leprosy. 'And you, as per usual, were a silly dupe.'

'There's a cellar too,' said Carol in desperation. 'Good for storing wine, and all that.' She reached into her black and white handbag and pulled out a key.

'I wonder how many corpses we'll find buried down there,' said Benjamin, wincing as he squeezed through an open door leading out to the back yard.

Carol unlocked a rickety door, and moved her hands around inside searching for a light switch. She flicked it and there was a loud pop as all the other lamps around them fizzled out.

'Surprise, surprise!' said William. 'The electrics are kaput as well. Well, I'm certainly not going down there to get eaten alive by rats and fleas and heaven knows what else.'

'I have a light,' said Benjamin, pulling a matchbook from his trouser pocket.

William shot him a look. Benjamin had only recently come out of rehab for a drug problem and it was obvious that William had an idea possessing matches might be drug-related.

'Thank you, Benjamin.' Theresa whipped the matchbook smartly out of his hands and walked past him. If William and Benjamin were going to have a row, Theresa would prefer them to have it in their own time. 'They'll be very useful.'

She tore a match from the pad and struck it, then, tentatively, step by step, made her way down the creaking wooden staircase into the darkness. Just as a cobweb brushed her face the match burned down to her nail, and she yelped.

'Are you all right down there?' called Carol from the top of the steps.

'Fine, thanks,' said Theresa, wondering why she was the one who was doing all the scary work, especially as she wasn't even in on the project.

She wiped her face, then lit another match and continued her descent.

The cellar was not damp, but it was very dusty and looked tiny.

'It's not very big,' she cried.

Just as Theresa struck match three and reached the bottom step, a wobbly beam lit the cellar from behind. Carol came quickly down the wooden steps.

'I am now the proud possessor of a "*J'adore Bellevue-Sur-Mer*" flashlight.'

Carol pointed the beam into the darkness. Now Theresa saw why the place had seemed so small. What she had perceived as a brown wall was a stack of large cardboard boxes.

'I wonder what these can be?' said Carol in her thick American drawl.

'Probably lots more lovely novelty gifts,' said Theresa. 'At least you'll never run out of "I heart Bellevue-Sur-Mer" tea towels.'

'What's going on down there?' William called from the top of the steps.

'If you're so interested, come down yourself,' said Carol, digging again in her handbag so that a small beam of light was bouncing all over the floor.

'We've had enough of this, Carol.' William wrapped his jacket tightly round himself. 'You can do what you want. Benjamin and I are going home to do some serious thinking about pulling out of this entire project.'

'Please yourself,' said Carol. 'I've been madly impulsive, I know, but it's my signature on the contract, so I'm the one who'll be liable.'

Theresa could tell that the plan looked like disintegrating or becoming a dreadful millstone round their necks. She could not see how this horrible shop could ever become the cosy little bistro she had been imagining for them all.

'Hold this,' said Carol, thrusting the torch into Theresa's hand. 'I do have a gorgeous Swiss army knife in here somewhere.' After a few seconds more, Carol pulled the knife from the bottom of her bag, quickly flicked open a blade and brandished it in the air. 'Twenty-one functions and at last I've found a reason to use it – apart from opening wine bottles, that is.'

She applied the knife to the top of a four-foot-high carton. Once the cut was made, Theresa helped her pull open the flaps. After removing some wedges of polystyrene padding, all that they could see was a flat stainless-steel surface.

'What *is* that?' whispered Carol.

'We'll have to get the lot off, I think.' Theresa ripped a large strip of cardboard from the side and threw it behind her. Carol joined her and the two tugged, pulled and tore until they had exposed the contents of the box – a brand-new top-quality industrial German oven.

It was an omen, Theresa believed. What good was her money just sitting in a bank? Wouldn't it be more fun to be part of a team, working here, cooking up a storm and maybe, if they were lucky, making a little profit? What else was she going to do with her days? Sit in her armchair and read the papers, and shuffle around in her slippers? What could be worse than that? She might be getting old but that didn't mean she had to give up trying. She wanted to fill her days with rewarding work. This job would be a real challenge. Risky, perhaps, but there was always excitement in taking a risk.

Theresa made up her mind there and then to join the restaurant team.

4

'I DON'T UNDERSTAND.' SALLY hunched up in the wheelhouse of a tiny fishing boat that ran on a small outboard motor. 'Why on earth do you need me to help you with this?'

Jean-Philippe smiled serenely as he swung the wheel round and pushed the throttle, taking the boat up to maximum speed as they pulled out of the harbour and into the bay.

'I saw you there all alone, and I thought I would like you to join me,' he said. 'And, to be truthful, I was let down by someone else.'

Sally felt a little scared. She only knew the man through lessons at his sea school. She knew nothing of his personal life. What if he was a serial killer or rapist?

She hadn't questioned his offer at all and now here she was out at sea with him in control. But unlike the distant days of her helmsman instruction, there would be no record of this journey. She was utterly at his mercy.

Sally smiled and tightened the buckle on her life jacket. 'Shall I take the helm?' she said.

Jean-Philippe shook his head. 'You don't know where I'm taking you,' he replied, opening the throttle and riding into a huge oncoming wave. 'It's the most exclusive place I've ever been to.'

Sally put her head down and made herself extremely busy tidying up the ropes on the rubber fenders.

The small boat took another swerve and was now heading due east.

How many private coves and secret inlets were there along this coast? wondered Sally. How many locked-up estates owned by absentee Russians, Germans, Arabs and Americans where the landing stages led to hidden caves and dark grottoes?

Jean-Philippe pointed. 'That's where we're heading.'

They had been navigating the waves with a fair wind behind them for probably forty-five minutes, Sally estimated. Suddenly she could see a vast cream house perched on a rocky promontory. All the shutters were closed. The villa was surrounded by a high wrought-iron fence topped with sharp-looking golden spearheads.

'It's all locked up,' said Sally.

'I know. All the better for what we have to do.' Jean-Philippe touched Sally's shoulder. 'Take the wheel, please, while I put out the fenders,' he said.

Trying to keep her eyes on him, Sally steered towards the little stone jetty, taking down the speed and running the boat alongside.

She cut the engine.

Jean-Philippe jumped out and wound the fore-line around an iron capstan.

Sally pocketed the keys and threw him the other line.

He held out a hand and helped her on to the concrete landing.

'Follow me!' he ordered, marching away towards a small pine wood behind the house.

Sally started undoing her life jacket but he turned and shouted, 'Keep that on. It will be necessary.'

She tried to feel for her mobile phone in her jeans pocket, just in case, but the life jacket was in the way. If she needed to grab for her phone, she couldn't.

'*Allez, allez,*' Jean-Philippe slapped his thigh. 'We're late as it is.'

With some trepidation Sally followed him into the dark copse.

He was walking very fast, so she had to run to keep up with him, then quite suddenly they both emerged from the trees, temporarily blinded by the strong sunlight.

Jean-Philippe stood with his hands on his hips and tossed his head. 'Well, what do you think?'

All Sally could see ahead was a large white wall.

She looked up and from side to side.

'This is the baby we are taking for a test run.'

Sally gaped and realised that the white wall was in fact the side of a huge super-yacht.

'But I thought . . . ?'

'You didn't think that I needed help with that tiny launch? *Non*, this is a private motor-yacht, which we're going to put through her paces.'

Sally couldn't believe her eyes. It was the largest motor cruiser she had ever seen up close.

'What is this?' she asked. 'A three-million super-yacht?'

Jean-Philippe pouted. 'Perhaps more. Seven million-plus.'

'Whose is it? A rock star's?'

He laughed. 'Not many rock stars would bother with this beauty.'

'Then who?'

'She's owned by a Russian zillionaire. Just sold by the owners of the villa behind us.'

'Good Lord!' Sally bit her lower lip. 'And he's trusting you and me to take her out to sea?'

'Uh-huh,' said Jean-Philippe. 'Let's get busy.'

Sally sat at the helm of the mega-yacht.

She felt like a mini-toy, one of those tiny plastic people they put into architects' landscape plans to make the false look real.

Jean-Philippe had walked her around the yacht. Together they explored its four decks and impressive en-suite staterooms, the grand dining room with vast plasma screen and incredible sound system, the swimming pool and jacuzzi, the cosy cocktail bar, the sunbathing decks, the galley – which looked like a luxury kitchen and was three times as big as Sally's own kitchen. When they reached a large nursery with all kinds of rocking horses and teddy bears, Sally asked how many kids the new owner had.

'None, as far as I know,' replied Jean-Philippe. 'But, with his money, no doubt within a week this will be converted into a disco.'

Sally laughed. 'To lure the young ladies he meets on the beaches, I suppose.'

'I imagine his reputation would be lure enough. He's a famous playboy, I'm told. Son of one of Russia's richest oligarchs. Plus of course – and the real reason I am so excited – he just bought my favourite football team: Walsingham Wanderers.' Jean-Philippe chuckled. 'I would like very much to be invited to drinks one night when he has Monsieur David Beckham aboard, or Monsieur Mickey MacDonald. *Mon Dieu*, my heroes of *le foot*!'

'I'm sorry; you've lost me. I don't follow football.' Sally sat on a cream leather chair, trying to pump up the height so that she could actually see through the multiple windscreens. Around her were so many electronic displays, each showing a different thing – radar, sea depth, fishing shoals, satnav maps and charts . . . and the rest – that she didn't know where to look. It was more like NASA HQ than a boat. What's more, before this, the largest boat she had ever seen was her own 28-foot sports boat, which had nothing more than a key, two thrust handles and a small radar display.

From her position, balanced on the edge of the seat, holding a small steering joystick, the sea seemed so far away.

'Jean-Philippe? Do you really know how to get this thing moving?'

Sally could see that Jean-Philippe himself appeared to be rather fazed by the size of the boat and its complex controls. He was kneeling, slowly moving along from screen to screen, inspecting each of them one by one.

'What happens if we crash it?'

Jean-Philippe made a small noise from the back of his throat, then said calmly, 'We only have to take it to Cannes and back.'

'What do we do in Cannes?' asked Sally. 'Please don't say we have to take it into that port and try to moor it with all the tourists staring up at us.'

'No,' said Jean-Philippe. 'We have to pull in, pick up the owner and take him out for a run.'

'If he's rich enough to own this, he must already have a team of people to drive it, doesn't he?'

'That's the thing,' said Jean-Philippe, taking the other helm seat, at last happy that he recognised the purpose of all the controls. 'He only bought the boat yesterday. He hasn't even seen it yet.'

Sally was open-mouthed. 'How could anyone buy something so enormous as this before even going aboard?'

'I'm told he made a lot of money by buying some painting, a Van Gogh or a Matisse or a Picasso, or something really famous like that. He put it into a bank vault for five years, then took it out and made a cool twenty million. He bought this with the change.'

Sally sighed. 'To those that have . . . Though I rather disapprove of paintings being locked in the dark and used only as investments, don't you?'

'I don't think about it.' Jean-Philippe shrugged, turned some knobs and flicked some switches on the massive control panel. 'Your disdain would show on your face, and you end up losing the job.'

Sally apologised.

'Don't worry. In this case, hopefully he will be so busy exploring his new baby that he won't be that interested in what we're doing. But we'll both get a good day's pay out of it.'

Jean-Philippe turned on the engines.

'Now, Madame Sally – you can choose whether to stay here at the controls, or go out and cast off.'

Sally made her way out on to the aft deck.

5

Theresa was in her worst clothes, complete with apron and rubber gloves, clearing rubbish into an area near the front door, ready for collection. She couldn't believe how Carol could make even dungarees look glamorous. She was decked out like a modern-day Hollywood version of Rosie the Riveter, in blue jumpsuit and red and white polka-dotted head-scarf. A transistor radio in the adjacent shop was blasting out French pop songs and Carol was happily singing along.

'Those two boys are such wimps,' Carol said, tearing open a cardboard box and pulling out a handful of coloured plastic windmills. 'Look at all the marvellous stuff we have to find a home for!' She whirled around making the sails spin. 'Do you think there's a children's orphanage near here or somewhere that would like them?'

Theresa looked around at all the piles of postcards, badges, T-shirts and ornamental ashtrays. 'It would certainly be nicer to find someone who'd like to have a bit of fun with all this rather than just dump it in a skip with the rotten stuff.'

Theresa was on her knees ready to start pulling up the hardboard beneath the lino to see how the floor looked underneath. Carol knelt behind her.

'Let's do this,' said Theresa.

'Please God, let it be parquet,' said Carol.

'One two three – pull.'

The two women stared down at a dusty grey surface.

'What is that? Concrete?'

'I'm not sure,' said Theresa, turning around in her squatting position to grab a dustpan and brush.

'I'll need to make use of another lovely souvenir flashlight key-fob,' said Carol, jumping to her feet and rifling through a nearby box. 'Here.'

She handed Theresa the tiny torch and together they yanked the board up again. Theresa gave the exposed area a quick dust-off, then Carol turned on the beam.

Both women gasped.

'Is it real?' Carol knocked it with the end of the torch.

'It's beautiful,' said Theresa, running her fingers along the surface of a turquoise mosaic floor. 'Quite modern-looking,' she said with a sigh of relief. 'I don't think we'll have the archaeologists down here shutting the place down for months while they dig for Roman artefacts.'

'Cover it up again.' Carol dropped the end of the lino. 'It's a lovely colour, that blue. We could match the décor to that floor and create quite a cool ambience.'

Theresa smoothed the lino back down into the corners. 'And we certainly want it well protected when we get the old kitchen stuff dragged out.'

'I think it's time for a tea break, darling,' said Carol. 'We'll have this room empty by aperitif time, so let's get the men in to clear the kitchen later, then we can spend the whole week scrubbing and painting it, ready for the electricians to put in the new equipment.'

Theresa agreed. It was important to get the kitchen installed as soon as possible so that all the necessary certificates could be obtained.

'Let's spend an hour at my place, phoning plumbers and electricians.'

'And we'll see whether there are any local shops who might like the old stuff.'

'And if no one wants to pay us for it, let's give it to a charity.'

Carol thrust out her hand. 'Let's shake, partner! To the restaurant. What shall we call it, by the way?'

'Thinking caps on!'

The two women shook.

Stanislav Serafim stood waiting on the quay at Cannes. He was in his fifties, six foot tall, with black hair and dazzling blue eyes. He had one of those sly Sean Connery smiles, the lips slightly cocked upwards on one side, a perfect physique – and decked out, by the look of the sleek cut, from head to toe in Armani.

Sally quite melted at the sight of him.

She threw out a rope for him to catch and loop round a capstan.

He grabbed it, then, to her surprise, instead of tying it, simply leapt aboard.

From all her sea-going lessons she knew he had just broken a golden rule. She wondered whether Jean-Philippe would have given him a telling-off?

Once aboard, Mr Serafim reached out to take her hand. Did she imagine it or did he give her a little wink?

'It's as beautiful as I imagined,' he said in excellent English.

'How did you know . . . ?'

'I heard you say "oops". A Frenchwoman would have said "*ouf*", or something else. You are English, are you not?'

'I am English born and bred,' said Sally. 'And have a passport to prove it.'

Stanislav smiled and strolled into the large rear lounge, sliding his sunglasses down his nose to see better. He glanced at his watch. Sally noticed his elegant hands; she realised she hadn't taken her eyes off him.

'We'd better hurry up. I have a lunch date with a very important person.'

Sally escorted him along the plush pristine carpets through to the control room, where Jean-Philippe obeyed his boss's instruction and revved the vessel up to its effortless speed.

'You aren't going to ask who?' said Mr Serafim.

'It seems impolite,' said Sally.

'I want you to ask,' the Russian replied.

'So, Monsieur Serafim, with whom are you taking lunch today?'

'Marina Martel.'

Sally laughed. 'Wow!'

'You think I don't know anybody so renowned?' Stanislav put on a chagrined expression, then he too laughed. 'You're right, madame. I do not know her . . . yet. But I have offered to put some money into her latest project, a film she wishes to direct. Today she flies into Nice and we're meeting there to discuss it over lunch at the Negresco.'

'How exciting!' said Sally. 'I adore her films. She is a great star. I suppose she's over for the film festival?'

'I know nothing about the movie business,' said the Russian. 'I know only oil. But I believe she is buying an estate here.'

Sally was on the verge of informing him that she had once been an actress and did know a fair bit about how it all worked, but decided against it. Today she was strictly here as someone helping her instructor drive a boat. Delivering the owner to the bridge, Sally then stood behind Jean-Philippe, ready to help operate the controls.

Mr Serafim turned to Sally.

'Now you could bring us a pot of tea.'

Sally was about to tell him to get it himself, when she caught eyes with Jean-Philippe, who slightly inclined his head, meaning 'just do it'.

Sally realised that, for all her qualifications as an ex-actress and a helmswoman, this morning she was, in effect, a servant. She made her way down into the galley, where she found a teapot, a kettle and a packet of tea. There was no milk in the fridge, so she hoped he liked it black. But there was an unopened packet of biscuits in one of the cupboards. She lay everything out on a small tray and carried it through to the helm. The way Stanislav, a Russian, spoke English reminded her of a line from Shaw's *Pygmalion* in which she had played Clara Eynsford-Hill up in

York: 'Can you show me any Englishwoman who speaks English as it should be spoken? Only foreigners who have been taught to speak it speak it well.'

She stood in the galley for a while, wiping down the tops, then made her way up to the aft deck and sat alone, gazing out on to the boat's wake cutting a white path through the navy-blue sea, letting the morning sun beat down on her face.

There were worse ways to earn a living.

Theresa and Carol were at Theresa's flat, busily circling names in the *Pages Jaunes*, when Theresa's phone rang.

It was Imogen, Theresa's daughter.

'We'll be coming out for half term,' she shouted down the line. 'Which is in about three weeks. To house-hunt.'

Theresa said, 'How lovely. Whenever you like.'

'So if you could gather any details and get a list of properties ready, that would be good,' Imogen barked. 'I'll have my work cut out getting everything arranged this end, but now that you're retired . . .'

Theresa decided against telling her daughter that she was herself very, very busy trying to get a new restaurant created, organised and open in record time.

She hoped to agree with her, say she was doing everything, then do nothing till the day before Imogen arrived, when she could rush around and quickly gather some details of places to look at. After all, it would be folly getting leaflets for flats that were for sale now – within those three weeks they might well be sold.

'Maybe, Imogen,' she said aloud, 'you could first have a little look online, and sort out which type of places interest you.'

'When would I find the time for that? Mummy! Do you know how busy I am now that I'm a single parent? And, after all, you're the one with expertise in the matter.'

'I'm looking forward to you coming out here,' said Theresa. 'And to seeing the children. Will you stay with me, or shall I get you rooms at the Hôtel Astra?'

'Don't be silly, Mummy. We wouldn't want to put you to any expense.' Imogen laughed. 'I'm sure you can find room for us in the flat – if you haven't any murderers staying, of course.'

Theresa clenched her teeth. Yes, Imogen was right; Theresa had made an error of judgement in her last lodger, but all her friends here in the town had been taken in too. She glanced across at Carol, who was sitting at the table, going through the *Pages Jaunes*, underlining names and numbers. She had just about lost everything as a result of having the wool pulled over her eyes by the same conman.

'Look, Imogen, I've got Carol over to lunch today and it's a bit rude to be chatting to you. Let's talk later.'

After a few more parting comments, Imogen hung up.

Carol grinned. 'After those Goodwill people come and pick up the things and the men take away the old machines, let's hire a car. If I had any money I'd buy one. But if we get a car this afternoon we can buy paint and scrubbing brushes and all that stuff, bring it back here and then if we're suffering from insomnia we can work overnight.'

'Let's stick to organising this place this afternoon. We can get a car first thing in the morning.'

'OK,' said Carol. 'I see your point. Let's get back to clearing.'

'Actually, Carol, we'd be better going there by bus. It takes you right to the door and it will save us about a hundred and fifty euros.'

'It won't cost us anything,' Carol smiled. 'We just give the receipt to William and it goes on the company account.'

'We are the company account, Carol. Every cent we spend is set against our profit, i.e., what we get paid.'

'So how will we carry all those tubs of paint back here?'

'We'll take a taxi. It'll be much cheaper than hiring a car.' Theresa indicated the markings in the phone book. 'What about arranging the plumbers and electricians, etcetera? We need to get them organised.'

'Do you know any? Who were those nice men who did this place?'

'Oh yes, he was very sweet. I got him through the estate agent. Now I think about it, she told me that he runs a whole building company – brickies, electricians, carpenters, the lot.' Theresa got up and rummaged through a drawer in the kitchen. 'I've got his invoice somewhere, with the guarantee.'

She pulled out a piece of paper.

'Here we are!'

Theresa dialled the number. After a slow stammering start from Theresa, in her intermittent French, the plumber put his wife on the line. She spoke rather good English with an extremely thick and guttural French accent. Theresa explained everything, and asked whether Monsieur Leroux could have a look over the place and give them an estimate. By lucky chance, he was on his way to Bellevue-Sur-Mer now, his wife replied, to look at another job his firm were doing. Would she be there at the property in the next half hour?

Theresa assured her she would.

'*Ah, mais . . .*' Madame Leroux made a harsh noise of regret. 'He has a big job starting. He could begin in two months' time.'

At the end of the call Carol flicked through the *Pages Jaunes* again. 'William won't be happy unless we get some rival quotes.' She sighed. 'Do you have a computer? There's a website where you can find English-speaking builders, you know. Wouldn't that be easier all round? No misunderstandings?'

As Theresa fired up the laptop, Carol opened her diary.

'Two months. That's a long time.'

Carol took the phone and tried a few numbers. She chatted gaily with two Englishmen and arranged for them to come to give estimates that evening.

When they got back, Monsieur Leroux was waiting outside the front door of the restaurant-to-be.

'*Le chauffage, il marche bien?*' he enquired.

Theresa understood that he was talking about the boiler and heating in her flat, and assured him that he had done a fine job.

She opened up and let him in.

The boxes of plastic windmills and tea towels had toppled over, and their contents were spread again over the floor.

'What the . . .' said Carol, stepping around the mess.

'It'll be kids,' said Theresa. 'I'll show Monsieur Leroux around.'

Carol started cramming the things back into boxes while Theresa took Monsieur Leroux into the kitchen. He peered down at the pipework, rubbing his chin. Theresa led him down to the cellar and showed him the new machinery.

He totted up some figures and scribbled them on to a scrap of paper which he handed to Theresa. It was a lot less than she had expected.

'*Mais . . . Je commencerai juillet?*'

'*Pas possible avant?*' said Theresa, hoping that she was saying 'not possible before'.

He departed with another handshake, leaving her with the decision whether to take up his offer to start work in two months' time – July.

Shortly afterwards a squat Brummie came, looked at the space and did much the same thing, and half an hour later a lanky Liverpudlian ran his fingers through his hair many times, and shook his head while making a sucking-in sound as he inspected the existing pipework.

They'd both need to do some sums, they said, and would put their estimates in writing, then drop them through the door tomorrow.

Sally trudged up the hill clutching a fistful of euros for her day's sunbathing (as she had not done much else it seemed a good way to think of the earnings). After tying the boat up, and driving them all back to Bellevue-Sur-Mer in Jean-Philippe's little boat, the smarmy Russian had given her another of those sparkly-tooth smiles as he bade her farewell. A few moments later, as the Russian climbed into a waiting black-windowed limo, Jean-Philippe had slipped the roll of notes into her handbag.

She thrust the money to the bottom of her bag, while pulling out her keys. As she looked up, she could see some woman sitting on the step of her front door. It was a shaded spot on an otherwise sunny street; many tourists sat there while reading maps or messages on their mobile phones. Sally sighed. She hated having to ask them to excuse her for going into her own house. They rarely responded with an apology, more a tut of irritation as though she was ruining their holiday. She shook her keys around a bit, trying to issue a warning, and moved forward till her shadow fell across the woman, who looked up.

'I'm so sorry,' said Sally, nodding towards her front door.

The woman clambered to her feet, broke into a grin and cried: 'Darling!'

Sally blinked in the evening sunlight.

'It's me, sweetie. Jackie!'

Sally was aghast. 'But you only rang this morning ...'

'I was phoning from Nice airport. Oh, sweetie, I should have explained myself better. Pip, pip, and all that! Dying for a cuppa. Let's go in and I'll tell you all.'

As Sally opened up she noticed that Jackie had a suitcase with her.

'Cup of tea?' Sally stepped inside, helping Jackie with the suitcase, which was surprisingly heavy.

'I wondered what had happened to you, actually. I must have arrived a mere hour after I called.' Jackie pulled out a chair and sat without being asked. 'Still, I managed to have a little wander round your pretty village. It's ever so nice. Though I have to say, I couldn't live here myself. I'd feel totally cut off from reality.'

'That depends, Jackie,' – Sally was filling the kettle – 'on what you consider "reality".'

'Well, the business, for one.' Jackie paused while she clicked open her case.

Sally filled a tray with some biscuits and the pot of tea.

Jackie had started pulling out large buff envelopes.

'These are some of my flyers,' she cried as she dropped a handful of them on the table. 'Perhaps you'd like to join me tonight, distributing them round Cannes?'

'Cannes is some way away, you know,' said Sally, hoping to get out of it.

'Oh, don't worry, old chap, I've looked it all up. It's just a chug away on the train.' Jackie slid a brightly coloured leaflet from one of the envelopes.

'Really, Jackie. You'd be much better to start fresh in the morning. It's a law of ergonomics, you know.'

'I say, old girl, where did you pick up lingo like that? Ergonomics indeed!'

Sally wondered where Jackie had picked up her own 'lingo'.

'So you didn't manage to find a hotel then?'

'Oh, Sally darling, don't be absurd. That would be so boring. It's going to be such fun catching up. We're going to have many glorious larks, old chum.'

Sally took a gulp of tea, and smiled wanly.

Part Two

TOMATES à la CHAPELURE

Ingredients
6 tomatoes
4 cloves chopped garlic
2 diced anchovy fillets
50g breadcrumbs
1 teaspoon chopped fresh parsley and another of basil
salt and pepper
olive oil

Method
Cut the tomatoes in half, remove pips, sprinkle with salt, rinse. Place on a well-oiled baking tray and pop into a warm oven (90–100°C) for about 15 minutes. Mix garlic, anchovies, breadcrumbs and herbs. Lay now-soft tomatoes open side up in a well-oiled baking dish, making sure they are close to one another, filling the bowl. Stuff each tomato with the herb and bread-crumb mixture. Season with salt and pepper and drizzle with olive oil. Bake in a hot oven at 200°C for about 20 minutes or until the edges of the dish caramelise. Eat hot or cold.

6

NEXT MORNING, THERESA AND Carol were climbing on to a bus and heading up to the huge shopping centre at Lingostière to buy scrubbing brushes, large containers of industrial cleaner and pots of paint.

'Sister,' said Carol, raising a hand to Theresa in the passenger seat. 'We rock!'

As they pushed their trolley around the vast *brico-lage* shop, William phoned Theresa.

'Stop everything!' He spoke loudly down the line.

'I'm sorry, William.' Theresa held the phone away from her ear. 'Why do we stop when we know we are in a rush against time?'

'All right,' said William. 'So who pays for all this work if we don't take up the sale? We are effectively doing up a wreck of a property for nothing.'

'We've not spent much, yet.'

'You're there buying paint, which isn't a huge expense, I admit, but it is money going out. If we decide not to continue after the rental period, do we get the money offset against the rent, or our deposit? Have we even paid a deposit? It's all a joke.'

Theresa could see that William was talking sense, but it was difficult to reason with him while standing in a hypermarket, speaking into a mobile phone, and especially when he was on high doh.

'I don't mind covering the paint,' said Theresa. 'And we are saving a fortune doing it ourselves, you know.'

'That's not the point, Theresa dearest. What about the plumbers and electricians? We do need to use professionals or we won't have the necessary certification, as I discovered this morning at the *mairie* . . .'

'We've already got three estimates on the way.'

'How did you do that in the time?' William calmed for a second. 'It's impossible.'

'It does seem unlikely, but we were just lucky. We phoned around twenty but we hooked up with the three builders who happened to be in town, or nearby.'

'You're making it up. I know women like you are prone to fantasy.'

'William! I am standing in the aisle of a supermarket, pushing a trolley full of cans of paint. This is not the time. But I do agree we must talk about it . . .'

William had hardly drawn breath.

'I know Carol doesn't have two rupees to rub together. So I suppose it'll be muggins here—' William went on. 'Therefore, to safeguard myself, today I am consulting a lawyer and putting measures in place by which I can protect my investment.' He left another pause before adding, 'Unless, Theresa, you wish to pull out now.'

Theresa gripped the phone tightly. 'Now calm down, William. I have some money and am due some more very soon. I have already put up the deposit on renting the building and am quite happy to go halves with you on any further outgoings.'

She caught Carol's eye and grimaced.

'It's a hare-brained scheme, anyhow,' William continued. 'Benjamin and I are feeling distinctly out of our depth.'

Theresa could sense that William was going through exactly the kind of jitters she had initially gone through while alone, lying in her bed the night before last. But the morning usually brought sanity. She decided that silence was the best policy.

But William was still at it: 'Shall we go ahead, Theresa – or are we all going to lose our shirts?'

'I wonder, William, if you feel so worried about it, whether perhaps you should pull out now? On my part, I have no desire to lose my shirt or any other part of my clothing. I used to work in the law myself. I know we have to keep strictly within the laws of the land. I realise that we also need a mutual agreement. But I do not believe that we should start to move separately now, one against the other. I want us to be safe, to have a clear contract and to cover ourselves against losses. But as for any extra fripperies of law – I do know how much it costs.'

It was William's turn to be silent.

'Why don't we meet at my place at one o'clock? Bring some bread and cheese.'

'Receipts! *S'il vous plaît*,' said William and hung up.

After putting the phone away Theresa rolled her eyes. 'I don't know why men are so difficult. We know there are risks. But there are risks in everything. Just crossing the road is a risk.'

Carol took control of the trolley and shunted it along at a lick. 'I do wish William would look on the bright side and stop being so pedantic about everything. I mean, Theresa, look at the deal I got us. It's almost too good to be true.'

'You're right.' Theresa ran along at her side, trying to keep up with her. 'Anyhow – let's have a go.'

'And if we fail . . .'

'"We fail? But screw your courage to the sticking place . . ."'

'Ssshhhh, Theresa, don't tempt fate.' Carol crossed her fingers and ducked. 'You've quoted from *that* play.'

'I'm not superstitious,' replied Theresa, steering the front end of the trolley towards the cash desks. 'And anyhow, doesn't it only apply to actors in theatres?'

'Ah, but the restaurant will be our little theatre, really, won't it? We don't want to jinx the place before we start.'

'You're not having doubts, Carol, are you?'

'None. I love a project, especially now, when I've nothing else left in my life. It's so good to keep busy. And, you know, it's exciting!' said Carol, heaving a twelve-litre can of paint from the trolley and dropping it on the checkout's conveyor belt. 'I'm happy as a clam.'

An hour or so later, Theresa stood alone in the potential kitchen of the new restaurant, dropping off the paint and cleaning materials while Carol paid the taxi driver.

William was already there, inspecting the possibilities of the reception space.

'Excellent. You're back. Let's go to your place and talk,' he said calmly.

* * *

Having successfully dissuaded Jackie from an evening's 'jolly old flyer jaunt', Sally found herself, right after breakfast, on a train rattling along overland in the direction of Cannes, listening to the story of her old friend's enormous TV success. 'Five series; any number of BAFTAs and People's Choice Awards, three for me personally, and then the broadcaster decided to pull it. We were all poleaxed, to say the very least. I mean, the ratings were high, we were delivering primetime quality TV on a pretty tight budget and we had totally won the hearts of the British viewer, everything was tickety-boo. The whole matter was a pretty bad show.'

'I thought you said it was a good show?'

'No, I mean, it was pretty bad show of them, the broadcasters – the nasty blighters.' Jackie gave a wry smile. 'Been in the blinking series rather too long, old chum,' she said. 'Got in the way of speaking the lingo, you know, old bean.' She gave Sally a wink and said: 'Plus – it's part of the image, you know. What my public expect.'

'What about the new project?' asked Sally, edging the heavy package of flyers from one knee to the other. 'Is that all tickety-boo too?'

'It's fairly spiffing,' said Jackie, in all earnestness. 'We were on an all-women air crew, delivering planes during World War Two and, after the network went bonkers and we got the elbow, a few of us banded up to make a little drama-doc based on the real-life lady-flyers. Do you like the title? We've called it *The Lady-Birds*.'

'And it's been chosen as part of the main programme at Cannes!' Sally was genuinely impressed. 'Well done!

Will you have to walk up the red carpet in a glamorous gown?'

'Not exactly.' Jackie gave a little cough. 'But we do have a showing in what they call the Marketplace.'

Sally raised her eyebrows.

'If it does well there we could make a lot of money in overseas sales. The European market is pretty huge, but we really want to crack the USA. I mean – look at *Downton Abbey*.'

'I don't get English TV here,' said Sally. 'I'm afraid I've rather missed out on what's going on back at home.'

'Oh, you see, I couldn't bear that.' Jackie made a face of exaggerated horror. 'Being so cut off. Stuck in some postcard-pretty backwater. I need to be in the thick of things.'

Sally resisted the urge to reply, and instead looked out of the train window.

'Oh, look,' she said. 'The *hippodrome*.'

Jackie peered out through the dusty window. 'Is that a theatre?'

'No, old bean, it's a racecourse.' Sally laughed. 'Where they trot.'

They spent the morning wandering around Cannes, getting their bearings while dropping leaflets anywhere that would let them.

'Come on,' said Jackie, 'it's gin slings on me when we're done. What larks!'

As they walked down from the station, the streets were buzzing with people. Every bar was loud with laughter and business chat.

'I want to capture all these people,' said Jackie dreamily.

'But they're not here for the film festival, Jackie. That doesn't start till next week.'

'Surely they're like me – here early to get a good start on everyone else?'

Sally pointed up at the canopy outside the Palais des Festivals. 'Look! This week it's a conference on taxation.'

Over bread and Theresa's favourite cheese, Comté, William, Benjamin, Theresa and Carol held their meeting.

'The widow Magenta's son had been living in Sardinia for years,' said Carol. 'But he died a few years back, before his mother. And now it's the grandson who's in charge. He just came of age, and so he can finally get rid of it. Costanzo told me he didn't want a shop, a café or a restaurant or any kind of premises in France. He just wants the cash so he can go home and settle down, in Italy.'

'Can I speak to him?' William doodled on a pad while they sat around Theresa's table. 'To get clarity.'

Carol shrugged and scrolled through the contacts on her phone. She gave William the number and he walked through to the back of Theresa's flat, phone to one ear, finger stuck in the other.

Theresa felt relieved suddenly; she knew all this was for the best. So far they had been blundering blindly into the project with all the unchecked enthusiasm of Mickey Rooney in those old films: 'Hey gang, let's open a restaurant – and let's do it right here, right now!'

Benjamin was looking through the estimates. 'Two of these are ridiculous,' he said.

'I agree,' said Theresa. 'They're the ones who speak English. The reasonable one, a Frenchman, can't start for two months.'

'Pity I didn't train as a plumber,' William replied, swishing back to the table. 'Our vendor is going to the estate agent now, and they're getting the lawyer to draw up an agreement about any work we do between now and the end of our contract.' He sat and looked over towards Carol, smiling. 'I am very sorry, Carol. I totally underestimated you.'

'Are we mad?' asked Theresa.

'Of course we are,' said Benjamin. 'Isn't that the whole point?'

'A profit might be useful too.' William piled up the papers on the table.

'We'll never do it,' said Carol with a deep sigh.

'We jolly well will,' said Benjamin, now sounding more fired-up than anyone else in the room. 'If those pop-up restaurants can do it, so can we.'

'So can we start painting?' asked Theresa.

'Benjamin has a friend with a scrap lorry. He's going to clear out the old equipment the moment I give him the call, which is when I have the new agreement in my hand. After that, off you go, gals! You can kick off by painting the walls where the new cookers are going to go.'

William began stacking the paperwork on top of his briefcase.

'Once we have all the assurances that while we're renting it we'll be covered for expenses, I will start the ball rolling. It would be mad to lose an opportunity like this – it's almost too good to be true.'

Theresa started at this phrase. Only a few hours before, Carol had said precisely the same thing. Was this fear like an infectious fever that they would all feel, one by one? Or was there really something to be afraid of because the deal they had been offered was so good? Tonight, alone, she would go through everything once again and put her mind at rest.

She pressed her hands, palms down, on the cool of her table's glass top. 'Anyhow, as soon as you give us the nod, Carol and I can spend the rest of the day being scrubbers, cleaning out that filthy kitchen, so any company would be welcome.'

She winked at Carol.

'Oh, and by the way, I think Carol did very well with that deal; the place couldn't be more perfect for what we want – the size, the location. It's ideal, and you know we have every chance to make it work. So let's press on, shall we?'

William rooted about in his briefcase, then said, 'I seriously think we should start looking around for a mortgage and putting in all the legal paperwork to buy. It'll probably take about a month, three at the most. We'll continue to rent until the purchase is complete, with a proviso that if the deal falls through we can either continue to rent or have compensation for any money we spend on materially improving the property.'

So, having tried to put the brakes on all morning, William's foot had slipped on to the accelerator, and he was now proposing they go straight in and buy the place. Theresa felt worried about committing to more expense while they were still pouring out money and with no hope of an income in some weeks.

'Are any of us in a position to buy?'

'Look,' said William with a sigh. 'The property is being offered to us at an absurdly cheap price. Once we buy we can always sell and, after the work we're doing, we should make a profit. It would be mad not to continue at least looking into the terms we could get.'

Theresa realised that William was right, although she knew that they were all going to be cash-strapped for a bit. But there would be some time in hand while William investigated mortgages and contracts and, whichever way things went, rent or buy, they needed to get the restaurant looking and working like a restaurant.

'What do we do about the building-work estimates?' she asked.

William looked over the papers again. 'I say we go for the Frenchman, even if we have to wait. Call him now, Theresa. Before he gets booked out for July.'

'What?' screeched Benjamin, as Theresa moved towards the back of the room to make the phone call to Monsieur Leroux. 'We won't get to open till August? We'll have lost half the season . . .'

Theresa dialled.

'Hang on, Theresa!' yelled William. 'Benjamin's right. We can't wait that long. We'll have to go with the second one. It'll cost us more but we'll have more time to recoup the money once we're open.'

At that moment Theresa got through to Madame Leroux.

'I'm so sorry, Madame. We'd very much like to go along with your husband. But, unfortunately, as he cannot start before July, it means we have to say no.'

Then Madame Leroux said something that changed everything.

'What a shame. I gathered you were in a rush. Are you not able to use him immediately, this week? His other job doesn't start till the end of next week. He is free from tomorrow, but would have to finish by Thursday. You can have him for a week . . . if you want?'

Sally took a late lunch with Jackie in a small café opposite the Palais des Festivals.

'I really need to see whether I can get into the Martinez. I'll treat you to a drink there.'

Sally knew of the hotel's reputation as the most select on the Croisette.

'The Martinez isn't the kind of place that has leaflet displays, Jackie.'

'There's always a first time,' said Jackie, brightly. 'Courage, cheerfulness and resolution will bring us victory!'

Sally stirred her coffee. Why bother to give advice when it was ignored? 'Leave some with a doorman there, then,' she said.

'You know as well as I do that that never works.' Jackie shrugged. 'They just drop them into the nearest litter bin.' She took a sip of tea, leant back in her chair and sighed. 'Crikey! It's so much tougher than I thought it would be.'

When the bill came Jackie smiled and said, 'Thank you so much, Sally,' even though Sally had said nothing like 'Let me get this'. So, yearning to go on strike from leafleting, Sally paid up.

She glanced across the road at the workmen who were working under arc lamps, hanging a huge sign above the steps to the left of the main entrance of the Palais des Festivals.

'Do you have your pass for the actual festival on you?'

'Rather!' said Jackie.

'You should go and see whether they'll let you inside. You could perhaps find someone who organises the leaflet stands.'

'What a jolly good idea. It looks so much like a fortress, I suppose I was daunted, but we must stand firm in our resolve, mustn't we?'

Sally wondered whether going into character might have an effect. She channelled Celia Johnson and said energetically: 'I think you should do it yourself, Jackie. Have an explore. Get a feel of the place.'

'But . . .'

Sally gave a benign smile. 'I have a book. Really, I don't mind waiting.'

Jackie was still hesitating.

Another spurt of Celia Johnson from Sally: 'Jackie, crack on, old girl! Give it a whirl. That's your best bet. Never say die, eh? The worst that can happen is that they don't let you in. And maybe it would be good to get some leaflets in there before the deluge arrives.'

'I say, Sal, you really are a ripping pal.'

Sally waved as Jackie moved off. 'I'll be here or around, don't worry.'

While she watched Jackie cross the forecourt to the main entrance, Sally sorted out some coins for the tip.

At the central glass door Jackie pushed but no luck. The place was closed.

A security guard followed her, his hand raised.

Jackie held up her pass.

He seemed to argue with her for a moment, then pointed to another building along the way. Together they walked along, Jackie gesticulating all the while. Obviously she was giving him some cock and bull story; Sally knew that the passes meant nothing till the festival started.

As Jackie disappeared into the great echoing halls, Sally came out of the bistro and strolled along the Croisette, gazing into the expensive and fancy shops. It was a lovely sunny day. Not too hot or windy and, unlike the duration of the film festival, Cannes was all but deserted, bar a few camera-toting tourists walking along in a crocodile. They must be on a coach trip – Cannes in the morning, Monte Carlo in the after-noon.

After a while Sally decided to go back to wait by the entrance to the Palais for Jackie to come out.

As she stood at the foot of the steps looking up, it wasn't hard to imagine herself doing it officially, smil-ing right and left, stopping to pose for the photog-raphers. It was funny, but although, for most of the time, Sally managed to convince herself that she didn't miss being in the business, somewhere hidden deep inside she realised that a tiny flame still burned.

'Sally?'

As though at a distance, she heard the female voice say her name.

'Sally Doyle?'

It was peculiar to hear the form of address again at that exact moment – it had been her acting and maiden name, so she hadn't immediately responded. Now she looked across at a woman she recognised instantly. Most of the population of Europe, if not the USA, would recognise her too, as she was the star of some hugely successful TV series and many films.

'You don't recognise me, do you?' said the woman.

'Of course I do!' Sally, like everyone, knew Diana Sparks.

'It's Diana! Diana Sparks! Don't you remember, I was Iras to your Cleopatra all those years ago at Frinton?'

'Diana!' Sally's eyes popped out of her head. 'Of course!'

The truth was that till this moment Sally had wiped the whole season at Frinton from her memory. It had been fraught with drama, affairs, and actors getting drunk on and off stage. The director was a nasty little wasp who for the entire rehearsal period had given her a hell of a time and driven her almost to give up.

If Sally remembered it at all, it was only as a horrible dark patch in her career.

'What an awful time!' laughed Diana. 'Do you remember that dreadful short little director with acne and bad breath, what was his name? Eddy something?'

'He was so rude to me.'

'He was so rude to *all* the women. Vile misogynist. And he walked out halfway through the dress rehearsal and the production got taken over by the chairman of the board.'

'Who didn't have a clue about anything to do with the stage.'

'And those terrible costumes that were like the Bluebell Girls starring in *Carry On Up the Nile*!'

Sally had forgotten all these details. The Frinton job was one she dropped from her CV quite early on. She genuinely had no recollection of it. But now that Diana reminded her, she recalled the lot.

'It was like being in the porno version of *Antony and Cleo*.'

'So cold! Shivering in the wings, all blue and goose-bumpy!'

'Lord, I do remember that. Trying to do those long speeches while I could hear your and Charmian's teeth clacking behind me.'

'That was Marcia Montague. She gave up about six months after that job. Became a homeopath.'

'Good grief,' said Sally. 'I had no idea.'

'And that filthy old pervert playing the fig-seller.'

'Some long-forgotten comedian, wasn't he?'

'That's right. Kept telling us how as a youngster he had headlined for Mike and Bernie Winters. And as for Enobarbus!' snorted Diana. 'Old grope-hands! Always feeling us up in the wings.'

'"Whoopsie, can I be of assistance, methinks I spy a lacy brassière a-peeking out!"'

They both laughed so loudly that several passers-by stopped to look round.

Then, as though by magic, a circle gathered, people thrusting notebooks and pieces of paper towards Diana.

'I'm sorry about this, Sally. Don't go.'

Diana switched on a brilliant smile and turned towards the little crowd. She answered questions and signed for a good five minutes. Sally kept glancing up at the doors to the Palais des Festivals, expecting Jackie to emerge. She wasn't sure how good a combination this might be – Jackie and Diana together. But meeting Diana again, and recalling that awful season, was such fun.

As the crowd dwindled away, Diana clutched Sally's hand. 'Look I've got to run, but are you over here for the festival? Are you in something?'

'No.' Sally saw Jackie just inside the entrance, looking around. 'Actually, I live near here.'

'Really! How wonderful! Lucky you.' Diana pulled a business card from her handbag and handed it to Sally. 'Look – give me a ring. I'd love to catch up and you can show me around somewhere saner than Cannes at *le festival* time. Where do you live?'

'A tiny place. Bellevue-Sur-Mer.'

'Never heard of it – but all the better,' said Diana, moving away. 'Once the madness starts I'll need to escape. As the week drags on this place becomes like the ninth circle of Hell.'

By the time Jackie arrived beside Sally, Diana had disappeared into the crowd.

'Wasn't that . . . ?' said Jackie, standing on tiptoe to look.

'Yes,' said Sally. 'She just stopped to sign some autographs.'

'Wait! Sally!' exclaimed Jackie. 'You were getting her autograph?'

'No. No.' Sally decided not to explain what had really happened. 'I was just standing here. Waiting for you. So how did the leafleting go?'

'It was smashing,' said Jackie. 'I met a lovely man in there who's going to look after it for me.'

Sally looked at her watch.

'Look, Jackie, I really must get back. Why don't you stay on for a few hours while I go ahead?'

'No!' Jackie shrieked dramatically, causing several heads to turn in her direction. 'I'd get lost. I may play Maisie the navigator in *Skirts Fly Over Suffolk*, but really, I cannot tell my east from my west. I'd never find your place again.'

'You found it easily enough yesterday morning,' said Sally, not without malice.

'But that was in daylight, darling. I don't think you have the best street lighting in Bellevue-Sur-Mer.' She grabbed Sally's arm and linked her own round it. 'Pretty please?'

'The festival starts next week, doesn't it?' Sally sighed.

'The earlier I get these around the place the more chance I'll have,' said Jackie, pulling an unappealing winsome face.

Sally knew there was no way out. 'Come on. Give me a handful.'

'Now, what time's the last train? I'm looking forward to getting back myself, actually. I'm feeling ever so peckish and I'm sure you're going to cook up a storm for us – *à la français*, of course.'

Sally took a deep breath and started striding up into the town.

William had made the new agreement at the *immobilier*'s office – regarding the work they were about to do on the property – right after lunch.

He phoned the others and told them it was full steam ahead.

Having spent the rest of the afternoon clearing the place of all the boxes and watching the dirty, ancient cookers being hauled out on to the scrap lorry, Theresa set to work in what was the old kitchen as evening descended.

Carol had rushed up the hill to the Huit-à-8 to buy them some more anti-grease spray and a couple of bottles of water and some biscuits to keep them going.

Theresa wished she had brought her transistor radio from home. Even some Europop would be better than this lonely silence. The shop next door was shut now. It was always cheering to have noise while you cleaned, especially when it was dark and you were working in the back room under a solitary bare strip-light.

She filled a bucket with warm water and detergent and started work on the dirtiest wall.

She had been at it about five minutes when she heard someone come in through the front door. Carol could never have made it back that quickly. Still fearful after her recent troubles with the burglar, Theresa peered through the strip curtain. Someone was in the front room. She could see a man's silhouette against the window.

She armed herself with a broom and flicked on the light.

'*Allô?*'

The man spun round.

She caught a glimpse of him: dark-skinned, brown hair, slim and tall, dressed in denim. But he turned away, and in a flash he was out of the door.

74

With pounding heart, Theresa went after him. She pulled open the door and looked both ways, but there was no sight of him running, nor could she hear footsteps.

She came back in and turned the key in the lock.

Better safe than sorry.

She worked on for a few more minutes, then wondered if she hadn't been overreacting. Perhaps it was someone who had seen the light and thought the shop was still open. After all, no one had bothered to remove the old sign saying that it was a souvenir shop and sold ice creams.

Theresa was out in the yard refilling the bucket and mixing in the heavy-duty cleaning fluid when there was a loud rapping at the front door of the restaurant.

She moved gingerly through the kitchen and into the front room – the dining-room-to-be. A tall figure was silhouetted against the window.

'Who's there?' she cried timidly.

'It's me, of course, darling,' said Carol. 'Who else were you expecting? Jack the Ripper?'

Theresa moved to open up.

'Sorry about that, Carol, but I left it unlocked earlier and discovered some young man rooting around in here.'

'Really?' said Carol. 'I wonder who that was?'

'He ran like the devil when I came after him with a broom.'

'Maybe it was one of the men who helped cart stuff away today. Must have been; no one else has been in here. Perhaps he'd left something behind.'

'So why didn't he say so? He just took one look at me and scarpered.'

'Or some chancer who saw an open door and hoped there would be something to steal. But look, the place is stripped bare. Nothing to nick.' Carol rolled up her sleeves. 'I wouldn't worry about it, darling,' she drawled. 'Now where are those rubber gloves?'

The two women worked till the ceiling and walls were clean enough to paint, and what was once a thick layer of brown grease on the ceiling was white ceiling with a mere hint of yellow.

'At dawn tomorrow we paint,' said Carol, looking at her watch. 'And now, as we've worked so hard, I'm going to treat you to a late snack and a drink at the brasserie.'

'Ooh! How lovely.' Theresa pulled off her rubber gloves. 'We'll have to run.'

Before she went to bed that night Theresa made herself a nightcap cup of chocolate, all the while mulling over Carol's words, 'It's almost too good to be true.' Too good to be true. William had said it too. That was right. When you thought about it, the deal *was* unbelievable.

Relishing her aromatic comfort, she moved to her desk and pulled out her copy of the contract for the restaurant together with the new addendum. She sat down and read as she sipped. Of course it was all in French, but she could make most of it out; in particular the financial figures. It really did look too good to be true. Theresa couldn't bear it if something went wrong just because they hadn't really delved into the contract.

Just to be safe, she scanned the document and sent copies off to Mr Jacobs, her former employer in England, and his friend the French *notaire* who had helped her with the purchase of her apartment. She attached a small note consisting of one sentence: 'Is this too good to be true?'

7

S ALLY GOT UP VERY early and pottered around on her own before her house-guest awoke. She thanked God that the Cannes Film Festival started soon and only lasted ten days.

Meeting up with Jackie had brought on a bout of depression. Sally wasn't sure whether it was stirring up doubts about wanting to go back into acting herself or what. It had been quite a turn-up, too, meeting Diana yesterday. And how strange that in all the intervening years Sally had never put two and two together and worked out that the actress who now ruled the world of showbiz was that same timid girl who every night handed her the snake at the end of *Antony and Cleopatra*. They'd shared a dressing room, along with Marcia, who played Charmian. Sally remembered that Marcia was quite a bit older than both of them, and obviously resented Sally for having the greater role. Diana had dyed her hair since those days, and had lost quite a bit of weight too. Nonetheless, Sally felt quite foolish for not remembering her while watching her in all those terrific movies and seeing her regularly brandishing shiny awards on the front pages of glossy mags.

But somehow thinking about Diana's success had also added to Sally's depression. She had once played the lead to someone who was now a world-famous actress . . . maybe, if she had stayed on in the business, working? Sally snorted to herself. Now she was sounding like that dreadful fig-seller comedian! 'I was somebody . . . once.'

Sally fingered Diana Sparks's card. She didn't think she'd ever phone her. What would she say to her? They'd had their little catch-up on old times. What else was there to talk about, really, and how long could they reminisce over a single play at Frinton? Of course Sally knew all about Diana's subsequent work, but to talk about that would put her on a par with the most cringey of fans. It would be embarrassing and awful.

Sally slipped the card into the wastepaper basket.

She picked up the phone and rang her daughter to find out how the house-hunting was going. Marianne told her baldly that she and Ted weren't looking to live here in Bellevue-Sur-Mer any more and that instead they had decided to fly back to London 'and see how things pan out'. Marianne was going to help Ted get a new literary agent and a book contract while she herself was planning to explore some new business opportunities in the City. 'There are too many bad memories here for Ted, Mum.'

Bad memories for Ted? All he did here was sleep with as many women as possible.

Sally wondered whether this didn't really mean that Marianne, knowing that Ted was such a womaniser, wanted to get him out of the way before the tourist season kicked in. Marianne would be wise to keep him in her sight; after all she knew only too well how, once the wife was away, Ted would play.

Marianne rattled on: 'And as Sian is ejecting Ted from the house . . . ' Marianne sighed down the line. 'We even have to put up with the indignity of house-hunters being shown round the place while we're here. It's humiliating.'

'Perhaps you could buy the house yourselves?'

'Don't you hear me, Mother? We want to leave Bellevue-Sur-Mer. To escape from the past . . . and *her*. In fact we're at the airport. The plane leaves in half an hour.'

'It's just that . . . well, I'll miss you.'

'You have Tom here, don't you?' Marianne snapped. 'And who knows, perhaps we'll be back for the summer.'

Sally put the phone down feeling more depressed.

She rang Tom.

The call had a foreign ringtone.

'Hello! Mum? I'm on a train to Genoa. Lots of tunnels. Sorry if we get cut off.'

'Genoa?' Sally balanced on the edge of a stool wondering what was coming next.

'I change trains there. I'm off to Venice.'

'Venice? What for?'

'I've got this . . .'

And the call cut off.

Sally wasn't sure whether to ring back, or would that be annoying?

She was about to pick up the phone when she heard the footfall on the stairs.

'Good morning, my old china!' Jackie clomped into the kitchen and slumped into an armchair by the window. Sally noticed that she was wearing her dressing gown. She must have taken it from the back of the bathroom door.

'What are we having for breakfast? *Café* and croissants, I presume.' Jackie stretched and yawned. 'I have to say I do love the French way of life. You have it so easy down here. Sun, sand, glorious sea, delicious food. It almost makes me tempted to give up the business, like you did.'

Sally bit the inside of her lip.

'Still, better put our shoulders to the wheel and get things shipshape and Bristol fashion. I've now got the name of the important woman at the festival place. No time to waste, eh?'

'Pip, pip,' said Sally, wishing she could biff her over the head. 'The trains to Cannes go once an hour. Next one's in twenty minutes; if you get your jolly skates on you could just about make it.'

Jackie looked up at Sally, bewildered.

'Chop-chop!' said Sally. '*Tempus fugit*, and all that.'

8

Theresa arrived to work at a little after 7 a.m. She could hear noises coming from the space at the back, so moved gingerly, in case it was the visitor from last night, but it was Carol, who was vigorously applying the paint roller to the walls.

'You're on the go early,' said Theresa, looking with amazement at the room, which was practically finished.

'I couldn't sleep,' said Carol. 'I got home last night, glowing with happiness and that lovely wine at dinner, to find a legal document waiting for me.'

'What kind of legal document?'

'My husband, of course. Divorce, or rather annulment papers, and legal notice to quit the house.'

This news was not unexpected. Since Carol's husband had gone back to live in the USA, he wanted nothing more to do with her.

'Where will you go?'

'That's the thing, honey.' Carol sighed and turned, roller swinging at her side. 'I don't want to leave Bellevue-Sur-Mer. I certainly don't want to go back to the States. All my friends are here, and what with the restaurant . . .'

Theresa knew what was coming.

'I wondered, perhaps, once the fateful day comes around, could I maybe stay with you just a little while, between being chucked out and finding somewhere else to live?'

'My daughter's coming over soon with her kids. But it would be possible before that.'

Carol smiled. 'I'm going to have to get a second job, on top of working for the restaurant.'

'Doing what?'

'I don't know. Shop assistant. English teacher.'

'Is your French up to it?'

Carol sighed again. 'Not really. No.'

'Listen to that English-speaking radio station. They have jobs that come up. Mind you, they're usually long-term and involve going away. Hostesses on boats, things like that. But, look, Carol, let's hope it doesn't come to that. This restaurant has to make money. We have to make it work. And we need you working with us.'

'What if it fails?'

'That's what we're all thinking.' Theresa knew she never spoke a truer word. She herself had been lying awake fraught with worry for most of the night. 'It would certainly be better to work for us than some stranger. We all have a great incentive to make sure it doesn't fail. And you have such charm, Carol. You'll make a lovely hostess, welcoming our customers in.'

Carol dipped the roller and swung back to work on the wall. 'At least we have this way of getting our niggles out of our system. It's quite therapeutic throwing paint around all day. I'd much rather this than sit in an office in town applying for a licence, like William's doing.'

'We're lucky to have someone who willingly offered to do all that.' Theresa pulled her work clothes on over her top. 'Believe me, the legal stuff is a tough job.'

'I imagine it would be very boring and tiring. I simply refuse to do things I don't enjoy.'

Theresa was about to chide Carol. Every success story involved doing things you didn't quite fancy doing, but they simply had to be done and that was that.

'Anyways,' Carol continued, 'as I don't have any money to invest in the capital project, I'm really only a pretend partner with nothing to lose and nothing to give except my exertions.'

Theresa was torn. She remembered that in the last few weeks Carol had lost her husband, her home and her income due to the recent shenanigans with the same burglar, which had left them both injured and embarrassed. When Theresa thought about it, the principal difference between their situations was that Theresa had received a large pay-off from an English tabloid for her version of the story – the very money she was investing in the restaurant.

Carol had gained nothing and lost all.

'Carol,' said Theresa, sloshing the paint on to the side wall where the cookers would go. She didn't want to dig too deeply. 'What did you do before you married David?'

'What do you mean, exactly?'

'Well, what did you do . . . with your time? Did you work?'

'I went to art school. Got my diploma. Then I was in the building trade for a bit. Then . . . well, things took a bit of a turn, and I had a bit of time off. Then I met David.'

'And you stopped working?'

'All but . . .'

'Same thing happened to me. I worked. Then I married and had my daughter. Then after Peter, my husband, left me and ran off with the nanny – what a cliché – I found myself in a situation where I went to work again.'

'Work is good,' said Carol. 'It takes your mind off things.'

Theresa wondered whether the 'things' might be loneliness and not having someone to come home to in the evenings. Work might well be good, but it would certainly be nicer to have a partner with whom to share the ups and downs, the tears and laughter.

Theresa picked up a thick square brush and dipped it into the paint pot.

Having rid herself of Jackie, for the morning at least, Sally took herself out for a walk by the quay. She watched the train pull out and disappear into the tunnel on its way to Cannes; relieved, she sat on the harbour wall in her usual place and gazed out on to the tranquil sea.

She couldn't believe her morning – both children had announced that they were leaving or had left town, and now she was stuck with this wretched woman and her jolly-what-ho prattle.

She watched Theresa come out of the old widow Magenta's place and walk briskly across the car park towards her own front door. She now felt slightly envious of the others with their restaurant project, although when it had first been proposed she hadn't been interested.

She thought of the day before yesterday, out on the boat with Jean-Philippe. That had been fun too, although it had been rather annoying when the Russian had assumed she was merely his tea lady.

'Morning!'

Sally instantly recognised the swooping tones of Zoe.

'I'm off to town, to an auction,' she said.

Sally noticed that since Zoe's visit to the hairdresser's her forehead had become remarkably smooth and shiny and her lips enormously bigger.

'Fancy joining me?' Zoe cocked her head to one side, sunlight creating a glass-like sheen across her brow. 'It'll save you from accidentally signing up for a course in mechanical engineering or birdwatching.'

The word 'bird' caused Zoe's mouth to wobble, as though the nearby muscles were incapable of lifting the weight of the newly filled lips.

Rather than hang around feeling sorry for herself, Sally accepted the offer, and a few minutes later was in a taxi heading towards the Hôtel des Ventes in Nice.

The saleroom was jammed with people, sitting in rows on black folding chairs.

Sally and Zoe squeezed in at the back.

'Creep over there,' whispered Zoe in a voice loud enough to wake the dead. 'I want to inspect the jewellery.'

Sally blushed when everyone turned to look at them, but nonetheless obeyed Zoe's orders and shuffled along, pressing past people till they reached the jewellery exhibits.

Everything in the glass display box looked pretty worn and dusty, but what did Sally know? The only jewellery she had ever possessed that was worth anything was her wedding ring, which she kept in a box full of junk on top of the wardrobe.

'It's rubbish of course, Sally, but you know me. I love a bit of bling.'

Sally knew that Zoe was perfectly capable of whispering properly, unless she wanted people to hear her usually quite funny comments. Sally wondered why she was being so loud now, but suspected that she must be after something good and wanted to put off the competition.

She examined Zoe's face for clues; never easy, as she had had so much plastic surgery and Botox that it was always set in one expression: surprised.

Zoe threw her the nearest she could do to a frown, indicating that Sally should look forward.

The bidding was currently for a painting. The assistant was holding aloft some old thing featuring stormy seas and a tossing ship, all set off in an ornate gold frame.

Sally watched the nods and winks, the flap of a catalogue, the shaking of a head – all signs indicating who was in or out of the competition. The auctioneer in his blue shirt balanced on a high stool and waved his gavel in the air. What a masterful job it was – recognising when someone was simply scratching their nose and when it was a bid.

From where Sally was standing she could see that most of the bidders were eccentric-looking. Fat bald men in denims, bomber jackets and hobnailed boots, women in multicoloured patchwork-quilted coats, women with little dogs on their laps, which they stroked between bids, a man with a long grey ponytail, in a sweeping leather coat. Sally realised that she was probably the youngest person in the room, save for the people who worked here. There was one man who looked younger, sitting in the middle of the front row. She could only see the back of his camel cashmere jacket, but unless he'd done a spectacular dye job, he at least had hair that was not grey.

Suddenly Sally realised that Zoe was bidding. Her head was nodding occasionally and her eyes were fixed on the auctioneer. She realised too that the man in the camel jacket was bidding against her. She could see his hand slightly raising from his lap in a counterpoint rhythm with her head.

'Someone's being very stubborn,' Zoe hissed at Sally. 'This should be mine by now.'

The man turned his head to see who was bidding against him.

It was Stanislav Serafim. He caught eyes with Sally and his eyebrows shot up. He gave her the merest flicker of a smile, then turned back to the auctioneer.

After this he stopped bidding and Zoe raised her fist in the air and called out her name.

The item was put into a box and one of the porters nodded towards Zoe, who nodded back.

Stanislav, meanwhile, was beaming in Sally's direction, also nodding.

He rose, and made his way to the exit, walking behind Zoe, who was scuttling after the porter. Sally followed.

While Zoe paid up and took possession of her painting, Stanislav sidled up to Sally. 'How lovely to see you again so soon,' he said. 'The pretty English who prefers her France.'

'Ah, yes,' said Sally. 'I am happy here. I wouldn't move back to England for a fortune.'

'Really?' Stanislav shrugged and smiled. 'I wonder if you would call me sometime. Let's have lunch.'

He handed Sally his business card and returned to the saleroom.

Holding her new acquisition, Zoe turned to Sally and said loudly, 'My God, you've pulled. Really good-looking too. Now let's scarper.'

'It's wonderful for us,' William perched on a large paint pot rereading the small print of the contract, 'but what's in it for him?'

'As Carol said, he just wants shot of the place.' Theresa shook the roller and applied it to the paint tray. 'He's young. To him it's a lottery ticket.'

'All right then. I suppose there's no point holding back.' He placed the contract on the floor and wiped his hands. 'My French lawyer says it's fine, but I wonder if you might get it checked out by your lawyer friends, Theresa.'

'Already have done.'

'And ...?'

'I'm awaiting their reply, William. Don't forget to organise the electricians and plumbers for tomorrow,' said Theresa. 'As early as you like.'

'I spoke to him yesterday evening. Monsieur Leroux has agreed to start today. As soon as the paint is dry. He says there are things he can get on with.' William glanced at his watch. 'In fact, he should be here in three hours' time.'

Theresa felt slightly put out that, after she had sorted all the arrangements with Madame Leroux, William had still thought fit to make a follow-up call. But she decided to say nothing.

Carol suddenly spoke. 'Hey, guys, if the grandson is so keen to be getting any money he can, we'd better make sure we don't lose it to someone else. We should put in an offer, get a mortgage, something. Just a thought.'

William stopped in his tracks and turned on her. 'I really don't think, Carol, that, having risked nothing at all in this project, you've much say in it.'

'I've put in plenty of time and effort and thought . . .'

'You've nothing to risk; no money equals no loss. If this thing goes wrong we're all going to lose our shirts and you can sail off to pastures new.'

'But I . . .'

Theresa stepped forward to stop this developing into a major row.

'She's right. We should press ahead.'

'It's a quandary,' said William. 'Should I sign and commit us, or wait till you hear back from your lawyer friend? Mine has OKed it.'

'Your lawyer says it's kosher?' asked Benjamin.

William nodded.

Theresa looked across to Carol, who stood, head bowed, eyes brimming with tears. She had seen how keen she was, how much time she spent and how much energy she threw into it. It wasn't entirely Carol's fault that she was broke.

'Carol, could you just help me find that letter?'

'What letter?' Carol obviously had no idea.

'Follow me.'

Theresa went into the kitchen and hastily whispered, 'I've decided. I'm going to give you half my share from that newspaper article.'

'You what?' Carol mouthed back in disbelief.

'That is the equivalent of my share of the money I'm due to put into the restaurant. I got the money for being taken in by the same vile crook as you, so . . . Think of yourself as an equal partner.'

Carol threw her arms tightly around her friend.

'Oh my gosh . . . I don't know how I am ever going to be able to thank you . . .'

'When we go back, simply agree with everything I say.' Theresa winked.

They returned to William and Benjamin.

'Can't find the ruddy thing,' said Theresa. 'Carol reminded me it's in my kitchen at home. But Carol is due to be paid a large sum in compensation for . . . what was it, Carol?'

Carol opened her mouth to speak. She managed to grunt one syllable before Theresa continued.

'Let's not bother about details now; the important thing is that Carol will be putting in as much as I am, and therefore has equal rights with all of us. I have to add that I also think her efforts so far have been extraordinary; so, William, a little consideration please.'

'If you knew about this money, why didn't you mention it earlier?' asked William, appraising Carol with a beady eye.

'Well, I . . .' said Carol.

'Carol is superstitious, William. We all know that. She didn't want to jinx it before it came through. Now then, let's take a vote,' said Theresa. 'Who's for signing today?'

All hands went up.

'Fine,' said William. 'I will head right up there. Come along, Benjamin. You're a signatory too.'

'Not yet.' Benjamin shook his head. 'I want to have a go at painting.'

William frowned at Benjamin. 'I do hope you're not going to paint in that shirt. It's a New & Lingwood.'

Benjamin sighed and stripped the shirt off. He faced William, hands on hips. 'Better?'

'The jeans were expensive too,' said William.

Benjamin undid one button.

'Enough!' cried Theresa. 'This is not the launderette.'

When Sally got home, Jackie was nowhere to be seen. Sighing with relief, she made a pot of tea and settled down to read a book. When she realised she had left her reading glasses in her handbag, she reached out for something to use as a bookmark and picked up Stanislav's card from the tabletop. She read it. Stanislav had a St Petersburg home, a Paris apartment and an address in a village up in the hills, near Vence. It was too tempting, so she opened up her laptop and, using Google Maps, took a tour of all his properties – well, all the ones on the card.

Should she phone him? She slammed the card down again. If she phoned now it would look too, too desperate. She'd wait till this afternoon. But then, later on Jackie might be in earshot, which would be difficult. Sally realised her heart was beating fast. How silly! The man probably only wanted someone to make tea for him on his next boating excursion. But that smile he had given her! Zoe was no fool, and she'd seen it too.

A rap on the front door.

Sally slipped the card into the book and, gearing herself up for more 1940s-style chitchat, went to open up.

'How is the mother of the deadly adulterous serpent?'

On the doorstep, shading her eyes from the setting sun, stood Sally's old friend Sian.

Seeing Sian was always rather daunting. She was brusque to the point of rudeness and prided herself on her acumen as a businesswoman.

'I thought you were in London.' Sally tried to give a bright smile.

'I lied.' Sian swept past her and took a seat at the table. 'Like everyone else in this sordid little caper, I'm spying on my husband and your daughter.'

Sally gulped and closed the door. How to cope with this? How did one behave when having the wife of the man your daughter was sleeping with to tea? She didn't know where to put herself or what to say.

What could she say?

She hovered behind Sian, staying silent.

'I do hope Marianne finds another job soon, or they're both going to struggle.' Sian took the lid off the teapot, peered inside and looked up at Sally. 'Ted eats up money, just like he eats up women. Well, aren't you going to offer me some tea?'

Sally scuttled into the kitchen and grabbed another cup.

'You can warn the little slapper you spawned that Ted won't stay with her long. He's used to being kept in a certain style.' Sian reached for the teapot and filled her own cup.

'I am so sorry, Sian. Truly, I knew nothing about it.'

'You're hardly going to tell me you were the pimp. Anyway, I'm here to get my house back. I've filed an order.'

Sally hung her head. 'I know.'

This was beyond embarrassing.

Another, louder rap on the door.

Hopefully it would not be Marianne, returned from London.

Sally opened up.

'Bad show, darling. Awful kerfuffle at the venue. Nothing doing till tomorrow now.'

Jackie came inside. Sally's stomach went into an even tighter knot.

'Hello there!' Jackie held out her hand to Sian. 'I'm Jackie, Sally's best friend, over from Blighty.'

Sally realised that she was so nervous about this clash of personalities happening here in her dining room that she was making an odd whimpering sound. Jackie could not have picked a worse moment to arrive.

'Her best friend?' Sian sipped her tea. 'I always thought that was me.'

'The more friends the merrier, eh, old girl?' Jackie took off her jacket and strode over to the table. 'Shove up, old chap. I'm dying for a brew.'

Old chap! Old girl! To Sian, sitting there in her pristine designer suit. Sally winced and turned to look at Sian, expecting an outburst.

But Sian was grinning from ear to ear.

'Good Lord!' Sian stood back to get a better look. 'You're Maisie Reilly, aren't you?'

Sally feared that this was going to be another faux pas, this time in the other direction, but Jackie was still beaming.

'Maisie the marvel! That's me, old bean.'

'How exciting. Jackie Westwood in the flesh! Why didn't you tell me, Sally? Oh Jackie, you're one of my favourite actresses and *Skirts Fly Over Suffolk* is my absolute top TV programme.'

Jackie glowed.

Sally went to fetch another cup.

After Monsieur Leroux called to take measurements and inspect all the equipment in the cellar, Theresa left Carol and Benjamin to paint the skirting boards and window frames, as it was too much of a squeeze with the three of them. She went home to prepare something to eat for the others. Once they had finished the gloss painting they would come over the road and join her. While she was chopping and stirring, the phone rang. She hoped it would be Mr Jacobs, but it was Imogen.

'Mummy! You'll never guess what?' She left a pause then said, 'Aren't you going to ask?'

'Well, tell me then.'

'Annunziata has left Daddy!'

Theresa was astonished. Nowadays she never thought of her ex-husband. The humiliation she had faced when he divorced her so that he could marry the au pair had faded into a mere shadow of a far-away memory. The whole episode was so long ago, and it seemed almost to have happened to another person and therefore no longer meant anything to her emotionally.

'Where has Annunziata gone? Didn't she depend on your father keeping her?'

'Oh, Mummy, you're so behind with the gossip. No. I think the thing that drove Daddy into the arms of the cleaner was Annunziata's independence, financially.'

Theresa sat down. 'I'm sorry, darling ... "Into the arms of the cleaner"?'

'Yes!' Imogen spoke excitedly. 'Annunziata caught him at it with the cleaner, an elderly Filipino woman.'

'I don't know why you say "elderly" like that. He's hardly a spring chicken. The cleaner! Good Lord, how sordid.'

'Anyway, it means Annunziata's moved out and left him all alone.'

'But he still has the cleaner.' Theresa chuckled.

'No. You see the cleaner has family of her own and has no intention of moving in with Daddy, or losing the money she gets from him as a cleaner. She sends it all home to her family in the Philippines, apparently. She's looking for another job.'

'So Dad's left alone, licking his wounds,' said Theresa. 'Serves him right.'

The doorbell rang.

'Someone at the door, darling.'

'Don't worry, Mummy – just had to let you know. Speak soon.'

Carol and Benjamin stood in the street holding up white-paint-stained hands.

'Sweetie! We forgot all about white spirit. Got any to hand before we smear all your goods and chattels?'

They followed Theresa through the flat to her back door. She went out into the small yard and got a bottle of white spirit from the little box shed.

While they cleaned up, Theresa laid the table for supper.

'Smells heavenly, darling,' said Carol.

'As usual,' added Benjamin.

They gathered round the table and discussed the whole project. In three days they had accomplished so much and from now on it was all systems go. Tomorrow, first thing, Monsieur Leroux and his team would begin fitting the gas cookers, the sinks and making the lavatories decent. Theresa, Benjamin and Carol meanwhile planned to start work on the front room, where the actual restaurant dining room would be – the shop window, the heart of the place.

Over dinner they discussed colour schemes and furniture; how to do it cheaply while looking stylish. Benjamin had some good ideas, having worked for a while in the second-hand furniture trade. He suggested, if they couldn't afford new, they might go for an arty, random look.

'There's a good antique market we could go to tomorrow morning down in Beaulieu. What do you think?'

'We really do need a small van,' said Theresa. 'Not only for this, but for daily collections of vegetables and going to the cash and carry.'

'There was a deal in today's paper.' Benjamin left the table and rooted about in his knapsack. 'I must have left it at the restaurant. I'll go and get it.'

Theresa tossed him the keys and he rushed out.

'We still haven't named the place,' said Carol. 'So much easier to say Le Jardin or La Cygne than constantly saying "the restaurant" as if there were no other restaurants in the world.'

'We don't have a garden and where is the swan?' Theresa dealt another helping of her standby penne, mozzarella, olive and tomato dish on to Carol's plate. 'And why does it have to be a French name?'

'Who lives here, and what kind of food will we be serving?'

'Oh, yes.' Theresa took a quaff of wine. 'I see what you mean.'

Sally felt quite left out. Sian and Jackie were getting on like a house on fire. Sian was already talking about backing Jackie's next film project and was putting pencil marks in her diary to make sure she didn't miss the showing at Cannes.

'I am so excited. I've never been to Cannes.'

'But it's just up the road.'

Sian laughed. 'I meant the festival. Do I need to get a gown?'

'Crikey, no,' laughed Jackie. 'I'm in the Marketplace. Not much glamour, I'm afraid, old bean. We're below stairs, in the business end of things.'

'And that, Jackie, is where I am most at home.' Sian smiled as she gathered up her handbag and phone. 'So sorry, Sally, to have to cut and run like this, especially when we were having so much fun.' She pecked Sally on both cheeks, then handed a business card to Jackie. 'Phone me in the morning, Jackie, with all the details. I can run you over there in my car.'

'Good show, my old china.' Jackie stood and swayed from side to side in what Sally suspected was a wartime manner. 'Toodle-pip! TTFN, old girl. Ta-ta for now!'

As she left, Sian was still smiling benignly. It was as though she had totally forgotten that she had come here to shout at Sally as a kind of proxy for her daughter.

Before Sally had a chance to ask Jackie about her day in Cannes, the phone rang. It was Jean-Philippe.

'Sally, are you mad?'

Sally was taken aback. What had she done wrong now?

'You must phone Stanislav. He's been on to me. You were supposed to phone him. He's an important man. He told me he gave you his business card and asked you to call him ASAP, but you failed to reply. Did you lose it?'

Sally wished Jean-Philippe would give her long enough to answer him. She found herself mumbling, 'I've been busy.'

'Sally, my livelihood and possibly yours lies in this man's hands. No one has any money any more – but he does. And he's looking for people to do things and he pays well. Phone him . . . now!'

Sally shrugged towards Jackie as she replaced the receiver. 'Sorry about this.'

She slid out Stanislav's card from the pages of her book and dialled his number. She got a machine, waited for the beep and spoke quietly: 'Hello, Stanislav. This is Sally here, from the boat . . . And the auction. You asked me to phone. And, well, here I am. Perhaps talk tomorrow. Bye.'

When she put the phone down Jackie was heading for the stairs.

'Awfully sorry, old chap, I'm pooped. Would you mind awfully if we don't chat and I just head on up to Bedfordshire?'

Sally waved and found herself saying, 'Toodle-pip!'

She started to tidy up the table, all the while wondering what Stanislav wanted of her that was so important he'd called Jean-Philippe. She offered no service like Jean-Philippe. The only things he'd seen her do were make a pot of tea and drop the fenders over the side before docking the boat.

She laughed. Perhaps he was smitten and she'd end up marrying him and living in a huge castle outside St Petersburg.

She smiled as she packed the dishwasher. Then her thoughts returned to her children. What was Tom up to now? Sally hoped his business in Italy wouldn't keep him away too long. On the other hand, despite all this difficulty over Sian and Ted, she found herself thankful that Marianne was in London, if only for a while, till the emotions had cooled down. What a terrible mother she was – to wish her daughter to go away. But Marianne had brought this whole trouble upon herself and it was too uncomfortable – especially with Sian, a dragon at the best of times, on the warpath.

Sally opened the fridge and pulled out a half-empty bottle of rosé. She poured herself a very large glass and flopped down in front of the TV to watch the news.

This is what it had come to! She had turned into a couch potato taking solace in alcohol.

She flicked over and reached the news channel. War, famine and all the usual horrors. Then there was a crowd of people peering into the waters of the harbour. The dead body of a young man had been discovered by fishermen this morning. She recognised the location immediately. It was down in the old port, round the corner from her hairdresser's and Jean-Philippe's sea-school. The drowning was something to do with a drug cartel. The dead boy was only seventeen. People were urged to keep their eyes open. She thought of Tom at that age. Like a baby. It made Sally remember that her problems were minuscule; nothing more than social inconveniencies really.

She downed the rest of the wine and headed up to bed.

9

WHEN THERESA ARRIVED AT the restaurant next morning she again found Carol already ensconced, sitting on the floor of the kitchen with a large cup of coffee, reading the local newspaper.

'*Bonjour, cherie!*' Carol drawled.

Theresa set her things down in the corner. She could see a few cigarette butts lying on the quarry-tiled floor.

'I didn't know you smoked, Carol.'

Carol looked up. 'I don't.'

Theresa took a step back and pointed to the floor. 'So whose are these?'

Carol got up and inspected the butts. 'Even if I did smoke I wouldn't be dragging on roll-your-owns. How low can you go?'

'So whose are they? They weren't here when we locked up last night and they're certainly not mine.'

Carol flopped down again. 'They must belong to Benjamin. Remember he came back to pick something up.'

'The newspaper.' Theresa checked the date on the one Carol was reading.

'I bought it this morning,' squealed Carol. 'He wanted yesterday's.'

'Well, he's a dirty puppy.' Theresa swept the butts on to a piece of paper using a paintbrush. 'I shall have words.'

A rap on the door signalled the arrival of two plumbers from Monsieur Leroux's team, who'd come to check out the taps for the sink and the gas pipes for the hobs. One was the same man who had fitted Theresa's new boiler in her apartment. They greeted one another fondly, though formally, and Carol went out to get them some coffee from the brasserie up the road.

While Theresa pottered around in the cellar, spray-cleaning the equipment that needed bringing up today to be attached, William arrived to help.

'Benjamin's running behind,' he said, pulling off his jacket as he came down the cellar steps. 'But he'll be with us in no time.'

'He's been a naughty boy,' said Theresa. 'Left some cigarette ends on the clean floor.'

'He what?' William stood frozen to the spot. 'Where are they?'

Theresa immediately felt bad for mentioning it. 'Oh darling, it's nothing so serious, just something not to be repeated once we're up and running.'

'I'll be the judge of that.' William raced up the stairs, Theresa scrambling behind him.

He came upon the bucket where the stubs were, just as Benjamin walked in gripping a couple of coffees, Carol at his side.

William held up a cigarette end, inspected it, sniffed it, then waved it at Benjamin.

'I thought I paid good money for you to give up drugs,' he said tensely.

'But I . . . I . . .'

'Admit it,' said William. 'You came in here when no one was about so that you could get back on your old habit?'

'No. I didn't. I swear. Really, William. I haven't touched anything since I came out. Really.'

William screwed up his eyes. 'As far as I know, there are three sets of keys to this place. I have a set, Theresa another and Carol the third. Whose keys did you steal?'

'I didn't. I didn't. Theresa lent me the keys to come for my paper last night and I gave them right back to her.'

William rounded on Theresa. 'So you're encouraging him?'

'Honestly, William, I came in, fetched the paper and went right back.'

'After you hung about for a few drags of marijuana?'

Theresa put up her hand. 'William. Please. If you must quarrel, let's not do so in front of . . .' She nodded towards the younger of the two plumbers, who was carefully avoiding them by running a metallic tape measure along the wall.

William moved into the kitchen to ask the chief plumber whether his work would all be finished by the end of the day and if it would be possible to continue at the same time as the electrician. He shrugged his shoulders while nodding confirmation that his colleague the carpenter would arrive shortly so that they could work together on fitting the sink into the countertop.

Theresa couldn't believe it was all going so well. Weren't there all those tales about workmen not showing? How lucky they were to have found this crew who contributed their own expertise to the project.

She wished now she had brought a kettle along and some camp stools so that while the men were busy next door they could sit in the dining room and discuss the works.

'Look, guys,' said Carol. 'While we're hanging around, why don't we get this hardboard up and have a peek at the floor. It looks great round the edges, but for all we know it's a foul mess in the middle and we'll have to estimate for some new *carrelage*.' She laughed. 'You see, I know that here in France there are two names for tiles: *carrelage* for floors and *faïence* for walls.' She smirked and rolled up the sleeves on her dungarees. 'So there!' She pulled out a pair of heavy work gloves from her pockets and turned to the others. 'Anyone going to help me?'

Purse-lipped, William came through.

'He's got to use blowlamps and drills and things, so the electrician can't start till tomorrow.'

'That's no surprise, William. He needs room to move. It would be chaos to have both things going on at once.'

William gave her an icy stare. 'Theresa, I need to set a date for the health inspector and that cannot be till the basic work is done. And you and Carol still need to pop into the estate agent's and sign your names to the rental agreement.'

Theresa feared that William was spoiling for a fight, but that it was more to do with his worries over Benjamin than anything else.

'Hellooooo!' cried Carol, who was down on her hands and knees tugging at the corners of the hardboard. 'Is anyone going to help me?'

'It'll be fine, William. Let's get our diaries out and set a date for the inspectors next week. I think we should have got the place looking decent enough by then. It's psychological – the better the place looks, the cleaner he'll find it. Now let's have all hands on deck.'

Benjamin was already beside Carol, and Theresa moved to the far corner.

William glanced at his watch.

'I'm sure you can manage without me. I need to get back to the *mairie* before they go off for the interminable lunchbreak.'

And he was gone.

Benjamin took the middle section of the hardboard and was keen to take command. He glanced at each woman and nodded. 'Shall we count to three, then haul it up as high as we can go?'

'All very well,' said Carol, 'but how will we then see the floor?'

Benjamin got the point.

'I need to haul it up from the centre, then you jump into position either side and we walk it up.'

They took breaths and Benjamin counted to three. With a concerted effort they raised the hardboard, walking underneath to lift it from the ground.

'My God!' exclaimed Theresa, glancing down. 'It's ravishing!'

'The décor will have to be worked around it – it's a masterpiece.'

They all stood, holding the hardboard up with their heads, looking down at a brilliant mosaic, created with vivid background of ultramarine glazed tesserae. The central motif was a swirling sun in chrome yellow, with flashes of orange and red. The irregular patterns along the edges showed Greek key motifs made from gold pieces and shards of broken mirrors. All around the sun were several circles and oblongs depicting the signs of the zodiac.

'This is brilliant,' said Benjamin. 'How do we protect it?'

'I suppose we carefully put this hardboard back down, and make no attempt to lift it up again till the very last minute.'

'OK – let's go,' said Benjamin. 'On three, gently lower ... One, two ...'

'Wait,' yelled Carol. 'Let me take a photo.'

She reached into her dungaree pocket, pulled out her phone and with one hand quickly took a few shots. 'Fine,' she said. 'Let's do it.'

Sally was heading out for the market when the phone rang. The suave voice of Stanislav asked her why she was avoiding him and invited her to lunch in a famed restaurant in the heart of Old Town, Nice.

So she went back upstairs and spent the rest of the morning changing into something smarter and putting on make-up.

As she applied her lipstick she thought about him – so dashing and handsome and rich. No! She must not think about the rich part. She didn't want to turn into one of those grabby women who only went after men for their money.

She couldn't believe that, after waiting for her to phone yesterday following the auction, late last night he had gone to the bother of phoning Jean-Philippe to get her number. He really must be keen.

She grabbed her handbag off the bed. She was glad that Jackie had left early for Cannes so she wouldn't have to explain herself. She paused for a moment in the hall. Would she need a shawl for later, if it got cool in the shade? She decided no, and if it did, well then she'd just have to shiver.

She took the bus into Nice and realised she was a little early, so strolled slowly through Old Town and the market before entering the restaurant.

The restaurant was not full.

Stanislav was there, sitting at a large circular corner table.

As Sally approached, he stood and bowed slightly in her direction.

'Looking beautiful today, Sally.' He took her hand and kissed the back of it. Sally felt the hairs rising on the back of her neck. 'I can hardly believe you are the same woman who was heaving those plastic balls out of the water on my boat the day before yesterday.'

'Fenders,' she said, and thought that she sounded like some awful seamanship know-all.

She decided also not to mention how many times she had walked past this restaurant, really wishing to come in but feeling too intimidated to try.

'By all reports the manager is a tigress,' said Stanislav, as though reading her thoughts. 'But that way she keeps out the riff-raff.'

Sally gulped and realised she was that 'riff-raff'.

A waiter hovered, handing out menus. 'Aperitif?' he asked.

'Champagne,' said Stanislav. 'Dom Pérignon.' As the waiter moved off he leaned towards Sally and whispered into her ear, 'Only the best for you.'

Another waiter flicked Sally's napkin on to her lap, which gave her an opportunity to look the other way. She really didn't want Stanislav to feel how her heart was beating or see the blush rising on her cheeks. He really was the most charming and sexy man she had ever met.

'So, Sally,' said Stanislav softly. 'Jean-Philippe tells me you are not married.'

Sally nodded and shifted slightly in her seat.

'I am very glad,' he said with a twinkle in his eye. 'I wouldn't want some terrifying English squire coming after me with a gun.'

The wine assistant approached the table with an ice bucket. Behind him the sommelier cradled the bottle of champagne as though it was a baby. As he tackled the foil wrapping, and prepared to pop the cork, another waiter was on Sally's other side placing a hot, bulging paper bag in front of her.

'*Du pain!*' he said. '*Attention! Chaud!*'

She peered inside.

Stanislav moved closer and she thought she heard him say the word 'Destiny'.

Sally gazed up into his eyes.

But he was looking past her, across towards the entrance.

A young, garishly dressed, super-tanned woman on incredibly high heels was scanning the room.

'Oh lawks! How was I supposed to find this place when the taxi can't get up to the front?' The new arrival staggered between the tables, heading towards them. She was cradling a little lapdog. 'Bloomin' France. Why can't they all speak English, like us?' screeched the young guest to anyone who was listening.

Sally turned back towards Stanislav and saw that he was in the process of rising from his seat, smiling brightly at the brash girl with the loud voice.

'Ooh, Don Pérignom!' squealed the girl. 'My fave. Pour us a glass, Stanny darling; my throat's as dry as a camel-driver's jockstrap.'

She stooped, grabbed a glass full of champagne and downed it in one. She then wiped her mouth with the back of her hand and gave a little burp before flopping into the empty seat next to Sally's.

Stanislav took the girl's hand and kissed the back of it, as he had done for Sally. 'Destiny! I'm so glad you could make it.'

Destiny put out a hand and touched Sally's forearm. 'You must be Sally. Stanny here's been telling me all about you. How you're a boat driver or something.'

Sally, nose out of joint, felt rather miffed.

'Hello. I'm Destiny MacDonald.' The girl thrust out her hand for Sally to shake. 'So you're Sally Connor. You know Stanny, and best of all, you speak-a-de-English and live in de France.' She laughed appreciatively at her own joke.

From the girl's demeanour, Sally could see that she was supposed to have had some kind of reaction to the name, but to be honest, it meant nothing to her.

She did her best to sound enthusiastic as she said: 'How lovely to meet you.'

'Destiny is married to the footballer I was telling you about on the boat. Mickey MacDonald? Walsingham Wanderers?'

Sally was still in the dark.

'Perhaps you had the conversation with Jean-Philippe, while I was making the tea? I know nothing about football, I'm afraid, Destiny.'

Destiny laughed so loud that her little dog jumped with fright. 'Me neither. He's just a wicked hunk, that's all I care about. Now shut up, Stanny sweetie, and let's order.'

Sally prepared for a long hour during which she was unlikely to taste a morsel.

10

THERESA SAT AT HER glass and wrought-iron table with a large clean pad of paper. She wanted to jot down menu ideas, recipes. The danger of this DIY-style rush to open a restaurant had caused her to lose the point of why she had agreed to be part of it in the first place. She should be cooking, experimenting.

As she wrote down a pretty random list of dishes, she realised that they hadn't even really discussed a theme for the menu. Would they be serving typical Mediterranean dishes, or perhaps traditional British fare? They could even look into presenting local specialities. Then an idea struck her. How about fusing the best of British and Niçoise food – let's say mashed potato and onion champ with red mullet, for instance?

It seemed a good plan. She made a list in two columns: Local and British. Afterwards she could write them on to index cards and assemble some interesting blends.

She was right in the middle of dreaming up those scrumptious ingredients, lost in her culinary world, when the phone rang.

It was Mr Jacobs calling from the office in London.

'Theresa! I am fascinated by this whole project you're involved in. The one thing that keeps coming to the top of my head is what's in it for the vendor?'

Theresa moved away from the paper-littered table and sat in her armchair.

'Do you mean that everything is all right for us?'

'Well, yes,' Mr Jacob's voice betrayed doubts. 'I simply don't understand the lessor's position.'

'He is very young . . .'

'He may well be, but this document is legally tight. It's just that the terms seem to favour you very well. I was so worried by this that I did make a little check on the French registry to be certain that the young fellow wasn't in the business of renting you London Bridge or the *Mona Lisa*.'

'Are you saying that the place isn't his to dispose of?'

'No. That's the whole problem, for me. It is legally his and the contracts are watertight. But something just doesn't feel right. I was wondering about money laundering, and all that kind of thing.'

Theresa took a deep breath. 'Now you're worrying me, Mr Jacobs.'

As Theresa spoke, she doodled on the pad by the phone and saw that her answering machine was blinking. A message was waiting.

'I don't mean to worry you, Theresa. As I say, everything is fine. It sounds a very interesting, not to mention romantic, project. And I wish you very good luck. Perhaps when holiday time comes around I'll nip down to the South of France for a weekend and visit the restaurant once it's up and running.'

After the call, Theresa remained in the armchair for a while, gazing out at the harbour and thinking.

It was all taking on a strange dreamlike quality and she wanted to pinch herself to make sure she was awake.

She stood up and pressed play on the answering machine.

'Mummy, it's Imogen . . .' For some reason Imogen seemed to be whispering into the machine. 'Can you ring me . . . asap?' Then her voice changed to a loud call – 'Coming!' – and she was gone.

Theresa picked up the phone and started dialling Imogen's number.

A hammering on the door interrupted her. She put down the phone and went to answer it.

It was William. He strode in, put his briefcase on the table and clicked it open. 'We need an alcohol licence. There's a special one, I'm told, which is for restaurants, and gives us the freedom to sell wine, liquors less than eighteen per cent proof, aperitifs, rum and spirits. It's naturally the most expensive one, but we cannot think of opening without it.'

'Of course,' said Theresa, fiddling with her coffee machine and laying out cups. 'Even Disneyland, here in France, had to get one. No self-respecting French person would dream of eating anywhere unless it's possible to have a glass of wine.'

'We also need to acquire a Protection of Minors notice, an official list of opening hours approved by the *préfecture*, a *commission de sécurité* from the mayor, have inspections by the fire brigade, police and the consul general, blah-blah-blah.'

Another rap at the door, and Theresa was relieved to see Carol and Benjamin.

William stood at the table, fingering through the papers. 'You see, I've not just been sitting on my arse. We also need a safety and hygiene inspection and they obviously have to continue on a regular basis. Plus we need to join the National Restaurant Association. Do we want a music licence?'

'No,' said Theresa, at the same time that Benjamin said yes.

'Planning a Friday-night karaoke session are we, Benjamin?' asked William.

'Actually, William, I was thinking about ambient music, some jazz or cocktail piano music. That always adds to the atmosphere.'

'I think we'd better think about that once we're making a bit of this outgoing money back,' said Theresa, remembering her early days in Bellevue-Sur-Mer, when Carol had cajoled her into giving cookery classes to balance the necessary and sometimes extravagant expenses of her move. 'How long will all those things take?'

'I would hope, if I hang around making sure we stay on the top of the lists and we don't run into any major roadblocks, about ten days. Thank the Lord this venue once had a licence before. Apparently if you want to get one from scratch, it's perfect hell.'

'Small mercies,' said Theresa, putting the cups on to a tray and carrying them over.

'And we were very lucky that the old girl Magenta kept paying the licence – even from the retirement home. That's saved us a lot of time and money.'

'Lucky?' said Theresa, reminded again of Mr Jacobs's call. 'It sounds rather odd. Why would she do such a thing?'

'Oh, you know what happens,' said Carol. 'No one actually believes that they're getting too old for anything. She probably thought she'd get better and come back to it.'

'Perhaps she hoped her son would continue the trade,' said Benjamin, picking up a biscuit and dunking it into his coffee.

'I thought we were dealing with the grandson?' said Theresa. 'I was also wondering who bought all that equipment in the cellar. It's not that old, you know.'

'Maybe whoever was running it as a giftshop also had dreams of opening it again as a restaurant,' suggested Benjamin.

'Carol?'

'The boy didn't say anything about that to me. Perhaps it was his father?'

'Hmmm.' William hooded his eyes. 'Well, it's there and it's part of the deal so . . .'

He looked round the team expectantly.

'Right, if you agree we should continue – Carol, Theresa – Benjamin and I will head back to the *mairie* to get everything officially submitted.'

Theresa glanced towards the clock.

'No one's going to be there till at least two-thirty, William. Why don't you go over everything that has to happen next with Carol and Benjamin while I rustle up the lunch?'

11

S ALLY COULD NOT BELIEVE what had just happened. Stanislav had paid the bill saying, 'Now, Sally, I'm sure you'll enjoy giving Destiny a tour of all the local tourist hotspots.'

There was no way to wriggle out of it.

Putting on a bright smile, she walked Destiny through the winding alleys of the historic quarter.

They strolled first past the remaining perfumes of the morning's flower market, now swept-up little piles of petals and stems. As they crossed the Place Pierre-Gautier, Sally pointed out the magnificent Palace of the Kings of Sardinia, gloriously bright-white against the China-blue sky.

'Sardinia?' said Destiny. 'I've been there. It's in Italy. Why does the King of Italy have a gaffe here in France?'

Sally tried to simplify the complicated history in words of one syllable. 'This area used to be owned by them. There isn't a King of Italy any more. It's now the *Préfecture*, a kind of official city hall.'

'My husband's over here looking for a place. Do you think they might sell up?'

Sally couldn't even start to explain.

'Doubt it,' she mumbled, 'but I do know a bit about the property market over here. What kind of budget were you thinking of?'

'Oh I don't know, Sally. Probably around six mill.'

'Six thousand?' asked Sally, translating the French *mille*.

'No, didn't you hear? Million. Six million.'

Sally gulped as they turned into one of the narrow alleyways.

She knew about the local property market but not for values over a million.

'So where is your husband now, Destiny?'

'Boys will be boys, Sally. He's been hooking up with his football mates for lunch, and he's due to take the afternoon off, larking around with Stanny. I think they're going out on his boat. I don't like boats, myself. I only have to look at the sea to be sick.'

Changing the subject, Sally gave Destiny the spiel she always gave friends she was showing round the Vieille Ville, pointing out the good cafés and ice-cream parlours, the churches and ancient buildings.

'It's very old-fashioned, this place, don't you think?' said Destiny, finding that her stiletto heels were not very effective when walking on cobbles.

'It's the Old Town,' replied Sally.

'Well, that explains it. I like new things.' Destiny leaned on Sally's arm to help keep her balance. 'Isn't there a New Town, or a more modern bit of Nice we could go to?'

'What do you like?' asked Sally, at a bit of a loss now to know what to suggest. Extricating her arm and instead taking Destiny's elbow, she offered faintly, but not holding out much hope: 'The Modern Art Gallery?'

'I like shops,' said Destiny. 'Shoe shops, fashion boutiques . . .'

Sally took a deep breath and steered Destiny towards a steep flight of stone steps. 'Then we need to go across the new gardens. You'll enjoy them. Surprising fountains and mist you can walk through, comfy wooden seats. It's very pretty. Green lawns, flowerbeds where only a couple of years back it was a horrible concrete bus station and car park . . . Many years ago it used to be a dried-up old river.'

'I'm not fond of nature,' said Destiny. 'I prefer buildings. You don't get so many insects in buildings.'

'So I'll take you to Rue Paradis.'

'Paradee?' said Destiny. 'My dad used to say a word like that. It was something to do with his drum kit. Paradee . . .'

'Paradiddle,' said Sally, recalling her Saturday-morning TV shows, when she was made to have a go at playing the drums. 'This Paradis is a street. All the fashion shops are along there.'

'Paradiddle, paradee,' said Destiny.

'There's – Chanel, Armani, Hugo Boss. Paradis is French for Paradise.'

'That's what I love about the French,' Destiny smiled. 'They really know the meaning of words.'

12

THERESA TRIED PHONING IMOGEN's mobile a number of times during the afternoon and evening but always got the machine. She tried phoning the home line too, which also switched instantly to voicemail.

She started getting worried. What could have been so urgent? And why was Imogen whispering to her but calling out cheerily to some mystery person in the background? Theresa's head flooded with images of burglars and other criminals holding Imogen and the children hostage in their kitchen.

She wasn't sure whether to try contacting one of her friends and asking them to drop round.

She slept fitfully and woke very early the next morning. Allowing for the one-hour time difference, it was certainly too early to phone anyone in London.

To keep herself occupied, she got up and went across to the restaurant. She was impressed by what she found. The plumbers had worked hard all day the day before, and the sink and hobs were now installed. The washroom still looked a mess but was obviously coming together, and once the basins and toilets were installed it would only take a tiler to make the place look wonderful.

Today, while they would continue work on the plumbing for the washbasins and lavatories, electricians would move in and start putting in the electric oven and wall sockets around the countertops in the kitchen.

The whole place looked bright and cheery, she had to say.

The only dismal area was now the dining room.

Theresa went down into the cellar. Now that most of the equipment was out of the way, she could see that the space was much more capacious than she had at first thought. It would be a very useful storeroom.

Carol and Benjamin could start whitewashing the walls today, then they should look at getting some shelving put up and installing some wine racks and perhaps a small desk to act as an office.

As Theresa turned towards the stairs something skittered away from her feet and she looked down to see a somewhat fancy red and golden Zippo cigarette lighter lying on the tiled floor. Someone must have dropped it yesterday when they were lugging the equipment up the steps.

She picked it up, and slipped it into her pocket.

A rap on the front door indicated the arrival of the electricians and plumbers. She ran up the steps to let them in.

As there was nothing much she could do in the restaurant while it was filled with a gang of electricians, carpenters, plumbers and plasterers, she went back to her apartment to work on other things and soon try Imogen again.

William was waiting on the doorstep.

'Do you have any idea how much a *grande licence* costs?'

'I have no idea, William. This was your area.' Theresa ushered him in and cleared a space on the table.

'Have a guess,' said William, crossing the threshold. 'Go on.'

'I really have no idea, William. Perhaps a thousand euros.'

'Not even in the right ball park.' William gave a braying mock-laugh. 'Wait for this, Theresa. I think you'd better sit down first. A *grande licence* costs between ten and twenty thousand euros.'

'Whoa . . . maybe we should get a not-so-*grande licence*.'

'Ha-bloody-ha, Theresa. A *grande licence* is the restaurant-standard alcohol licence.' William paused, pursing his lips, allowing Theresa to register before carrying on. 'And in case you didn't hear me the first time, I said between ten and twenty thousand euros. Money up-front *before* we can open. Who is going to foot the bill for that?'

'We'll have to find a way. Yes, it's expensive, but we can't open without one. Go ahead William – your department, end of subject,' said Theresa. 'Coffee, or something stronger?'

William thrust up his palm. 'Don't even mention alcohol. I'll have a *café crème*, please, Theresa.'

A knock on the door.

Carol stood there with a huge suitcase and a duvet wrapped over her shoulders.

'The repo men – or whatever they're called over here – just hauled me out of bed and threw me into the street. I'm officially one of the homeless.'

She sank down on to the chair beside William and burst into tears.

While she was sobbing there was another knock on the door. This time it was Benjamin.

'I just saw Carol, lugging a suitcase like a bag-lady ... Oh, you're here.'

He sat in the third seat.

As Theresa once more walked to the table with a tray of coffees, the mobile phone in her pocket started vibrating. She staggered across the room, put down the tray and fumbled in her pocket. The phone was right at the bottom. She pulled out her bus pass, a small packet of tissues and the lighter she had picked up this morning before retrieving the phone.

'*Allô! Allô!*' But the phone had stopped vibrating.

She looked at it.

It had been Imogen.

Damn.

'One minute, guys. If I may make a quick call.'

She turned and dialled Imogen, but, annoyingly, it switched immediately to voicemail. Imogen must have started another call. Theresa left a message: 'It's Mummy, darling. I know you're trying to get me. I hope everything's all right. You know where to find me. Keep trying and so will I.'

When she got back to the table Benjamin was admiring the Zippo lighter.

'I always wanted one like this. It was a limited edition, you know.' He flicked it open and lit the flame. 'But isn't it gorgeous. Look at those crosses and skulls. Wow!'

'You don't need a lighter any more, though, do you, Benjamin?' William gave a tight smile. 'Not now that you're off the drugs.'

'I don't *need* one, no. But it is still lovely. I could use it to light birthday-cake candles and things.' William glared and Benjamin placed the lighter back on the table, leaving Theresa to pick it up. 'Not what I'd expect you to have, Theresa.'

'No, it's not mine, actually. I found it this morning on the floor in the cellar at the restaurant. I was wondering whether it might have been yours.'

'If only,' said Benjamin.

'Then it must belong to one of the workmen.' As Theresa slipped it back into her pocket she noticed William giving her a sidelong glance.

They continued the conversation about money, as William sat with a calculator and large ledger, jotting down notes and doing sums.

They spent the morning working out plans for the decorating, and maybe the hiring of extra staff. They discussed advertising and marketing and finally chose a day to open.

'I think we should open quietly, like a trial run,' said William.

'Then have a grand opening night,' said Carol. 'With stars and glamour and popping paparazzi taking photos for all the big magazines.'

'We should be so lucky.' Theresa scribbled on a piece of paper. 'We should make sure to invite all the reviewers too – Michelin, Gault et Millau, *Time Out*, Amex, local papers . . .'

'You're right,' said William. 'Carol, will you organise that?'

'Meanwhile,' Theresa said, 'it might be helpful if we came up with a name.'

'Le Chat sur le toit?' suggested Benjamin.

'I hate those humorous names,' said William. 'And *toit* may, in fact, mean roof, but, the word, in English, has a rather unfortunate homonym.'

'Twat!' Theresa and Benjamin spoke in unison, and laughed.

'OK, gang, I've got it,' said Carol, after a short pause. 'La Mosaïque.'

Part Three

CAVIAR NIÇOISE with MELBA TOAST

Ingredients
250g black olives, stones removed
1 clove garlic
2 anchovy fillets
a few basil leaves
1 tablespoon capers
100ml olive oil
black pepper or *piment d'espelette*
ordinary white sliced bread

Method
First make the caviar. Chop the olives, garlic, anchovies, basil and capers together, until they reach a fine consistency. Put the mixture into a bowl and pour in the olive oil, stirring all the time. Add pepper or *piment d'espelette* to taste. Set aside and make the melba toast as follows. Toast the slices of bread, then remove all four crusts and cut laterally – i.e., through the moist centre of the bread, creating two fine slivers per slice. Place on a baking tray, moist side up, and grill for a very short time till crisp. Spread the caviar on slices of melba toast and serve.

13

Sally squinted in the sun, trying to find a table for lunch at the brasserie by the quay. The terrace was as usual packed, but on such a lovely day she didn't fancy sitting inside. She felt nervous, and hoped her daring mixture of guests would approve of her choice.

Jackie had been up late working on her laptop into the night and when Sally left was still snoozing, promising that she would join her after 'a jolly old soak in the tub'. Today was Sunday, the festival three days away, and Stanislav was once again due to spend the day playing on the yacht, leaving Sally to 'look after' Destiny. To ease the situation Sally had decided to invite Sian to lunch, to make up the four.

The brasserie owner came through to greet her, with arms outstretched.

'Madame Connor! How can I help?'

Sally explained the situation and he told her that he would have a table ready in about twenty minutes, and in the meantime if she'd like to sit up at the bar, she could have an aperitif on the house.

He took her by the elbow and whispered in her ear.

'In fact, I was hoping to talk to you.'

Sally gave him an enquiring look.

'Your friends, the other English . . . I hear they are hoping to open a restaurant a few doors along at old widow Magenta's place. Is this true?' Marcel's face was wrinkled.

Sally felt her palms go all hot. She hated being put on the spot like this. Especially as she had sidestepped the project herself.

'I believe they are looking into it,' she replied, hoping it was a vague enough response. But Marcel was not to be put off so easily.

'It's just that Bellevue-Sur-Mer is a small town, Madame Connor. I'm not sure whether I can take such competition. There is only so much of a clientèle, especially in these hard times of austerity. Think of the winter . . .'

Sally knew she had to be straight with him or this would turn into a conversation that would spill all over her possibly high-tension lunch.

'I'll have a word with them, Marcel. Get them to come over and talk to you. I'm sure they must have some plans that will work in a complementary way so that you can both exist together. But truly, I have nothing to do with it.'

Marcel, temporarily pacified, went over to greet another potential diner. Sally squeezed her way through the tables on the sunny terrace and, as she moved past one, a hand flashed out and grabbed her by the jacket.

'I have a bone to pick with you, madam.'

It was Diana.

'Oh, Diana! Hi! What's up?'

Diana patted her lips with her napkin. 'What on earth entered your brain, giving out my email address and phone number?'

Sally was mystified.

'I didn't.' Sally heard her voice two octaves higher than usual.

Diana focused her famous glare on Sally. 'You most certainly did. And worst of all, you gave it to that tiresome woman from that ghastly TV soap about the female aviators. *Birds Fly Over Broadstairs* or whatever it's called.'

'*Skirts Fly Over Suffolk*,' Sally mumbled, wishing she could fly off out of it right now. 'Jackie Westwood.'

'Exactly. Now she wants me to come to some pathetic little screening at Cannes Marketplace, and pose with her for photos and all kinds of things, and you know, Sally, it's embarrassing to refuse her when I know you recommended her to me.'

'But I didn't . . .' Sally's mind raced. How on earth had this happened? Then she remembered the card Diana had given her. Hadn't she thrown it into the bin? But how could she tell Diana that? Obviously Jackie had gone rooting about in the wastepaper basket and found it. Worst of all, she was about to arrive here on the scene, any second.

'Look, Sally, darling, you know me, I'm a big softy, but I have to refuse her. You do understand, don't you? And please don't do anything like that to me again.'

The young woman sitting opposite Diana went into a coughing fit, drowning out all conversation.

'Oh, Sally, this is my daughter, Cathy. She's come over with me to have a little break and get a bit of sun on her skin. Cathy, this is Sally. We were in rep together, sweetie, during the Stone Ages. Cathy is a librarian.'

The girl rose and shook Sally's hand. 'Hello, Sally. Cathy. Don't mind me. I don't like to be noticed. That's Mama's job.'

Cathy sat down again and started vigorously attacking the food on her plate.

'So, Sally darling, it's all forgotten and forgiven. But it won't happen again, will it.' Diana nodded slightly.

Sally started to explain and realised she was making it worse. She did manage to convey that Jackie was staying with her and might suddenly arrive for lunch.

'You won't mind if I have words with her, then.' Diana gave a radiant professional smile. 'Thanks for telling me about this little town. It's gorgeous here, and so lovely to get away from the madding crowds.'

Cathy started coughing, quite violently, as though she was choking.

'Are you all right, Cathy?' asked Sally, glad of the diversion.

'I'll be fine,' said Cathy in a squeaky voice. 'This foreign food is very rich for me. I prefer something a bit more plain, you know. Gluten-free, if possible. What with my allergies . . .'

'Still friends, darling? I know you understand.' Diana blew Sally a kiss and, ignoring her daughter, turned once again to her plate.

Sally was dismissed. She started to walk away.

'You must show me your place, sometime. What are property prices like?' Diana called after her. 'Is property cheap? It might be quite cosy to get a little bolthole hereabouts.'

Sally's heart quivered with horror at the thought of Bellevue-Sur-Mer being filled with old acting friends from England. Some escape that would be!

When she got to the bar, she found Sian already perched on a stool, sipping an aperitif.

'Marcel told me we were waiting for a table.' She nodded in Diana's direction. 'Isn't that . . . ?'

Sally nodded.

'You must introduce me to her. I'm *such* a fan.'

Sally's stomach clenched.

Sian went on staring in Diana's direction.

'Who's that girl with her? Is she famous too?'

'No,' said Sally. 'It's her daughter.'

'Ah, so *she* managed to raise a child who isn't a man-eater, then.' Sian knocked back the rest of her Noilly Prat. 'Quite sickly looking, isn't she? Like a nun.'

Before Sally could reply, a loud screech came from the pavement, silencing all the diners on the terrace. It was Destiny.

'Hi, Sally! Which is our table?'

Marcel scurried forward and guided Destiny through to the bar as all heads turned to gawp at her.

'Destiny MacDonald!' Sian muttered under her breath. 'My God, Sally, suddenly you're the new "and friend" of *OK!* magazine. What happened? You've become celeb central.'

'It's all a coincidence.' Sally felt embarrassed and uneasy. She changed the subject and mumbled, 'However long are they going to take with that table?'

Sally saw Diana's head turn to watch Destiny's arrival as she slipped herself between the tables. Simultaneously, in the distance, she noticed Jackie swaggering towards the brasserie terrace.

'I am so excited,' said Sian. 'What a lunch date this is. It's the best Sunday ever!'

In the midst of the terrace Marcel raised his hand and pointed to a table.

Sally grabbed her bag and nodded to Destiny and Sian.

They were all seated as Diana rose from her chair and made an elegant sashay towards them.

'Hello, girls!' She pushed her sunglasses down the bridge of her nose and peered over the top. 'Here we all are, living the glamorous Riviera life.'

'Rather!' said Jackie, stressing the last syllable. 'Girding our loins before the battle commences.'

'Oh, darling . . .' Diana beamed down at Jackie. 'I'm so sorry I won't be able to make your little film, I'll be at a junket all day.'

Jackie opened her mouth to speak, but Diana got in first. 'After that I've promised my daughter that I'll take her to the Cocteau Museum at Menton, and the Matisse and Chagall at Nice . . . Oh, I have *such* a full week. And the rest of the time of course, like you, I'll be rushed off my feet at the festival. I'm so sorry, sweetie.' She bent low to the table and stage-whispered: 'And, except for duty, one wants to spend as little time as possible in Cannes, don't you think? It's just a sweaty meat market.'

Sally was aware that most of the other diners on the terrace were staring at their table with its array of stars and celebrities.

A waiter lurked, wanting to take their orders.

Diana sensed the moment and took her leave. She turned back and headed to her own table in the shade.

'I know her. She's a famous actress, isn't she? And what the bloody heck's a junket?' asked Destiny.

Jackie said, 'She is. Yes. Oh, and it's a sort of Q and A.'

'Q and A? What's that? Isn't it a cheap high-street clothes shop?'

Jackie picked up the menu.

Monsieur Leroux was technically breaking the law by allowing his men to work on a Sunday, but he was keen to get the job finished as soon as possible, and in his words 'what went on behind closed doors stayed there'. He was thankful that it wasn't a flat with downstairs neighbours having nothing better to do than complain or, worse still, report him. But he had to be out of there this week and didn't want to leave them with anything unfinished.

So, while his men fiddled about fixing worktops, installing lavatories and basins, and testing all the electric points and equipment, Carol and Benjamin worked alongside Theresa, painting the walls of the dining room a bright white.

Theresa had tried to call Imogen a number of times both on her home line and her mobile and got nothing but the answerphone. She now had a constant internal niggle. What had happened? And why no word from her since that one enigmatic message?

While there was nothing she could do but wait and keep trying, she knew she had to concentrate on the work in hand.

'If we get a move on, while the men fit the lighting in here tomorrow, we can visit all the furniture shops for tables and chairs and we'll be practically ready for inspection by the end of the week.'

Carol took a few steps back and admired the work. 'What we really need is a huge piece of art on this side wall – bright and shiny with big splashes of vivid colour. A Patrick Heron, a Terry Frost or an Albert Irvin.'

'On our budget, you'll have to do it yourself.' Benjamin dunked his paint roller in the white vinyl. 'We'll be the only place that can boast an original Carol Rogers.'

'I went to art school, I'll have you know,' said Carol. 'Though I must admit I did not graduate.'

'How about Sally's son Tom?' suggested Theresa. 'His work was rather good, I thought.'

Carol gave a deep throaty laugh. 'We are not using his huge canvas of naked Zoe, however colourful.'

'Worth asking, though.'

Theresa noticed that Monsieur Leroux's men were sitting in the little back yard, eating home-made sandwiches from plastic boxes. She glanced at her watch. It was late for lunchtime.

'We're almost done here, aren't we? Let's wash the brushes, and get over to my place and have an official break.'

'Sod that,' said Benjamin. 'Let's go to the brasserie.'

'I'm with Benjamin.' Carol was already unbuttoning her dungarees. 'Let's get waited on.'

'I'll phone William,' said Benjamin. 'See if he has got any further with the business stuff.'

'On a Sunday?' said Theresa. 'Unlikely.'

'Well, he can join us anyway.'

While the others were washing their brushes, Theresa had one more go at calling Imogen.

This time she got through.

'Imogen? Are you all right?'

'Can't talk now, Mum,' she replied. Her voice was tense, and slightly out of breath, as though she had been running. 'It's dire. Soooo much to tell you. Cressida, leave that alone! Get in, Chloe.'

'But, Imogen . . .'

Imogen said, 'Talk later,' and hung up.

As they strolled along the road together, Theresa looked up to see Marcel standing on the pavement watching them approach.

'Full,' he said, waving his arms, shooing them away. 'No space.'

Theresa could see a few available tables, and others where people had finished their coffee, paid the bill and were picking up their things, ready to leave.

Marcel stepped out on to the street, blocking their way.

'No room for traitors here,' he said. 'No room for people who stab you in the back.'

Carol took the lead. 'Marcel darling, don't get so hot and bothered! We'll be no competition for you, sweetie. Look at your fabulous view and your huge terrace. Our place is tiny. We'll have about forty covers.'

'If we're lucky,' added Benjamin.

Marcel did not calm down.

'In the winter, I'm lucky if I get forty covers. Especially if it rains.'

Theresa stepped forward. 'Please, Marcel, let's talk, but just not now, in front of everyone.'

'I will not tolerate the treacherous!' The brasserie owner was red in the face and looked as though any moment he might explode. 'Go!'

'All right, all right,' said Theresa, putting up her right hand in a halting gesture. 'Let's go to my place.' She turned and spoke quite calmly. 'You just lost yourself four covers for lunch today, Marcel. Seriously, we don't want a war. There's no reason why we cannot exist together.'

Sitting around Theresa's glass table, they discussed the problem, and Benjamin made a good point. 'What did he do when old Ma Magenta was in charge? Presumably she was here first. Or were they both running along in perfect harmony?'

'Maybe Marcel was at war with them too,' said Carol.

'Perhaps that is the real reason the grandson is so keen to ditch the place,' said Theresa.

Sally had seen Marcel shouting at Theresa and the others and wondered what was going on. She was sorry to see them walking off, as she would have liked them to be at an adjacent table where she could talk to them.

Jackie, Sian and Destiny had been deep in conversation for what felt like hours. While they munched through the starter, the main course and now the dessert, they talked about show-business publicity agents and marketing strategies and all kinds of things that Sally knew nothing about. Even in those faraway days when she was actively in the business, no one she knew had a publicity agent. Everyone just muddled through. Nowadays, it seemed, everyone's lives were dictated by stylists and managers and PAs as well as the compulsory agents.

While they talked, currently on the subject of which designer labels provided you with the best loans for premières and parties, Sally watched fishermen sitting on their boats, tucking into their lunch and mending their nets. There was a row of small fishing boats and beside them another row of gin palaces.

'Destiny?' Sally spoke for the first time in half an hour. 'Why would you prefer lunch with us to being on that fabulous yacht with your husband?'

'Oh, Sally, love, I only have to look at a glass of water and I'm seasick, remember. Boats! Can't stand the things. If God had wanted us to mess about on the water, we'd all have been born with flippers, I always say.' Destiny paused to sip her wine. 'Anyhow, hun, nothing beats a nice chinwag on a sunny Riviera terrace with the girls. Stanny gets a bit too intense for me.' She took another gulp of wine then gave Sally an enquiring look. 'Didn't Stanny say you had your own boat, Sally?'

Jackie's head swung round. 'Crikey, Sally, you're a dark horse. Maybe you could run us over to Cannes in it. That would be ever so glamorous, don't you think?'

'Where do you keep it?' Destiny pushed her sunglasses up onto her head.

'It's over there.' Sally stood and pointed towards it. 'It's moored alongside the red and green fishing boat.'

'It's the boating equivalent of a garden hut,' said Sian.

'I like it,' said Sally, feeling quite defensive, being the only person at the table who was not rolling in money.

'It's hardly a gin palace, darling, is it?' said Sian, laughing and turning to the others. 'And as Sally is part-owner with my soon-to-be-ex-husband, who I am about to take to the cleaners, perhaps it'll soon be mine. You only own the licence, don't you, Sally? The structure of the boat belongs to Ted.'

Sally knew that this was true, but she had planned to buy out Ted's share.

Sian put her hand out and rested it on Jackie's arm. 'You'd be lucky to get to Cannes in two hours in that little thing. And that's with a calm sea and a following wind. I'll run you to Cannes in the car when you need to go, Jackie. It'll take all of half an hour. We'll put on headscarves and dark glasses and wind the top down and pretend to be 1960s *filles BCBG*.'

'You really are a sport, Sian. I think I'll take you up on that.'

'When's your showing?'

'Weeeelllllll . . .' Jackie screwed up her mouth. 'I'm not absolutely sure. But I think it's on Wednesday or Thursday.'

Destiny interposed. 'When you're all saying "Cannes", do you mean Cannes the film place, with the red carpet up all those steps?'

'That's the one,' Sian smiled. 'You must be pretty used to red carpets by now, Destiny.'

'I am, Sian, I am. Perhaps I could come with you both?' Destiny blotted her red lips with her napkin. 'I adore everything to do with showbiz. I'm never happier than when I'm in a lovely dress and people are taking pictures of me.'

Sally looked out to sea again and wished she was bobbing about on her boat – or was it Ted's?

14

T HERESA WOKE VERY EARLY on Monday morning. She felt exhausted; in her dreams she'd been running up and down ladders all night long.

But yesterday had been productive. They had discussed and made decisions on several things: the menus – both the look and the content; which wholesalers and meat and fish suppliers they would use; the cutlery and plates; even the laundry where the napkins and tablecloths could be washed daily.

William had made enormous spreadsheets, and pages of costings that covered everything from staff rotas to profit margins.

Carol had presented a magnificent portfolio about advertising, complete with designs and ideas for the layout of the dining room. Theresa wondered where she had found the time. Maybe Carol didn't need sleep, even after a heavy day's painting. She was now staying in Theresa's box room. Theresa had definitely seen a light on in the early hours this morning, and heard, through the door, the swish of bits of paper being torn from a pad, followed by the fevered movements of rubbing out. Carol was obviously still at work on the design.

Last thing yesterday, before locking up, Theresa and the gang had gone to see the wonderful work Monsieur Leroux and his team had managed to accomplish in such a short time.

Apart from finishing touches – fitting downlights into the holes that were wired and ready in the ceiling – it really was now a case of furnishing the place. Carol was going to decorate the plain dining-room walls to give the restaurant, in her own words, 'a bit of oomph!'

Theresa rolled over in bed and looked up through the window to the steep dark well leading up to the Hôtel Astra. She could hear a couple arguing. 'I want to go to Grasse, to see the perfume places,' said the young female voice. 'But I thought we'd agreed we were going to Monte Carlo?' said the man.

'Monte Carlo – I know you're only wanting to get tickets for the Grand Prix.'

Theresa laughed. The young woman pronounced the X, giving it an altogether different meaning.

'Typical man!' said the woman.

'Well – you know what they say,' said the man, his voice rising. 'All cows go to Grasse!'

Then she heard a slap.

Oh dear, thought Theresa. That was what holidays were all about – falling out with your nearest and dearest.

She sat up and yawned, then shuffled into her clothes and had a quick wash before making her way across to La Mosaïque to let everyone in.

When she got there, she found the front door ajar.

She hadn't knocked on Carol's bedroom door, knowing that she'd been up working into the night, but maybe the woman was a complete insomniac and had crept out and was here before her. Or perhaps William was inside, measuring up for table sizes or the welcome desk.

She walked through the empty dining room, and pushed open the swing door into the kitchen.

Things were not as they had left them last night when they all locked up.

The doors to the oven, fridge and cupboards were hanging open.

What on earth was going on?

She hurried on through to the yard, calling, 'Hello?'

The back door was ajar and the outside store cupboard was also open. Theresa noticed that the padlock had been forced.

What the hell?

She turned and noticed that the drain cover had also been removed, and not put back flush to the ground. She was about to make her way into the cellar when there was a rapping on the front door. Instinctively, before going through she picked up the broom.

Monsieur Leroux was standing just inside the open front door holding out a hand for the ritual morning shake.

'Madame Simmonds, *bonjour!*'

'Monsieur Leroux, *venez!*' Theresa indicated to him to follow her. '*C'etait vous qui a fait ça?*' she asked. 'You did this?'

'*Mais non! Bien sûr!*' Monsieur Leroux looked around the kitchen as he pursed his lips and shook his head. He inspected his work more closely for damage.

'*Les jeunes,*' he said. '*Les mecs.*'

'Young troublemakers?' asked Theresa. Bored kids with nothing to do, she presumed. Local ruffians with little else to fill their time except by causing trouble. That must be the explanation.

But somewhere deep inside Theresa knew there was more to it than that.

She phoned William to let him know about the pranksters, then asked Monsieur Leroux if he could change the locks and reinforce all the entrances.

Theresa thought about her row yesterday with Marcel and wondered if he had been behind all the little things that had happened since they started work on the place – the young man she saw in the dark, the cigarette butts, the Zippo lighter and now this. Could his anxiety about a rival restaurant opening just up the road have led him to employ scare tactics? Perhaps he wanted to make them fear opening so much that they pulled out? Maybe he was simply being nosy and wanted to see what he would be up against?

But then why not just ask Theresa to show him round? She'd have been only too willing. Surely Marcel was man enough to speak up.

Theresa put down the broom, which she realised she was still gripping. She would not be scared out of this place. They'd all invested too much now, both in time and money, to start being intimidated, whether it was by kids or Marcel or whoever.

They were days away from being ready for inspections. Once they passed successfully, and had the certificates framed and plaques put up outside, they would be able to open their doors to the paying public.

Theresa felt proud, but that feeling was diluted by this fresh worry.

In one week they had all worked wonders. They could not surrender now, not when they were so close to achieving what had at first seemed impossible.

15

S ALLY COULD HEAR JACKIE moving about downstairs. She was tempted to turn over and go back
to sleep but did not want to be seen as a really hopeless
hostess, even when the guest was uninvited.

She was pulling on her blouse when the phone rang.
It was Diana. 'How's life with Miss Jolly-What-
Ho?'

Sally couldn't help but laugh.

'Downstairs,' she whispered. 'Making breakfast.'

'Well,' said Diana. 'I saw her cosying up to all those
others at your table yesterday and wondered if, now
that she has some new friends, she might leave you
free today to join me for lunch somewhere along the
coast. I've got three more days left to play before work
really kicks in. I saw a lovely little place hanging from
a rock down near Cap-d'Ail or Cap Martin or one of
those obscure zillionaire-inhabited Caps. Fancy it,
Sal?'

'I'll call you back in an hour, Diana. But I think the
answer is yes.'

Sally put down the phone and went downstairs to
find Jackie seated at the table, sipping a cup of tea.

'Hope you don't mind, old bean,' said Jackie. 'But I helped myself.'

'No problem,' said Sally, actually feeling a little put out. 'Is there enough in the pot for another cup?'

Jackie winced. 'Oh dear. Only filled up for one. Waste not want not and all that.'

Sally gritted her teeth and refilled the kettle.

While her back was turned away from Jackie she asked her if she would be busy today.

'Oh, rather!' said Jackie, biting into a piece of toast. Sally realised that Jackie must have raided the freezer too, as that was the only place in the house she could possibly have found a sliced loaf. Tom had bought it and put it there and Sally had forgotten all about it. 'Sian is going to drive me up to see the hillside towns – tourist stuff, you know – and then help me do a bit of marketing on the old film. We have to go into Cannes too, so that I can try to get her a last-minute festival pass.'

Sally wondered how many film credits Sian could prove. Or perhaps, being at the marketing end of things, she could get in as a finance person.

Outside in the road a car pulled to a stop and there were a couple of toots on the horn.

'That'll be Sian now.' Jackie sprang from her seat, cramming the remains of the toast into her mouth. 'See you this evening, old girl.'

After an hour, when she had eaten her own breakfast and washed up for them both, Sally phoned Diana and agreed to be waiting by the quay at a quarter to noon.

Zoe was down there, sitting on the sea wall, swinging her legs and rooting through her capacious handbag.

'Hey, Sally!' she called brightly. 'Off to your motorcycle-maintenance class?'

'Zoe!' Sally laughed. 'Will you *ever* give up on that old joke?'

'How's the gorgeous boyfriend?'

Sally perched on the wall next to her friend. 'I wonder, Zoe, if he doesn't prefer the boys, you know. He's been at sea ever since with that footballer.'

'Ah yes,' Zoe peered over the top of her specs. 'While you "cavort with his busty model wife, Destiny, twenty-four". Isn't that how they put it?'

'There'll be no cavorting on my side,' said Sally.

'I knew a Russian once. Lived up in Èze. Wife had a *huuuuge* b . . .'

Zoe's lips started to vibrate and she was unable to finish the word.

She tried again: 'A huge b . . . b . . .'

When the stammer recurred Sally suggested: 'Bosom? Bust?'

'No,' said Zoe decisively. 'A huge b . . .'

'Bottom?'

'No, no,' cried Zoe. 'She had a huge balalaika.'

Together they watched William and Benjamin cross the car park and go towards the Magenta building.

Zoe sang: 'Bill and Ben, Bill and Ben, off to work they go.'

'I thought that was *Snow White and the Seven Dwarfs*?'

Zoe glared at Sally and pulled her spectacles even lower down the bridge of her nose. 'I swear I won't ever tell *anybody* you just said that,' she said. 'We don't want the LGBTQXYZ community baying for your blood now, do we?'

'I meant the song was from . . .'

'Do you know, Sally, I wouldn't touch that Magenta place with a fifty-foot pair of tongs.' Zoe's head swerved in the general direction of the restaurant. A signwriter, up a ladder, was slowly painting its new name above the frontage – La Mosaïque. 'Too much history, you know.'

As Sally was starting to regret not being part of the gang working to create the new restaurant, she was glad to hear this.

'Why do you say that, Zoe?'

'That Magenta bird was a wily old thing. Very tricky.'

'And I suppose that you, Zoe dear, are a breeze.'

'I am! I am!' Zoe's voice swooped like Dame Edith Evans's famous 'handbag'. 'But compared to Magenta I'm a soothing southern zephyr. Franca Magenta was the mistral, a maelstrom, a hurricane, a nasty piece of work.'

'Really?' Sally was always unsure whether to believe anything Zoe said, as she was so keen on exaggeration. 'Why do you think that, exactly?'

'Why?' Zoe was back into the 'handbag' mode. 'Why not? All that voluptuous Italian thing, for a start. The wobbling flesh, the plunging necklines, the ever-so-slightly too tight and short skirts and tops. Always on the pull. And on top of that there was the usual southern Italy culture . . . you know.'

Sally did not know; involuntarily shrugging one shoulder, she let Zoe know it.

Zoe flapped her arms about. 'Italians, you know, Sicily, Sardinia, horses' heads on doorsteps, "He sleepah with the feeeshes." All that stuff going on but with a row of dribbling lusty-eyed men in her wake. She was hell.' Zoe sniffed.

'You're just jealous, Zoe.'

'Not me. Too much intrigue around that one. Flies around . . . And let's just say, she was not a woman's woman.'

'I always thought that Franca Magenta was just a simple peasant type. Salt of the earth. Come to Mamma. Eata your dinna!'

Zoe laughed so hard Sally feared she might fall off the wall.

'Darling Sally, always the innocent lambkin. I'll tell you something. She had lovers in every cupboard, popping in and out of windows. Her particular penchant was for the famous rich elderly.'

'Well, that's a new definition,' Sally smirked.

'I think the old bitch was hoping to feature in somebody's will. Don't think she managed it. But she took her tits out for those mad old boys and they did give her things in return: jewels and stuff. She had a fair old stash by the time she was shoved into the home.'

'And there's me thinking she got her money from the restaurant.'

'That place? God, no. For starters, the food was repulsive. I wouldn't have put it past the woman to have served up her enemies' body parts in those famous ragouts of hers. The French didn't have such strict meat laws then, remember. There were quite a few men who vanished.'

'They probably just caught a boat back to Sardinia, Zoe. They do leave from here daily all year round.'

'Not from here, Sally. You have to go along the coast to Genoa.' She tutted and shook her head. 'The vibes that place must still have.' Zoe shivered. 'Before I opened a new enterprise in that building I'd get the place exorcised. There's probably a skeleton or three under the floorboards and another down the drains. So anyway, Sally . . .' Zoe paused and looked Sally in the eye. 'What's all the gossip about you knocking around with all these famous people? Marcel is full of nothing else; he's telling everyone about you sitting at a table with the whole front page of *Hello!* magazine.' She paused, then added, 'Well, that and the Magenta place opening to ruin his business.'

A taxi swerved down the hill and swept along the front.

'Come on, Sally, spill the goss.'

Sally stood.

'I'll have to tell you next time, Zoe. I'm off on a lunch date.'

'Not with that Russian Handsome Harry, I suppose.' Zoe peered into the back seat of the car as it came to a stop.

'Aha!' she said with an inscrutable smile. 'No. Not a boyfriend, then. Off to join the rich and famous. Well done you! Ta-ra, old girl!'

Sally stepped forward to open the back door.

Although she rather resented being called 'old girl' by a woman easily old enough to be her mother, if not her grandmother, Sally was delighted that Zoe now had a new game to play next time they met.

As the car pulled out, Sally thought she heard Zoe say: 'You and Franca Magenta – one thing in common: fame by proxy.'

Diana greeted Sally warmly, although her daughter Cathy did not turn her head from the front seat to say hello.

'I get carsick if I change direction,' the daughter said in a quavering voice. 'But Ma is so looking forward to seeing you. I hope you don't mind me sitting in the front, do you?'

Sally noticed Cathy was clutching a half-opened packet of low-salt, gluten-free crackers.

Diana, as usual, looked radiant and utterly glamorous.

Sally bit her lip and wished she'd remembered to check her lipstick before getting in. What was she going to talk about over lunch? The whole day ahead was rather daunting.

Diana poked the driver's shoulder.

'To lunch, to lunch!' She threw her arms up and cried: '"There is no sincerer love than the love of food."'

'Oh God!' Sally instantly recalled a moment in another of the plays they'd done together at Frinton. '*Arms and the Man*! "Ann loves you that way . . ."'

The two women continued in unison: '"She patted your cheek as if it were a nicely underdone chop."'

As the car sped up the hill, they both threw back their heads and laughed.

No, thought Sally. This wouldn't be so difficult after all.

16

THERESA HAD PHONED IMOGEN'S mobile repeatedly, only to be greeted with 'Not now, Mum. Not a good time.' Imogen's voice had seemed pretty tense on every occasion and at the end of the last attempt Theresa had signed off with 'Ring me when you like, darling. I'm always here.' When Imogen had responded with 'Fine. Whatever you say,' and then hung up, Theresa had made up her mind to stop trying her daughter for a while, and wait for Imogen to call her.

For Theresa and her colleagues the next few days were fraught. William had decided he would have to fork out for a car. He added it to the restaurant's initial expenses by way of his mother's favourite maxim: 'You have to lay out to pick up.' She had abided by this in the betting shop or on the racecourse. William had come to realise this catering venture was always going to be as big a gamble as betting on the horses anyway, so as he got accustomed to his new white Peugeot Bipper, he felt completely justified. He efficiently busied himself whizzing everyone around, dropping them off at various shops, outlets and catering suppliers.

In between taxiing the others, William swung his time between the *mairie* and the accountant's office. The opening date had been fixed for ten days away. William had also brightened up. Everything in the legal department was, amazingly, running to schedule, and without any hitches. If the building work also kept on track, some inspectors would be making their rounds on Friday and the rest on Monday morning.

Benjamin, meanwhile, sat in La Mosaïque all day, making sure that the workmen kept on at it, assisting the telecom engineers who were installing the restaurant's official phone line, and being there to sign for deliveries. With his phone always on, he was ready to help co-ordinate the others, while he unpacked chairs and assembled tables.

Theresa was at home working. She had a plan. Before the official licence came through, they would have a few test runs with some friends. They couldn't officially take money for such a thing, and if the friends wanted wine or any other alcoholic beverage they would have to supply their own. She hoped they would do the decent thing and leave a little 'gift' in the pot to cover the cost of the raw materials.

Later in the week they decided they had better gather to interview some local people for positions assisting in the kitchen and to wait at the tables, to cover themselves if ever one of them was ill or needed time off. They were all facing the reality of this round-the-clock commitment. Adverts were in the local papers and the interviews would take place as soon as the building work was complete. That way they could show the potential employees around the premises.

Carol was working away to match the exact lettering from the sign outside, copying it on to a foldaway sandwich board which they could place on the pavement displaying the day's menu. All the designs she had come up with were based on the theme of the mosaic. She had already started painting little zodiac motifs on the dining-room walls. William had not been happy with the receipts she had handed him for acrylic paints and sable brushes.

'One hundred-plus euros for a few tubes of paint?' he cried. 'What are they made from, liquid gold?'

'The colours had to match the floor, William,' Carol said. 'I can't help it if those were the most expensive colours. The pigments in them must be pricey or something.'

Theresa was also worried by Carol's apparent lack of concern about splashing out, rather than searching for cheaper alternatives. It was all very well for her. It wasn't her own money going up in smoke.

Meanwhile Theresa had assembled and costed menus to last at least a fortnight. While balancing the prices, she made up her mind to use only the fruits and vegetables of the season, which, in a place like Bellevue-Sur-Mer, wasn't all that difficult.

Theresa was also refining her original idea for the food: local specialities – *socca, pissaladière, tourte de blettes sucrés* – mixed with very traditional English dishes like toad in the hole, lemon syllabub and summer pudding. That way she also hoped they would appease Marcel and the folk at the brasserie, where they served what was known locally as Mediterranean cuisine – salads, pizzas, fish and meat.

Theresa felt guilty. She knew she should be actually practising the recipes. Sometimes these things looked all very good on paper but then didn't work out on a plate. Other times it was technically impossible to make these dishes without a huge team of helpers, pastry cooks, sous-chefs and the rest. She knew she had to try everything out before officially committing it to the menu. It was simply finding the time and space.

Despite her extravagance, Carol was a fine lodger. She offered some inspired suggestions towards Theresa's work, like making fish and chips using battered sea bream, with *panisse* chips – *panisse* being another local dish, not unlike *socca*, made from chick-peas. She also made sure not to get under Theresa's feet and spent a lot of her time in the small box room. She rose early most mornings, and often when Theresa came into the main room there was a pot of coffee brewing and a fresh baguette waiting on the table, laid ready for breakfast.

And in the evening, when they were both dog-tired from working on preparations for the opening, it was lovely to have someone to chat and share a bottle of wine with before turning in.

Added to which, Carol was always so droll and amusing.

It was Carol who had the idea that to refresh their heads they should not have their next meeting at the usual places – the restaurant, Theresa's apartment or William's – but instead go into town and meet on the terrace of a bar on the Cours Saleya in Nice. That way they could share a drink in a buzzy ambience and discuss everything in a neutral space.

They all carried their portfolios to the bar – William's consisting of the certificates and an appointment schedule, Theresa's her menus and costings, Benjamin's a checklist of what had arrived and what was still to come, and Carol's her designs.

Although they sat on a busy terrace, bathed in the warm rosy evening sun and surrounded by other people, while techno music played softly from nearby speakers, its repetitive beat drowned out by laughter and chatter, they conducted the meeting as though they were in a boardroom and put forward their work one by one, followed by a joint discussion.

In the centre of the table was an ice bucket with a large bottle of rosé wine. Beside it there were four small plates of olives (both large green and tiny, local black Niçoise), pizza slices and *pissaladière* squares for them to nibble on.

When William talked about the licence, his holy grail, he turned and pointed to a red, white and blue enamelled plaque on the wall of the bar. 'There you are. That's the precious thing we're after. *Grande licence* level four. Displayed by law.'

All four of them spent a few seconds staring up at the licence.

'It's both hard to get, costs an arm and a leg and even when we get it we cannot serve alcohol for several weeks.'

They looked away from the plaque as though it had disappointed them and turned to Carol, ready to hear her plans.

She pulled out her portfolio. Inside were drawings for the menu decoration, all sketched and linked into the mosaic theme. For her own reference she had also painted a replica of the floor, in its full glory. It reminded Theresa of the vivid blues, reds and yellows of a stained-glass chapel window.

'As you can see,' said Carol, 'I have taken as my main inspiration the patterns of the original floor. It's almost there,' she said as she laid the drawings out one by one. 'I just have to refine them a little.'

'Glad you opted for grey and white, in the end, for the actual menu design, Carol,' said William, picking up the top one. 'Colour printing is prohibitive.'

'It's also pretty naff,' said Carol. 'A multicoloured menu smacks to me of desperate tourist places. Next thing we'd have fading photos of the food displayed outside, and little language flags everywhere.'

'There's somewhere up the road which has actual plates of food on a table outside the restaurant,' said Benjamin, full of glee. 'They look like four plates of sick.'

'We won't be trying that,' said Theresa.

'Amazingly, the place always has customers.' Benjamin sat back in his seat, surveying the crowds drifting past the bar.

'Let's hope we do.' William flicked through Carol's work, then topped up everyone's glass.

'Oh look, there's Sally,' said Benjamin, rising to his feet. 'And – OMG – check out the handsome hunk she's with. Who *is* that? I've never seen *him* around the place.'

Sally was with Stanislav.

He had called Sally that morning, asking if she'd care to join him, along with Destiny and her husband, for dinner. Since her fun day out with Diana, her new motto was 'Why not?'

Benjamin whispered to the table: 'What goss! Sally has a new secret beau. But not so secret for long.' He raised his voice and waved frantically. 'Sally! Sally! Come and say hello, stranger!'

Sally glanced across the crowded terrace and saw them all assembled, faces beaming in her direction. 'You don't mind, Stanislav, do you? Come and meet my friends.'

They squeezed between the diners to reach the back of the bar, and stood beside the table.

'Glass of rosé?' William stood up, holding the dripping bottle, while Sally introduced everyone to Stanislav.

Theresa couldn't help noticing that when he shook hands with the Russian, Benjamin put on his best pout.

'No, thank you,' said Stanislav. 'Sally and I are on our way to dinner with some friends. What are you up to? It looks interesting.'

He picked up one of Carol's sketches which lay on the table.

'Lovely drawing. What is that?'

Carol blushed. 'Oh, it's not really me. It's all based on a thing we're doing in Bellevue-Sur-Mer.'

'A restaurant,' chipped in Theresa, already wanting to spread the word, especially to someone who liked to eat out. 'La Mosaïque. We open next week.'

'*Deo volente*,' added William.

'What's the problem?' asked Stanislav.

'No problem,' replied William. 'We're just waiting on our licence.'

'Do you have a card with opening hours, etcetera?'

Theresa was already rooting in her bag for the packet of business cards, which had arrived from the printer's last night.

'Here you are,' she said, placing a card in Stanislav's hand. 'Maybe you'd like to book for our opening night?'

Stanislav turned to Sally.

'What do you think, Sally?'

'I was hoping to go anyway. But yes. If you'd like to come with me?'

'A table for two please.' Stanislav made a slight bow, and started to move away. 'Now we must go, I'm afraid, or we will be late for our friends.'

As they walked off Benjamin whistled under his breath. 'What a corker.'

'I'll say,' said Carol. 'Lucky old Sally.'

Theresa waved her diary in the air. 'Who cares about that,' she cried. 'We just made our first booking.'

The adjacent table of four Irishwomen, every exposed plump piece of flesh rose-pink, giggled and nudged one another, clinking glasses at the sight of Stanislav's retreating back, then bellowed their approval with laughter.

'To business!' William replaced his spectacles and picked up Benjamin's delivery papers. 'Now, Benjamin, which items are still to arrive?'

Theresa could feel her phone vibrating in her handbag. Surreptitiously she took it out and glanced at the screen, just in case it was a supplier. It was Imogen.

Well, it hadn't been convenient when Theresa had phoned her, and now it wasn't convenient to take

Imogen's call, so Theresa pressed the red button and slipped the phone back into her handbag.

She would ring back after the meeting was over.

When she reapplied her full attention to the discussion, Carol was suggesting she have a go with the chairs, which were plain white. 'I thought I could apply little painted simulated pieces of the mosaic here and there. To keep up the theme. I also found a set of serving plates with a mosaic motif.'

'Too pricey.' William glanced at the paperwork and slid it back to Carol.

Benjamin moaned. 'I like them.'

'All right,' said William. 'Perhaps when we have some money coming in.'

Carol uttered a disgusted sigh. 'William, sometimes you are so tight.'

'Madam,' he replied. 'I want us to earn a living.'

Finally they turned to publicity. Benjamin had arranged with a girl from the local newspaper to do a small article, while Carol had got on to all the main restaurant guides: Michelin, Gault et Millau and the rest.

'They don't give you any warning,' she said. 'But I was tipped off that one reviewer is in the region at the moment. We just have to look out for a man eating alone with a notebook!'

'If only it was that easy,' said William. 'We actually have to make sure we're *always* at our best.'

After an hour, when the business was finished, William called the meeting closed and they all put away their papers and relaxed. The main subject of conversation was Sally's date.

Sally was really enjoying herself. The candlelit restaurant with its soft piano music was chic and romantic. The food was divine.

Mickey MacDonald, with his thick Liverpool accent, was quite the clown, and his repartee with Destiny was very amusing and affectionate. Many of the other diners, both male and female, were giving him admiring looks.

Sally thought about how a footballer played to massive audiences, where, in true Aristotelian form, he could be the beloved angel or the cursed demon. She remembered one of her tutors at RADA talking about how he wished theatre audiences could have more of the atmosphere of the crowd on the football terraces. Despite all those years in between, until now Sally had never met a footballer.

Mickey was funny, and somehow his downbeat droll way of speaking complemented Destiny's brash scattiness.

Stanislav was, as usual, the attentive host.

But today, Sally noticed, maybe because Destiny had a husband to look after her, he was very much more attentive to her.

They talked about Sally's kids, asked where they lived and what they did. She was rather perturbed when she realised that both of her children were essentially wanderers, of no fixed abode. He asked questions about her career as an actress and whether she missed the attention and the fame. Was she perhaps tempted to move back to London and start it up again?

Sally explained that it was an odd thing. For the most part she couldn't think of anything worse than going back there and living the on-off life of an actress, waiting for the phone to ring, being rejected at auditions, packing your bags when you suddenly got a film part which meant you'd be on location in the Orkneys or Turkey in two days' time and have to arrange people to come in and look after your pets or water your plants. But then, unexpectedly, acting friends would reappear, as Jackie and Diana had done, and a strange yearning returned. A desire for the hobo life, the never knowing what would happen next.

Stanislav was amused by this.

Did she miss London? As she lived permanently in France, would she consider giving up her British citizenship?

'Do you know, Stanislav, it's only the red tape that puts me off getting a French passport. All that stuff about pensions and so on. I couldn't face the paper trail. I'm happy to let sleeping dogs lie.'

'A strange way of putting it,' he said, and laughed. 'But this way, I suppose, you have the best of both worlds.'

Stanislav then asked Sally about her friends in Bellevue-Sur-Mer and their plans for the new restaurant.

'They asked me to join them, but you know, that kind of thing doesn't interest me as much as the theatre or movies or boats, so I declined.'

'What's this?' asked Mickey. 'Your friends own a restaurant?'

'They're setting one up. It's going to serve Provençal dishes with an English twist.'

'What the blithering heck does that mean?' asked Destiny.

Sally hesitated then admitted she hadn't a clue and everyone laughed.

Sally took one of the delicious *petits fours* being offered her with the coffee. 'I think it's important to be passionate about anything you're investing in.'

'I completely agree,' said Stanislav. 'For instance, I have just bought a large share of Mickey's football team, and I am fully backing the new project he is starting with kids around the globe.'

Mickey looked up and raised his glass for a toast.

'To the "Kids Have Goals" project!'

Destiny, Sally and Stanislav echoed his salute.

'He's having a big do next week at the local stadium, Sally,' said Destiny. 'I'll be there as support. Fancy coming? It's a gala football game, to raise funds, you know.'

Sally told Destiny that she'd look in her diary and get back to her. She hoped that way she could avoid it. A football match didn't seem much of a fun afternoon to her.

When it came to the time to pay the bill it turned out that Stanislav had settled it even before sitting down. Sally was impressed. The man might have money, but he also had style.

'And now I have a car waiting to deliver us to our respective homes,' he said. 'But first I would like to take you all somewhere special.'

'Oooh, not that ruddy boat, Stanny, please.' Destiny gathered her clutch bag and stood up. 'I'd hate to lose that lovely supper into the Mediterranean.'

'I'm quite aware of your preference for dry land, Destiny.' Stanislav held Sally's chair as she too rose to her feet.

'Shut yer face, Ligorish Boy,' said Destiny.

'Does he like liquorice?' asked Sally, as they got their coats.

'Dunno,' said Destiny. 'It's just something he's always saying when he speaks Russian on the phone. It's ligorish this, vigorish that.'

A shiny limo waited for them outside the restaurant. Stanislav held the door open as they all climbed in the back. Stanislav himself got into the front with his chauffeur and the car revved away along the Promenade des Anglais and then headed inland along steep winding roads, while loud rock music thumped out from the magnificent sound system.

After about fifteen minutes' drive, the car turned in to a pair of high gates that opened by remote control.

'This is my Riviera pied-à-terre,' said Stanislav as the limousine pulled in beside the front door. 'Welcome to my *domaine privé*.'

The house door opened and a butler and maid stepped out, ready to assist Stanislav and his guests.

'Champagne and a few canapés in the lounge, thank you, Cecile. Then you can both retire for the night.'

Mickey stepped forward. 'Actually, Stanislav, could I have a pot of PG Tips?'

'What's that?'

'What's that?' echoed Destiny. 'A cup of good old builder's tea is what it is.'

'Builder's tea?' Both Stanislav and the butler looked bewildered.

'He just means a pot of strong tea,' explained Sally.

'English Breakfast?' asked the butler.

Destiny laughed. 'Breakfast at midnight. But yes, love. That would be gorge. Ta.'

As Sally moved across the hall she could see a billiard room to the left and a large kitchen ahead.

They turned right and walked through a stone-walled dining room equipped with antique oak table and carved chairs all draped in plush maroon velvet. Sally thought it so archetypal a dining room it was almost a joke.

Then they took a few steps down, passed through huge double oak doors and arrived in a large room with fur-strewn sofas and a widescreen TV big enough for a small cinema.

Stanislav picked up a remote control and music came on, late-night jazz, and the lights dimmed.

Sally felt strangely distanced from reality. It was like being in a James Bond film.

'What an amazing place!' she said, wondering if perhaps she was dreaming.

'You're not thinking of selling, are you, Stanny dearest?' Destiny flopped down in the middle of one of the sofas. 'This is exactly the kind of place Mickey and me are after.'

'Comfortable, Sally?' Stanislav came and sat near her on the sofa. She could feel the warmth of his body and hear his breathing. His aftershave was musky and sensual.

The doors opened and the two servants came in wheeling a trolley laden with trays of food and a magnum bottle of champagne in a silver cooler.

The maid poured tea for Mickey, while the butler tackled the champagne.

After the bottle was popped and the delicate crystal glasses filled, Stanislav gave a nod to Stephane and he and Cecile left the room.

'May I propose a toast?' Stanislav served his guests then sat beside Sally and raised his glass. 'I'd like to say that I feel I couldn't be in more splendid and welcome company.'

Destiny went 'Aaaah!' and lifted her own glass.

'You're lovely too, Stanny.'

'It's difficult to talk about, but when you have been born with a silver spoon in your mouth, as I was, people tend not to relate to you as a person. But I have to say that you and Mickey have never treated me any different from all the other millionaires you know.'

Mickey laughed, an explosive locker-room sound.

Stanislav turned to Sally.

'And as for you, Madame Connor, I know you're not a rich woman, and although you once were famous throughout your own land, now your flower has faded, but you're elegant and always full of humour and grace. Here's to you, Sally. You have a beautiful and kind soul. I feel privileged to have met you.'

Short of pinching herself to make sure she was not dreaming, Sally did not know how to respond. She knew she was blushing. She looked at Stanislav, who was beaming at her in a dewy-eyed way.

Was this a joke? Where were the hidden lenses? Surprise, surprise, you've been had! Smile, you're on *Candid Camera*!

But nothing like that happened. Instead, Stanislav reached out, took her hand and squeezed it while never stopping gazing into her eyes.

Sally was amazed to realise why the feeling was so familiar. She had played Helena in *A Midsummer Night's Dream*, and now she finally knew exactly how that character felt when the man she had been chasing suddenly turned round and protested his undying love. Sally wasn't stupid, and knew that Stanislav had probably had a few too many glasses of champers, and, if he had one, would probably be saying these romantic words to his dog. But it was odd that when a man you fancied started making public protestations, it was nothing short of humiliating.

'Oh my word. Thank you,' Sally stammered. 'Really! It's been so lovely to have a bit of company.'

Stanislav drew Sally's hand to his lips and kissed it.

'Oi! Stanny dear,' yelled Destiny. 'If you're going to start canoodling, for God's sake let us out of here, and . . . "get a room".'

17

EARLY NEXT MORNING THERESA was sitting with Carol at one of the tables in the restaurant, working out advertisements to put in the local papers, when her phone rang.

'Mummy! Finally!'

Theresa was glad that she had at last made contact with her daughter.

'Is everything all right, darling?' she asked. 'You sound frantic.'

'Frantic is not the word for it. I'm frazzled.'

'What's happened?'

'You won't believe it.' Imogen's voice went quiet, as though she was cupping the phone with her hand and whispering. 'It's Daddy.'

Theresa made no sound.

'He's moved in.'

'With whom?'

'With me, Mummy. With me and the children. And it's vile. He is such a liar. And a hypochondriac. And he's so demanding.'

'Where's the cleaner? I thought you said he was living with the cleaner?'

'Oh God, Mummy, don't you listen to a word I say? That's history. He wants Annunziata back. But she's skipped the country and won't even take his calls. She's in Turin, I think, north Italy.'

'Her family home, I suppose.'

'No, no, Mummy. Don't you recall she came from some countrified island, Sicily or Sardinia or Capri or somewhere?'

'Now you mention it, I do remember her talking about a tiny island called La Maddalena. Because she was so often maddening and . . . oh I don't know. It seemed funny at the time.'

'Anyway, she's gone to the business end of Italy. And she's utterly washed her hands of him.'

'So why is he not living in his own home?'

'He tells so many lies that I have no idea. He *claims* that Annunziata is a witch and that she has put a curse on the place.'

'A witch? Has he lost his marbles?'

'Oh, it's because she came from some clannish village where they believe in all that superstitious stuff. Don't you remember, she used to tell our fortunes all the time?'

'Oh God, I'd forgotten all that.'

'She showed him a book of spells, apparently, and ever since, he's been sure she sticks pins into his wax model.' Imogen sighed. 'What I do know for a fact is that the house is on the market, 'cos I went there yesterday to get him some clothes – he stinks, by the way – and there was a huge For Sale sign on the gate.'

Theresa was having difficulty taking this in.

'Do you mean he plans to live with you for ever?'

'That is his proposal, yes. When I protested, he kept repeating, in that awful sorry-for-himself voice he uses, "You only have one father, Imogen. Only one father, who begat you," until I had to be restrained from whacking him with the frying pan I was using to cook the children's breakfast bacon and eggs.'

Theresa, still trying to make sense of the information, was about to offer some words of consolation when William burst in to the restaurant, white-faced.

'The mortgage company's turned us down,' he said, flinging his briefcase on to the table they sat at. 'So either we've wasted our time and energy doing this place up, or we're going to be enslaved to someone who may well kick us all out after our six months is up, when we've done all the frigging work.'

Theresa felt winded at dramas coming in on both ears at once.

'I'm sorry, Imogen, I have to go. Let's talk later today. Love you. And the kids.' She put the phone away.

William said, 'Rejected! End! *Finita la commedia!*' and slumped down beside them.

Carol groaned.

Right from the start, Theresa had dreaded something like this happening.

'Did they give any reason?' she asked.

William shrugged. 'Why would they need to? We're a disparate group with no official affiliation. We're not French-born citizens. Some of us have only been living here a matter of months. We're too old. We have no track record. You name it, it will work against us. Look at it from their perspective. We don't have a leg to stand on, especially in this miserable financial climate.'

'Is there anything else we can do?' asked Carol.

'We could win the EuroMillions,' said William. 'Or start an affair with a multibillionaire who wanted to indulge our every little whim and shower us with money. Easy.'

Theresa patted Carol's knee to stop her reacting to William's slightly hysterical outburst. Though her own stomach was a tight knot, she knew someone had to be the reasonable one.

'Before we give up altogether we must have a brainstorm.'

'I think we already had that, dear,' snapped William. 'A month ago, when we embarked on this crazy ill-judged scheme.'

'Let's draw up a list of backers,' suggested Theresa.

'You've heard of crowdfunding?' said Carol. 'Well, why don't we try our own version of that? If we pool our own money, and see if we can get others to add to it . . .'

'And whose name will we put on the deeds? Bill Brewer, Jan Stewer, Peter Gurney, Peter Davy . . .'

'William, stop!' Theresa tried to drown him out, but on he went, relentlessly.

'Daniel Whiddon, Harry Hawke, Old Uncle Tom Cobley and all?'

William picked up his briefcase and walked to the door. 'I'm going home. If either of you need me, that's where you'll find me.'

He turned and slammed out of the restaurant, leaving Carol and Theresa in stunned silence.

Theresa got up and rooted in the cupboard under the welcome desk for a clean piece of paper.

Carol spoke first.

'Who *are* those people he was reeling off?' she whispered. 'Do they live round here?'

Theresa laid the paper on the welcome desk and pulled a pen from the penholder.

'We're a load of bumbling amateurs,' she said. 'I've been terrified to admit it to myself, but what are we thinking of?'

Carol rose and gave her a quizzical look before moving towards her.

'Don't give up now, Theresa darling. We're not utterly washed up, you know. And everyone has to start somewhere.'

'But William's right. We're too old to be starting out.' Theresa sighed. 'Things like this get kicked off by young people gushing with enthusiasm and energy – people naive enough not to realise that life is finite. Not people like us. We're living under the delusion that we can have a fresh start, when really we're so near the end.'

Carol put her fingers in her ears. 'La-la-la-la,' she sang out. 'I will not listen to this kind of talk. We're not washed up. We've had a setback and we have to regroup and press on. We've come this far. We have to give it a chance.'

'I wish I had your spirit, Carol.'

Theresa was still unconvinced.

'I'm going to write a letter to the agent's and see how much of the money we've already laid out we can try to claw back.' She picked up her bag. 'Let's go,' she said to Carol. 'We're getting out of here and going to sit in the sun for a while.'

When they hesitated by the brasserie terrace look-ing for some empty seats, Marcel came out and waved them on.

'Oh Lord,' Theresa said a little too loudly. 'Some people can be so small-minded. Couldn't matter less. We'll have to go to my place for a coffee.'

As they were opening Theresa's front door, Benjamin came panting along, yelling their names.

They moved inside.

'William's about to go to the agent's to get his deposit back,' he said between gasps.

Carol pointed a gloved finger in Theresa's direction. 'So is Theresa.'

Benjamin threw his hands up. 'What is wrong with you lot?' he exclaimed. 'We're down, but we are most definitely not out. There are people who'd back us.'

'Like who?' Theresa snapped, opening the fridge and bringing out a cake. 'The Crown Prince of Ruritania?'

'Well,' Benjamin looked flustered but reached out for a slice, 'what about Sian? Isn't she a businesswoman? Perhaps she has contacts who are looking for just such an opportunity. And Sally's daughter Marianne ...'

'She's in London,' said Carol.

'Really?' said Theresa. 'I'm sure I saw her this morning.'

'We cannot have both Sian and Marianne – they hate one another.'

'Wherever. We just phone them, one by one. Haven't you ever watched *Dragons' Den*? Come on. We have to work fast. We can do it.' Benjamin crammed his mouth with cake. 'I know we can.' He spoke with such convic-tion he sprayed the room with crumbs. He swallowed.

'This is delicious, Theresa. Where did you get it?'

'I made it last night,' said Theresa.

'There you are then,' said Benjamin. 'Who wouldn't want a hunk of that to take home?'

Theresa felt flattered but knew that selling a few slices of cake would be better done in a patisserie than a restaurant.

Carol said suddenly, 'Where is Ruritania?'

'Make-Believe-Land,' said Theresa.

'What day is it?' Benjamin asked unexpectedly. 'Is it Wednesday or Thursday?'

'Thursday!' Carol and Theresa spoke in unison.

'Thursday's child has far to go,' mumbled Theresa. 'Rather like us.'

'Isn't something meant to be happening on Thursday?' Benjamin patted his pockets for his phone, which instantly started to buzz. 'Oh damn, who's this?'

Theresa watched Benjamin as he looked at the screen. He mouthed 'William!' then pressed accept.

'Uh-hum.' Benjamin nodded, winced and said, 'Oh dear, darling. What a shame. See you.'

He smiled and slid the phone back into his pocket.

'So, he's gone to the lawyer's and it turns out that we cannot get out of the first six-month contract, which is great news. So we either leave the place to rot until Christmas, or try to make a go of it for the duration.'

He plonked himself down at Theresa's glass table. 'Well, what are you both gawping at? Let's get the coffee going and start compiling our list.'

'List?' said Carol. 'Of potential backers, you mean?'

'That too,' said Benjamin. 'But what we really need is a list of ideas that are going to get us noticed.'

Theresa filled the percolator, knowing the energising aroma of coffee always helped to spur her on. Secretly she was pleased that they had tried to pull out and been thwarted. There was nothing to direct the mind so much as having your back to the wall. However, at the same time she couldn't prevent a sinking feeling.

'It's going to be hard to press on with total enthusiasm when you know it'll be all over almost as soon as you get started.'

Carol made a quiet sound, indicating that she agreed.

Benjamin crossed his legs deliberately. 'Losers!' he said. 'Where's that Dunkirk spirit? Get on. We've got a chance to have fun for six months. We might even make a bit of money out of it. And if we prove ourselves, we can find somewhere else, can't we? Cannes? Monte Carlo? When things go wrong, we just have to get over ourselves.'

Benjamin's phone buzzed again. The call was short and, during it, Benjamin rose and indicated that they had to hurry out.

'Bye, William,' he said as he slipped the phone back into his jacket pocket.

'Come on, you two!' he called, heading for the door. 'William's on his way to the agent's. He wants to see whether we can sublet La Mosaïque to someone else.'

'Oh no we won't,' said Theresa, following him. 'We're going to stop William in his silly-billy tracks.'

18

S ALLY WOKE IN HER own bed and, despite drinking rather a lot of champagne the night before, she
had only the vaguest glimmer of a hangover.

She could hear banging around in the kitchen
downstairs and at first was alarmed. She'd been having
such a good time with Stanislav, and Sian had taken
over Jackie's welfare and entertainment to such an
extent, she'd forgotten she was there.

But she was clearly downstairs now and the noise of
clanking pots seemed rather loud.

Sally climbed out of bed and looked at herself in the
mirror. How on earth had Stanislav gazed at that tired
phizog and declared her to be beautiful? She shook
her head and went downstairs.

Jackie was dressed up to the nines: full make-up, drop
earrings, hair up, long dress and very high stilettos.

'Going anywhere special?' Sally joked.

'It's my première this afternoon,' said Jackie. 'Then
tonight I've been invited to the smashing new movie
starring Marina Martel.'

'Marina Martel! Oh Lord!' Sally shuffled over to the
sink to fill the kettle. Hadn't Stanislav talked about

Marina Martel on that first day when she was on his boat with Jean-Philippe? Wasn't he financing one of her films or something? Sally wondered whether he'd be there at Cannes today, with the glamorous Miss Martel on his arm, strolling up the red carpet, smiling for the banks of cameras.

As she poured her cup of tea, Sally noticed that Jackie was preparing a packed lunch. It was really rather moving seeing her old friend all tarted up like this, and knowing that she was planning to spend her lunchtime hiding in a corner of the Palais des Festivals, gobbling down a home-made stack of sandwiches, smuggled in an old-fashioned Tupperware container.

'Now, Jackie, is there anything I can do to help?'

Jackie swayed from side to side in a movement that would have looked quite good in uniform but in evening dress looked slightly mad.

'Well, Sally, old bean, I was actually wondering if you'd chum me.'

'Chum you to what?'

'All of it,' said Jackie. 'To my première, then to the big screening tonight. It's a formal red-carpet affair. You have to wear evening gown, high heels and everything. I've wangled two tickets and I don't want to give it to just anyone. We've got invites to the after-party too, if you'd like.'

'Marina Martel's after-party? What about Sian?' Sally dreaded the idea of a thwarted Sian arriving at her front door for a scene. 'I thought you'd promised to take her.'

Jackie winced.

'The situation re Sian is all a bit delicate, as a matter of fact, Sally. When we were parking the car last night, after a very jolly day together, there was this man standing on the pavement grinning in her direction. Sian used the car to try and ram him up against a wall, while shrieking the most dreadful things at him. I thought she'd gone quite barmy, but it turns out the man she was trying to kill was her husband.'

'That would be him.' Sally remained quiet about why Ted actually deserved any foul language he'd got from his wife, as she felt so ashamed that her own daughter was 'the other woman'. 'It's all a bit of a mess.'

'I'll say.' Jackie pressed the lid down on her box of sandwiches. 'But after the little marital drama finished it was as though I'd never been there. I hung about, to say thanks and all that, but Sian just locked the car then chased after him, screaming at the top of her voice, and the pair of them disappeared up the hill. You could hear them yelling for some time. It was obvious she wasn't coming back. So I left it at that and came home and went to bed.'

The lights had all been out last night when Sally was dropped at her door by Stanislav's driver. Jackie must have been already tucked up.

'Did you try to call Sian this morning?'

Jackie shuddered. 'I'll say. Got a right earful down the line. Anyhow, the upshot was that Sian told me she was too busy to do *anything* today. Which is smashing, Sally, 'cos I'd much prefer to be with you.'

Sally couldn't help smiling at Jackie's clumsy attempt to flatter her.

She wondered how the episode between Sian and Ted had ended, and also where it left her daughter Marianne. Sally realised there was no point phoning Marianne, as that was bound to make matters worse. Better to get out of town for the day.

'I'd love to accept your invitation, Jackie. But I'm clearly not as brave as you. I don't think I could face sitting among all the tourists on the train in full drag. Is there anywhere for me to change in the Palais?' she asked. 'If so, I'll bring my clothes in a bag.'

'No problem. If you don't mind using the ladies' powder room to get dolled up.'

'Do we have to dress up for your film too, or can I come to that in civvies?'

'My screening will be ultra-casual,' Jackie laughed. 'That's the spirit, old girl. But it's all guns blazing for the evening show. That's the only place we have to dress posh.' The wall clock struck ten o'clock. 'Golly!' said Jackie, grabbing her sandwich box. 'Look at the time. I'd better be skedaddling. Train departs in five minutes.' She pulled a card from her clutch bag. 'Here's the invitation and details of my screening this afternoon. Don't be late!'

Theresa and the others had dragged William out of the *immobilier*'s office before he reached the desk. Luckily for them all, there was an American couple ahead of him, going through brochures of lots of very expensive estates, and the solitary girl working there this morning was not going to let small fry like William interrupt the possibility of netting two such bigger fish.

Theresa and Carol let Benjamin give the pep talk as they walked back down the hill to La Mosaïque.

Zoe was resting against a bollard outside, holding her face up to the sun.

'Looking forward to opening night,' she said, giving them all a wave.

'Really?' said William, pushing open the front door of the restaurant. 'You deal with it. I'm not in the mood.'

Benjamin, Carol and William went inside. Theresa decided that it was worth keeping one potential customer sweet and stayed for a moment to chat.

'We hope you'll be a regular, Zoe,' she said.

'As long as you don't serve that bright-green soup of yours.' Zoe adjusted herself and brought up a hand to shield her eyes from the sun. 'Too *Exorcist*-like for me.'

'There will always be a choice on the menu.' Theresa gazed out to the harbour. 'Fresh fish, salads, puddings, I hope, something to please everyone.'

'And can we pay in kind?' asked Zoe, trying for a feline smile, which was rather limited, due to her recent lip filler.

'What's that mean?' asked Theresa.

'The old girl used to take things as payment. Saved herself a hefty tax bill, I should think, while cleaning up at auctions.' Zoe lit a Gitanes.

'She reportedly had little Picassos, van Dongens, Chagalls and Dufys stashed away at the back. There was a Léger on the wall in the dining room at one time, and a Cocteau. I remember a huge photo signed by Brigitte Bardot and Salvador Dalí and Grace Kelly and all kinds of glamorous types.' Zoe took a puff of her cigarette. 'Must have been worth a packet. What a girl! She was something else.'

'Rather clever of her, don't you think?' Theresa felt excited again now, to think that they were opening a restaurant in a room where such celebrated people had once visited. 'They must have loved her.'

'Oh, she was clever enough,' said Zoe, exhaling smoke through her nostrils. 'But she was probably blackmailing them all. Terrible family connections, you know.' Zoe stroked her nose and gave Theresa an old-fashioned look.

'What kind of connections?'

'Old Mama Magenta come from Sardeeenia.' Zoe spoke in an exaggerated Italian accent. 'I'd say eff you spent any time in her prezzence you'd 'ave been wise to hold on to your eahrrs.'

'Do you mean the Mafia?'

'Not quite,' said Zoe, her face deadpan. 'But she was certainly part of a family of bandits and kidnappers, and they were all bound together by a secret code of honour.'

'You seem to know an awful lot about her, Zoe. Why don't you come inside and share some of your stories with the others.'

Zoe gave the restaurant a glance.

'I won't, thank you all the same. But I'll definitely be a regular for dinner . . . Once you've had the place exorcised.'

'After it's been sprayed with green soup, you mean?'

'I'm sorry.' Zoe looked at Theresa as though she was mad. 'I haven't a clue what you're talking about.' She stubbed out her cigarette with her shoe and moved away, shaking her head and chuckling to herself.

Theresa walked over to the front door of La Mosaïque.

The failed green-soup joke had reminded Theresa of what had slipped her memory, but was due to happen today – Thursday. She looked at her watch. They had about five minutes to get ready, but that was no worry, as the workmen had recently finished and the whole place was pristine.

Today at eleven was the time of their first visit from one of the health inspectors.

Theresa opened the door and entered, calling out: 'Quick, everyone. Action stations! The health inspector is due to arrive at any moment.'

But the tableau which greeted her rooted her to the spot.

William cringed in a corner, stabbing frantically at his mobile phone; Carol, her face frozen in an expression of horror, held her gloved hands up to cover her wide-open mouth. She was whimpering.

In the centre, at the threshold of the kitchen, stood Benjamin.

Like the Cellini statue of Perseus and Medusa, Benjamin held his left hand aloft, while his face was turned away.

Theresa gasped.

The thing that shocked Theresa and the others was dangling from Benjamin's hand.

It was the bloody decapitated head of a pig.

Part Four

PANISSE CHIPS

Ingredients
2 teaspoons olive oil
150g chickpea/gram flour
salt and black pepper

Method
Grease a few saucers and arrange them in a row. Boil
500ml of water in a pan with a pinch of salt and the
olive oil. Slowly pour in the chickpea or gram flour,
stirring all the while. Keep stirring and in 5 or more
minutes the mixture will thicken. Pour it into the
saucers, filling right to the top. *Take care, as the mixture
sets very quickly.* Leave to set and put in the fridge for a
while to cool, then slide the individual *panisses* off the
saucers and slice them into chips. Deep-fry till golden.
Drain on kitchen towel and serve with finely ground
black pepper and salt (NEVER ketchup!).

19

SALLY HAD PACKED A small bag with her evening clothes and was heading for the door when the phone rang.

It was Marianne, and she was in tears.

'Oh, Mum,' she sobbed. 'I've done an awful thing.'

'It can't be that bad,' said Sally, fearing the worst.

'I hit Ted.'

'Sorry?' Sally took a seat. This was not going to be a short call. 'Did you hurt him?'

'He has a black eye.' Marianne sniffed.

'What did he do to deserve that?' asked Sally, knowing that Ted had been here in Bellevue-Sur-Mer yesterday and trying to put two and two together. 'And where are you?'

'I'm at the Hôtel Astra.'

'And where is Ted?'

Marianne wailed down the line. 'Gone!'

'You'd better tell me all,' said Sally, torn between her need not to be late to Cannes and being a good mother. She hoped in vain she might hurry her. 'And how long have you been here without letting me know?'

'He came in very late last night. After midnight. He told me he was going into Nice to see a film, so I wasn't worried. He got into bed and then in the morning I saw that he had a black eye.'

'Did you do it in your sleep?'

'No. It wasn't me, Mum.'

'I thought you just said that you gave him the black eye.'

'Wait, Mum. You never let me speak,' Marianne continued. 'It turns out he hadn't gone to Nice at all but spent the evening chasing after his ex-wife ...'

Sally just prevented herself in time from correcting her daughter and saying 'wife', because Sian and Ted were still married.

'And he actually spent the evening with her, at their old home, and then she gave him a black eye so he came back to me.'

Sally left a pause. It was obvious what was coming.

'When I pressed him this morning, and got the whole story out of him, he admitted that he'd slept with her last night. So I hit him.'

'And now what?' asked Sally, hating being in the middle and dreading the knock on the door which might be Sian coming to tell her version of events.

'I'm packing up and going back to London, of course. Without him.'

'You could come down here and see me ...'

'No, I could not, Mum. I've booked my plane ticket and the taxi should arrive any minute. I just wanted to talk to someone.' Sally heard a voice in the background calling, 'Taxi for Connor,' then Marianne said, 'Oh, and if you happen to see Ted, please will you tell him to drop dead.'

20

Benjamin managed to smuggle the pig's head out in a black plastic bag just as the health inspector arrived.

While William and Carol dealt with the inspector, Theresa and Benjamin debated how it had got there.

It seemed that while they were out of the restaurant this morning, somebody had let themselves in and left the pig's head resting on the kitchen worktop in a pool of its own blood.

'Who locked up?' asked Theresa.

'We were so concerned after William's announcement, I wonder whether we left it to one another. And nobody actually did it.'

'And, anyway, at the moment there is nothing inside worth stealing. The place is a shell.'

'No one would break in to steal tables and chairs. There's nothing else.'

'From now on we make better security provisions.'

'Perhaps we need an alarm,' said Carol, joining them as the inspector had his final few words with William. 'Someone is clearly out to get us.'

'More expense!' said William, when they sat down to discuss things after the inspector had gone.

'Better locks wouldn't cost so much,' said Carol. 'It's like being hunted. We need to protect ourselves.'

'From whom?' said Theresa, thrown into doubt about the project once more. 'Or what?'

'It's not hard finding out, if we get the right system.' Benjamin explained that video security wasn't that expensive these days. 'We can link it to our home computers,' he told them. 'Then we'd have them on film.'

Suddenly Theresa saw a glimmer of light. 'I understand that the very fact we're talking security,' she said, 'means we are going to press forward with the restaurant and give it a go?'

William gave a reluctant shrug.

'Do you think it was Marcel or someone from the brasserie?' asked Carol. 'A kind of Mafia threat.'

Benjamin was shaking his head. 'Did they go out and kill the pig or did they just find it dead, then think what a good idea it would be to cut its head off and leave it here?'

'Either way, it's unspeakable,' said William.

'Whoever did it is perfectly ghastly,' said Carol.

Theresa had sat listening to them but mulling over her earlier conversation with Zoe. She spoke up. 'Actually, Zoe was telling me this morning about some Mafia-like connections with the old widow.'

'But she's dead,' said William. 'If they had a grudge against her, why take it out on us?'

'Maybe they're taking it out on the grandson, Costanzo.' Theresa looked out of the window and watched some tourists stroll by. 'He still owns it, after all.' She turned to Carol. 'Could you get hold of him? Bring him in so we can talk to him about all this stuff?'

'So that's that matter discussed.' William looked serious. 'Are we all going to avoid any mention of the inspector's visit?'

Benjamin muttered under his breath, 'Always the drama queen . . .' then said out loud: 'Tell us . . .'

'He wasn't a health inspector at all,' said Carol. 'He was here about the alcohol licence. We're approved, and in two weeks he'll give us the plaque, which we need to put up before we can sell drinks.'

'Two weeks!'

'That's the law.'

'Perhaps we should delay the opening.'

William slammed his fist on the table. 'We have worked like Trojans. And we will open, as advertised, on Sunday.'

'Sunday. Three days. Come on.' Theresa stood up. 'We'd better get some bleach on all the places where the pig's head might have dripped. I'm glad we kept the dustsheets down to protect the floor while the furniture was unpacked.'

'It wouldn't be hard to clean. The pieces are glazed. Better than wood, really.'

'It's not that.' Theresa was rolling up her sleeves. 'Don't know why, but that mosaic feels to me like our lucky mascot.'

'Lucky or unlucky,' said Benjamin, putting on a spooky voice. 'Time will tell.'

There was a knock on the door. It was another delivery. This time it was the brightly coloured blue, yellow and red, varying-sized plates, spanking-new pots, pans and sparkling cutlery. Later, neat wooden wine racks, a grey office desk and filing cabinets arrived to be carried down into the cellar, and boxes of fresh white table-cloths and napkins piled up near the door. Carol had suggested firmly that nothing beats the pleasing sight of bright-white napery, when Theresa had started getting carried away with the idea of trying to match even those to the colours of her 'lucky' mosaic floor.

It took four of them the rest of the afternoon to unpack everything, and arrange it, ready, in the kitchen cupboards.

It was getting dark when they decided to call it a day.

'Night all,' said Benjamin, sitting down on the floor. 'I'm your security guard for the evening. And tomorrow morning I'm afraid I'll be taking time off to buy a security system.'

There was no arguing with him. Theresa and Carol waved off William, who was heading up to his place to get blankets and pillows, and walked across the street towards Theresa's apartment.

Carol grabbed Theresa's arm.

'There are people hiding by your gate. Look!'

Theresa could see shadowy figures moving about, apparently crouching down, behind the low wall.

'What shall we do?' Theresa pulled out her phone, ready to dial 17 for the police, as they edged nearer.

'There's a whole gang,' said Carol. 'We wouldn't stand a chance.'

'After that pig thing . . .' Theresa started to stab in the numbers. '*Allô!*' she said into the phone. 'Police?'

One of the shadowy figures stood up and hollered: 'Mummy? Where the hell have you been?'

By the time she had finished her conversation with Marianne, Sally knew she would be late. She grabbed her bag and ran for the train, only to watch it disappearing into the rock tunnel. It was nearly an hour before the next one arrived.

Once she was in Cannes, Sally hurtled through the streets, careering down through the town towards the Palais des Festivals.

She ran to the main entrance and presented her ticket for Jackie's film showing.

A guard blocked her way.

'Your pass?'

'What pass?'

'You need to have a pass before we can let you inside the building,' he said. 'You'll have to go down those stairs to the registration hall.'

Sally stumbled down the stairs, following the signs.

'I need a pass,' she said, holding up her ticket to the screening.

'Do you have screen credentials?' asked the supercilious woman at the desk.

'I don't want to join the festival,' explained Sally. 'I just need to get it to view my friend's film.'

'This is strictly professionals only,' said the woman. 'Name?'

'Sally Connor,' said Sally.

After a minute or two of the woman fiddling around on her computer she said, 'No. No profile. You are not in the cinema business.'

'But I need to . . .'

'No!' said the woman.

Sally walked away from the desk, her mouth dry. Why hadn't Jackie thought of this?

She started slowly to climb the steps back to the street. Then suddenly had an idea and went back to the desk.

This time a young man came to assist her.

'The name's Sally Doyle. I left the business some years ago, but I am returning to work on a project and am expected at a screening, which I helped to finance, and which starts in approximately four minutes.'

The young man stabbed at his computer.

'Oh Lord!' he said. 'You have been out of show business for a long time.'

He started printing out Sally's pass.

'That will be ninety-five euros.'

'Blimey,' Sally mumbled. With her new pass, Sally arrived in the seething lobby of the Palais. Some film was clearly just over as she faced a tide of chattering people coming towards her.

She followed the signs leading her down and along past niches covered in posters for films from every country in the world.

She turned into a wide corridor with doors leading off into numbered screening rooms. She grabbed her invitation and made her way down the far end to number twenty-two.

The door was closed. She could hear the sound of music and machine-gun fire, and edged the door open.

A haughty young man stepped out.

'Can I help you?'

Sally held up her invitation.

'We don't usually allow latecomers, but, lucky for you, there is space,' he said, opening the door and ushering Sally into the small dark screening room.

She took her allotted place at the back, and tried to concentrate on the screen; as she settled into her seat, she realised it was the most expensive film to which she had ever been given a free ticket.

Having prepared a little supper for the children before putting them to bed, Theresa and Carol sat in the front room listening to Imogen's tales of her father taking over her house and drinking.

They were now on their second bottle of local rosé.

'He invited six of his cronies over to play cards till the small hours.' Imogen topped up her glass. 'Which of course kept the children awake practically all night. Naturally enough, at school next day they fell asleep and I got notes from the teachers all but telling me to be a better mother.'

'Unfair,' said Carol and Theresa in unison.

'Meanwhile I had to put up with Daddy staying at home all day sitting in the lounge listening to a recording of the Carpenters singing "Solitaire", at full volume and sobbing.'

'How ghastly!' exclaimed Carol. 'That awful anorexic woman with a voice like a quarterback. He might at least have used the Andy Williams version.'

'That's not all,' continued Imogen, happy, it seemed, to be the centre of attention and sympathy. 'When the final long note was over he would continue wailing and return the track to the start.'

Carol groaned.

Theresa said, 'Typical of him. Always liked to be the martyr.' She took another swig of rosé. 'Why on earth did I marry him?'

'Thank God you saw the light, dear,' said Carol.

'The poor children were utterly perplexed. Was Granddaddy injured? Why was he always crying?' Imogen finished her glass and grabbed the last fistful of olives. 'What was I supposed to tell them?'

'How about "his au pair walked out on him because she caught him shagging the maid"?'

They laughed till tears came into their eyes.

'Thank heavens for France,' said Imogen, helping herself to a refill. 'It's lovely being able to laugh about it.'

As she listened to Imogen's descriptions of her father, Theresa couldn't help but feel rather smug about her ex-husband. The biter was bit.

'What about school?' asked Theresa. 'It's not half term for a few weeks, is it?'

'School cannot have it both ways, Mummy. I'm staying here till Daddy gets back with Annunziata.'

'Or somebody,' added Carol.

'Anybody – if they would have him,' Theresa laughed and walked towards the kitchen to top up the bowl of her favourite little black Niçoise olives.

'Anyway, I'm here till he moves out of my home,' said Imogen, wiping her mouth with a napkin. 'Time for bed now. Will I be in the box room, as usual?'

Theresa had put the children to bed in her own room an hour ago. She hadn't really thought about the practicalities till now. Where were she and Carol going to spend the night?

'Oh, Carol, I should have thought!' Theresa rose. 'Last time I had my family staying I slept here on the floor, under the table. But, even if you fancied it, there won't be room for two.' Theresa felt rather badly, but thought better than to correct her daughter, who was bustling towards the bathroom.

'I've already thought about it, darling.' Carol was gathering her things together. 'There is no problem at all, Theresa sweetie. Of course I understand that family come first. And if I'm going to sleep on a floor I think it would be quite useful for me to join Benjamin at La Mosaïque. Two security guards on the prowl will be better than one.'

Sally kept herself at the back of the screening room as the audience squeezed out. Many people were congratulating Jackie, who stood near the door, shaking hands and handing out further leaflets.

'We're still looking for distributors,' she cried. 'So if you're in a position to help, jolly well do!'

Sally thought that some of the audience members had a very strange sense of style. There was even one man who, despite the heat, sat in the front row wearing a mackintosh, with collar turned up, a trilby hat and dark glasses. He had kept these on throughout the screening. It was very irritating, as from where Sally was sitting the hat had blocked out the lower-right quadrant of the screen. Sally wondered whether he might be a member of the cast. It was as though he was dressed in costume for the event, although the sunglasses definitely had a modern look to them. But then perhaps vintage sunglasses weren't that easy to find. Did they even have vintage sunglasses, especially during the war?

By the time Sally reached the exit he was nowhere to be seen.

Sally congratulated Jackie on what was a sweet little film. She was genuinely moved both by the film itself, the lives of the heroic women it depicted, and Jackie's dedication at seeing it through and getting on with it. It really was a great achievement.

'You must be very proud,' Sally said. 'So well done to you and the rest of the team. Were they here to support you?'

'No. I was a bit browned off about that, to say the least. Other work came up – one of them is doing the summer season in the Park and the other is on holiday. So muggins here had to get the whole show on the road.'

'A holiday doesn't seem like a very good excuse,' said Sally as they strolled along the passageway past all the movie Marketplace stalls.

'Fair do's,' said Jackie. 'She'd just finished a six-month stint in *Wicked*, so I suppose she needed to get out of town.'

'Isn't Cannes and the glorious French Riviera out of town?'

'Not when you've set your heart on a beach in the Seychelles.' Jackie nodded at a man who ran past, saying: 'Congratulations! Sweet little film.'

'I am so brassed off with all these people who insist on calling my film "sweet" and "little". Would they say that to Steven Spielberg? No they would not.'

Sally hoped she had not actually said the words out loud.

'So, once I've changed, shall we go somewhere for a drink before the evening screening?' Sally could think of nothing she'd enjoy better than a glass of wine on the beach.

Jackie came to a halt.

'Oh, Sally, I forgot to say. Well, there's this chap, a potential backer, and I . . .'

Sally felt disappointed, but understood.

'Don't worry.' Sally wondered if it might be Stanislav. 'I do understand how these things work.'

'I've got a meeting up at the Martinez. I'll see you at your place in the cinema.'

'Can't we pal up and do the walk of shame up the red carpet together? I shall be nervous on my own. Like an impostor.'

'Oh, I would have thought you'd have leapt at the chance of being able to go up the grand staircase alone, all those cameras clicking away,' said Jackie.

'Oh no, I couldn't.' Sally was cringing inside.

'Come on! After all, you're an actress, for goodness sake – act. By the way, I must tell you, I have a very nice eligible man who's asked to take my arm. He was at the screening – didn't you see him?'

'It was dark.'

'You couldn't miss him. He was in a hat and dark glasses. I met him on the train, actually. He was ever so kind to me. You don't mind, do you, Sal?'

'It's important to be seen with people who are in the loop. I know that.'

'Oh no. He's not part of the festival. I bought him a pass. Seemed the least I could do for someone who helped me carry my leaflets down from the station and who gave up his seat for me and had to stand all the way from Nice.' She rooted about in her carrier bag. 'Here's your party invitation, in case I forget. You won't get in without one. I should have introduced you earlier, after the screening. But he's just gone to buy himself a dinner jacket for tonight. You'll get on famously, I know. He is *such* a flirt!'

When Jackie left for the Martinez, teetering down the street in her evening gown, Sally went back into the Palais, which now seemed strangely calm after the frantic scenes out along the Croisette, where jostling crowds of fat tourists shoved past anxious young people in evening dress who were holding up scribbled notes reading 'Invitation for *The Stranger*', 'DESPERATE for invite to *HELL*!' and '*Pigs Might Fly* PLEASE!' and waving them at everyone who emerged from the Palais.

She grabbed a reviving coffee in the exclusive Nespresso bar upstairs, then went to the ladies' powder room to get dressed up for the movie.

Being in this world again – rubbing shoulders with the actors, the producers and directors – was giving Sally an unexpected buzz.

She regretted now all the years she had withdrawn from showbiz.

Standing in front of the mirror in the cramped ladies' room, putting on her rather worn-down make-up, was also reminiscent of many a night in shady touring venues from her past. She recalled arriving at venues where no one had thought that actors actually needed somewhere private to change into their costumes. And a shabby Theatre in Education group where most of the actors came to work on the bus dressed as bears and scarecrows rather than have to change in school toilets, being jeered at by the kids.

Her phone rang. Marianne.

'Are you back home now?' asked Sally.

'In a way of speaking,' said Marianne. 'There was some air-control strike on and I couldn't get a flight today, so I'm at yours.'

When she was done making herself look smart, Sally sidled out of the Palais. Having waved her invitation to one of the doormen, she was hustled along the Croisette, about half a mile, pushing through the milling throng. Then a prompt U-turn and into the main entrance drag, joining the others in evening dress.

She hung her head slightly, embarrassed at being stared at by leering crowds.

'Who's she?'

'Nobody,' she heard.

Along with all the others she arrived at the red carpet. Here on either side were decks of professional journalists, cameras whirring and flashing. Some people, mainly women in very expensive scanty gowns, were stopping and posing for the cameras.

Sally scanned the other faces in the red-carpet area, hoping to find Jackie, but she was nowhere to be seen. She carefully climbed the plush steps into the Cinema Lumière.

Taking her seat inside the magnificent red and black auditorium, Sally looked around. She recognised many of the people sitting near her: directors, actors and actresses seen in magazines, or familiar from television and cinema. She had an aisle seat and on the other side of the aisle were rows of empty places. These, she presumed, must be reserved for the director, producers and artists who had worked on this film.

The buzz was thrilling.

She looked anxiously at the two empty seats beside her, praying that Jackie wouldn't be late.

Suddenly a ripple went through the audience, and all heads turned.

Marina Martel, surrounded by a posse of producers, strode down the aisle, head held high, smiling radiantly at everyone.

People around her stood, offering an ovation. Clapping, Sally too rose to her feet.

Before she moved into her row of seats, the Hollywood actress stopped and turned, waving at the audience. She then headed for her seat, but for a flash of a moment she did the tiniest of double-takes, and glanced back in Sally's direction.

Sally cast around to see who she was looking at, but at that minute the applause subsided and the lights dimmed.

The huge screen showed floating red steps, first underwater, then against blue, then up into the stars – the Cannes palm logo came on to the screen and the audience burst into applause.

As the production titles came up an usher appeared out of the darkness at Sally's side.

'*Pardon, madame!*'

In the pitch-black, first Jackie, then the man in dark glasses were shown to their seats. Sally stood to enable him to pass. It was when their faces were a foot away from each other that she realised the man was her best friend's husband, her daughter's lover, Ted.

* * *

Theresa sat and listened to Imogen's stories about life at home in London since Annunziata had walked out on her ex-husband and he had moved in with Imogen.

Annunziata, however, had turned out to be quite a gal, and not the brain-free sex bomb that Theresa had thought her. But while Annunziata used all her wiles to get a well-paid job in fashion publishing, Peter, Imogen's father, had let everything go, and coasted along on Annunziata's achievements, which appeared to be considerable.

Theresa had to keep pinching her hands and biting her cheeks to try and stay awake. But for Imogen all this piffling stuff seemed so important.

When at last Imogen yawned and declared she was off to bed, looking forward to a lovely relaxing Riviera day, Theresa gathered her spare pillows and beach futon roll and tucked herself in down under the front window.

She lay in the dark and thought about La Mosaïque, and really how exciting it all was. As for the strange visitations – the fag ends, the open doors, the dead pig's head – who could it be? Surely Marcel from the brasserie up the road wouldn't be quite so demonstrative of his displeasure because they were opening what he saw as a rival establishment.

She remembered Zoe's tales of – what was it she called them? – those Sardinian bandits who were related to Old Mother Magenta. She'd seen *The Godfather*, and leaving animal heads around the place as a threat was surely part of the Italian brigands' repertoire. But what were they threatening?

Theresa couldn't imagine what she and her friends were doing wrong. Would the distant relations of the boy who was selling really prefer him to be letting out a shop peddling tourist tat to owning a fancy local restaurant, which would stay open even during the cold, rainy winters?

Her mind strayed to their financial predicament. Who could they approach as backers? They could certainly go back to Sally; in fact, William was probably on the blower to her right now, and what with her new friends, who all seemed to be celebrities, there must be some interest somewhere. Theresa certainly recognised the two actresses from TV shows back in London. Perhaps they would like to invest.

Theresa turned over and realised that she was not going to sleep.

Why not go and join the other two – perhaps they would be in the same state of nervous excitement and it also left them sleepless?

Quietly Theresa got up, wrote a brief note to Imogen, explaining that she was at La Mosaïque. As she'd probably read it when she got up for breakfast, how was she to know her mother was going to join the midnight dorm, rather than getting up early for work? She rolled her futon, put a pillow under her arm and let herself out.

The night was cool and clear. Every star imaginable pricked the black sky. She could hear the waves softly lapping on the harbour wall as she took the short walk along the front. As she approached the restaurant she thought she saw someone moving stealthily near the windows of La Mosaïque.

She stopped, took a position behind a parked car and watched.

She could see the silhouette of a man, stooping, peering inside. Then the man stood up and moved furtively towards the door.

Theresa put down her bedding, except for the pillow, and walked as silently as she could in the direction of the restaurant.

The man was now standing tightly against the door. From his stance, Theresa believed he was about to try opening it, but she could see that he was braced, as though he intended to move suddenly.

What if Benjamin and Carol were both asleep?

She could not let this man jump them.

As the man gripped the handle and pushed the door open, Theresa rushed forward and shoved the pillow into his back, causing him to lose his balance and fall flat on his face. At the same time she heard Carol shout out and Benjamin yelled, 'Gotcha!' The lights flashed on inside and as she entered Theresa could see both Carol and Benjamin on the floor, splayed out on top of the intruder, who turned his head and said quietly, 'Back off, you idiots. It's me. William.'

21

S ALLY FOUND A SET of blow-up chairs on the edge of the beach, just under the awning of the large marquee in which the after-party was being held.

She had adored the film, a quirky wild tale set in the seventeenth century. It reminded her of a production of *The White Devil* in which she'd played Isabella, a wife who was poisoned by kissing her own husband's portrait. This film had all those Jacobean elements – murders, unfaithful henchmen, deceitful, greedy relatives – and also finished with a bloodbath. Marina Martel had been superb as the crafty evil leading lady who ended impaled on a huge golden crucifix.

Unfortunately Sally's enjoyment of the movie had been slightly marred by the arrival of Ted. In fact at first she found the plot of the film quite hard to follow after spending five minutes seething with anger about him showing up. She thought too about Sian, and also Marianne, now sitting in her home in Bellevue-Sur-Mer.

Ted was at this minute standing in the centre of the party, his arm around Jackie, talking to a gaggle of laughing people. The room seemed to be full of people who knew one another. She felt rather lonely and embarrassed. Sally accepted a glass of champagne from a passing waiter and turned to watch the waves lapping up the sand in the darkness. For a moment the sound in the party seemed to dip.

She turned to see why, and, as she did so, everyone started applauding. Marina Martel, with an entourage of bulky minders wearing earpieces, had entered the marquee and was escorted to a roped-off corner, where luxury sofas and tables laden with treats awaited her.

At that moment Sally saw Stanislav standing at the bar, chatting to a young boy in a very fancy white-sequined tuxedo.

At last someone she knew!

She went over.

'Sally!' he exclaimed. 'How lovely to see you.' He bent to whisper in her ear. 'Which one is your friend Jackie? I must apologise to her for missing her screening this afternoon.'

Sally gritted her teeth and said, 'She's with the man in dark glasses.'

'Rather affected of him,' said Stanislav. 'The lighting in this place is pretty mellow. How can he see where he's going? Too much posing for his own good.'

He laughed, showing off his wonderful row of perfect teeth. The young man in the sequined jacket edged out to sit with a gang of people on a nearby bench.

'I'm sorry,' said Sally. 'I didn't mean to interrupt.'

'I don't know him,' Stanislav replied. 'We both happened to be trying to get vodka from the barman at the same time. The official waiters have only champagne.'

'How do you know Jackie?' asked Sally.

'Oh, she said you'd suggested she ring me, as you thought I might like to invest.'

How embarrassing! Sally wondered where Jackie had found his number and felt more than a little edgy at the possibility of Jackie going through her things when she wasn't around. Stanislav put his hand in the small of Sally's back and guided her through the crowded party towards Jackie and Ted.

As Ted saw them approaching, Sally was relieved to see him slink away, leaving Jackie alone.

'Hello, my old china! Isn't Ted funny, he just cracks me up!' Jackie laughed and swapped her empty glass for a full one from a passing waiter's tray. 'I cannot imagine why Sian left him. I'd think he was a keeper.'

While Sally groped around for a way of explaining that Sian had not left him, but he had run off with her daughter, Stanislav stepped forward, presenting his hand to shake.

'Stanislav Serafim. Miss Westwood, I am so sorry I missed your screening. Sally tells me it went very well.'

'Tickety-boo, I think. I have a meeting with some people from Brits in Film about funding the day after tomorrow. Excellent feedback from all concerned so far, and it does look as though we might get a slot on British TV. Mind you, they'd be doolally not to show it.' Jackie knocked back the whole glass of champagne. 'Thirsty work, this film-promotion business. It's hot in here, don't you think? Oh, and Sally, don't

wait for me getting back to BSM, will you? I'm going
to stay in Cannes tonight with that chap I met on the
train.'

Sally squinted at her watch. The last train back to
Bellevue-Sur-Mer would leave in about forty minutes.
She'd have to leave pretty smartish. If she were to get a
taxi on her own it would cost a fortune.

A young man in spectacles edged in on the circle,
and handed Jackie a card. He jabbered away, a prac-
tised patter: he was in promotion, impressed by Jackie's
track record, could they swap ideas . . . Jackie directed
all her concentration on the young man and Stanislav
used the moment to steer Sally away.

'I will drive you to your front door,' he whispered.

'You can read minds too,' said Sally. 'Talk about an
all-rounder!'

Just when Sally was starting to relax, she was interrupted: 'Sal! I had no idea you'd be here!' It was Diana
Sparks. 'I am simply exhausted, aren't you? What a
movie!'

They discussed the film for a while, occasionally
glancing towards the roped-off corner where Marina
Martel sat with her entourage.

'That footballer's wife was a right one,' said Diana.
Destiny – Stanislav's friend! Sally kicked Diana's foot
and flashed her a look. Diana immediately picked up
the hint and turned the subject. 'She can really tell a
joke, can't she?'

'Oh sorry, have you two met?' Sally felt all tingly
being able to introduce such a dish to her old pal.

'How is Cathy?' asked Sally. 'Cathy is Diana's daughter, Stanislav.'

'Bored out of her mind, I fear.' Diana took a glass from a passing waiter. 'She wanted to come to the South of France but doesn't quite realise that all this socialising is work just as much as being in the studio or on location.'

'You should have brought her tonight.'

'She doesn't like parties, I'm afraid. Not that I do, but, as you know, Sal, I must. Hey, what are you up to tomorrow?'

Sally felt excited. Her last outing with Diana had been such a laugh.

'Nothing at all. I am at your command.'

'Phew!' Diana touched Sally's forearm. 'So you wouldn't mind taking Cathy out somewhere. She hates the freneticism of Cannes, but she loves your "Blissful"-Sur-Mer. I really don't like leaving her on her own, day after day. I'd be much happier if she was with someone I cared about.'

Before Sally could respond, the same spectacled man who had approached Jackie now arrived and offered Diana his card.

'Oh, no. I'm sorry,' Diana handed his card back, 'I already have a PR company looking after me.'

As he moved away, she rolled her eyes at Sally. 'Being in places like this is also like being a sitting duck.'

'So let us find somewhere a bit more discreet.' Stanislav escorted the two women to the edge of the beach and they stood at the water's edge gazing out to sea at all the twinkling lights of moored motor-yachts.

'Is your boat out there?' asked Sally.

'You have a boat?' exclaimed Diana. 'How marvellous.'

'Temporarily out of action. Something wrong with the fuel pump. Jean-Philippe had to go all the way to Marseille today for parts.'

A woman in a tail coat and top hat tapped Diana on the arm.

'Honey pie!'

Diana whooped. 'Helen! How fabulous!'

They moved off, deep in animated conversation.

Stanislav and Sally remained on the sand, standing in silence, enjoying the ambience. A waiter arrived at their side with canapés.

Sally turned and watched Marina Martel in her private space, surrounded by her cast and producers.

'It must be funny to be one of the most famous faces in the world, don't you think? I wonder if she can ever do anything normal like going to the shops or taking a walk without a bodyguard present.' Sally sighed, trying to imagine such a life. She looked at Stanislav.

'How did your meeting go? Didn't you say you had a meeting with Marina Martel?'

'It wasn't very interesting,' said the Russian, suppressing a yawn. 'Just money talk. I feel like Cinderella,' he added. 'I really ought to be thinking of leaving soon. I have a very early start tomorrow.'

It was a strange reaction. Sally realised that Stanislav had not been invited into the magic square with friends of the actress. Perhaps she had cancelled. Something had certainly not gone his way.

Stanislav was certainly mysterious.

'I'm happy to go now, if you like.' Sally had had enough of today and was worried about Marianne, waiting for her at home in Bellevue-Sur-Mer. 'Let's go.'

They moved back into the crowded space and pushed through the partygoers, heading for the exit.

'Are you off, Sal?' Diana was still with the woman in the tail suit. She mimed a phone and mouthed: 'I'll call you.'

A group of men shouting too loudly obstructed their getaway. Stanislav took Sally's arm.

'I'd better say goodbye to Jackie,' she said.

Jackie was standing alone, grinning. As they got near, she lunged in their direction and flung herself at Stanislav, wrapping her arms round his neck.

'Bob's your uncle,' she cried. 'And Fanny's your aunt.' She was clearly very drunk.

A split second later, Ted was at their side. He too looked the worse for wear.

'What are you doing to my woman?' he leered.

'Nothing,' Stanislav smiled, still trying to pry Jackie's arms from around his neck. 'She appears to be attached.'

'You've got your hands all over her.'

'Perhaps, sir, if you took off your sun-specs, you could see better.' Stanislav was still wrestling with Jackie. 'It is rather too dark in here for those glasses, surely.'

'You're full of it.' Ted lurched towards Stanislav and growled, 'Don't you come the raw prawn with me.'

'I'm sorry. I don't understand you,' said Stanislav. 'Could you speak English?'

'For God's sake, Ted.' Sally didn't like the way things were moving. 'Stanislav, stop provoking him.'

'That's right, bossy-boots. You tell him.'

'Ted, do shut up.'

'You can belt up too, mother of the dried-up twig that is Marianne.'

Sally slapped Ted, and his sunglasses fell to the floor. As Stanislav stepped forward, he trod on them, smashing them to smithereens.

'Hey, you drongo, that's my sunnies ...'

Ted pushed Stanislav, who staggered backwards and, still attached to Jackie, lost his balance, then lay sprawled on the floor with Jackie writhing on top of him.

As Stanislav crawled to his feet, Ted raised a fist. He flailed out, missing Stanislav and hitting only the air. But Stanislav's defensive punch landed hard on Ted's chin as he fell. Pulling herself up using Sally's legs, Jackie staggered to her feet.

Instantly, bodyguards sprang forward, detaining both men, while Jackie swayed, took a step to the side and was violently sick.

After a night sleeping on the restaurant floor Theresa felt oddly content. The sense of camaraderie was lovely.

Carol rose early and went up the hill to get them all coffees and croissants, and they sat together at one of the tables to eat.

William was excited because he had asked Sian to help finance the purchase of the building and she had phoned him very late to tell him she was happy to buy into the business.

As Theresa prepared to nip back home to have a wash and say hello to her daughter, she found a note that had been slipped under the restaurant door.

It was in English, addressed 'To the owners'.

She opened it and read it aloud to the others.

'You have twenty-four hours to hand it over.'

'Hand what over?' asked William.

'We're not the owner, are we?' said Theresa. 'That, for the moment, is still Costanzo.'

Carol was already on the phone.

Costanzo arrived within minutes, looking pale and tousled. He read the note.

'I know nothing,' he said. 'It's ridiculous. Who left this? Did you see?'

Years of working in a law office had taught Theresa to recognise all the tics that betrayed a liar – the swallowing, the licking of lips, the pauses, the extra phrases put in to give time. Costanzo was lying.

'What do they want you to hand over?' asked Theresa.

'And whatever it is, please do so immediately,' added William. 'We really don't need problems like these at this stage. We open for business in a few days.'

'There is nothing here for them,' said Costanzo. 'I checked myself, over and over and over.'

'Checked for what?' Theresa was right. The boy knew more than he was letting on.

'Is it something you left here?' asked Carol.

The boy ran his fingers through his hair, then shrugged. 'I do not know.'

'You know something, though.' Theresa proffered a chair for the boy to sit. 'Perhaps we could help you.'

'I went through everything myself before I put the place on the market. They take me for a simpleton, but I am not green.'

'Who?' asked William. 'Who are "they"?'

'Idiots.' Costanzo splayed his hands out in a gesture of incomprehension. 'If anything was here, why do they imagine I did not take it for myself?'

'But you must know, Costanzo.' Carol leaned forward, and spoke in a soothing voice, as though trying to entice a wild animal out of hiding. 'Who are they?'

'People in my family.' Costanzo blurted it out as though relieved to have someone to share it with. 'People who think my grandmother should have left this place to them.'

'They could still buy it,' suggested Benjamin.

William shot him a filthy look.

'They don't want it,' said Costanzo. 'It's too much responsibility and expense.'

'This is ridiculous!' Theresa threw her arms up. 'They want it or they don't want it? Or they should just go home and leave us alone.'

'They don't want the building. They want the thing that my grandmother left behind.'

'So tell us exactly what that is, Costanzo. What do they want? If we have it, we can hand it over and put an end to this silly siege.'

'What have they done to you?' Costanzo wrapped his arms around himself. 'Tell me what stage they have reached.'

'First it was just coming in, searching the place,' said Theresa. 'They dropped cigarette ends, a lighter, left cupboards open.'

Theresa went to fetch the lighter from a drawer beneath the welcome desk.

Costanzo nodded. 'I see. Nothing more?'

'A dead animal head,' said William.

'A head dripping blood all over the lovely clean floor,' added Carol.

'Oh.' Costanzo shook his head and swallowed. 'Then they are getting desperate.'

Theresa presented the lighter to the boy.

'I will return this to its owner.' He took the lighter from Theresa. 'Are you sure you do not have what they want?'

'Have what?' Theresa almost bellowed the reply. 'If we had even a notion of what they were looking for, and we had it here, I am sure we would hand it over instantly so that we could get on with our lives in serenity.'

'If you know, tell us what they want?' asked William. 'You obviously know. But no one has told us.'

Costanzo looked round at the four faces waiting for his reply.

He licked his lips, shrugged and said, 'A medallion.'

William marched around laughing hysterically.

'The old girl loses a locket and your Sicilian family come over here making our lives hell?'

'Sardinian,' said Costanzo. 'I agree with you. And you can be sure that I searched high and low before I sold. While I was a kid my Uncle Vito was running the place. I was sure they'd already cleared out everything of value. But apparently not the medallion. I suppose they thought you might have come across it when you were moving the cookers or clearing the cellar.'

'So a barking old bag mislays a trinket . . .'

Theresa stepped in front of William, blocking him from Costanzo.

'Tell us what is so important about this medallion?' she asked. 'Is it made from solid pink diamonds? Why are they making such a fuss?'

'I don't know anything about it.' Costanzo again shrugged his shoulders. 'They only found out about it recently in some old letter or diary of hers, and threatened me for it. It was given her by one of her lovers.'

'Some sentimental reasons? And they cause all this trouble. Really?'

'No. Not that,' said Costanzo. 'It is worth some money.'

'But is there even any proof that she still had it when she died? Perhaps it was among her things she left behind in the retirement home. Have you tried asking there?'

'They seem convinced it remained here when she left the place. She planned to come back for it. And that is why I decided to sell up. I searched too and did not find it. They plagued me. I just wanted to get them off my back.'

'Thanks a bunch,' said Benjamin. 'So now we have them on ours.'

Costanzo looked as though he was about to burst into tears. 'Please tell me? Did you find a medallion?' He regarded each of them. 'It was a birthday present. I beg you to tell me the truth. Do you have it?'

Theresa realised this quest for the medallion was one of those things, like suspicion and jealousy, which could never be satisfied by anything but the presentation of the thing itself. They could go on denying finding it, because they had not found it. But no one would ever believe them. The only satisfactory answer was to present these people with a medallion. Only then might they go away.

'I may have it,' she said.

Everyone spun round and stared at her.

'It's in a bank in town.'

William, Benjamin and Carol gawped at her, mouths ajar.

'Sorry, Costanzo,' she said. 'You'll have to come back on Monday.'

When he had gone everyone turned to Theresa.

'Why didn't you say you had it to us?' demanded William.

'I was lying,' said Theresa. 'Wasn't it obvious? I knew that while we said we didn't have it, he would never go.'

'There is still no medallion and no bank?' William's eyes were popping. 'And what the hell are we going to do when they come back for it?'

Theresa sank down on to the nearest chair.

'I don't know,' she said.

'Maybe we just go to an antique shop, fork out for a medallion and present it to them?' suggested Benjamin.

'And when they say it isn't exactly the medallion they were after?' said William, still the sceptic. 'In fact, not in the slightest bit like the medallion they're after?'

'We play dumb,' said Theresa. 'We tell them we found it in the cellar and we truthfully thought it was what they were looking for.'

'So now, where do we find an antique medallion, enhanced with air de gangster?' asked Benjamin.

Carol stepped forward. 'That'll be my job. I'll go to the Monday antique market in Nice and pick up something suitably worn, with swirly engraving, preferably of the old girl's initials.'

'Which are?'

'FM,' Theresa sighed.

'Then I get "Happy Birthday" inscribed . . .'

'In Italian, remember . . .'

'No, French.'

'Then we give it to them.'

Theresa shrugged. It was tricky, but this plan actually might work.

22

S ALLY HAD HAD TO wait outside the *gendarmerie* for around twenty minutes before taking their advice and heading home. She walked up to the top of the town, looking for a cab rank. So many streets were barred off for the festival she didn't know where she might find one.

Then she remembered that there was a night bus, which would be damned cheaper and get her as far as Nice airport, where there were sure to be taxis. She had been standing at the stop for quarter of an hour when a car pulled up.

'Are you stuck?' The driver leaned over and pushed open his door. 'So get in.'

Sally took a step back, then recognised the man at the wheel – Jean-Philippe.

During the twenty-minute drive they talked of Stanislav.

'I am surprised he got into a fight,' said Jean-Philippe. 'I didn't see him as that type of man.'

'Too strait-laced?' suggested Sally.

'Too precious of his reputation,' said Jean-Philippe. 'I'm beginning to think he is quite the Artful Dodger.'

Men! thought Sally. Always think life is a competition.

'I'll tell you something else, Sally.' Jean-Philippe spoke hesitantly. 'I don't believe he is entirely truthful.'

Sally shifted in her seat. 'What makes you say that?'

'He has, let us say, fibbed to us.'

She wondered what was coming next.

'I cannot be sure, but I think he does not own that boat we took out for him. I think he is renting it.' Jean-Philippe flicked his indicator and turned off the Grande Corniche into a steep succession of sharp downhill zigzag bends. 'I had to go to Marseille to get the spare part, and when I gave the part number the man at the chandlery needed the name of the boat. He went off to get the part and the boy working behind the counter told me it's a charter boat from Italy.'

'I thought it was owned by the people in that villa?'

'Actually, it turns out they were renting both the villa and the boat.'

Sally wondered why that mattered so much to Jean-Philippe.

'Maybe Stanislav isn't even a Russian,' she said. 'Perhaps he's an Italian. Maybe he's a spy!'

'Just keep an eye on him,' said Jean-Philippe.

'I will.'

Jean-Philippe didn't say much after that but took Sally right to her front door.

When she got in she found Marianne asleep in an armchair.

'Ted is a rat!' she mumbled as Sally helped her upstairs towards the bedroom.

'He is,' said Sally, and left it at that.

Next morning she was woken by Marianne, looming over her holding up a copy of *Nice-Matin*.

'And who is this slut?' she exclaimed.

Sally wiped her eyes and peered at the newspaper.

The red-carpet shot was of Marina Martel.

'Well, it's the world-famous megastar, Marina Martel,' said Sally, hauling herself into a sitting position. 'I don't know why you should think she's a slut, though.'

'Not her.' Marianne bashed the paper with a finger, jabbing it into the photo. 'Her!'

Sally took the paper, and put on her glasses. She looked closely.

Oh God.

Standing not far behind Marina Martel, held back by a red rope, was Jackie. But the thing that had stirred up Marianne's ire was the fact that grinning at her side stood Ted, his arm clutched tightly and possessively around Jackie's shoulder.

'She's an actress,' said Sally, trying to be vague. 'She's in a TV series.'

'I know all that.' Marianne snatched the paper from her and took another close look. '*Skirts Fly Over Suffolk*. I watch it all the time. But why does Ted look as though he owns her?'

'Who knows?' Sally climbed out of bed and whisked to the bathroom to retrieve her dressing gown. She didn't think that now was the time to confess that they were friends and that Jackie was staying here. 'Let's make breakfast,' she said.

'I wonder if Sian has seen this?' Marianne followed Sally downstairs. 'And I wonder where he is now, the little bed-hopping bastard.'

Before Sally had time to fill the kettle, the phone rang.

It was Sian, and her voice shrieked down the line, ear-splittingly loud.

'That ungrateful, grubby, deceitful, grabbing, phony little bitch!' she bellowed. 'Sally, did you know about this?'

Sally knew that Marianne would overhear everything she said, and undoubtedly most of what Sian said as well.

'How could I? Look, Sian, I'm so sorry. I have people here and I'm late.'

'Make your mind up,' shouted Sian. 'You're either late or there are people there.' Then there was a slight pause before she added quietly: '*She's* not there, is she?'

Knowing that Marianne was just as bad a 'she' to be present as Jackie, Sally said, 'I'm due at the restaurant. La Mosaïque. It's terribly exciting, don't you think?'

'I'm a major investor,' snapped Sian and hung up.

Now that, in front of Marianne, Sally had committed herself to going to the restaurant, she was in a quandary. Should she go, and risk leaving Marianne here, with the ever-present threat of Jackie coming in, using her own key, while Marianne was here alone? Jackie might even arrive with Ted in tow. Sally inwardly groaned at the thought.

Sally decided that from now on, until she had a confirmed location for Jackie's whereabouts, wherever she was going, Marianne would have to come too.

'They're doing a great job down there,' said Sally. 'They're looking for investors. Perhaps you'd like to come in as a partner? You know them all – Theresa,

William, Benjamin, Carol. I know they're looking for people to finance the purchase of the building, which is very sweet, and they've done so much already to . . .'

'Mother,' snapped Marianne, 'will you stop babbling and get dressed.'

Sally again panicked. If she went upstairs maybe Jackie would arrive while she was up there.

'Why don't you come up with me?' she said.

'Mother!' Marianne tapped her watch.

Sally ran upstairs and flung on her clothes as quickly as possible. She skipped washing and dashed down again.

'Okey-dokey! Onwards and upwards!' The words were barely out of her mouth before Sally realised she was starting to sound just like Jackie.

Marianne gave her a sideways glance.

Sally picked up her handbag and they left together.

As they walked down the hill Sally's phone rang. It was Tom.

'Mum! *Ciao, bella! Non è una bella giornata?*'

'Tom? I'm sorry, you'd better speak English. I'm with Marianne.'

'Why, doesn't she approve of me *parlare Italiano*?'

'Are you coming back to Bellevue?'

'Not immediately, no. I've got this lovely job here in Milan now, Mum. So, how is my old sis? Still shagging the Ozzie renegade?'

'Listen, you.' Marianne snatched the phone from Sally's hand. 'That vile Australian is dead to me. Dead!' She thrust the phone back towards her mother.

They turned the sharp corner into the alleyway that led down, via some steep stone steps, into the Old Town.

'So anyhow, Mama, I am working for a great new magazine, linked up with a worldwide credit card, so that my drawings and designs will be seen now in households from Adelaide to Arkansas, from Zagreb to . . . where else starts with a Z? Uh-oh, she who must be obeyed has entered the office. Must go, Mum. Talk soon.' And he hung up.

Sally could hear fury even in Marianne's breathing. She prayed that they would not bump into anyone else involved in this seedy affair. There was a chance they'd not only stumble into Jackie but Ted, or Sian. Following events at the after-party last night, even Stanislav was now a time-bomb in the Sian/Marianne/Ted scenario.

They turned another of the sharp bends. Sally heard footsteps and feared the worst, but ahead, along the lane, coming up towards them was Cathy, carrying a large cardboard shopping bag emblazoned with the MaxMara label.

'Hello, Cathy!' Sally gulped. She had utterly forgotten that Cathy was due to spend today under her care. 'You're earlier than I expected.'

'When were you expecting me? I didn't think Mummy had arranged a time.'

'Well . . .' The girl was right. Sally didn't actually even remember agreeing to having her at all. In fact, as Cathy was all of nineteen, Sally wasn't sure why she needed a chaperone. But it was now a fait accompli. 'Cathy, this is my daughter Marianne. Marianne – this is Diana Sparks's daughter, Cathy.'

Cathy flung her shopping bag on to the ground.

'I do happen to be a person in my own right, you know. Not just the daughter of some actress or other.' Sally felt embarrassed but at the same time panicked. How else could she introduce her? Just 'Cathy', she supposed, but then Marianne would only have enquired how they knew one another and they'd be back at square one.

'Been shopping?' asked Sally, in a feeble attempt to change the subject.

'Obviously,' said Marianne and Cathy in unison.

'We're heading down to offer our services to the people who are opening the new little restaurant on the quay. Fancy joining us?'

Cathy shrugged.

'Why not? I've nothing else to do. Mummy's off all day doing interviews and other boring stuff, while I hold the fort here.'

When the three women arrived at the front door of La Mosaïque, they saw a young man leaving.

Sally entered first. 'Knock, knock!' she announced as they came round the entry screen. She stopped to survey the scene – the tables in position, the white walls decorated with painted fragments of the mosaic pattern from the floor in blues and reds and yellows.

'Wow!' Sally cried, twirling to get a better look. 'Haven't you lot all worked hard? My goodness, it's a miracle.'

Marianne and Cathy gathered behind her.

Benjamin stood and William rushed forward. 'Sally, darling, it's been an age.'

Theresa moved towards the door to greet them and Carol surveyed the artwork – which she had hand-painted.

'We came to offer our services,' said Sally. 'Each in our own way.'

'How lovely!' Theresa felt happy, but William prevented her from speaking.

'What exactly can you do?' he asked.

'If you like, I'll take a look at your business plan,' said Marianne.

William scowled.

Sensing the atmosphere, Carol said, 'How's Ted?'

Marianne shot her a look and said, 'Who's Ted?'

The atmosphere chilled further.

Both Theresa and Sally laughed, and muttered niceties about how things were coming along.

'I was so excited to hear you'd been dining with Diana Sparks,' said William. 'Wow. She is my A-number-one actress in the world . . .'

'Cathy is . . .'

Cathy yawned. 'Here we go – the Mummy Fan Club.' She raised her eyes to the ceiling.

' . . . Diana's daughter. But I do happen to be an individual human being too, you know.'

'A new dress?' asked Theresa, spying the shopping bag.

'A coat,' said Cathy.

'Can we see it?' asked Carol.

'Oh, you wouldn't be interested. It's just a coat. Nothing special.' Cathy looked around. 'Who's the artist? It reminds me of Chagall.'

'Me, unfortunately,' said Carol. 'If it was Chagall, we'd all be quids in. And I, for one, want to see your coat.'

'Oh, no.' Cathy held the bag close to her body. 'Nobody wants to look at *me*. It's too embarrassing. I can't do it. I prefer to lurk in the shadows. I'm not used to being stared at.'

'Well, good,' snapped William. 'Then we should get on. I'll just say to everyone present that we are looking for backers – in a practical sense. People to buy the bricks and mortar, so it's not just investing in a business that may or may not succeed. If you or anyone you know has a little spare cash they'd like to put into property, please tell me.'

'If we invested, what return would we get?' asked Marianne.

'You'd own a piece of the restaurant,' said William.

'If you're asking people to help you buy a place and then they don't get paid back until you sell, there's no investment. You're just begging for a free loan. What if you forget to insure the place and next day a plane crashes into it? What would the investment be worth then? Nothing.'

Theresa wished this conversation had not started.

'Is there a ladies' room?' asked Cathy. 'When I'm stressed I get IBS.'

Theresa pointed to the sign that said WC.

'If I were you,' continued Marianne, 'I would go for an extension of the lease and carry on renting. Go for five years or longer.'

'The boy who owns it is keen to sell and have the money. If we don't buy, somebody else will.'

'Especially after all the work we've done,' added Benjamin.

'Boy?' asked Marianne. 'Which boy?'

'He's Italian,' said Theresa.

'He inherited it from his grandmother,' Carol chipped in.

'Not the widow Magenta's grandson?' said Marianne.

They all nodded.

'And you still expect other people to stump up towards it, with their family history?'

Without thinking, Theresa blurted out, 'Sian Kelly is investing.' She instantly realised the faux pas.

'That bitch?' said Marianne. 'Then you are sunk before you even start.'

A deathly silence reigned.

Theresa caught eyes with Sally, who winced an apology.

A knock and Marcel entered.

Knowing the tension which had been stirred up by their plan to open a new eatery near his brasserie, the four in the restaurant team stood braced.

Theresa took a pace forward, blocking his way. 'We don't want trouble, Marcel. I have already explained that we have no intention of stepping on your toes.'

William stood beside her. 'Besides which, I wonder whether we'll even make it to opening, let alone outlast our six-month lease. So how about leaving us alone, Marcel.'

'I want there to be no more bad feeling,' said Marcel, with a shrug. 'It's just that nobody thanked me for the present.'

All four proprietors said: 'Present?'

'My gift to you?' Marcel grinned.

'Gift?' said the four.

'The *tête du porc?*'

'Pig's head?' Theresa said, the penny dropping.

'My peace offering.' Marcel rooted about in his shopping bag. 'I knew you said you wanted to prepare local specialities. So I thought you might also like these?'

Marcel grabbed Benjamin by the elbow, then held his arm aloft.

He proffered a brown paper bag, tinged with blood-stains.

'Testicles. Very tasty, especially sliced, battered and deep-fried.'

Benjamin flopped to the floor in a faint.

At this moment Cathy emerged from the ladies' room wearing her new coat.

She paraded into the centre of the dining room and gave a twirl.

'Well, everyone,' she said. 'What do you think?'

Along with Marcel, Sally, Marianne and Cathy were shown round La Mosaïque. They cooed at the neat but effective cellar, with its desk and filing cabinets on one side and large wine racks and fridges on the other. The kitchen, with its white walls and stainless-steel appli-ances, also met with great approval. Sally felt quite jealous of them and their project and really wished she had joined them at the start.

After the little tour it was clear that Theresa, Carol and William wanted to be alone to get on with things. Benjamin sat quietly in a corner sipping a glass of water, so Sally took her leave.

Rather than go straight back home, she invited Cathy and Marianne to an early lunch at the brasserie. Today was becoming a nightmare of anticipation. She wished Jackie would text or leave a message, so that she at least knew her whereabouts and could avoid an embarrassing scene with Marianne. There was also no way of knowing when or if Sian would pop up and pick a fight.

After an anxiety-ridden lunch, she arrived back at the house, with Cathy and Marianne still in tow. A huge bouquet was waiting, tucked in behind her front wall.

'If those are from Ted,' said Marianne, stepping over the threshold, 'they can go straight into the bin.'

No doubt from Jackie, thought Sally, to apologise for the debacle last night.

But Cathy picked them up. 'I'm used to doing flowers. My mother gets so many bouquets.'

She pulled off the small card and handed it to Sally, who tore open the envelope and quickly read: 'Forgive me please. Dinner tomorrow night? Call me. Stanislav.'

Well, there was a turn-up!

While Cathy was mid-arranging, with flowers strewn all over the shower-room basin, her phone rang, and she moved to the living room, where she sat under the front window, talking. Marianne rolled her eyes in Sally's direction. She mouthed: 'How long are you stuck with her?' then said aloud, 'I wonder where that rat is now.'

In her fluster over the flowers from Stanislav, Sally was unsure for a moment to whom Marianne was referring.

'I'm looking forward to making a scene with Ted, and humiliating him in public. I was hoping he would roll up at the brasserie. That terrace is a perfect stage.'

Sally swallowed. All she wanted was a quiet life, and here she was in the middle of a maelstrom.

Her phone rang. It was Sian. 'Fancy lunch?'

'I already ate.' Sally shuffled from foot to foot, praying that Marianne couldn't hear who was on the line. 'I'm a bit busy now, I'll call you back.'

She hung up.

'Sian, I assume.' Marianne flopped into an armchair. 'Presumably she also saw the photo in *Nice-Matin*.'

Cathy advanced, holding her phone out ahead of her. 'Mummy wants a word with you.'

Sally was glad of the diversion. 'Sal darling, Cathy has been telling me what a wonderful time she had at your friends' restaurant. Now look, could you approach them for me? She tells me they're looking for backers. I am willing to put in some capital, but also to pay the wages and taxes or whatever for an apprenticeship, for a waitress/kitchen assistant, anything that would be useful to them.'

'Oh, Diana, how kind.' Sally was delighted she could go to her pals with such news. 'I'll go right down and let them know.'

'There is only one condition. Cathy will be the apprentice.'

Sally glanced across at the girl, and foresaw problems. She said, 'How lovely. But won't you both be heading back to the UK soon?'

'There's the thing, Sal. You know how this business goes. It's all so random. I've just been offered a movie, which is shooting a little way along the coast in Liguria, and I thought it would be nice if I rented somewhere in Bellevue-Sur-Mer to come home to at weekends, and Cathy could stay there full-time.'

'Cathy wouldn't go to Liguria with you?'

'No, darling. You know what those location shoots are like. Different hotel every night. We're all over the place: Genoa, San Remo, La Spezia. I think we even go up to Turin for a few days. Then there's the four-thirty a.m. calls, don't get back till nine p.m., have to learn the sides for the next day. It's hell for me, and she'd be bored out of her mind. She said she adored the place and the people there. Much nicer if she could be busy in a lovely place and earning a little pin money for herself.'

Marianne came over to Sally and mimed that she was going out. Sally tried to gesture at her to stay.

'I suppose you're right,' Sally said absently into the phone. Diana was talking, but Sally had stopped listening. She was trying to communicate with her own daughter, who just waved and left, slamming the door behind her.

'It's so kind of you, darling. I'll owe you a big one.'

Sally's attention was right back on the call as Diana continued: 'And most important of all, Sal, I'm so glad it's someone like you keeping an eye on her for me. I do adore her, but, as daughters go, she is very innocent.'

Theresa brought in a box of sample ingredients and moved into the kitchen. While Carol finished decorating – putting up curtains, arranging the table linen and deciding on the place settings – and William was off getting Benjamin some air, Theresa used the small time she had left to work on some of the recipes and dishes which, so far, she had only created on paper.

Although Marcel had offered them a table this evening at the brasserie, Theresa knew that she had to do this, and it would be better if they all sat in the dining room here, tasted, and then offered her a critique, so that she could improve everything in time for the dress rehearsal on Saturday – when they had invited a few friends in to try everything out.

Sunday was D-day, the official opening; for the general public, if they turned up, and hopefully with local papers covering the event.

Theresa spent half an hour or so laying out the preparation tables: working out where she would chop and plotting where to keep things like sieves, which would be needed at an instant's notice. It was only when everything seemed perfect that she realised she had forgotten to leave a workspace where the plates would be dressed.

She started again.

Once things looked good, she started washing, peeling and preparing the ingredients for several different dishes, which she would serve to the others this evening.

She had just finished chopping a large onion when Imogen appeared in the kitchen. She had heard voices but was so involved in her work she hadn't realised it wasn't William and Benjamin returning after his little dizzy spell.

'Thank God I found you in time,' said Imogen, flopping into one of the dining chairs, while Chloe, Lola and Cressida, Theresa's grandchildren, streamed into the kitchen. 'I've managed to get myself an appointment at this wonderful hairdresser's in Nice and I have nowhere to leave the children.'

'But Imogen ...' Theresa noticed Cressida pulling at a saucepan handle, and reached out to prevent the heavy pan tumbling down on her head. 'I really have too much on my plate ...'

'Do you have any of those chocolate yums that you made for us before?' asked Lola, pulling open the fridge door.

'*You've* too much on your plate?' said Imogen, running her fingers through her hair. 'Do you know what it's like waiting twenty-four hours a day on your miserable whining geriatric ex-husband?'

'He's your father, Imogen.'

Chloe had pulled open the pantry steps and used them to clamber up to peer at the prepared pots of ingredients. 'What are these, Grandma?' she asked, putting her fingers into the bowl of whipped egg yolks.

'I'll pay you back, Mum. Don't worry. And I won't be long.' Imogen was up and backing in the direction of the door as she spoke, heading towards the way out. 'You know how the kids love you, Mummy, and adore all this cooking stuff you do.'

'Imogen ...' she called.

But Imogen was already gone.

Theresa raced around trying to corral her grandchildren, who were now running about, laughing and playing tag.

She had to rush to stop a bowl full of prepared strawberries crashing to the floor.

Carol arrived at the pass, and peered through.

'Oh my!' she said. 'How will this work out?'

'Grandma?' asked Lola. 'Will you take us to see the fat lady's bare bottom?'

'Please, Brandma,' echoed Cressida.

'I won't even ask,' said Carol, stepping into the kitchen and shooting a wink at Theresa. 'Now, you little renegades like chocolate, I gather?'

All three children put on winsome smiles and looked up at Carol.

'We like making tiffin with Brandma,' said Cressida, with a coy chuckle.

'If you stay very quiet and help me do a bit of napkin folding and leave Grandma to do some cooking, I promise to buy you some tasty chocolate. Deal?'

She held her hand out to shake.

Chloe shook first, then Lola.

Cressida, looking up, stepped forward and said: 'You're funny. You've got a voice just like Brandad's.'

'*Brandade!*' Theresa rubbed her hands together. 'Now there's an idea.'

Sally phoned William with Diana's proposal.

'Diana Sparks?' he said, excited. 'Then she'll come to the opening?' He squealed then said quietly: 'Oh, but God, the daughter is that ghastly girl. I cannot let a frump like that appear front of house.'

Sally tried to talk over him. It was difficult to explain that Cathy was standing only a few feet away.

'I'll leave it with you, William, and I'll phone you again this evening.'

'Let me have a think and talk it over with the others,' he said. 'On second thoughts, what the hell. If it's free, what's the problem?'

Before he had hung up, Sally heard a key turn in the front-door lock.

Jackie appeared, mouse-like, cringing before Sally.

'How will I ever deserve your forgiveness, old bean?' she said, holding out a small bouquet of flowers. 'It really was a bad show, wasn't it? I genuinely didn't notice how much I was drinking. And then there was that awful kerfuffle when the men went doolally. I mean, they shouldn't just keep refilling your glass like that. I blame the waiters.'

'How's your head?' asked Sally, moving towards the kitchen. 'Fancy a cup of tea?'

Cathy took the bouquet from Sally and went into the shower room to arrange the new flowers in another vase.

'I'm a bit peckish,' said Jackie. 'I could murder some toast, if you don't mind. They don't give you anything except coffee in the police station.'

'You were arrested?'

'Not exactly. It's because it was such a high-powered event, I suppose. They took us all away and left us to sober up in a waiting room at the *gendarmerie*. You should have seen the place. Thirty or more people in evening dress, all out of their mind on drink and drugs. It was there that I realised that Ted isn't quite so much fun as he first appears. He's quite the womaniser, isn't he?'

'Here in Bellevue-Sur-Mer he is known as the Lizard of Oz,' said Sally. 'He's a big kid.'

'Oh, I picked that up. A maudlin boozer too. He went on and on and on about some woman who he was in love with. He was like a broken record. Apparently this woman is very ambitious.'

Marianne, thought Sally.

'And there's someone else on the scene too, but she's a non-starter, now. Rather sharp-tongued, I got the picture.'

And that would be Sian. It was really quite interesting to hear. Sally had no intention of interrupting Jackie's spiel with any information about Marianne.

'And she has a mother who's dried up with disappointment.'

Sally was amazed that while banged up for drunkenness Ted would find the time to moan about Sian's mother. Incredible how booze loosens the tongue.

'My daughter has arrived unexpectedly to stay with me—' Sally was unsure how much Jackie knew and how much detail she should pass on. 'So I wondered how long you're thinking of being here.'

Jackie hung her head.

'I know I deserve you to chuck me out to sleep in the gutter, Sally. I really do. But I like you so much. I always admired you as an actress. Your marriage and giving up the biz was the world's loss. That Russkie fellow, by the way . . .'

'You mean Stanislav.'

Jackie laughed. 'Yes, I kept calling him Stanislavski by mistake! Force of habit – all those years pretending to be trees! Anyhow, he's putting money into my project – sight unseen. How about that!'

'Congratulations!' Sally handed Jackie a tray with a plate of toast and a mug of tea.

'Thanks, sweetie. And thank you so much for introducing me to Stanislavski.' She took a bite of toast. 'I have to say, I do think he's rather keen on you, Sally. To tell the truth, I think that's the only reason he's backing me. He wants your favour. He kept telling me what a lovely woman you are.'

Sally glowed inside. But hesitated at letting herself believe it. Maybe it had been the drink talking, and he was having a Slavic moment of sentiment.

'I know you have a tendency to exaggerate, Jackie. So I'll take it all, but with a generous pinch of salt.'

'Seriously, Sally. He's keen as mustard. Why else did he go on and on and on about you? Honestly, my old darling, I was rather jealous.'

Sally purred inside but still chose to keep her distance. It might not be what Stanislav thought at all. Perhaps Sally reminded him of his mother or something awful like that.

Jackie sipped at the tea, hastily putting the too-hot mug down again. 'Do you know what he said?'

'No,' said Sally, dreading the reply.

'He said he'd give up all his wealth if he could find a wife exactly like you.' Jackie paused and looked Sally in the eye. 'How about that for a result? "Exactly like you".'

Oddly, on hearing this information, Sally felt as though someone had punched her in the stomach.

Jackie was looking rather sorry for herself.

'So, it's OK, old girl. I know I have to go. I do know where I'm not wanted. I'm prepared for the worst. But if you're chucking me out, please do it quickly. My bags are all but packed.'

Sally knew that it would be very difficult to put Jackie out without feeling really terrible about it.

'It is problematic, Jackie . . . My daughter . . .'

'But, old bean, if you could be so sweet and just let me stay on till the Brits in Film party on Sunday night. I promise I'll vanish like a wraith on Monday morning. But it really is important for me to be seen at that party . . . You can come too, if you like. I can get you invited. I mean, even though it's been years, you never know.'

Against her better judgement, and in a whoosh of excitement thanks to the news about Stanislav, Sally found herself saying yes to everything without thinking. After all, Marianne might never get to know the details of Ted cavorting with Jackie, and Sally supposed she should be quite glad to hear what Ted was saying about her to almost total strangers.

While Theresa was making tiffin with the children, William arrived in the kitchen. She had decided that it was worth trying anything to keep them quiet so that she could get on with the job in hand. But William didn't see it that way.

'Will someone tell me what the hell is going on?'

Theresa put down her wooden spoon and wiped her hands down her apron.

'I'm just babysitting the grandchildren for a little while.'

'This is not a nursery, Theresa.'

'I know that, William, and I am continuing to prepare the dishes for tonight's tasting, as agreed.'

'Theresa, this is not a crèche or a playgroup. It's not Theatre in Education or Watch the Kiddies Go A-Cooking. This is supposed to be a restaurant. We open in two days, for God's sake. There is absolutely no time for messing about.'

Little Cressida grabbed him by the trouser leg. Her hands were smeared with chocolate fudge; William's trousers were pale blue, now with brown patches.

'We like it here,' she said. 'There's a nice tall lady with great big feet.'

William wiped the child's hands away.

'This, Theresa, is the final straw. Absolutely the last. I am sorry to have to say it, but you have really not been pulling your weight.'

Theresa was shocked to hear him doubting her efforts. She'd worked like a trooper. What hadn't she done?

'William, I've given this place every moment of my waking life. I've been in cleaning, clearing, painting, overseeing plumbing and electricals all hours of the day and night. I've gone through phone books for advertisers. I've had no life at all *except* this place.'

'None of us have, Theresa. The difference being that you have done all those other things but, until now, have given no thought at all to the one and only job that is yours and yours alone, and in fact the *only job* that is vital in a restaurant – the preparation of the food.'

'But I . . .'

'No buts. Without food we are not a restaurant at all, are we?' He turned on his heels. 'Now pull your finger out. Get rid of these brawling brats and get on with it.'

'Mummy!' Lola started crying. 'I want my mummy!'

'The nasty man called us brats,' said Chloe, running through to Carol. 'He's a bad man.'

'I planned to give us all a tasting session this evening,' said Theresa, wiping the sweat from her brow. 'But as you see, things went awry.'

William stood in the doorway between the kitchen and the dining room. 'Regardless of your familial complications and however "awry" things might be, Theresa, we have no option but to continue with the tasting session tonight.'

Carol came up close behind him and leaned against the doorframe.

'He's right, Theresa. It's always been a race against time. And we're coming up to the finishing line. No one in a race slows down when they're coming into the home straight. That's when they really put a spurt on. Have you never watched the Kentucky Derby? It's the final seconds that clinch it.'

Before Theresa had a chance to reply, the restaurant door burst open and then slammed shut.

Everyone turned to see Ted emerge round the screen. He stood at the welcome desk, a hat pulled down low over his forehead.

'Hi everyone! Lovely day out there!' he called. 'Any room in here for a refugee? Preferably at the back where no one can find me.'

'And that is it!' shouted William, pushing past Ted. 'I'm off. It's like a Carry On film in here. I will see you later, Theresa, for the tasting session. I'll send Benjamin to help.'

He was gone.

'No time to waste.' Ted scampered into the kitchen. 'I'm up a gum tree with three women braying for my blood. I tell you, Theresa, they're mad as cut snakes.'

Theresa's three grandchildren were huddled in a corner of the kitchen, sobbing. Ted's arrival silenced them.

'What have we here? A trio of blubbering ankle-biters.'

They stared up at him in wonder.

Theresa realised her prayers had been answered.

'OK, Ted. I'll make a deal with you. There's a small yard out there. You will entertain these three darlings for the rest of the afternoon, leaving me to get on with the cooking.'

'My stomach thinks me throat's cut.' Ted looked around the messy tops. 'Can we take the chocolate stuff out there with us?'

Theresa looked at the earnest expressions on the children's faces and saw that they were already colluding with the Australian. She handed him the pan of tiffin.

'Now, Theresa, my old mucker, you promise you won't lag on me if Marianne, or my wife, or that limey bird off the telly-box turn up, will you?'

'I really don't want to know the details of your private life, Ted.' Theresa gave him a wink and held the back door open. 'But you are definitely not in this restaurant. Now, shoo, so I don't have to lie.'

While Jackie went up to bed for the afternoon, to sleep off the effects of both the Cannes party and her night at the police station, Sally took Cathy down to La Mosaïque to offer her services.

Carol, aware of Sally's relationship as mother of one of Ted's three inamoratas and the perils of letting her know that the guilty party was playing nanny in the yard, explained that Theresa was up to her eyeballs with work and did not want to be disturbed, which was the truth.

She sat them down at a table in the centre of the dining room while Sally went through Diana's offer to subsidise Cathy's apprenticeship.

'I would be so happy here,' said Cathy, 'working among normal people.'

Carol exchanged a look with Sally.

'The truth is that today, Cathy, there's not an awful lot to do out here.' Carol stacked the pile of plastic menus into which she had been inserting the change-able paper pages and put them on an adjacent table. 'However, if you are serious in this endeavour, I can explain how things will work. And later Theresa can show you round the kitchen. Another thing you could join in with will be tonight's sampling of the dishes we hope to have on the menu this week.'

'*This* week!' said Sally. 'I'm impressed. So you'll change the menu every week.'

'The plan is to keep everything seasonal and accord-ing to what's looking good in the market.'

'How exciting,' said Sally, looking forward to many evenings in the restaurant. 'Don't you think it's fun, Cathy? I fear I'll be eating in here all the time and put on stones, if not tons. I can never resist tasty grub.'

'As a matter of fact, Sally darling, I was about to email you inviting you to be our guest tomorrow night. We're having a kind of dress rehearsal. Just to try it all out without a paying public.'

'Count me in; I could rustle up some numbers if you like,' said Sally. 'You'll have to let us pay you a nominal sum, though, to cover your costs. Start as you mean to go on or you'll all be broke in a fortnight.'

'It's only a preview, Sally. More for us than you. We'll be using you as guinea pigs, and giving ourselves a warning of how things may turn out. So it should really be on the house.'

'Who else will be coming?'

'The usual gang,' said Carol.

'Oh yes. Zoe? Sian? How about Marcel?' As Sally spoke, she noticed that Carol's eyes flicked towards the closed kitchen door. Sally thought she looked slightly agitated.

Carol stood up. 'So, Cathy, shall I begin by showing you the ropes?'

Cathy asked, 'What ropes?' and Sally's phone started buzzing. She flipped open the case and looked at the caller's name.

Stanislav!

'I'm sorry.' Sally got up and backed away. 'I'll just take this outside.'

Sally had no intention of letting either Carol or Cathy hear this call.

'Hello! Could you hold the line a moment?'

She started heading towards the back door.

Carol signalled quickly and whispered, 'Boxes of vegetables piled out there, Sally.'

She turned around, left the restaurant and crossed the road to sit on the harbour wall.

'I don't have the words to describe how sorry I am . . .' he said.

Sally left him in silence.

'I thought perhaps I could pick you up and treat you to dinner,' he went on. 'Only this time there will be no one else there to stir things up. I would like to propose . . .'

Sally held her breath.

'…dinner on my yacht. Just you and me. Out in the harbour at Cannes, watching the fireworks display.'

Sally loved boats, fireworks and food …

'I adore fireworks,' said Sally.

'Then it's a yes?'

She didn't want to appear to be the keen teenager she felt she was. 'When would this outing take place, Stanislav?'

'Tomorrow, of course.'

Tomorrow! Sally had only just promised herself at La Mosaïque. Good. Better to play hard-to-get, to seem cool.

'I don't think I can do tomorrow, actually.'

Sally heard Stanislav inhale deeply.

'I would be so disappointed,' he said.

Wow! How keen was *he* being? Perhaps Jackie had not been exaggerating.

'That's all right, Stanislav. Couldn't we do another night?'

'But the fireworks are tomorrow!'

Now she was torn. Perhaps she should take up his offer. She'd have to wait a whole year to have the same possibility.

How romantic, anyhow, to be out on the harbour at Cannes, dining in a great white gin palace during the film-festival display? Who knew, maybe Steven Spielberg and George Clooney would be on an adjacent boat.

She accepted. She was sure her friends at the restaurant could manage their 'dress rehearsal' without her.

* * *

With the new nanny in place, the afternoon at La Mosaïque turned out well. The three kids loved playing with Uncle Ted in the yard, and Theresa cooked up a storm, doing the preparation for every dish that would be on the menu for the next week. She made things like the cakes, which did not need to be done immediately prior to serving. She parboiled and blind-baked and did all the jobs she was going to have to do in the mornings before lunch service. This, she knew, was why she wanted to be part of the project. She was happy working.

She could hear Carol in the next room explaining how to lay the tables and how to serve; how to note down a telephone booking; how to take a coat and present a receipt. From what Theresa could tell, Cathy looked as though she would be quite an asset to the business. She simply needed to brighten up the hangdog expression and put a bit of a spring into her slouchy walk.

A knock on the door and Carol entered, suggesting that from now on, while she finished painting a few more motifs on the dining-room walls, Cathy should help out in the kitchen.

Although happy in her work, Theresa was hot and tired from being on her feet all afternoon. She welcomed the offer of an assistant, especially as she had already overheard, from the dining room, how good Cathy was at picking things up.

She showed her where everything was kept, and told Cathy not to take it personally if she barked out orders. Running a kitchen was a bit like being in the army, she explained. It had to run smoothly under enormous pressure.

'Oh I know about that,' said Cathy, tying the bow of her apron tightly. 'Mummy also says being an actress is like being a soldier. You do as you're told, you turn up on time, you go where you're sent and you need enormous self-discipline.'

Theresa couldn't quite understand what she meant, but smiled anyhow.

'Do you know how to make a roux?' she asked.

'I can learn,' said Cathy, the faithful, keen puppy dog.

Theresa called for ingredients: 'Butter, flour, milk, salt . . .'

Cathy ran around the kitchen presenting packets and jars, while Theresa sought out a pan and whisk.

By the time of the evening rendezvous, between them they had managed to get everything perfectly prepared. Once the others arrived it would be on with the live cooking – 'Which can only work with an audience,' said Cathy.

Theresa nodded. Perhaps the girl had a point. There were a few similarities.

William and Benjamin appeared, and were surprised to see order reigned, even with the surplus people present.

Theresa suggested that Ted stay for the tasting. William thought it was a good idea. 'As long as you're not expecting kangaroo burgers,' he added.

'Hey there, mate,' said Ted. 'I'm not a total drongo, you know. I've probably eaten in more posh restaurants than any of you. If you recall, my wife is a very successful lady of business. It's five-star all the way with Sian.'

And that silenced any further comments.

William looked doubtful about including the three grandchildren in the notating. But at that exact moment Imogen arrived and offered to help sample the dishes too. 'I live in London, you see,' she said slowly, as though addressing primitive people, 'where we eat out constantly.'

'I think we should shove the tables together,' said Carol. 'Remember, this isn't the dress rehearsal, this is strictly sampling. While Cathy was in the kitchen helping Theresa, I made some cards, which we can use to mark everything out of ten.' She handed out the cards to everyone, including Theresa. 'I've drawn columns. It's important, Theresa, that you also join in the marking.'

While William and Benjamin talked to Imogen and Ted, Cathy and Theresa went back into the kitchen to make the final touches to the dishes.

There was a rapping on the front door and Ted bolted for the kitchen.

Benjamin went to answer.

Diana Sparks stood on the threshold.

Benjamin opened and closed his mouth a few times.

'I . . . I . . . hello!'

'I believe my daughter has taken a job here,' said Diana, still on the doorstep.

'Oh?'

'Cathy? She came here this afternoon, with Sally Doyle, I mean Connor.'

William appeared behind Benjamin and gasped loudly.

He went into something like a curtsy.

'Miss Sparks,' he said breathily. 'How lovely to meet you. Please come on into our little bijou abode – I mean, um, eatery. Oh no, that sounds awful . . . I . . .'

Diana stepped in and William stopped talking.

Theresa and Cathy were rushing back and forth from the kitchen to the long table laying down plates. Imogen and the children had gathered round one end, sitting with empty plates before them and pencils ready.

'Ooh, what's going on?'

'We're having a bit of a tasting session,' said Benjamin. 'Cathy is helping Theresa in the kitchen.'

'Oh, dear,' Diana smoothed her hair back. 'I don't want to intrude.'

'No, no, you're not intruding at all. Please come in.'

'Can I wait for Cathy to finish?' said Diana. 'I'll just sit here, quiet as a mouse, I promise.'

'Don't be so silly,' said William, unable to stop smiling.

Diana raised an eyebrow.

'Oh, I'm sorry. I didn't mean to . . . I mean . . . Do join us. If you like . . . ?'

'We're marking the dishes out of ten for how much we like them.' Carol leaned forward and handed her a card. 'One to ten on appearance, taste and balance of dish.'

'And putting in opinions and comments, and that stuff,' said nine-year-old Chloe. 'It's going to be very professional.'

'Glad to hear it,' said Diana, taking a seat. 'Professionalism is sublimely important.'

'OK – all clear on the western front!' Ted put his head round the kitchen door as Theresa appeared with the last of the starter dishes. 'May I join in the fun?'

'The more the merrier,' said Theresa. 'Pull up a pew.'

Ted took the seat next to Diana and held out his hand. 'Ted Kelly, poet, man of the world, childminder and general factotum. Pleased to meet you.'

'Australian! I adore Australia. I toured there years ago. We had a hell of a good time.'

'I'll take all the credit for that,' said Ted.

'It's a very beautiful country. So excitingly young.'

'Unlike us,' said Ted.

'We're young,' said Chloe indignantly.

'Very important to have balance in all things,' said Diana.

William clinked his fork against his glass of water. 'Now, the sole point of this exercise is to help Theresa, who has been at it all day.'

'At it?' said Ted, laughing. 'Thought that was my job.'

'We really do want to know your opinions: would you like to pay for this? Would you come again? Which do you like most? Is anything wrong – not enough seasoning, too much, too dry, too heavy, etcetera?'

'Give them the bad points, why don't you?' said Carol, picking up a pencil and a fork. 'I think it would be very useful to enter positive comments also.'

For the next half hour the dining room was quiet except for the scrape of cutlery on china and the licking of lips. Theresa and Cathy took turns in announcing the names of the dishes.

Once the starters were eaten and marked, Theresa and Cathy served up main courses followed by the desserts. Everyone scribbled away. Cressida sat between Ted and Carol, and they both gave advice on how to put her opinions on the form.

When everything was done, Theresa, Carol and Cathy served the adults with a coffee and the kids with a glass of freshly squeezed orange juice, while William and Benjamin totalled up the scores and fixed the comments to separate papers marked with the name and description of each dish.

Theresa sat and talked to Carol and tried to act naturally with Diana. Both told her that her recipes were delicious and original.

Theresa felt tingly inside, and wondered why it seemed like triple praise coming from such a star as Diana Sparks.

'When's opening night?' the actress enquired.

'The day after tomorrow,' replied Theresa.

'How do I book a table?' asked Diana. 'I'd like to be there.'

Carol fetched the bookings ledger.

'Make it a table for four,' Diana added. 'I'll bring Sal, if she's free.'

Theresa dared herself; she hesitated before asking but, as she knew well, nothing ventured nothing gained.

'Might we be able to let the local paper know?'

Diana flinched and her famed smile became brittle.

'Let's think about that,' she said.

Theresa was aware that if they thought about it they would certainly miss the moment. But getting a photo of a celebrity exiting the building might be just as good publicity as a celebrity being announced beforehand.

While the women were deep in conversation, the men busy marking and the children giggling and running around Nanny Ted, the front door opened and in stepped Marianne.

'I knew it!' she said. 'You had to be hiding in here. It was the only place left.'

She strode up to Ted, who cowered behind the three goggle-eyed children, and slapped him across the face.

'You're a bastard,' she said. 'If you want to talk, I shall be at my mother's.'

'You want to talk to me along with Jackie Westwood?' said Ted. 'She's as mad as a box of frogs. While she's staying there, no way am I coming in to that house and have to deal with two of you at once.'

Marianne's eyes widened. 'Jackie Westwood is staying with my mother?'

Ted winced. He had clearly only just realised that Sally had not told her and that Marianne was in ignorance. Now he had four women to worry about.

Marianne turned on her heels and left.

'Marianne,' cried Ted, rising from the corner where he crouched. 'Don't go there making trouble.'

'Order!' cried William. 'Order, please!'

Ted grabbed his hat from the coat stand and ran out after Marianne.

Sally was sitting in the kitchen, deep in conversation with Jackie about Stanislav's invitation, when Marianne burst in, chased by Ted.

Chaos ensued.

While Marianne yelled profanities in Jackie's direction, Ted threw his arms in the air and hollered.

'I had no idea he actually belonged to anyone, old bean.' Jackie was backing up behind a dining chair.

Sally tried to thrust herself between the warring parties.

Marianne spat at Sally, 'And you are as bad. Sheltering, aiding and abetting ...'

'It was the excitement of being at Cannes,' exclaimed Ted, as Marianne wrestled with him. 'And, be fair, you'd told me to bugger off. Nothing happened except that I had a boxing round with Sally's new boyfriend and we ended up spending all night banged up in the cooler.'

Marianne rounded on Sally.

'What new boyfriend?'

'Nobody,' replied Sally. 'Not that you know, anyhow.' She reached out for her daughter. She didn't care what happened to these other two but had no desire to drive Marianne away.

'He's sweet,' said Jackie.

'And loaded,' added Ted. 'And younger than me.'

'That is just weird,' said Jackie, glancing from Sally to Marianne. 'But he is charming.'

'And Sally's a beautiful woman,' added Ted, realising his gaffe.

Marianne stared in horror and disgust, then said to Ted, 'I suppose you're after my mother too?'

A hard rap on the door.

'I'll get it,' said Jackie, glad to find an excuse to edge towards the exit.

She opened up.

On the doorstep stood Sian. She took one look at Jackie and slapped her cheek, then calmly stepped over the threshold to see where the yelling was coming from.

Sally, Ted and Marianne were pulling hair, jabbing at one another, jammed up in a corner looking like a St Trinian's rugby scrum.

'Just as I expected – a writhing nest of vipers,' said Sian serenely. 'Except that you are supposedly mature adults. Are you feeling quite sane?'

Ted extricated himself from the fight and stepped forward.

He flung himself on to his knees before his wife.

'Take me back, darling,' he cried. 'It was always you and only you. I made a big mistake here.'

Sian looked at her prostrate husband, crooked her finger in his direction and said, 'Does my big bad Teddy want his honey?'

He nodded. She held out her hand. He took it. They left.

Marianne said, 'I think I am going to be sick.'

'Well, please don't do it on my Turkish rug,' said Sally.

'Oh lawks, so it was his wife he was on about,' said Jackie. 'I obviously got it all wrong. When Ted told me the lover he wanted to ditch was a sharp-tongued non-starter he must have meant you, Marianne, and the mother he thought was a dried-up old twig was obviously . . .'

'That's quite enough, Jackie, thank you,' snapped Sally, twisting the metal lid off the gin bottle. 'Does anyone else need a drink?'

Theresa spent a lovely evening with her family. After the tasting at La Mosaïque was over and they had cleaned up the kitchen, leaving everything prepared for the dress rehearsal tomorrow, they all sat out on the terrace of the brasserie enjoying a drink and a snack.

Imogen was very impressed to have met a celebrity, and even the kids were bubbling with excitement, as they had realised that Diana had played the big bad witch in one of their favourite films. On hearing about this, Theresa ordered them bright-green drinks – Perrier Menthe – which they glugged down joyfully.

'Tastes a bit like toothpaste,' said Lola. 'But I like it.'

'It's a very witchy drink,' agreed Cressida.

Imogen leaned back and took a deep breath as she gazed out over the darkening harbour. The sun was setting in a haze of red, and, on the navy-blue horizon, little boats, their lights flashing white and red and green, bounced over the waves heading round the capes in the direction of Cannes or Monte Carlo.

'I can really see why you wanted to move here, Mum.' Imogen sipped her chilled glass of local rosé then stabbed at an olive from the small bowl that had arrived with the drinks. 'They know all about service, don't they? A drink needs nibbles. You shouldn't have to ask.'

'And then be charged three additional pounds for a packet of crisps, salt and vinegar or prawn cocktail only.'

'They do come cheaper than that, I believe, Mum.'

'You've mellowed, Imogen,' said Theresa. 'Or is that just the Bellevue-Sur-Mer effect?'

'It's a wonderful place. But since Michael buggered off with the nanny, and since I've had to deal with my self-obsessed father, who's still grieving for his lost girlfriend, I must admit I've started looking at things in a slightly different way. I mean, really, Mummy, you either have to laugh or cry. And I don't like crying, it plays havoc with my mascara.' Imogen smiled. 'The kids have been brilliant about everything. I think seeing other people behaving like pigs does tend to wise you up. They were very happy to be coming out here to see some woman with a fat arse ...'

Theresa winced.

'Not you, Ma.'

'Oh Lord!' Theresa grinned.

'It's a statue, or rather a bas-relief, in town. Set into a concrete wall. It shows some local heroine.' Theresa sighed and took another sip of wine. Although there was much work ahead, everything was going smoothly. The tasting session had scored a 'bingo', or a '180' or whatever the latest name was for practically perfect. Now all she had to do was keep it up.

'But the thing that puzzles me,' continued Imogen, 'is why, when you came here escaping the rat race, you want to join the race again, only this time with so much responsibility? Isn't that ruining a good thing?'

Lately Theresa had wondered this herself during many a sleepless night.

'Look at your friend Sally,' said Imogen. 'She didn't want to get mixed up with this stuff, and now she's got someone chasing after her. That won't ever happen while you look so frazzled. It's too much for you at your age.'

Theresa didn't like the 'at your age' tag. But sometimes when she lay awake at night she did fear being old and alone. Not helped, she guessed, by her old

261

bones being in her current *chambre* on the mattress on the floor.

'Work, work, work!' Imogen continued. 'Wouldn't it be better if you had someone here with you full-time? Someone with whom you can share your twilight years?'

Twilight years? A shudder went through Theresa. Euphemistic phrases like that made her feel rather nauseous. Theresa could only think of the *Twilight Zone* and that haunting tune. She found herself humming it.

Maybe it would be nice to have someone to share things with. But there was no one on the horizon and she knew that if she just stayed here and lounged around, doing nothing with her days, she would go mad with boredom. Everyone, even older people, had to have some aspirations and some place where they were going to be needed. What was sadder than reading about an elderly person who had died at their breakfast table and remained there undiscovered for weeks? Theresa wanted to be busy and to have somewhere to go each day. She liked the idea of having to turn up at work, and knowing that, if only she and the others could get it right, they might even make some money from it.

'If I don't like it I can stop,' she said, realising that this was not entirely true, as all her money was now tied up in the project. 'But while it lasts – I like the work.'

Chloe sat forward and said, 'Professionalism is sublimely important.'

Theresa shot a look at Imogen and they both laughed.

Theresa could not be happier.

23

S ALLY WOKE EARLY NEXT morning wondering why she felt so nervous. She then remembered the list of reasons.

The rapprochement between Sian and Ted had led to a high storm from Marianne, who, even though it was late at night, had packed her bags and ordered a taxi to the airport. She was leaving for London and, 'as long as she lived', never wanted to see Bellevue-Sur-Mer again. This left Sally feeling very hurt. Was a short dalliance with a childish man like Ted really worth the drama? Sally feared it was loss of face for her daughter, more than anything. Even as a tot, Marianne had always loved to win. And in this case she may have won Ted, but too soon afterwards she had lost him again.

She also remembered, rather crossly, how, according to Jackie, Ted had described her while in the Cannes police station. Was she really 'dried up with disappointment'? She knew that inside she felt lost and unwanted. She wanted work, or love, or something. Marriage and motherhood had come and gone as a form of quasi-employment anyhow, leaving her free, but with nothing to do with her days.

She felt sorry again that she had not become part of the team at La Mosaïque. She imagined them now busily preparing for their opening, just like you did for a first night, stomach a-flutter, totally tense, but excited too, rushing around getting cards and make-up, laying out your place in the dressing room, arranging the telegrams . . . Oh no, times had changed. No one sent telegrams any more.

She climbed wearily out of bed and went to put on her dressing gown, aware of the lingering perfume left on it by her house guest.

Jackie's door was closed. Sally wondered if she was cowering inside, scared to come down after yesterday's embarrassment.

She shuffled into the kitchen and filled the kettle.

An urgent rap on the front door.

She opened up.

Four *gendarmes* with sniffer dogs stood in the street.

'Madame Sally Connor?'

Sally nodded. What on earth? She prayed nothing had happened to Marianne, or to Tom. But why dogs?

The lead officer presented an authority to search and she took a step back, allowing him to pass.

One man and his dog ran upstairs; the other started at the front door and worked his way back on the ground floor.

'I have a friend up there,' shouted Sally, wishing she'd had time to get dressed. 'She is probably asleep.' She turned to the commanding officer. 'What's going on?' she asked. 'What are you looking for?'

'You are acquainted with Jean-Philippe Delacourt?'

'Yes.' Sally nodded. 'He was my instructor at sea-school.'

'He drove you to this house late at night last Thursday?'

Sally thought back to the ghastly evening at Cannes, and Marina Martel's after-party.

'Yes. But what . . . ?'

'Monsieur Delacourt is currently in police custody. He was followed by the Marseille drug squad and, after a search of his car, it was deduced from the trace elements we discovered that the main stash of cocaine had been deposited elsewhere. He claims to know nothing.'

Sally stood open-mouthed in disbelief.

'Perhaps, Madame Connor, you might tell us where it is.'

'I know nothing too,' she said. 'And I don't believe Jean-Philippe would . . .'

She was interrupted by the two dog-handlers. '*Rien,*' they said. 'Not a trace.'

One of them turned to address her.

'Your friend is not there in the bedroom,' he said. 'The bird has flown.'

The chief held out his hand to shake.

'Apologies, Madame Connor, for disturbing you.'

And they were gone, leaving Sally to wonder what on earth was happening.

Why had they arrested Jean-Philippe and how was Jackie involved, or was the officer simply making a joke? Had Jackie upped and gone without letting her know? After last night's shenanigans it would not have surprised her.

Sally went up to check the spare room. Jackie's things were still there, and the bed lay unmade. What day was it? Saturday. Perhaps something was on at Cannes and Jackie had left early for that.

Sally returned to her own bedroom and got dressed.

She was being silly worrying about Jackie, when the real problem was Jean-Philippe. She wished now that she had asked where he was being detained and upon what charge.

The phone rang. It was Tom.

'Hi Mum, I'm thinking of coming down to see you for a few days.'

'How lovely.' Sally was still worrying about Jean-Philippe. Had she accepted a lift from him while he was carrying drugs back from Marseille?

'It's semi-work, actually, Mum. After you told me about all your friends opening that restaurant of theirs, I put the idea to my editor, who wants to start a column where I draw the establishment while my boss does a little write-up. We're only going to glamorous locations, holiday hotspots, haunts of the rich and famous, so where better to begin than BSM?'

'So when will you arrive?'

'Tonight?' asked Tom.

Sally snatched her diary. She suddenly remembered that tonight was her date for the Cannes fireworks.

'Isn't that when you said the place opens?'

'No,' said Sally. 'Tonight's the dress rehearsal. They open on Sunday. I'm going. Why don't you phone William? I'll give you his number. He has the low-down.'

'That's the thing, you see, Mum. We don't like to forewarn the proprietors, otherwise they tend to play it up a little. So anyhow, I'd ask you to keep it under your hat.'

'Of course. Shall I make up your room?'

'No. They put us up in the nearest posh hotel.'

Sally laughed. 'There is no posh hotel in Bellevue-Sur-Mer.'

'So they'll probably taxi us into Nice. No probs. See you soon.'

And he was gone.

William greeted Theresa with an early phone call, informing her of the latest news: Sian had now changed her mind and decided to take all of her money out of La Mosaïque.

'We are back to square one,' he announced. 'Any ideas?'

Theresa sank back down into her armchair and told him no.

'So what's the gen today?' he asked. 'I will be off my projected route as I now have to sniff around again for money.'

'What about the van?' asked Theresa. 'You're supposed to be picking up the supplies.'

'No can do.'

'How about Carol?'

'She's going to be at my side, on the phone all day, trying for adverts and reviewers.' There was a pause. 'How about Benjamin drives and you give that Sparks girl the list?'

'Excellent idea, William,' said Theresa.

'I'll ask him once he gets back from his midnight tryst with Carol.'

'Oh, are they still doing that?' Theresa herself was sleeping on the floor, but had forgotten that the other two were as well.

'The threat hasn't gone away, has it? Unless you've discovered the lost medallion stuck behind a wine rack and returned it to them?'

'You know that I haven't,' said Theresa. 'Except Carol's plan.'

William groaned. 'So, better safe than sorry,' he said. 'Until the security people can get in to fit up the new system at least. And we have the money to pay them for it. So, that's it then, Theresa. Benjamin and the Sparks girl can go to cash-and-carry or whatever . . .'

'William,' said Theresa, 'as you are so ready to fawn over the mother I do think it's about time you remembered that the "Sparks girl's" name is Cathy.'

'Who got out of the wrong side of the bed this morning?' said William. 'Oh. Forgot to ask. How many people have we rustled up for the rehearsal?'

'I left it to Carol,' said Theresa. 'But I think we're just about full.'

'Good,' said William, and hung up.

Theresa took it easy for the morning; after all, it was going to be a very hard night. She drew a map for Imogen, who wanted to go into Nice for a salad lunch in the Old Town. She put an X to mark the spot in the street where they'd find the statue of Catherine Ségurane, so that the kids could show their mother the woman with the bare bottom they were always talking about.

When Theresa arrived at the restaurant, Benjamin and Cathy were unloading the van. Theresa helped carry crates of fresh vegetables, while Cathy emptied packets into the jars marked flour, rice, salt, etcetera.

Theresa picked up one of the printed menus, which Carol had dropped off earlier, and pinned it up in the kitchen.

She laid out her preparation worktop and started chopping.

Sally was so nervous about her date that she spent almost all morning in front of the mirror, changing in and out of every piece of clothing she possessed. Some things looked classy, but too dressy for what was supposed to be a casual evening on a boat watching fireworks. After all, she had not been invited to the Prince's Ball at Monaco or even Royal Ascot. It was an evening jaunt on a gin palace.

When she tried to dress down, then it looked as though she was about to traipse round the supermarket or take the bins out.

Eventually she went for the slightly nautical but still glamorous look and adorned herself with pieces of jewellery and a bit of make-up.

While she was inspecting herself, she wondered what Stanislav would do now that Jean-Philippe was unavailable to drive the boat. Would he expect her to navigate, or even take the helm? Maybe she had got quite the wrong end of the stick altogether about this evening. Perhaps Stanislav wanted her there as a practical asset. Maybe he was throwing a proper party, with Destiny and Mickey and a shipload of celebrities. Isn't that what people did at Cannes? Perhaps she would simply spend the evening throwing out and pulling in the fenders.

She had a light lunch then went back to the wardrobe and tried again.

She thought about Jean-Philippe. She couldn't imagine him taking drugs, let alone dealing. He just didn't seem to her the type. He was so outdoorsy. But like all these secret things, you never really could tell.

She picked up another top and held it against herself. No. That wouldn't do at all.

Three outfits later, Sally heard the front door open, and went to the stairs to look down.

Jackie came in, peered up at her and wolf-whistled.

'Phwoar!' she said. 'You look corking, old girl. Off on a date?'

'I was worried about you, Jackie.'

'You silly old goose. Whyever?'

'When I couldn't find you this morning.'

'No probs, old bean. I had to tootle over to Cannes, remember . . . I told you days ago. Meeting with the British funding people. Left at sparrow's fart. Didn't want to disturb you.'

Sally knew the next question was going to be tricky. She doubted anyone ever answered truthfully.

'Do you take drugs?'

'Drugs?' echoed Jackie.

'Cocaine?'

'No,' said Jackie emphatically. 'Tried it once at drama school. Went green and was sick in a lift and never felt tempted again. Why? Were you about to offer me something?'

'No, no.' Sally now felt foolish for asking. After all, the sniffer dogs would have picked up the smallest trace, if there had been any in Jackie's room.

'In fact,' said Jackie, 'I'm rather down on all that illegal stuff. Once had a pal who was attacked by a loony on crack. Really don't approve of druggies at all.'

Why had Sally suspected Jackie? The only person they were looking for was Jean-Philippe.

Sally thought back to the car ride home from Cannes that night. There had been a box on the back seat. Was that full of drugs? Or were they stashed in the boot?

'Are you all right, Sally?'

Sally realised she was just standing there gripping the banister and that Jackie had offered to make a cup of tea.

'No, no. I'm fine,' she said. 'Got to get ready. As you said – I'm off on a date.'

'Who with?' asked Jackie. 'As if it was any of my business!'

'Stanislav.'

'Ah, the handsome Stanislavski,' said Jackie. 'I told you he's funding my film, didn't I?'

'He's a very generous man,' said Sally.

While Carol and Benjamin laid up the tables, Theresa and Cathy worked next door, blind-baking the pastry and preparing the desserts, boiling potatoes and rearranging things when they realised that the layout wasn't suiting them. Cathy was proving to be a very good worker. She took orders quietly and whenever Theresa called on her, she was ready.

Just after six, when Theresa, Carol, Benjamin and Cathy had just sat down to take their own light supper, William arrived, grinning, with a crate of champagne and another crate of mixed wines.

'We can't sell or serve liquor till the terms of the licence start,' he said. 'But as we are not actually open this evening, and this is essentially a private party of invited guests, I have brought some wine.'

He walked around with a distinct spring in his step and put a bottle on each table.

'Who's coming, Carol?' he asked, sitting and taking a plate. 'Do you have a table plan?'

Carol got up and fetched the piece of paper.

'Zoe and three guests, no doubt young men she pulled in some disco in Beaulieu last night,' said Benjamin.

'Sally, plus three.' William pointed to the table nearest the door. 'Will that include the Russian hunk? Oh, by the way, he left a message. He wants to invest in us!'

'Wow,' said Theresa. 'That will certainly help. Did he say how much?'

'It was a short message and the line not good, but I think he said "name your figure", then he laughed and added "within reason".'

'We can ask him when he gets here,' said Carol. 'I'd say "Beware of Russians bearing gifts."'

'Marcel and his family are coming,' said Theresa, who also thought that you shouldn't believe anything till it was all done and dusted and the money in the bank. 'I think that's nice that Marcel's supporting us tonight. I hope he likes us! And that table is for my daughter and three grandchildren. They adored everything they tried yesterday.'

'Who are all the other bookings?' William had his glasses on and was inspecting the table plan.

'Friends of friends,' said Carol. 'Oh, and that four, there, is for Costanzo and companions. To keep the peace, you know.'

'The most important thing,' said William, putting his spectacles back in his pocket, 'is that we use this night for ourselves. We need these people's reaction to help us make sure we get things right. Dishes should arrive in a timely fashion, wines and food served from the left, and taken away from the right. That's what I was taught. I . . .'

Benjamin interrupted. 'It's not school, William. We have all been preparing for this moment too, darling.'

'What time do we open the doors?' William looked at his watch. 'Oh, my God, we're going to be late.'

'According to our cards we're open noon to two p.m. and seven p.m. to ten.' Benjamin brushed a little flour off his boyfriend's lapel.

'So we open the doors in three minutes.' Theresa leaned back in her seat. 'Calm yourself, William. Let's enjoy our last few moments of peace.'

Zoe was waiting at the door and was the first to enter. Benjamin had been correct. She had brought three spectacularly good-looking young men with her. They were extremely attentive, taking her wrap, holding out her seat at the central table; in fact, doing all the jobs that Benjamin should have been doing.

Theresa went into the kitchen to await the orders. She watched through the pass, where the waiting staff would collect the plated dishes, as Carol handed out the menus and told them about the 'specials', which she had earlier scratched on to a small blackboard that she now placed on a stand adjacent to the table.

'The wine is complimentary,' said Carol. 'As our licence is not yet operational.'

'I thought it was all complimentary,' said Zoe. 'Isn't this a dress rehearsal for you lot?'

William appeared, suddenly all smiles, and explained the peculiar legalities of this one-off evening.

Theresa waited like a greyhound in the slips. She wanted to get on, to start cooking, and wished they'd order.

Other tables filled up; first Marcel and his family, then Monsieur Mari and his wife from the *boulangerie* up the hill.

Theresa tapped Cathy on the shoulder and she started lining up the *amuse-bouches*, tiny complimentary dishes that would be served to all diners at the very start. Tonight's were simply minute bowls of olive tapenade with slivers of carrot and celery to dip.

The orders started coming in and Theresa's hands flew from the whisk to the fish slice, from bain-marie to frying pan, as she served up the requested dishes.

When she placed two plates of the Niçoise 'fish and chips' on the pass she noticed that the table nearest the door had clearly been changed around, as Imogen and the children were seated there, not Sally and her guests. In fact she couldn't see Sally at all, but all the tables were full.

She pulled a paper order from the pass and returned to the range to fry up some more *panisse* chips.

* * *

274

As arranged, Sally waited at the harbour side for Stanislav. While she stood, she watched people going into La Mosaïque, pleased she had made her booking for the opening tomorrow. Then suddenly she remembered, and quickly got out her mobile.

'Jackie, I entirely forgot that I was meant to be at tonight's dress rehearsal for the new restaurant on the quay.'

'I did wonder when you went out,' said Jackie. 'Does that mean I can't go? I was rather looking forward to it.'

'No, darling, you go, please, and present my apologies. Trouble is I thought Sian and Ted would be with me, so you have two choices: cancel the other three seats or find some friends you can bring along.'

'Fantastic!' Jackie said.

Sally heard a chugging behind her on the water, and was surprised to see Stanislav arriving, alone on a small RIB, a little inflatable rubber boat with an outboard motor.

'I am driving my own tender,' he said. 'First time ever! I'll be grateful when you get aboard.'

Sally leapt in.

So her fears were right. She was here to provide nautical aid.

They arrived at Stanislav's yacht and climbed on to the back, pulling the RIB in after themselves.

'Phew!' he said. 'Glad that's over. I'm being very daring about everything tonight.' He flung his arms up in an extravagant gesture. 'Why not? You only live once.'

He turned to Sally and took her hand. 'So, Madame Connor, would you care to join me upstairs in the decent quarters?'

Sally followed him up the narrow steps and through the saloon towards the helm.

There was no one else to be seen. Her party idea was wrong, unless they were picking up the guests later, which at Cannes was quite probable.

'Who's taking the helm?' she asked.

'You are,' he said. 'With me beside you.'

'Oh Lord, Stanislav, do you think that's wise?'

'Jean-Philippe was unavailable,' he said. 'And I couldn't bear to have some stranger here, especially as the whole idea is to be alone with you.'

Sally wondered whether Stanislav knew why Jean-Philippe was unavailable.

'Have you spoken to Jean-Philippe at all lately?' she asked.

'Tried,' said Stanislav. 'No reply.'

'I see.' Sally looked at the big boat and was worried. 'Do you mean that you and I have to navigate our way to Cannes and back on our own?'

Stanislav nodded.

Sally gulped and took her place in the helm seat. She surveyed the array of controls, and was relieved to see that most of them were irrelevant to manoeuvring the boat. She could see multiple displays for fish shoals, sea and air temperature, and switches for stereo hi-fi systems and air conditioning.

'We don't have to moor,' said Stanislav, no doubt trying to reassure her. 'That is an advantage. We just drop anchor both ends.'

'So it's just us, then?' asked Sally. 'I'm hoping you've got someone in to cook the dinner, or do I have to do that too?'

Stanislav put up his hands in a gesture of surrender. 'I'm a man of simple tastes. I know people believe it's romantic to have servants running around, but I hate that idea of strangers listening in to your every word, don't you?'

Sally shook her head. Oh dear! This was not the romantic rendezvous she had foreseen. However, it was good to be out on the water, she loved fireworks, and when else would she get the chance to play about with a great big marine vehicle like this?

The anchor switch was plain enough to see. She pressed it and heard the motor spring into action. Another indicator showed her when the anchor was safely stowed.

'What can I do to help?' said Stanislav.

Sally looked around, then turned the key for the engine and put her hand on the throttle.

'Nothing,' she replied. 'Just sit there and look pretty.'

They both laughed.

24

Halfway through serving the main course Theresa knew that something was badly wrong. There had been the odd comment, brought up to the pass by Benjamin or Carol, about texture, and some about taste. But now the messages were flooding in. The batter was 'floppy and tasteless'; the sauce 'like wallpaper paste'. She herself had been wrestling with things in a way she never had done before: the roux seemed to be the wrong consistency, the pastry crumbled, the batter didn't go as crispy as it always did and the sauces somehow didn't gel correctly. She had no idea why, and whatever she tried, it failed to correct the problems.

William stormed into the kitchen. He was enraged, but instead of shouting – which the guests would hear – he half-mimed and grimaced his way through a verbal tirade of fury.

'There isn't one table on which someone doesn't want to send the food back, Theresa. What the hell is going on?'

Theresa looked around her. She had no idea why everything that had worked yesterday should turn out so different today.

'I can't imagine.' Theresa's stomach clenched in fear. This was like one of those nightmares. She prayed she was asleep and would wake up to find it was only a bad dream. 'Nothing's changed since yesterday.'

'Oh yes it has, Theresa, dear.' William still managed to snap while speaking in a hoarse whisper. 'I tasted the batter on the fish myself. It's like gnawing your way through a rubber wetsuit. And the pastry cases are like cardboard. Don't you sample things before you send them out, like you're supposed to?'

'Of course I do, but pastry cases and batter are two things you cannot taste on the dish. They were both fine in the previous runs. Everything I did is the same as yesterday.'

'I'm telling you, Theresa, it is not the same. Even the *fleur de sel*, in the little bowls on the tables, appears to have been replaced with something that tastes like dishwasher salt.'

Theresa went to the jar marked 'Flour' and unscrewed it. She dipped in a spoon and emptied a little into a saucer with some water, then stirred. She tasted the result.

'There's something wrong with the flour.'

Carol came in. 'Everything's ground to a halt out there. Even those children are saying the food is disgusting.'

Theresa wiped the sweat from her forehead with the back of her hand.

'Do you think it was those thugs who left the lighter and the fag ends?' said Theresa. 'Perhaps they let themselves in and changed everything in the jars.'

'How could they?' asked Carol. 'There has been someone here at all times, day or night.'

'Theresa,' said William. 'It's your kitchen. You are in charge. As you said, it's your domain . . .' William looked really distressed.

'Perhaps they came in when you were sleeping?' suggested Theresa.

'Oh, Theresa,' Carol sighed loudly. 'You and your gangsters.'

'We'd better call back all of the dishes,' said Theresa, thinking of the only other possible answer. 'Perhaps some of the dry ingredients have been contaminated.'

'Poison?' William's face filled with horror. He reached out and grabbed a countertop to steady himself. 'Oh my giddy aunt! We'll be sued to hell and back.'

'Someone go out there and tell them not to eat any more. We don't want a bunch of lawsuits on our hands,' said Theresa.

'Let's stop now,' Carol agreed. 'Let's just let them all go while we sort this out.'

'I don't mean to be alarmist, but maybe we should call the police?' said William.

Theresa flopped down on the folding steps, put her face in her hands and started to sob. 'It's all my fault,' she said. 'I'll pay for all the costs of tonight.'

'Including the complimentary wine, if you don't mind,' added William. 'That's around two hundred euros alone.'

Cathy took a step forward.

'I think I know what happened,' she whispered.

Everyone turned and looked in her direction, a timid grey mouse of a girl cringing in the corner. 'I didn't mean . . .' She shrugged her shoulders and hung her head, hiding her face. 'It was a surprise. I thought I was being helpful . . .'

The tension was palpable. No one dared speak.

Eventually Theresa took a deep breath and asked Cathy what she had done.

'I changed all the flour for gluten-free, the sugar for sweetener, the butter for low-fat spread and all the fancy salt for low-sodium. I thought it would make everything as tasty as before and, at the same time, much more healthy.'

By the time Sally dropped anchor in Cannes about an hour later, she was feeling very confident in her navigational skills. The most difficult thing about manoeuvring such a large vessel was being so high up above the water level. It was hard to see small rowing boats and RIBs, but Stanislav, sitting beside her in the navigator's seat for the entire journey, kept a keen lookout.

Once the yacht was safely at a standstill, Stanislav held out his hand.

'Now, my dear lady, follow me.'

He led Sally through the main saloon and up a couple of gangways, eventually emerging on the outer top deck.

They walked to the platform at the stern of the boat, which now faced the shore.

'Please be seated,' he said, pressing a button that brought up a table. He turned and opened a cupboard, took out a linen cloth and spread it with a flourish.

He then opened the fridge and presented a half-bottle of champagne, which he placed in a prepared ice bucket nearby. After a few minutes he had brought glasses, opened the bottle, poured them both a glass each and laid the table with two place settings and the most perfect picnic. Olives, a selection of cheeses and breads, some salads – potato, carrot, beetroot, tomato, cucumber, *mesclun* – and some strips of cold poached salmon with a little pot of mayonnaise.

'I had it made up at that little *traiteur* at the top of the town,' he said, taking a seat beside her. 'A light dinner. We even have dessert.'

The sun had set and, in the balmy gloaming, all the little lights of hundreds of boats twinkled on the black water surrounding them. Multicoloured disco lights from party tents the length of the Croisette added to the incidental illuminations, and the rhythmic beat of music from multitudinous revelries, both along the shore and in nearby boats, blended with the sound of seagulls and the lapping of wavelets against the hulls of all the seacraft in the broad bay.

Stanislav raised his glass and proposed a toast.

'To Sally, a woman beautiful and multi-talented, alone here with me tonight, but who really shouldn't be all alone in the world.'

The first spray of fireworks, pink, green, silver and gold, popped against the dark sky.

Theresa took it upon herself to make the announcement about the food. She told everyone that there had been a bit of a mix-up with the labelling and that they should all feel quite healthy, even if their taste buds had not been inspired.

She then went round to speak personally to all the guests she knew, while Carol, William and Benjamin did the same.

Monsieur Mari from the *boulangerie* talked to Theresa as though he was not surprised that the food was awful. After all, Theresa was English, not French; it was a different cuisine. She knew there was no point arguing with him, explaining how it should have been, how it had been yesterday. The fact is, today it was horrible.

Marcel from the brasserie could barely disguise his glee as he sympathised, telling her 'these things happen'.

She turned to address Zoe.

'Don't worry, Theresa. For a moment I thought I was back at boarding school,' said Zoe brightly. 'Next course: Spam fritters!' She laughed and the boys at her table joined in. 'Have you met my friends, um, Antonio, Raphael and Fabio? We met at the May Ball last night at Cap Ferrat.'

Theresa smiled at the assembled table.

'I was just telling the boys about the previous owner, how she made quite a wonderful art collection.'

'That's true,' said Theresa, glad to be able to change the subject. 'I gather the local painters who came in to eat used to pay for services rendered by donating pictures.'

Zoe laughed loudly, and the boys around her joined in.

She winked and pulled Theresa closer. 'She was paid for services rendered, all right, Theresa, but the services had nothing to do with the cuisine.'

She turned back to the boys and topped up their glasses.

Theresa went over to her family seated at the next table. Imogen was not quite as gracious as Zoe had been. 'Honestly, Mummy, I'd been boasting to those nice young men with the woman off that BBC thing – you know, *Girls with Flying Skirts in Norfolk* or whatever it's called. Anyhow, having been proud of you when I came in, I am now scarlet with embarrassment. Scarlet!'

Theresa moved on to speak to Jackie and her friends.

'Hello, I'm Theresa Simmonds and I'm sorry for this debacle. You're Sally's friend, aren't you? I've seen you around the town.'

'I love the artwork on the walls,' said Jackie. 'Very eclectic. Kind of Cath Kidston meets Marc Chagall!'

'That's by Carol, over there.' Theresa pointed towards Carol but didn't think she'd be very happy for her labours to be compared to Cath Kidston. 'She's worked very hard.' Theresa quickly wiped a sheen of sweat from her top lip.

'I'm sorry it turned out like this for you all,' she said. 'Hopefully we will be able to count on your patronage further along the line when we've worked out all our little hiccups.'

'Not me, old girl,' said Jackie. 'I'll be safely back in Blighty by then, I should think. But if Sally ever invited me over again—'

Costanzo clumsily interrupted. 'My grandmother would have loved to see the place looking like this.' He smiled and introduced the balding man with him as his Uncle Vito.

Theresa was relieved and smiled back, then she looked to the men who sat with Jackie.

Jackie said, 'Sally and her friends stood me up, so I brought along these fine gentlemen in their place. We'd got talking during my afternoon coffee in the brasserie and as they were so fascinated with this establishment I thought, well, why not? They're not very talkative. But then I no speekah di lingo.'

'French?' asked Theresa. '*Français?*'

'*Bien sûr, madame,*' said one of the men.

'*Vous souhaitez une carte de visite,*' said Theresa, reaching behind her for one of the restaurant's business cards.

'One for me too,' said Costanzo's uncle.

Theresa handed him one. He patted his pockets, took out his packet of cigarettes and lighter; then, from beneath them, his wallet. Thanking Theresa, he took the card she proffered and put it carefully away.

Theresa looked down at the lighter on the table in front of her. It seemed familiar.

She turned back to address the dining room and clapped her hands.

'So, everybody, I apologise once more for the upset, but assure you we'll be OK with the desserts, if you'd like to continue?' She looked around the room.

People were nodding; a few applauded.

Uncle Vito stood and said, 'First, I should like a word.'

He picked the cigarette lighter up from the table, and slipped it into his inside jacket pocket.

Costanzo rose from his seat and said hoarsely: 'No!'

Theresa knew at that moment where she had seen such a lighter. It was the exact model of Zippo that she had found on the cellar floor, left presumably as a threat – fancy red enamel, with a gold engraving of skulls.

After the firework display ended and all the little boats started up their engines and turned out of the bay into the darkness, Stanislav went to the fridge and brought out two small glass bowls filled with chocolate mousse dessert, and drained the bottle of champagne into their glasses. Sally had the last drop.

'Now you have the wish,' said Stanislav.

Sally closed her eyes and made her wish.

The dinner had been perfect, the fireworks sublime, and the ambience of this particular place at this time of year, with the film festival in full swing, was sparkling with excitement and anticipation.

Sally looked at all the people thronging the shores. How many of them would be celebrating tonight – perhaps they'd just signed career-breaking contracts, writers had sold their scripts, actors won awards, directors finally raised the finance for their next film? On every boat around her there were people looking thrilled and full of hope. No doubt many a boat was also full of those whose lives would change because of something that happened today. The atmosphere was intoxicating.

Sally had had a wonderful evening watching it all from Stanislav's yacht.

Now she sat back and looked up at the stars pricking the black sky.

'When you see all that up there in the heavens and know that each tiny pinprick is bigger than our Earth, it makes life seem so short and makes us seem so unimportant in the grand scheme of things. Don't you think, Stanislav?'

Stanislav raised his glass.

'Talking of heaven,' he said. 'I'd like to propose a last toast.'

Sally gazed at him.

'To the most wonderful, kind, beautiful lady, Sally. And thank you for making this a magnificent evening.'

'Oh, what did I do?' asked Sally. 'Don't be silly, Stanislav. You could have had all this without me.'

'That's what you don't understand,' he said. 'I have had all these things and been unhappy and lonely. Since I met you, I see a point to having all these things. When I am with you I am happy. At my age that is something unexpected.'

My age, thought Sally! He must be all of fifty.

Stanislav put his hand into his trouser pocket and pulled out a small box, which he presented to Sally.

He got down on one knee.

Sally wondered where the cameras were. Surely this time it was a gag, and any minute a crowd would jump out and shout: 'Had you fooled!'

She looked around. There was nothing but herself and him, on a boat in Cannes bay.

He held open the box, and wiped a tear from his eye.

Sally looked down to see a beautiful diamond and sapphire ring.

'Dear Sally. You have made me very happy. Please marry me. I want to be your devoted husband.'

Part Five

BRANDADE

Ingredients
500g salt cod
2 large potatoes suitable for mash (e.g., Maris Piper)
1 bouquet garni
150ml milk
knob of butter
3 tablespoons olive oil
1 clove garlic, crushed
juice of 1 lemon
150g Comté cheese, grated
ground nutmeg
salt and pepper

Method
Allow cod to desalt by soaking overnight in a bowl of cold water. Change the water several times. Peel the potatoes, cut them into cubes and boil for 15–20 minutes, till soft. Chop the desalted cod into pieces and poach for 3 minutes in a saucepan of boiling water, with bouquet garni. Drain the cod. Drain the potatoes and mash them, adding the milk and some butter. Discard any fish skin and bones that might remain and mix the fish with the potatoes. Mash the mixture with a fork, incorporating the oil, garlic and lemon juice. Add pepper and salt. Put into a baking dish, then cover with Comté cheese and a sprinkle of nutmeg. Place into hot oven (210°C) for about 15 minutes or until brown on top, and serve.

25

THE BALDING MAN GRABBED Theresa by the front of her white chef's overalls.

'Uncle Vito,' begged Costanzo, springing forward in Theresa's defence. 'Please!'

Vito put his face close to Theresa's ear and said: 'Give us what we are here for.'

Theresa stayed as still as she could, looked directly at him and said quietly: 'I told you I would get it for you. Today is Saturday. There is nothing I can do. The bank is closed.'

Vito kept his face close to hers. 'My men are all around me.'

The three men at Jackie's table got up and moved to the corners of the dining room. Theresa noticed Zoe slide gracefully to the floor and hide under her table.

'If you are lying . . .'

Vito shoved Theresa backwards, causing her to fall into William, Carol and Benjamin, who stood behind her. He put out his hand and said: 'So give me the key.'

'What key?'

'To your safe-deposit box.'

'I don't have . . .'

'So where is the medallion? You said it was in the bank.'

'It is.'

'So give me the key,' he repeated.

Theresa's mind raced. How on earth to convince him that any of her keys would work in a safety-deposit box? She didn't even know what bank keys looked like. For all she knew they were modern plastic digital ones, like you see in hotels. Her only hope was to give him the key to the restaurant's safe.

'I will get you the key,' she said.

From the corner of her eye Theresa detected movement. Jackie was crawling slowly, imperceptibly along the floor, commando-style, elbows doing all the work.

'You're a bad man!' shouted Cressida, her eyes full of fire. 'Go away!'

'Shut that child up!' barked Vito.

One of his men came menacingly towards the child.

'Don't you take another step towards her,' yelled Theresa, moving sideways to block his path. She turned to Vito. 'You should be ashamed of yourself, frightening children. You're a bully and a coward.'

'You owe me. I'm not giving up until I get it. Whatever it takes.'

'No sentimental medallion is worth enough money to justify you threatening us like this,' said Theresa.

'Oh, yes it is,' replied Vito gleefully. 'When it was made by Marc Chagall.'

Under one of the tables, Zoe coughed. As everyone swung to look in that direction, Jackie got herself to all fours and darted, round the screen and out of the front door, to freedom.

'Lock it!' shouted Vito. 'That silly Englishwoman doesn't matter. But now our time is limited. She will call the police. She has, how do you say, "put the heat up". Everybody stay still. We have guns. Next person who moves will be shot.'

'Let me give you the key,' Theresa pleaded. 'Please. I have the key. In the cellar.'

Vito nodded. One of his henchmen grabbed Theresa's arms and marched her slowly into the kitchen.

'This had better not be a trick.'

Theresa tried to think, as she stumbled forward.

'It's where you dropped your Zippo lighter last week,' said Theresa. 'You know it.'

She led them through the kitchen, which was just as she had left it when she came into the dining room to make her apologies, then made her way down to the cellar.

Rolled up in a ball in the corner, Cathy crouched, her face ashen, looking up at them with huge black eyes.

Theresa had no idea she was there, and didn't want the men to be surprised. She stood in front of her.

'There,' said Theresa. 'Look inside the cupboard at the bottom of the steps. Mine is the turquoise coat. Inside the right pocket. You'll find a bunch of keys.'

Vito's accomplice rushed to Theresa's coat and pulled out the key ring.

As he passed her Cathy shrunk further into her cocoon and whimpered. The man swung round and went for his gun.

'Who is that?' asked Vito.

'She works in the kitchen. An apprentice. Another child.'

Vito ignored Cathy and inspected the keys. He thrust them in front of Theresa.

'I need to sort them out,' she said. She was allowed to fumble with the bunch. She pointed at a smallish-size key. 'Take it. That one. The bank is in Nice – Rue Portmanteau.'

'There!' Vito snatched the whole bunch of keys. 'Better safe than sorry. In whose name? Don't we need to bring you?'

'La Mosaïque company,' said Theresa. 'You can give my name. Simmonds.'

There was a cry and sounds of a commotion coming from the dining room.

Theresa was steered back up the steps, and through the kitchen. A table had been upturned. Carol had dived for one of the men and both were sprawled on the floor. Theresa was pleased to see that Carol had the upper hand and that during the disturbance most of the guests had fled.

'We will check this bank of yours on Monday. If we don't find what we are looking for, don't mistake, I will return. And next time I will not be so kind.'

If navigating Stanislav's boat had been difficult during daylight hours, it was practically impossible to see her way in the dark. Sally made much use of the radar and nautical satnav screens on the control panel.

Stanislav was very helpful. He occasionally used binoculars to scan the horizon, while remaining standing up, scrutinising the darkness, searching for the lights of smaller vessels.

'I think it's better if we keep clear of the coastline,' said Sally. 'I remember from my time passing the test that there are notorious outlying rocks here. We're safer right out to sea.'

Stanislav nodded and smiled. 'Whatever you say, captain.'

Since his proposal, Sally's head had been in a spin. She had declined giving him an answer straight away for the simple reason that everything was too perfect: the night, the boat, the dinner, the champagne, the fireworks. She wanted to think about it and give him a reply when she was somewhere more like reality.

Stanislav had told Sally he didn't want to rush anything. She could take as long as she wanted to make up her mind. But life was short . . . If he had his way he would go into town tomorrow and marry her.

Sally knew she couldn't make any such decision alone. She had to discuss it with someone. That person should have been Marianne; Tom too. But it was certainly not a conversation to have on an international phone call. She felt excited, apprehensive. If she went ahead and said yes, everything would change, and yet . . . How lovely it would be to have someone to wake up with, someone to dine with and take to the theatre. Someone who, like her, loved going out on boats. She knew it was silly. She'd only known the man a few days. But she was no spring chicken. Whenever else in her life was a handsome hunk going to pop up and propose? She realised too that no one could say he was after her for her money or anything, because, compared to him, she had nothing – no Paris townhouse, no country estate at Vence, no property in St Petersburg.

All she had was two small houses here in Bellevue-Sur-Mer. If she traded them in for a London property, she might just about get a garage in Streatham.

'Watch out!' yelled Stanislav, raising his arm in front of her. 'There's something down there.'

Sally peered out into the black. She could see nothing.

'Look!' he said, pointing. 'It's a fishing boat or a RIB.'

'I don't see it.' Sally stared in the direction of Stanislav's finger.

'There are some kind of lights on it, but it looks as though they have no motor and no power.'

'Ah, yes, I can see,' said Sally. 'I'll tell you what the lights are, Stanislav. They're holding up mobile phones.'

She scanned the controls. 'There'll be a spotlight somewhere.' She located the switch and flicked it. 'There!'

As the light went on, she used the little joystick to swivel it round towards the smaller vessel. It was an open RIB with outboard. And it was drifting on the Mediterranean swell.

She heard faint cheering as a man and a woman stood up, waving their hands in the air.

'Keep looking at them,' said Stanislav. 'Don't get too near, so we don't send it under our wake. When I shout, turn the boat so that I can reach them from the rear platform and find out what they need.'

Sally knew that this was the correct procedure.

She waited for the call, never taking her eyes off the RIB, then pulled the yacht forward a small way.

She heard Stanislav yell something indistinct. She also distantly heard a reply. A few minutes passed. A small bump from the rear. This was probably Stanislav putting out the ship-hook and hauling the RIB in to touch the back of their boat. He could secure it behind.

Another, louder thump from the rear of the yacht.

Sally was suddenly frightened. What if these people were robbers? There were only two of them, but they could easily smack Stanislav over the head, throw him into the sea and board this boat. She would be powerless to stop them.

You heard about this kind of thing often enough on roads, where someone would feign an accident, stop a Good Samaritan, then steal their car. Surely the same thing was possible at sea?

She called Stanislav's name.

No reply.

She was torn.

Should she stay at the helm? Should she drop anchor? Should she go back and see what was going on?

She moved towards the saloon and looked out. It was impossible to see through to the back from there.

She edged forward.

Again she called Stanislav's name.

Still no reply.

She heard a distant splash.

Please God, let that not be the body of Stanislav hitting the water.

She could feel their boat drifting. She shouldn't have left the helm unmanned. They were far from shore, but what of other craft? Without the motor on or an anchor, they were at the mercy of the current. Anything might be in the way. She rushed back to the controls and looked out of the windscreen.

She flicked a switch, hoping it was a second search-light, and, as though by magic, five small screens at the far end of the control room flickered on. Each one showed a closed-circuit image of another part of the boat. Why hadn't she known about this before? She should have switched it on right from the moment when Stanislav left to go aft.

She inspected each glimmering screen one by one. There was a grey shot of the engine-room, a dark view along the gangway between the saloon and the master bedroom, another of the grand saloon itself, one of the upper deck, and the last showed the stern platform. They all looked like stills from those TV programmes where people go hunting for ghosts in damp base-ments.

Sally shivered.

Where was Stanislav? The stern platform was empty. She could see a taut rope extending from a cleat on the starboard quarter. That one must be attached to the drifting RIB. But no one was visible. Where had he got to? She should have been able to see him there.

A flitting shadow caught her eye on another screen. Was it the top deck? By the time she switched her attention she'd missed it.

Oh God, please don't let this be a modern-day pirate attack. A glamorous boat this size was an obvious target for thieves. Perhaps they had pulled Stanislav off the back and were now running around, silently invading, ready to take over.

Sally's heart was thumping and her mouth dry.

'Stanislav?' she called again from the doorway in the direction of the saloon.

She could hear more noises coming from the rear of the boat: footsteps, splashing, banging.

She rushed over to look at the stern platform on the closed-circuit screen.

Someone was out there. She glimpsed the outline of a head just as it passed out of the scope of the camera and into the door.

Somebody was heading her way.

Benjamin was moving around the room, comforting the few remaining terrified guests.

'The Magenta family were never good people,' said Marcel, brushing himself down and heading for the exit.

Costanzo apologised profusely and started to sob as he followed Marcel out.

'I see those three pretty boys of mine were first out,' said Zoe, hauling herself out from her hiding place under the tablecloth. 'Never can trust a man you meet at the Bal Masqué.'

Now there were only the four proprietors left. And Zoe.

'What happens now, for heaven's sake; do we have to wait for them to come back?' Zoe asked. She was appalled.

'You don't have to do anything,' said William, 'or be anywhere. They're not after you.'

'You can't help us, Zoe,' said Theresa. 'We know what they want. And we don't have it.'

'Oh, really?' Zoe stepped forward and stood in the middle of the circle. 'Sorry to contradict you, but we do have it.'

'We do?' Theresa, Benjamin, Carol and William spoke together.

Zoe fumbled in her handbag. 'I say we, because I am now buying in to La Mosaïque,' she said. 'I wish to own a fifth share. I will put in enough to cover the cost of the building, which I will own. I won't chuck you out and we can get a contract promising that. How much do you need? Two hundred grand?'

She pulled out a chequebook and flourished her fountain pen. 'Who is the estate agent?'

'Zoe? What is wrong with you?' William threw up his arms. 'Is this the time to be doing a business deal?'

'Now is precisely the time. The bastards will get what they are looking for and we'll all be happy.'

'Don't bother,' said William. 'That Russian boyfriend of Sally's has already told us he's going to back us. We don't need your money.'

'Safer the devil you know,' said Zoe. 'Let me help you.' She started scribbling a cheque.

'Cheques don't mean anything these days, Zoe dear, as you well know. The only trusted method is the bank transfer.'

Theresa felt all her energy rush back as she reminded everyone: 'The key won't work. They can search my house, they can go to the bank I told them about and they won't find anything there, not even a safe-deposit box. Carol hasn't even been able to buy some antique replacement medallion like we planned.'

A cold chill ran through her at the thought of what could happen next.

'Oh, you're right, Theresa.' Zoe spoke calmly and clearly. 'But you're also very wrong. They will come back here, of *course* they will – I wouldn't believe all that key-at-the-bank tosh – but then and only then will we give them what they want. Before that we have a lot to do.'

Sally stood behind the door as the heavy footsteps approached.

She should find something, something solid, which she could use to bash an intruder on the head. Her eyes darted around the room. There was nothing except her handbag, a squashy leather thing, with inside a couple of pens, a notebook, make-up, tissues and her mobile phone. It was better than nothing. She reached out and held it ready.

Whoever was out there stopped walking. She could hear breathing.

Then whoever it was started tiptoeing towards the control room. She heard the creak of a piece of flooring, and then a foot crossed the threshold.

Sally swung her bag with all her might.

The man, dripping wet from head to toe, staggered sideways and fell to the floor.

It was Stanislav!

'What did you do that for?' he cried. 'Are you mad?'

Sally flopped to her knees. 'Oh I am so sorry, so sorry! Are you hurt?'

Stanislav grabbed hold of the helm seat and pulled himself up.

'I'm fine, no thanks to you. Soaking-wet, exhausted, but fine.'

'What happened?'

'I could ask the same thing,' said Stanislav. 'I went to the back of the boat. It was a nice married couple out for a night jaunt along the coast. They'd rather underestimated how much fuel you need to keep one of those outboards going and run out. I had a spare tank for our RIB, so went down to give it to them, but fell in while climbing back aboard.'

'I saw someone . . .' said Sally, trying to explain her actions.

'Someone?' Stanislav looked at her intensely. 'Who?'

'I don't know,' said Sally. 'But there is someone else on the boat. Upstairs on the top deck.'

Stanislav laughed.

'Oh Lord. I forgot actresses are also dramatists! That was me.'

'But why?' Sally could not imagine why he had to go up above.

'Because they told me they were hungry. How could I leave them with a long wet journey ahead with no food when I knew we had plenty of leftovers in our fridge?'

Sally felt utterly foolish now. How kind and thoughtful this man was. How solicitous and caring.

'I suppose I'd better get us back to Bellevue-Sur-Mer,' she said. 'I'm so sorry! I thought you'd been kidnapped and I was being boarded by pirates.' As the words came out of her mouth she realised she sounded like an idiot.

'I was wondering,' said Stanislav, climbing on to the navigator's chair and looking her in the eye. 'Have you a reply yet?'

THERESA SAT WITH ZOE and the other members of the La Mosaïque team. Zoe had instructed them to stack the tables in the corner and they perched on chairs arranged around the side as though they were at a school dance.

'Does anyone remember the date of the old bird's birthday?' said Zoe, out of nowhere. 'I'm hoping we might be lucky on this.'

'We don't even remember the old bird,' snapped William.

'It'll be somewhere among the legal papers, surely,' said Zoe. 'Run along, dear boy, and find out.' She was rolling up her chiffon sleeves.

'Now,' she continued. 'We must start to destroy this rather magnificent floor. We will begin with the Crab.'

'No,' cried Carol. 'It would be criminal.'

'That is where I hid on the floor. You will find what they are looking for there. Chop-chop! Let's get digging.'

Benjamin and Theresa went to the kitchen to search out aprons and overalls, then any tools and implements capable of breaking through concrete.

'Is she mad?' asked Theresa as they pulled open drawers and cupboards, gathering hammers, knives, screwdrivers and chisels.

'It's a means to an end,' called Zoe, loud enough for them to know she had heard.

'But to destroy such workmanship . . .' said Theresa, yelling through the pass.

'We're not destroying. We will re-create. Just as the old cow did to hide her valued gift from her grabby family.'

'You still haven't told us. What exactly is this thing they want, Zoe?' asked Theresa, bringing anything she could find and handing the tools around. 'Is it hidden underneath the floor? And how do you know?'

Zoe shushed her.

'And if you do know,' added Benjamin, 'why didn't you tell us before all this trouble?'

'Anyways, I still don't understand how digging up a floor will give them what they want,' said Carol, between blows of the meat hammer on to a heavy-duty knife. 'Why don't we get the police in?'

'Pah!' said Zoe. 'They know nothing of these big bullies.'

'Zoe is right,' Theresa said. 'Giving them what they want does appear to be our best chance of getting them off our backs.'

'But what is the thing they want?'

Zoe raised a finger to her lips and said, 'Patience!'

William reappeared from the office in the cellar waving a piece of notepaper. 'Got it. Franca Magenta was born on the twenty-third of July 1920.'

'Ha!' said Zoe. '*Patronale* of St Marie Magdalene, another old whore. Anyone know their zodiacs?'

Everyone said no.

'What a useless lot,' said Zoe, rolling her eyes. 'Why on earth am I helping you?'

'That's what we'd all like to know,' said William.

'I think it's Leo,' said Benjamin.

'Leo?' Zoe peered down at the floor. 'Merciful God! This really could be our lucky day. I need to get on to that computer of yours,' she replied.

'It's still there, on the desk in the cellar.' William reluctantly took a screwdriver and started scraping at the cement between the mosaic pieces. 'Oh, and watch out for Cathy; she's down there too, curled up under the desk.'

'Is she all right?' asked Theresa. 'Shouldn't someone look after her? Shall I go?'

'She should be up here with us,' said William.

'Poor thing,' said Theresa, sorting out the implements near to Carol. 'She's only a kid.'

'No one ever said that about me when I was nineteen,' said Carol as she hammered at a copper line around the Leo mosaic.

'No one ever said that about you when you were five, dear,' said Benjamin.

Sally moored the boat along the coast in the marina where the whole adventure that first introduced her to Stanislav had started. She gathered her things together.

Stanislav put out a protective arm, and she let his hand slide round her waist.

They walked slowly through the dark saloon, towards the stern platform.

'It was very brave of you, helping those people,' said Sally. 'Poor old damp boy, you might have drowned.' In the bright harbour lights, Sally noticed for the first time slight greying at his temples, but even that she found adorable. She could feel herself slipping to the edge of that inexplicable moment when you're forced to decide whether to fall in love, or save yourself.

'You'd have to have a very hard heart indeed to leave people drifting at sea on a rubber RIB with no fuel and no radio,' he said.

'They had mobile phones,' said Sally, putting her hand on his. 'I suppose they could have called someone on the shore.'

'As they had been using them as beacons, I doubt there would be enough power,' said Stanislav. 'Or signal.'

He took her face in his hands and kissed her gently. Sally let the emotions flood right through her and slid her arms around him. He squeezed her tight.

'What a night,' she said. 'What a wonderful night. Do you know, I was feeling pretty badly about not being at the dress rehearsal of my friends' restaurant, but now I know I wouldn't have missed this for the world. It's been one of the loveliest nights of my life.'

'It could be lovelier,' said Stanislav, 'if you said yes to my proposal.'

'I want to very much,' said Sally. 'But you know I have to discuss it with my children first.'

'One minute.' Stanislav extricated himself from Sally's grasp. 'I just have to run up top and get something.'

Sally took a seat on the stern platform and watched the waves bobbing up and down, slapping gently against the sides of the boats moored in the marina. She loved the sound of the masts chinking, and the slight movement of a boat at rest.

The night was balmy for May; she knew that it could get quite chilly at this time of year. She felt so warm inside, though, she wondered whether she would notice the cold when she was this content.

Stanislav appeared, holding a pink and orange stripy beach bag.

Sally laughed. It seemed so incongruous for a man like Stanislav. 'Where on earth did you get that thing?' she asked.

Stanislav glanced down. 'I hadn't really noticed,' he said. 'I bought it in the *traiteur*'s,' he added. 'To keep the picnic cool.'

He helped Sally step off the boat. As they walked along he took her hand and there they were – like teenagers, thought Sally.

A car was waiting for them. Sally recognised the butler, or whatever his official title was.

'Good evening, Stephane,' said Stanislav. 'You remember my friend Sally.'

Stephane held the car door open and Sally slid into the back seat.

Stanislav got in beside her and whispered into her ear: 'Perhaps you would like to come up to my place in Vence?'

'Not this time,' said Sally, knowing in her heart it was the right decision, for now. 'But very soon.'

'So, I see you tomorrow?'

He spoke as though this was a date they had already set up. She didn't remember them doing it.

'Tomorrow?'

'For the football, remember? Soccer? Destiny asked us, remember, on that first lunch date.'

Sally did not remember. She, like most British women of her age, took no interest in football. But if it was another date with Stanislav, why not? She could only make up her mind about this proposal if she got to know him a bit better.

'Do we meet there?' asked Sally.

'Don't be silly,' said Stanislav. 'I'll pick you up about twelve-thirty. Destiny will come in the car with us.'

'No Mickey?'

Stanislav laughed. 'He will be playing in the match. He'll be like you all morning, a player, preparing in his dressing room.'

Sally smiled, thinking of Jackie calling him Stanislavski – not so far from the truth.

When they reached her front door, Stanislav gave her a quick kiss on the lips, which sent shivers down her spine.

She climbed out of the limo and looked back in through the rear window. As the car drove off it amused her to see Stanislav pulling the stripy beach bag on to his lap and holding it in his arms.

It was well after two in the morning when Theresa, William, Carol and Benjamin finished the digging of the mosaic floor.

Zoe stood over them as they levered out two oval pieces of mosaic zodiac signs. Both were bound in a copper band, and had obviously been made, like all the other zodiac symbols, as stand-alone pieces, then set into the floor.

Now that both ovals were out and leaning against the wall, two empty sunken circles of concrete remained.

'I was hiding right on top of it under that table when he said the name Chagall,' said Zoe. 'I recognised his work right away.'

'He made this floor?' asked Theresa.

'No,' said Zoe. 'That was some local hack, by the look of it. But he certainly had a hand in one of the inset medallions.'

'That sort of a medallion!' said Theresa, looking down at the floor with its clock arrangement of zodiac oblongs. 'Why didn't we work that out?'

'The word medallion is much more commonly used for jewellery,' said Carol. 'Though it is a term in art, like bas-relief.'

'Thank you, Professor Carol,' said Benjamin.

'If that's the kind of medallion they were searching for all along,' said William, 'some hope we'd have had if Carol had got to spend more money on some cheap bit of tat jewellery down at the antique market.'

'Do we have to dig them all up?' asked Theresa.

'They would be very greedy to expect twelve valuable works of art,' said Zoe. 'Especially when they only asked for one.'

While they were digging, Theresa had gone rummaging and found a small bag of sand and cement, left over in the cellar from the recent building work.

Carol's job now was to make the holes from which the medallions had been removed look as though they were undisturbed. And Benjamin, Theresa and Zoe had had to smash up a few of the blue, red and yellow serving plates in the yard. While the others washed and changed out of their overalls and aprons, Carol started putting the pieces back.

'My God, Franca Magenta was a wily old cow,' said Zoe, looking down at her calculations. 'Even when she had this floor made she was thinking of people coming after it.'

Theresa had now had enough of Zoe's air of mystery. 'Zoe, will you please tell us what we're doing?'

Zoe pulled her specs down her nose and peered over the top. 'Of course, my friends – or, should I say, business partners . . . Once you accept my offer to buy in.'

William said, 'I told you, Zoe. Sally's Russian is backing us. The full amount. We do not need your money.'

'You yourself have told us, Theresa, that a visit to that bank will quickly show them they are wasting their time with the key.' Zoe tried to pucker her very full lips in an expression of scorn, but ended up simply looking mildly surprised. 'So they will come back . . . And, once you accept my share and put that cheque into the bank, we give them what they're after.'

'Even they don't know exactly what they're after.' Theresa looked hard at Zoe. It was always difficult to know what she was thinking or what she was up to. But she certainly had an air about her that made Theresa trust her. After all, Zoe had lived here longer than any of them and knew the Magenta woman personally. 'Promise us you are certain about this.'

'"Cross my heart and hope to die" – that's what we used to say at boarding school. Though I certainly have no desire to die just yet.' Zoe sighed. 'I am as sure as a person can be that this is what they're after. I recall old Franca Magenta telling everyone about all those famous artists who had come here in her heyday: Picasso, Dufy and the like. Marc Chagall lived up the coast a bit. He was quite a hot-blooded fellow. God knows what went on between the two, but no doubt she asked him for a birthday present – perhaps threatening otherwise to tell his wife, a rather formidable Russian lady, some nonsense about herself and him.'

'So to shut her up,' said Theresa, 'he made her a mosaic.'

Carol surveyed the entire mosaic. 'And she had a whole floor constructed to hide it.'

'Enough history!' William clapped his hands together. 'So tell us why have we dug up these two, why two, and which one do we give them?'

'Her birthday was . . . ?' asked Zoe.

William spoke in a singsong voice: 'July the twenty-third.'

'Leo,' said Benjamin.

Everyone turned to look at the oval mosaic of a Lion standing up against the wall.

'Funny,' said Carol, 'but the Crab looks more Chagall to me.'

Theresa squinted her eyes as people did looking at artworks. 'It certainly has a familiar style to it.'

'But, according to them, it was her birthday present, remember. So Signor Vito and his gang will get exactly what they're looking for.'

'But they didn't really know what they were looking for,' said Theresa. 'Did they?'

'Medallion, birthday of Franca Magenta, Chagall,' said Zoe.

'Will this be enough for them?' asked Carol, wiping the sweat from her brow. 'I don't want to do all this and they still come after us.'

'Of course it will. They want a medallion that was gifted to her for her birthday and that has remained here ever since that day back in the sixties or seventies or whenever it was.' Zoe pointed at the Leo medallion. 'And there it is.'

'Is that Sparks girl still here?' asked William, on his knees, wiping dust from the Crab medallion.

'Unless you saw her pass through the room in the last thirty minutes, she's in the cellar. She was fast asleep when I was down there,' said Theresa. 'Seemed cruel to disturb her.'

Zoe walked over to the two mosaic medallions. 'Carol, dear, can you help me with this.' She took a pair of nylon shopping bags from her handbag – one red, the other lime green – and pulled them out of their tiny pocket sleeves. 'These things are frightfully useful, don't you think? Never go anywhere without my *sac de courses*. Slip the medallions in those, darling, would you? And hang the Leo under the coats. No, better in the kitchen somewhere. In the fridge, perhaps. Then put the Crab down in the cellar, on top of a cupboard or behind something so that it's really, really well hidden.'

27

S ALLY WOKE NEXT MORNING and lay awake for a
few seconds before the events of last night really
hit her.

And now she had to get up and tart herself up ready
to go on a date that was also a football match, her first,
where she would sit in the VIP box with a real-life
footballer's wife, and perhaps agree to marry her
second husband.

Thinking of Stanislav as her husband made her
tingle.

But really? What was she thinking? It was all too
sudden. She barely knew him.

What could he want from her?

Why on earth would he want to marry someone like
her? A small-town nobody, living on her wits in a
sleepy French village.

She went downstairs.

It looked as though Jackie was up and gone. Sally
supposed to another of those Cannes events or meetings.

When she was making a pot of tea, the phone rang.

It was Diana. 'Have you seen my daughter?' she
asked. 'She didn't come home last night.'

'Have you tried her mobile?'

'Goes straight to answering machine.'

'Have you tried phoning the restaurant?' asked Sally.

'Too early.'

'How about trying William?'

'Do you have a number? Have I met him?'

'He's the maître d', remember.'

'Oh, the fastidious little queen in the purple velvet jacket.'

'That's the one.'

'I think I'll have to agree to let them take my picture for the paper. But what the hell.'

'I'll just get his number.' Sally walked over to her desk to fetch her address book. 'How's Cannes going?'

'That Russian of yours put money into my new film,' said Diana. 'The producers are over the moon.'

Sally sat down.

'Really?'

'It was quite a substantial sum. Not enough to make the film or anything, but a serious enough investment. He told the producers he was doing it because you were my friend. So thanks, darling. And please do say thanks to him from me. Have you seen him lately?'

'As a matter of fact . . . ' Sally settled, plumping a cushion to lie against, to tell her the tale of last night's proposal on the boat.

'Oh darling,' sighed Diana. 'How romantic. And I was there only a few yards away at one of those ghastly parties in tents on the Croisette. You should have told me, Sal, and I would have brought my binoculars. Are you going to accept?'

'Last night I was all for it,' said Sally, curling up on the sofa. 'This morning not so much.'

'Oh no, why?'

'I don't know.' Sally stretched out and yawned. 'It was almost too romantic.'

'He is pretty gorgeous, Sal.'

'But why me?'

Diana made a growling noise. 'That was always your problem, darling: never could see that you were great. The answer to "why you" is that you are fabulous and he should be so lucky.'

'You think I should say yes?'

'I think you should leap at the chance. If it all goes wrong you can always divorce him.' Diana laughed. 'And take him to the cleaners.'

'Diana, you are awful. I just don't know. He could have supermodels or anybody.'

'Have you ever met a supermodel?'

'I'm so old and I'm nobody. Just an Englishwoman living alone in a tiny house in Bellevue-Sur-Mer.'

'Perhaps that's exactly why he wants you.' Diana paused. 'Don't take this the wrong way, Sal darling, because you know really I'm in much the same boat. I may still be working. But as for men – well, we're both over the age when men really look at you. For someone to fall head over heels . . . well . . . I don't expect it'll happen to me again in my lifetime. We'll never be young again.'

Sally wasn't sure whether to laugh or cry. Everything that Diana said was true.

When the phone call was over she went upstairs and took a bath. Today she was going to say yes to becoming

Mrs Stanislav Serafim. Sally Serafim. Sounded kind of silly really, but . . .

She was lost in thought, sitting at her dressing table putting final touches to her make-up, when the front door slammed.

She went to the landing and looked down to see Jackie come in.

'Jackie?'

'Oh sorry, Sally, I hope I didn't wake you.'

'No, I've been up ages. I thought you had gone to Cannes this morning. You were up very early.'

Jackie went straight through to the kitchen, ran herself a glass of water and noisily glugged it down.

'That's tonight,' she said. 'Evening-dress thing. The big party. I may not make it.'

'Are you all right, Jackie?' Sally thought she looked very nervous and agitated.

'I'm fine,' she replied, with the accent heavily on the 'I'm'. 'I should qualify that. I'm fine, apart from almost being killed in a stick-up last night and being threatened by gangsters this morning.'

'Stick-up? What do you mean? Where?'

Sally padded down the stairs.

'At your friends' restaurant. It was one of the most ghastly evenings of my life.'

'What on earth happened?'

'Oh, I ended up sitting at a table with a lot of men who wanted to do a robbery or something. Anyhow, I got myself out sharpish. I learned quite a lot about commando-style tactics and how to extricate yourself from dangerous situations while filming *Skirts*.'

'Is everyone OK?'

'There were guns being waved around,' said Jackie, 'So I scarpered. I was wondering what made you decide not to come last night. Did you know something was going to blow off?'

'No.' Sally was shaken by this news. 'In fact I went on a boat trip to Cannes with Stanislav to see the fireworks.'

Jackie took a step back.

'You're not serious?'

'He's a lovely man.'

Jackie's face took on an expression of horror so grotesque that it looked as though Godzilla was advancing to eat her.

'The Russian?' she said. 'No. No. No. No.'

Sally bridled. What had happened? What had Stanislav done to upset Jackie? Had he bankrolled Diana's film and eschewed hers, perhaps? She knew that Jackie was an expert in the art of exaggeration. And, anyhow, what contact had Jackie ever had with the man, apart from a few moments at Marina Martel's after-party and the subsequent night in the police station?

'I suppose you're excited about the Brits in Film party tonight?'

'As I said before: I may not make it.'

'Did you say you were threatened by gangsters, too? Was that at the restaurant?'

Jackie looked as though she was about to say something, then suddenly swerved into another subject.

'Due to events of the morning . . .' She spoke slowly and deliberately, as though thinking each word very carefully before saying it aloud. ' . . . before the party I may have to leave the country.'

'But you've been looking forward to the party. It was a deal-clincher, wasn't it?'

Jackie ignored her and sniffed.

'Did Stanislav decide not to put money into your film project?'

Jackie made a loud noise like 'HAH!'

'I presume that means he didn't?'

'No, Sally, it means yes, he did. Stanislav put money into my movie, yesterday afternoon. And that is what worries me today. It's dirty money.' She stopped, took a deep breath and said, 'Sorry. Forget I said that.'

Sally decided to take the bull by the horns.

'I'm going out with Stanislav today, as a matter of fact.' Sally put on the kettle. 'We're going to watch the football game with Destiny and Mickey. Should I thank him for you?'

'No. No. You must not say that you have seen me at all. Promise me.'

Sally now wondered if Jackie hadn't taken a knock to the head. She was behaving so strangely.

'Destiny and Mickey MacDonald! Yes, yes. They are exactly the types I would imagine are into that kind of thing.'

Sally was perplexed. 'What kind of thing?'

Behind her, Jackie sniffed again.

Sally turned, thinking Jackie was crying. But she wasn't. She sniffed once more.

'Do you need a handkerchief?'

'No, Sally.' Jackie put her face to the kitchen counter and made an even longer sniffing sound.

'Are you feeling all right, Jackie?' asked Sally, wondering if perhaps she had lost her marbles.

'I'm miming, aren't I? Miming.'

'Miming what?'

'Drugs!'

'Drugs?'

'Drugs.'

Sally cocked her head. 'And why exactly are you miming drugs, Jackie?'

'Stanislav,' was all she said.

Sally was mystified. From whence had this drama come?

'Stanislav and I went to Cannes last night, Jackie,' she said. 'On his boat. It was a lovely evening. He is a very wonderful man.'

Again Jackie sniffed the surface of the countertop.

'Stanislav is not a junkie, Jackie, if that's what you're saying. He is a very sweet and generous man.'

Jackie tapped her nose and said, '*Kogdá rák na goré svístnet*.'

'I'm sorry, Jackie,' said Sally, now exasperated and seriously worrying over the woman's sanity. 'What are you on about?'

'It's Russian. I had it as a line in a play once. *Kogdá rák na goré svístnet*.'

'Really?' Sally decided that the best thing would be to appease her. 'And what does that mean exactly?'

'It means, Sally, "When the crawfish whistles on the mountain".'

Sally waited for her to finish what appeared to be an unfinished sentence.

Jackie threw her arms in the air, as though utterly exasperated with Sally. 'Pigs might fly, sweetie. Pigs might fly. And it's very much more serious than that.'

Sally emptied boiling kettle water into the teapot.

'And when did this revelation hit you?'

Jackie mimed zipping up her lips, then opened them again to say: 'My lips are sealed.'

Sally poured the tea. She decided not to share the news about the proposal with her right now. But she was curious as to what had instigated this madness.

'When did you last see Stanislav, Jackie?'

Jackie made another show of not opening her mouth.

Luckily for Sally the phone rang. It was Tom.

'Hi Ma!' he yelled down the line. 'We swung it.'

Sally had forgotten what, if anything, was due 'to swing'.

'How lovely,' she said.

'Yep,' said Tom. 'We managed to get the editor of the magazine to let us do a little piece on Bellevue-Sur-Mer and we're going to include your pals' restaurant, La Mosaïque. They're all for new places, you see. Means they look groovy and in the swim.'

Sally wondered if those weren't rather old-fashioned phrases for a man of Tom's age to use.

'At least that's what the boss says,' he added. 'She's coming down with me. We've booked rooms at the Astra.'

'But Tom . . .'

'Don't be daft. The magazine's paying. They really wanted us to stay in Nice, but we decided it would be more fun to live down with the locals.'

Before Sally could reply, the doorbell rang. Sally looked at her watch. Dead on the proposed pick-up time.

Jackie gave a hoarse whisper. 'That's not him, is it?'

Down the phone line, Tom said, 'I heard the bell, Ma, don't worry. Sorry about changing plans. See you later.'

Fearing a confrontation between Jackie and Stanislav, Sally grabbed her bag and made her way to the door. But when she turned she saw Jackie crawling along the floor, hastily making her way to the stairs.

Before opening up Sally waved. 'Have a great day, Jackie.'

Jackie was now nowhere to be seen.

'Enjoy your party at Cannes.'

'Beware!' Jackie emerged cautiously from behind the newel post. 'Don't accept anything from him, Sally. Keep your distance. What must be done will be done. You must protect yourself.'

Sally said: 'I'm only going to the football, Jackie.'

'I am not a timorous mouse,' Jackie hissed from between the banisters. 'I will always stand up for justice and what is right.' As Sally put her hand on the door handle, Jackie ducked back behind the wall and said earnestly: 'Be safe, Sally.'

'There will be two thousand people there, Jackie. I'll be quite safe, I'm sure.'

Jackie scampered up the stairs, whispering, 'But beware of Russians bearing pink beach bags!'

Sally opened the door and walked straight to the waiting car, where Stanislav sat, along with Destiny.

28

AFTER THE ORDEAL OF the night before, the three children were still sleeping, huddled with their mother in Theresa's bed, while Theresa lay awake in the spare room.

Imogen had left a note explaining that because the three girls had been scared, they were all going in together, and that Theresa was welcome to sleep in her own guest bed, rather than on the floor.

It was a relief to get a good night's sleep after the evening's labours.

They were all so tired when they finished carrying out Zoe's mad plan, the restaurant gang had debated whether they should cancel or at least postpone tonight's opening. Theresa led the argument that to delay would be handing a great victory to the bullies.

In the cold light of day, as she lay thinking, she wondered if it was the right decision.

For all Zoe's protestations, Theresa had a sneaking feeling that Costanzo's Uncle Vito and his men would make a reappearance before the banks opened again on Monday.

Her mobile phone rang.

It was Carol.

'Another cosy night on the futon, darling?' she asked.

'No. They let me have your old room.' Theresa laughed. 'How about you?'

'I'm getting quite fond of camping. However, this mosaic seems less comfy since we hacked at it.'

'But you slept well?'

'Apart from almost jumping out of my skin this morning when I was just lying there minding my own business, and in comes Cathy. She stood on the threshold and shouted, "I'm sorry for ruining everyone's night. But does that mean I have to be ignored?" Really, darling, the girl is cracked. "Play your games," she said, "'twas ever thus", which I gather is some olde English thing, and went back into the kitchen "to forage for breakfast".'

Theresa wound back the events of the evening and realised that perhaps Cathy had misunderstood what had happened last night. She had gone down to the cellar after the gluten-free, low-salt, fat-free shaming and stayed there. After that she had witnessed Theresa's own brief arrival in the cellar with a man who wanted her keys. But from where Cathy was hiding it was quite possible she believed that Theresa was simply ignoring her.

'After the drama was over she spent all night in the cellar?'

'So it seems.'

'Oh Lord. Has she phoned her mother? Poor woman must be worried sick. I would be if she was my daughter.'

'She's chattering away to her as I speak. I gather we are bullies who scared her when she was only trying to help.'

'Let me talk to her.'

Theresa could hear Carol's footsteps as she marched through into the kitchen. After signing off with her mother, Cathy came on the line.

'How are you feeling, Cathy? You know you didn't have to spend all night in the cellar.'

'Oh, I do know,' said the girl breathily. 'I was fast asleep. Don't mind me. No one ever does.'

Theresa wondered if she was being sarcastic but realised it was probably a pattern of speech she couldn't get out of.

'Do you realise what happened last night?' Theresa asked.

'Not really,' said Cathy. 'A lot of fuss about nothing, I should think. Usually is. I really thought I was helping. Am I fired?'

'No,' said Theresa. 'Unless you want to go. I'll bet your mother was worried about you.'

'I told her I didn't phone because I couldn't get a signal down there, which is true. She does know about how hard scene-painters and backstage staff work just before opening night, so she appreciated that I needed to stay over. I didn't tell her what I did. Please can you not tell her.'

Theresa realised how hard it must be to be the nondescript child of a mother famed for her talent and her beauty. She also decided that if Cathy was in the dark about the events with Vito and his men, perhaps it was easier to leave her there. The girl seemed so earnest and well intended. Theresa actually felt very sorry for her.

And when Cathy wasn't swapping ingredients, her help in the kitchen really had been indispensable.

'All right, Cathy. I'd suggest you go back to your hotel and get washed and I'll see you later. About four-ish. Now could I speak to Carol again?'

Carol came back on, and Theresa asked her over for a bite of breakfast and a debrief before tonight's big event.

Part Six

SOCCA

Ingredients
500ml water
250g chickpea/gram flour
2 tablespoons olive oil
1 teaspoon salt
salt and pepper for seasoning

Method
Put the water into a bowl, and whisk in the flour, olive oil and salt, till smooth. Lightly grease a cast-iron skillet or pizza pan and pour in the mixture, to pancake thickness. Cook on a steady high heat, pricking any bubbles that might rise. When slightly golden, remove from heat, cut into strips and serve with salt and pepper.

29

S ALLY WAS VERY IMPRESSED by the sight of the
vast stadium, and the thrilling hum of the crowd.
She sat at an elegantly decorated table in the fancy
private VIP-only restaurant. There was much excitement all around her. Clearly, all the men who sat at the
other tables were very well known in the world of
football, even if they were unknown to her. Destiny
was in her element, passing from one table to another,
saying hello to other footballers' wives and older men,
whom Sally imagined were managers.

Stanislav put his hand on hers and squeezed it.

'Fun, isn't it? The anticipation in the air.'

'Certainly quite different from anything I've ever
witnessed before,' said Sally. 'It's hard to imagine playing
in front of such a huge crowd. Actors don't know they're
born. They could only ever dream of an audience this size.'

'Talking of actors, did you see your friend Jackie this
morning?'

'Why do you ask, Stanislav?'

'Because yesterday I put some money into her little
film, and wondered if she might have sent me a message
through you.'

Sally thought back on the mad diatribe she had witnessed from Jackie earlier and decided against admitting that she had seen her.

Mickey entered the restaurant and hurried over to the table.

'Shouldn't you be in the dressing room, or whatever they call it in a football stadium?' asked Sally.

'Just a bit of a rush on, Stanislav, mate.' Mickey patted the Russian on the shoulder. 'Seeing as how you've put a truckload of dosh into my little project, I wondered whether you might come out on the pitch before the match and take a bow.'

'No, no,' said Stanislav, lowering his eyes. 'It's not my way.'

'Oh come on, mate. Don't have to be so modest about it.'

Stanislav spoke firmly.

'I really don't like to, Mickey. But thank you for asking.'

Mickey made a gesture of exasperation and left the dining room.

'I hope I didn't upset him, Destiny.' Stanislav leaned towards Sally. 'I think it's more classy to give, but keep quiet about it, don't you think?'

A couple of men Sally hadn't seen before pulled up chairs and sat at the table. Destiny got up and loomed behind Sally.

'Hey, Sally, old girl, come and join me for a quick tour round the commoners' areas. I'm told you can get pizza and chips out there in the real world!'

Sally really didn't want to go, but Stanislav gave a quick nod and she thought that perhaps she had better let him talk business with the men.

'I always leave the room when men want to yak. It's so boring, don't you think?' Destiny linked arms with Sally and they swung into the public area of the stadium. 'Oh, you should have heard old Stanny in the car this morning, Sally. I was quite glad you got in. He was jabbering away with the driver, vigorish this, ligorish that. Sounded quite cross about something. But he's cheered up now, thank God. I hate a sulky man, don't you?' Destiny raised her hand and pointed towards a huge illuminated sign. 'Hooray! That was easier than I thought it would be. Look, they've written it in English for us: "Pizza".'

'So how are the bookings for tonight?' asked Theresa, who was busily doing advance preparations when William came into the restaurant kitchen. She had started work early, while Carol prodded about next door, sprawled on the dining-room floor, applying touches of paint to the dried cement, making sure that her new pieces of mosaic blended in with the old.

'Not great,' William replied, studying the large ledger. 'We have Sally and her Russian friend, a table for two under the name Simmonds. I suppose that's your daughter, and . . .'

Theresa put down the chopping knife.

'Imogen is married. That's not her surname.'

'Maybe once her husband left home, she resorted to her maiden name,' said William.

'No,' said Theresa. 'She didn't. She thought it would be too much trouble getting her passport and credit cards changed. Anyhow, she told me that if we were short tonight she would come and fill a table, if we wanted, but I was to phone her first.'

'Whatever! Enough family matters,' said William. 'We can only hope there will be a good turnout on the door, because that's it. Two tables for two. Let us pray for passing trade. Benjamin put ads in the local papers. "Grand Opening" and all that.'

'And we have Diana Sparks, remember,' said Theresa. 'Our celebrity guest.'

William's body tensed from top to bottom.

'Oh God! How did that happen? I was obviously so overawed, I'd forgotten she had promised to come tonight. How embarrassing. We have Diana Sparks arriving at an empty restaurant. We'll look like the village idiots.' He gasped and spun round. 'And I think Carol told photographers from the local press she was coming too. We'll be a laughing stock!'

William moved off into the dining room to consult with Benjamin and Carol about filling the place, should no one turn up. Theresa went back to peeling and prepping.

Simmonds? Could the Simmonds who had booked be her ex-husband? But he had reserved a table for two? Perhaps he was bringing a new girlfriend in to show off to her. He knew Imogen was here. Theresa certainly wouldn't put anything past him. She had a terrible thought that her ex-husband, having been thwarted in his attempts to woo back ex-girlfriends and wives, was about to descend.

Oh, she was being silly, imagining horrors out of nowhere.

And William was right. Perhaps Imogen had booked the table for herself and . . .

But why not a four?

Theresa picked up a bunch of leeks and a stainless-steel cleaver.

Why was she wasting time thinking about such stuff? Simmonds was hardly the most unusual name on the planet.

Maybe it was just an English couple, holidaying in Bellevue-Sur-Mer, who had seen the ad in the paper and fancied trying something new.

Theresa brought the cleaver down hard.

Sally sat on the concrete steps overlooking the bright-green football pitch with Destiny while she ate her slice of pizza. Sally was loving the sweet smell of the turf as it was being freshly hosed.

Outside the quiet calm of the VIP restaurant, the public area buzzed with energy and the soundtrack of cheering crowds. Kids bolted around, some bearing packets of hot chips, wearing team strips. Men stood in gaggles talking earnestly, gesturing and laughing; women sat in the fold-down seats chatting and eating *socca* off shallow cardboard trays and slugging back beer from plastic cups.

'I like sitting with the common people – like me – don't you?' Destiny took a bite of her pizza. 'The food they serve in those posh places is always tepid. Is that the word? Not much taste.'

Sally decided not to correct her.

'You're keen on Stanny the Russkie, aren't you, Sally? I gather he's talking about marrying you?'

'He told you that?' Sally thought this was all a big secret until she had made her decision.

'Nah. He told Mickey and Mickey told me. Men are bigger gossips than us, you know.' Destiny dabbed at her lips with the paper napkin that came with the pizza, pulled out a lipstick from her handbag and started refreshing her make-up. 'I suppose you'll have a nice life with him. He's quite rich.'

'Money doesn't matter to me,' Sally said, and instantly realised she sounded glib.

'Money always matters, hun,' said Destiny, as a bunch of men moved between them, heading down the steps looking for their seats. 'You wait till you ain't got any. Then you'll know how much it matters.'

'I really meant I wasn't after him for his money.' Sally felt weird having to say that. But, truthfully, his money had to be part of the equation, even if in a negative way.

'And Stanny certainly knows how to spend it, doesn't he? Thousands here, thousands there. My old mum always taught me to keep a grip on my spending and I do. No one is a bottomless pit. Or perhaps they are in Russia. I've never been tempted to go there. Too much snow. And I can't stand beetroot.'

Sally had to defend Stanislav. After all, he was being so generous with all her friends, sponsoring their projects so that they had the freedom to move forward. Sometimes money was a positive force after all. 'It's all investment money, though, isn't it?' she said. 'He's spending, but it's backing films and football initiatives. Presumably somewhere down the line, there's a pay-off for him. Think of those people who put money into *Star Wars*. A thousand-pound investment and now they're millionaires.'

'Suppose so. But it's a bit like roulette, isn't it? Mum always said the safest place to shove money in is houses. Like they say: "safe as houses". Even banks aren't safe, are they? That's why Mickey and me are looking to put our dosh into buying an estate out here.'

Sally realised that she had become very fond of Destiny, with her straight talk and lack of guile. In the short time she had spent with Mickey, he too seemed very candid and sincere. 'How did you meet Mickey?'

'At Boujis. I was a waitress. I accidentally spilled a drink on him, and the girl with him, some posh bird, got all cross and tried to get me sacked. Mickey just laughed and winked at me. He sent me a note, later, apologising for her and asking me out. And we just clicked. We made each other laugh. We had so much in common, see.' Destiny looked out at the stadium; Sally followed her gaze. 'This place is bloody massive, isn't it?'

Sally found the buzz of the stadium intoxicating. Rock stars and football players, she realised, experienced this on a daily basis. How she would have loved to have a try at playing in front of anything nearly as exciting as this huge expectant crowd.

'My dad used to bring me to football games since I was a tot. He wanted me to be a boy really, but instead he got this.' Destiny grimaced, indicating herself. 'There wasn't any of that princess thingy either. He tried to call me his Princess, but I stopped up my ears when he did 'cos I was frightened if I really was a princess I'd have to marry Prince Charles, with those jug ears.'

Sally laughed.

'Princes are generally quite ugly people, when you think about it.' Destiny snapped her bag shut and leaned back on the step behind her. 'Look at them: Prince Albert of Monaco, Prince Edward . . .'

'Prince William and Harry seem OK,' said Sally.

'Only because we know who they are and who their mother was. No one would look twice at them if they worked in the local garage. Not like my Mickey, or your Stanny. They're good lookers. You two will look great together.'

A bell rang and everyone started to walk briskly; some ran. Sally was frightened it was a fire alarm, but the general movement was towards the stadium seating, pushing past them down the steps.

'Yeah, Stanny is one good-looking bloke.' Destiny got up and put out a hand to help Sally. 'I don't like that Russian man who drives him about, though, do you?'

'I don't think I've met a Russian man with him.'

'Yes, you have. He's called Stephane. He was up at the house in the hills playing butler.'

'But he's French? Isn't he?'

'Not when he was jabbering away to Stanny this morning in the car. French is all "hon hee hon" and pouty lips, but Russian sounds like a tape going backwards. I'm sure they were talking Russian together. That Stephane bloke sounded quite cross. Anyone would think he was the boss and Stanny the servant. I wouldn't like staff talking to me like that. They'd have their cards in a jiffy.'

Out of the corner of her eye Sally thought she saw a man who looked just like Jean-Philippe. She turned to check but he turned too, so she could not see his face. Was it him? Had he been released from jail? Why was he here? She felt sure it was him.

Something felt wrong.

Destiny pushed through the doors of the VIP restaurant, with Sally in tow, just as Stanislav, and everyone else in the room, was rising from the table and moving into the viewing box.

Stanislav held out his hand. Sally took it. He raised hers to his lips and kissed it.

'You look ravishing,' he said. 'I'm sorry business got in the way. From now on it will be your day.'

He put his arm around her waist and pulled her close.

'We're going to be very happy,' he whispered.

Sally looked into his sparkling eyes and made her final decision.

Theresa was talking Cathy through the dishes for the evening. They had both learned some sharp lessons yesterday and now, hopefully, things would go more smoothly.

'Everything that happened was my fault. I do know that,' said Cathy, head hung low.

Theresa thought back to the terror of Uncle Vito and the Magenta gang and digging up the floor and thought, my dear, you do not know the half of it!

However, as Cathy knew nothing, Theresa still thought it best to keep quiet, especially as her mother was footing the bill for Cathy's wages, and also providing the much-needed puff of publicity that might make a splash in the local papers so that their opening would maybe mean something to locals and tourists alike.

Cathy was now in the middle of preparing melba toast to go with a caviar Niçoise tapenade, which they hoped to serve in place of the rather disappointing *amuse-bouches* they had had last night. Called *croûtes en dentele* in France, melba toast had been created by the local chef Auguste Escoffier. Its preparation was not hard, but required concentration. Theresa showed Cathy by making one piece herself, toasting the bread then cutting through it laterally, and retoasting the raw side. Unattended, it was very easily burnt and then came out like a Friesian cow, black and white, and had to be thrown away.

As she prepared carrots, Theresa could hear William, Benjamin and Carol next door, chatting amiably while they laid up the tables.

'It's a shame about Mum, isn't it?' said Cathy, laying the once-toasted slices of bread on to the grill rack.

'What do you mean? Has something happened to her?'

'No,' said Cathy. 'She'd forgotten that she had a prior arrangement tonight, and won't be able to make it.'

Next door the telephone rang and William took the call.

Theresa didn't want to have to break the appalling news to William quite yet. She bit her lip, turned and placed the carrots into salted water, then started shelling broad beans.

An eerie silence next door was followed by the sound of William howling at the top of his voice: 'The bitch!'

Theresa now realised who had been on the line.

She counted to ten, and sure enough, before she reached seven, William arrived on the threshold, smiling coldly.

'I gather your mother can't make it?'

'It's the Brits in Film night at Cannes,' said Cathy. 'She's one of the guests of honour. The dates were . . .'

'I know,' said William, cutting her off. 'Very confusing. She told me.'

He flounced out and Theresa turned to apologise to Cathy but before she had time to voice the word she screamed, 'Help!'

Cathy was standing by the open oven; the melba toast had not only burned, but tongues of flame licking out from the grill had caught the ends of her hair. Cathy was on fire.

Theresa grabbed a towel and threw it over her.

Sally sat in the stadium, almost deafened by the sound of cheering as a giant eagle appeared seemingly out of nowhere and circled the arena, swooping down to land gracefully on the gauntlet of a falconer who stood in the centre of the pitch.

The bird and his handler walked off and, to a tremendous roar from the crowd, the footballers jogged out through the tunnel.

'What was that? What was that?' Sally was getting really caught up in the theatricality of the whole event.

'That's their mascot, the Nissa Eagle, innit. And, look, there's mine . . . my Mickey mascot.'

Destiny clapped her hands together like a little child when she saw Mickey give the crowd a wave.

'Are you going to keep me waiting much longer?' Stanislav leaned in towards Sally and whispered in her ear. 'The anticipation is driving me wild.'

The crowd cheered again as a team of policemen and dogs on leashes came on to the pitch and stood around the entrances. At the same moment the doors of the VIP enclosure opened and a file of *gendarmes* marched down the stone aisle.

'Oooh,' said Destiny, patting Sally's lap. 'The guard of honour!'

A man in a camel-coloured coat and trilby hat walked out on to the green. Sally imagined that this must be the trainer, or manager of the visiting team. But when she looked at the footballers' faces they seemed puzzled and started giving one another strange glances. This presence was not expected.

'Well?' asked Stanislav, taking Sally's hand and squeezing it. 'If you thought that on the boat it was too romantic to give me an answer, this must be a better place. Please, Sally. I am yearning to know your decision.'

Sally turned to Stanislav. He was so debonair and charming. Everything about him was perfect. And Sally also knew that when she said yes to him she could have everything she ever wanted.

She clasped his hand and looked him right in the eye.

'It has taken up every moment,' she said. 'But I have made up my mind, Stanislav, and . . .'

Before she could finish, a policeman stepped down and put his hand on Stanislav's shoulder while another began reading him his rights. Stanislav started to rise, but two more officers appeared behind him and shoved him down. One of them pulled out handcuffs and locked them on to Stanislav's wrists.

'The answer is no, Stanislav,' Sally continued. 'I can't do it.'

'Madame Sally Connor?' asked one policeman, while another was asking Destiny's name.

As Sally struggled to stand, she too was handcuffed, and so was Destiny.

Sally saw Destiny glance down at the pitch and she followed her gaze. Policemen were also slapping cuffs on Mickey MacDonald.

All Sally could hear as she was dragged up the concrete steps was her heart pounding and the stadium ringing out with the thunderous sound of booing.

Theresa came in and slumped down with the others.

Cathy's hair had been extinguished swiftly enough not to have burned her scalp or face, but she was now left with a very strange hairstyle.

'Oh dear, I look weird,' she said, glancing in her handbag mirror. 'People will probably stare at me. I really don't like that. That's Mama's job.'

William rolled his eyes and Theresa kicked him under the table.

'A positively thriving business,' he said, tapping his watch in case it was wrong. 'Eight o'clock and not a sign of a soul.'

'What time is the first reservation?' asked Theresa.

'Eight-thirty,' said Carol and Benjamin in unison.

'It's not like it was yesterday, is it?' said Cathy.

'Thankfully,' said Carol. Now Theresa kicked *her* under the table.

'Perhaps we should have a phone around,' suggested Theresa. 'See who we can rustle up.'

'We're all here,' said William. 'Unless you want to get Zoe back. Sally was meant to be here. She didn't give an exact time but she said eight-ish.'

'She's late,' said Carol, twisting her watch round on her wrist. 'Surely we know somebody else. How about Monsieur Leroux?'

'The plumber?'

'Why not?'

William gave Carol a glacial stare.

'Benjamin darling, go and have a look at the brasserie and see if they've got the same problem?'

Benjamin followed orders and darted out. He came back in a jiffy.

'Buzzing,' he said.

'Somebody has to turn up eventually,' said Theresa. 'It's early days. Perhaps people don't know we're open yet.'

'You mean they cannot read the huge sign outside the door that says "Now Open"?' William went to the welcome desk and pulled out a bottle of wine.

'I'm going to have a drink.'

Benjamin leaped up and wrestled with him for the bottle.

'Come on, William. The licence doesn't allow us to serve drinks yet, remember?'

'I'm not charging anyone. It's for my own personal consumption.'

Behind the screen the front door rattled and opened.

'A customer!' Theresa jumped to her feet and r.
towards the kitchen.

A long-haired, tanned and tattooed man in scruffy
jeans and T-shirt shuffled in.

'*Vous avez une table pour une personne?*'

William picked up a menu and led Jean-Philippe to
one of the many empty tables.

30

'How long have you known Stanislav Serafim?'
'About a week,' said Sally, looking up at the clock and noting she had been here in this room for around four hours.

The questioning detective was giving nothing away but asked many questions about Stanislav that she had no idea how to answer. When the inspector reached another dead end, he started again from the beginning: How long had she known him? How did they meet?

Sally realised just before the moment of his arrest that she had never known him. It was Destiny who had made her realise that. She had been caught up in some romantic puff, simply because her days were empty and she had nothing better to do than play along. Destiny and Mickey had lots in common. That was the secret. What did she have in common with Stanislav? Nothing.

'You took him to a celebrity party at Cannes?' asked the detective. 'The actress Marina Martel's party.'

'No,' said Sally. 'I bumped into him at Cannes. He happened to be there. I was there because a friend had got me an invitation. I don't know Marina Martel.'

'The name of that friend who invited you?'

'Jackie Westwood.'

The detective picked up his pencil and scribbled the name. This was the first thing so far that had interested him.

'But you took a package from Mr Serafim that night and put it in the car of Jean-Philippe Delacourt when you accepted his lift home?'

'No. I had no package.' Sally realised he was now trying to implicate her in Jean-Philippe's arrest, though whether or not her sea-school instructor was in league with Stanislav she had no idea. She had met the Russian through Jean-Philippe . . . so perhaps . . . 'I was badly let down and couldn't get home. I was expecting to catch the night bus as far as the airport. I didn't have enough money on me for a taxi and all the cash machines in Cannes seemed to be drained dry. So I was waiting at a bus stop and Mr Delacourt came by and picked me up.'

'A strange coincidence?' said the detective. 'A man you know just happens to drive by while you are apparently stranded?'

'It was a lucky coincidence,' said Sally. 'But for him not strange at all. The bus route is on the main road through Cannes.'

'He could have taken the autoroute.'

'He had stopped off in town to get a bite to eat. He'd had a long day.'

'You had not arranged to meet up?'

'No. But, as I said, it was good luck. For me, anyway.'

'You introduced Mr Delacourt to Mr Serafim?'

'No. I met Mr Serafim on his boat. Mr Delacourt runs the sea school where I trained. He had been engaged as helmsman.'

'Mr Serafim has no boat. Mr Delacourt says he already told you that. Serafim had hired it for a month.'

The detective slid forward a photo of Stephane. 'Do you know this man?'

'That's Stanislav's servant. A kind of butler and chauffeur.'

The inspector looked over to the policeman at the door and grinned.

'And did you ever see this?'

He plonked down another photograph, this time of the pink and orange stripy beach bag.

'It contained a picnic,' said Sally. 'Salads and things, which we ate on the boat during the Cannes fireworks. He got it at a delicatessen in Bellevue-Sur-Mer.'

The detective chuckled to himself as he scribbled notes.

'You're sure you had the beach bag with you at Cannes during the fireworks?'

Sally cast her mind back. She really couldn't remember seeing it. But surely it must have been there. Perhaps it was stowed away in a locker. 'I can only truthfully say that he had it when we got off.'

'Was there anyone else on the boat with you that evening?'

Sally told him no.

'Strange, don't you think?'

'I suppose it is,' said Sally. 'But I do have the necessary certificate to take the helm.'

The detective shook his head. 'The man told you he was a millionaire and you never questioned why the boat was not crawling with staff. That is the usual picture for millionaires on boats.'

'I can't say I've had much experience of millionaires,' said Sally.

'Who has? Did you pull the boat into any coves or marinas on your way to or from Cannes?'

'No.'

'What do you know of this?'

The detective slammed down an estate-agent's details of a small mews house in Kensington. Very chic, two storeys, garage downstairs, living accommodation up.

Sally picked the papers up. 'It's lovely,' she said. 'Very Swinging Sixties.' She flipped the pages over. 'Quite a decent price, too, for somewhere in that area.'

'You have no memory of buying it?'

Now it was Sally's turn to laugh.

'Me?'

'Last week. True, contracts have not yet been exchanged, but if all goes well, in a few weeks' time it will be yours.'

'I know nothing about this.'

The detective opened a folder and showed Sally a legal document. 'That's not your signature?'

Sally looked down at her old signature – her maiden name, her acting name – Sally Doyle. Added to it was a hyphenated second name: Serafim.

Sally Doyle-Serafim.

Sally pushed herself back in her chair.

'Please will somebody tell me what's going on?'

* * *

William popped his head into the kitchen. 'Still only the one diner. He's enjoying it. A local. He tells me he taught Sally how to drive that boat of hers.'

'That'll be nice for her,' said Theresa.

'When she eventually arrives.' William pursed his lips and put his hands on his hips. 'Or will it be show-down time with that Russian? This French one is quite a hunk too. I don't know how she does it.'

Theresa and Cathy were sitting on stools by the back door. They were ready for orders, but, as there were none, they had decided to take a rest, ready for the fray, should it ever start.

Behind William the rattle of the restaurant door opening again.

'A second customer. Stand by!' he cried and twirled back into the dining room.

'It'll probably be someone asking for the Gare Maritime,' said Theresa. 'Let's not get overexerted before their order comes in.'

They leaned back against the cool white wall.

'Everything seems very quiet out there,' said Theresa. 'You see, Cathy, I was right. They came in, took one look and left. No one wants to eat in an empty restaurant.'

'It's not entirely empty,' said Cathy, trying to be help-ful.

'Sometimes one solitary diner is worse than having none.'

They sat back and closed their eyes, waiting. They knew the gen. William would show the guest to their table. Carol or Benjamin would bring them the menu. The guest would take an age to choose something, then Carol or Benjamin would appear in the kitchen with the order.

'I'm not sure what's worse,' said Theresa. 'Being too busy or too slack. It's tense work, waiting, don't you think?'

Cathy yawned.

Carol came in holding up the paper order.

'It's Tom!' she said, surprised.

'Who's Tom?'

'Sally's son. Tom.'

'Oh, Tom!' said Theresa. 'I thought he was in Italy.'

'Italy is only a few miles away, Theresa. And there are roads and trains back and forth all day long, you know.'

'Is he with Sally? The table for two?'

'No. He's got some woman with him. Never seen her before. Huge boobs.'

Theresa laughed and moved towards the cooker.

'What do they want?'

'The boobs?'

'No. Tom and "friend". Do they want to eat?'

Carol handed her the order for two sets of starters.

'No mains?'

'Can't make up their minds. I'm telling you, it's like a morgue out there, darling,' Carol said. 'One man at a single table, eating alone in silence. At least with any luck these two will talk to one another. I told William we needed a music licence. He never listens to a word I say.'

'Oh God,' said Theresa. 'It's all so nerve-racking.'

'Let's go over it once more and talk in detail about your night on the boat at Cannes.'

Sally told them everything. How they drove the boat to Cannes, took supper, watched the fireworks, Stanislav proposed to her and then they drove back again.

'No one boarded the boat?'

'No.'

'You two were alone together the whole time?'

'Yes.'

'You enjoyed some cocaine together?'

'Absolutely not. We had a half-bottle of champagne.'

'A half-bottle.' The detective laughed. 'Generous!'

'We both knew I had to drive the boat back. I needed to stay sober.'

'Which is why it is usual to bring a crew with you. Then you could have drunk a whole bottle. Stingy bastard for a millionaire.'

'He was always the gentleman to me, and very generous.'

'And yet he expected his date to drive his boat? Some gentleman!'

'As a matter of fact,' said Sally, 'he is a gentleman. And he can be quite brave too. He helped some people who were stranded at sea. He almost drowned.'

'That same night?'

Sally nodded.

'Where was this?'

'Coming round Cap d'Antibes.'

The detective leaned forward.

'Tell me more.'

Sally wondered if this interrogation about nothing would ever end. If Stanislav was a little eccentric and wanted to be alone with her, why was that a police matter?

'Can you tell *me* anything?' she asked. 'Or is it only me who has to tell you things? I want to know why I am here, what Stanislav has done and how I am implicated.'

'Tell me about the people you and Mr Serafim encountered on your way from Cannes. Can you describe them?'

Sally thought back to the dark night, the two people floating in a RIB and the view from the boat's bridge.

'It is like one of those scenes at the start of a *Dracula* movie,' said Carol, fetching a bread bowl for Tom's table, while Theresa wiped down the worktop, preparing for when she next had an order. 'Dead silence in the tavern. And every time the door opens all eyes turn towards it. What can we do?'

She pushed the door with her behind, and moved back into the dining room.

William was standing by the kitchen sink, glugging a glass of water, also escaping from the embarrassing silence next door. He'd even had time to go down and do a few things on the computer in the cellar.

'The money came through,' he said when he finished his drink. 'From the Russian hunk. So we're all but home and dry, even without Zoe's help.'

Then Benjamin slipped into the kitchen and whispered earnestly to them all.

'Things get worse,' he said. 'While his lady friend was going to the powder room, Tom has just let slip to me that the woman is in fact a critic from some new international glossy mag, here to do a thing about us.'

William swung round. 'What!?' He slumped against the cooker. 'God give me strength.' He turned to Theresa. 'Right. Pull out all the stops.'

'What stops? They're eating their starters and they haven't made up their mind about the main course.'

Both men left the kitchen in a flurry.

Carol came back in.

'The woman has changed her order about three times,' she said, passing over another chit of paper. 'She wants the last one, not the ones I crossed out.'

'She's testing us,' said Theresa. 'To see if we can cope during the high pressure of too many customers.'

'Too many? Any moment I'm expecting balls of tumbleweed to start rolling in. It's as dead as some old ghost town in the Midwest. No atmosphere whatso-ever. Uh-oh! Don't speak too soon.' Carol spun around. 'There goes the door again. With all three of us rush-ing to open it!'

Theresa put another pie into the oven and started preparing the vegetables for the plating up, while, at her side, Cathy whipped up a bit of *pistou*.

Carol turned.

'Don't get yourselves into a tizzy. We've another two tables for one. Zoe on one and some old man on his own ...'

'It's not Uncle Vito?'

'No, no. English tourist. Short and fat, with one of those old-fashioned moustaches like airmen in the war, you know like Errol Flynn. William's put him on one of the centre tables back to back with Big Boobs.'

Theresa laughed. 'And then there were five. Go fetch the orders, gal.'

'You still haven't told me about the house in London,' said Sally. 'What has that got to do with cocaine? Why did he need me? What part was I in all this? I swear I didn't buy it. Look at my bank account.'

'Madame Connor, we already have. Let's just say there will be many disappointed people tomorrow. Did he promise you money for anything – a project, some work you were proposing?'

'No. But he did to all my friends. And I really mean all of them.'

The detective leaned back and said the name Jackie Westwood.

Sally winced at the thought. She had been working so hard at getting her TV show on.

'Why did you ignore her warning, Madame Connor? She did try to warn you this morning, no? Don't you listen to your friends?'

Sally cast her mind back and realised that Jackie had warned her this morning, but at the time she had seemed so disturbed.

'I thought she was mad. But how had she known? She can't have seen Stanislav for several days.'

'She saw him this morning, Madame Connor. And as a result was not mad but scared,' said the detective. 'It seems she had taken a visiting card she found in your house and gone by taxi up to the villa he was occupying in the hills near Vence. She was going to thank him and ask if he could up the budget so that she could work on another, separate project. One which she wished to keep secret from you. She found the door open and wandered inside. She caught him unawares while he was testing his cocaine. The very cocaine he had picked up with you last night from the people in the RIB, which you believed was broken down. The cocaine that he stored in the pink beach bag. He tried to hold her, but she got away. She is trained as a military woman, no?'

Sally's mind raced as she tried to put it all together.

'So you have arrested Stanislav for dealing drugs?' Sally asked.

'From the drugs he earns a cut – what they call in Russia "the vigorish".' The detective leaned forward. 'But Mr Serafim is responsible for much more than that,' he said. 'He targeted this week to be here especially. Like those jewel thieves a few years ago. We have officers now going around Cannes and Nice, breaking the news to the many people involved in the innumerable projects he put money into. A few thousand here and another few there. It's a classic method.'

'You mean all his generosity was actually money laundering?'

'Exactly.'

'But the house in London?'

'By marrying you he could settle there as your husband, and start up business. You wouldn't even have known about it, as you live here full time. But he could claim anywhere he bought in England was a marital home. And he could sell, perhaps make a profit, and suddenly a huge amount of money would have been effectively "legalised".'

Sally felt punctured. So all of his romancing had been a filthy game in order that he could take advantage of her nationality to set up in England to launder his drug money.

'I thought he really liked me,' she said. 'I'm such a fool.'

'Not the only one. Many people have been taken in this week and let him run money through their work accounts. But any money that was paid by him is now being withdrawn by us, as it was illegally gained.'

'So all my friends, who I introduced to him, have been duped too?'

The detective nodded.

'They have nothing?'

'You got it.'

Sally imagined Jackie and Diana finding out that they had been taken for a ride, and felt crushed.

William came into the kitchen, went over to Cathy and flung himself on to his knees before her.

'Please, Cathy, phone your mother. Please beg her to come,' he said. 'We are a laughing stock.'

'What's happening?' asked Theresa, as she dropped pieces of battered fish into hot oil and watched them sizzle.

'We now have paparazzi by the door. They are screwing on their lenses waiting to catch this so-called celebrity restaurant opening, starring the famed Diana Sparks. And what do we have? A local sea instructor, a fat little tourist, Zoe and the son of one of our neighbours with some elderly floozie.'

'Elderly?' asked Theresa. 'All Carol said was large knockers.'

'She's in her fifties. Old enough to be Tom's mother.' William raised his eyebrows and clambered to his feet. 'Talking of which, where *is* Tom's mother?'

'To you, elderly is younger than I am, thank you, William. If she's "elderly", what does that make me? Or you, for that matter?'

'There's no point phoning her.' Cathy stepped forward. 'There is simply no hope of my mother coming tonight. She's in Cannes at that Brit party.' Cathy touched William's arm. 'Perhaps I could go out there to greet the photographers, as her daughter?' She started pulling her apron off.

William put up his hand. 'No. Thank you, Cathy, that will not be necessary. Paraffin to the fire!'

'It's like death warmed up out there.' Zoe bustled into the kitchen. 'In here is clearly where the action is.'

Benjamin popped his head round the door.

'Can I come in?'

'No!' they all whispered.

'Someone has to take people to the tables . . .' said William.

'And take their orders . . .' said Carol.

Benjamin pulled a face and returned to the dining room.

'Cathy,' William was desperate. 'Please see if you can get her on the landline.' He indicated the cellar, and Cathy duly went down the steps. 'Beg her!'

'I've still got that cheque for you, William,' said Zoe. 'And I thought you'd like to know what really happened here last night.' She fetched one of the stools from beside the wall and placed it in the centre of the kitchen. 'As you know, we dug up two medallions, the Crab and the Lion.'

'As they only asked for one,' said Theresa, 'it did seem a little strange.'

'There's a reason. It seems that old Ma Magenta was so worried about her family coming to claim her valuable little item, she herself did a double bluff, which is what we also intend to do.'

'So one of them really is genuine?' said Theresa, cutting a slab of *pissaladière* into small squares and arranging them with the salad on a plate. 'But which one is which and which do we give?'

'As William informed me, Ma Magenta's birthday was the twenty-third of July. As Benjamin pointed out, in usual years this is Leo the Lion. But I'm a child of the Sixties, you know, where we all wore kaftans and smelled of patchouli and had our palms read and drew up one another's horoscopes.'

William let out a noisy yawn.

'I recall having to search out an awful book called the *Ephemeris*, which to me looked like logarithm tables and smelled of old wet dogs, but you had to hunt in there to find rising signs and conjunctions and cusps, and all that guff,' Zoe continued. 'I also clearly remember that the dates given in the newspaper horoscopes are often not correct, not once you've consulted the *Ephemeris*. Thank God for the internet, because now you don't have to faff about with stinky old books, you can just Google it – which I did last night.'

Benjamin reappeared at the door. He opened his mouth to speak but everyone shooed him away.

'But let me . . .'

'Get out there, Benjamin,' said William. 'That woman is a critic, for God's sake.'

'But—'

'Go!' William gave Benjamin a shove and he spun round back into the dining room.

Zoe was still rattling on. 'I have checked and double-checked. Franca Magenta, an Italian who believed in all kinds of hoodoo, would know very well that her actual birthday – born on that date in that year, 1920 – fell under Cancer the Crab.'

'Not Leo? So the Crab is the Chagall?'

'And we're going to give them the Leo?'

'That's it.' Zoe nodded. 'They're no art experts. I doubt they've ever watched the *Antiques Roadshow* or spent an afternoon in the Musée des Beaux-Arts. What will they know?'

'But if they take it to an expert?'

'Then they'll have to believe that the old girl was playing a great big joke on them.'

'They might come back here and take them all, like Russian roulette . . .'

'And if they do?' said Zoe. 'They'll find none of them are a Chagall.'

'And two of them are genuine Carol Rogers,' said Carol.

'And what happens to the other one?' asked Theresa, placing two plates on the pass for Benjamin to deliver. 'The Crab.'

'Once William has cashed my cheque, we've settled with the estate agent and we own the building, when it absolutely becomes ours; being, as part of the floor, a fitting and fixture, naturally we sell the medallion. Up in Paris, at Sotheby's or somewhere,' said Zoe. 'And we split the dosh between us.'

'So that's why you wanted to buy in!'

The door pushed open again.

'I've told you once,' said William. 'Go back, Benjamin.'

But it was not Benjamin.

In walked Uncle Vito.

'I am so pleased I overheard that last conversation,' said Vito. 'Now you can hand over what is rightfully mine.'

'Hand over what?' said William, very badly feigning innocence.

Vito slipped his hand into his pocket and smiled.

'I'd like the Crab, please.'

Theresa had a wild try. 'Crab salad or the terrine?' she said.

'You know very well which crab.' He stepped further into the kitchen and spoke in an intense whisper. 'Don't mess with me, lady.'

'Look,' said Theresa. 'We are running this place in good faith. If you have a family quarrel, go and have it out with your relatives and leave us alone.'

'Shut up!' Vito pulled out a pistol and levelled it at Theresa, who took a step back. William tried to make a dash for the door.

'No you don't.' Vito turned the gun on William, then swung it to face Carol and Zoe, who cowered beside the fridge.

'Where is my Chagall medallion?'

'The Leo medallion, by Marc Chagall, is in the dining room,' said Theresa.

He thrust his face close to hers.

'I've told you once. I am not interested in being fobbed off with a fake. I heard what that old woman said. I want the genuine Chagall. I don't want the Lion. I want the Crab.'

'Don't shoot.' Zoe put up her hands. 'I'll tell you where it is. It's hanging up under the coats.'

Vito laughed.

'You really take me for a fool, don't you? I know you are hiding the real one. Whatever you have out there will not be the one I want.'

Theresa prayed that Benjamin was now dialling the police from the phone at the front desk. Then she realised that Cathy was on the line down in the cellar and he would not be able to. She hoped Benjamin could use his mobile.

'Right!' Vito advanced, pulling open cupboards, flinging things on the floor. 'You bring me the Crab now, or else . . .'

'I'm sure that we . . .' Theresa stood in front of the fridge door.

'Be quiet!' shouted Vito. 'Hand it over or I will go out there and start shooting your customers. After that no one will ever visit this stupid place. You'll be finished.'

Nobody moved.

'It's in the fridge,' said Theresa, stepping away from the door.

Vito pulled the set of keys she had given him yesterday from his pocket and flung them to the floor. 'Why should I ever believe a word *you* tell me?'

He held the gun up and herded everyone into a corner, while he pulled open the fridge door. He glanced inside and instantly saw the lime-green shopping bag lying on the bottom shelf.

He hauled it out.

'It's the real one,' said Zoe, trying to sound bright as he slammed the fridge shut and glanced into the shopping bag. 'Chagall.'

'It's a medallion, all right . . .' He held the gun up again and waved it about. 'Get back! Stay still.'

'Her birthday, remember?' said Theresa. 'She was a Leo.'

Vito advanced towards Theresa and the others.

'You have not forgotten that I overheard your whole conversation?'

He raised the shopping bag high in the air then flung it to the ground with a crash. All around hanging pots clattered and pans rattled.

Theresa could hear steps coming up from the cellar. She tried to warn Cathy not to come in, in case it made Vito scared and he accidentally fired.

'Cathy!' she cried out in warning. 'Watch out!'

But, regardless of her call, Cathy appeared.

'Watch out for what?' she asked, blinking in the stark kitchen light. 'Oo-er! Is something wrong?'

Cathy was clutching Zoe's bright-red shopping bag.

'Look what I found hidden down the side of the desk,' she said brightly. 'It's a missing part of the floor.'

Cathy peered around, saw the startled looks on everyone's face and only then noticed the gun, which Vito trained upon her.

'You! Girl!' he said. 'Open the bag!'

'It's just an old bit of flooring,' she said, holding the shopper open, displaying the contents: a blue and yellow mosaic medallion of a crab.

'At last. Just what I always wanted.' Vito snatched the bag and, still holding the gun up, backed out of the kitchen. 'It's that simple. Thank you all, and goodbye!'

William and Theresa ran to the door to watch Vito stride through the dining room, swinging the red shopping bag as he left.

'Should we go after him?' asked Carol, moving behind them and peering over their shoulders.

'What would be the point?' said Theresa. 'He has what he wants.' She turned to everyone. 'Now perhaps he'll go away, and we can run the place in peace.'

'But that thing was meant to be ours,' said William.

'No it wasn't. We were supposed to be opening a restaurant.'

'But we would have been rich,' wailed Zoe.

'Let's forget about it,' said Theresa. 'And try to make tonight work for us.'

'Perhaps the photographers will take his picture?' William said.

'Why would they? They save their shots for people they recognise,' said Carol. 'And anyway, how will that help? I can see the headline: "Man leaves restaurant with red shopping bag!"'

The front door opened again and through it they could all see a barrage of flashlights and the frantic sound of cameras clicking and whirring.

'Oh no,' whispered Theresa. 'He's not come back . . .'

Two people walked in and Benjamin stepped forward to lead them to a table.

'Why are the paparazzi snapping them?' asked William at the same time as Theresa said: 'Who are they?'

'A footballer and his wife,' said Carol. 'That's Mickey MacDonald and his wife Destiny. They're on the cover of *OK!* magazine almost every other week. They're friends of Sally.'

'Oh, well, something for the press coverage,' said William, pulling down his jacket and putting on his front-of-house smile. 'Beggars can't be choosers. It's now officially a quasi-celebrity opening.' He pushed open the dining-room door and swung into welcoming action.

On the train home Sally was forced to stand. Every compartment was full. People were crammed in the gangways, on the stairways and in the spaces near the doors. She was squashed against the lavatory wall by a horde of young film executives who were chattering non-stop in English about how Cannes was a waste of time, except for the parties. They then started arguing about the problem of finding trustworthy funding.

Sally wondered whether any of these young men had encountered Stanislav, and winced. Had she the room, she would have put her face into her hands.

When she arrived back in Bellevue-Sur-Mer, her instinct now was to pack a suitcase, head straight to the airport and fly away. But where would she go? And even if she found somewhere, wouldn't she be taking with her the thing she was mainly running away from – herself?

How gullible and idiotic could she be? Being taken in by such an obvious conman and all because she was stupid enough to think that he fancied her.

She wondered if Jean-Philippe felt as foolish as she did. He had been used as a drug-runner by Stanislav and not even known it. Stanislav's contacts in Marseille had put the bags into Jean-Philippe's car while he was in the shop picking up the spare part for the boat. It was all on CCTV. The police even wondered whether Stanislav and his friends hadn't damaged the boat part themselves so that they could send Jean-Philippe on this fool's errand. This was particularly likely because under the terms of the charter all repairs should have been done by the rental company. But Jean-Philippe was not to know that. The authorities had let him go this morning, just before they moved in to arrest Stanislav. He would be a witness in court.

A drunken young man pushed past Sally and pulled open the lavatory door, which let out a vile odour of stagnant urine.

Sally wondered how all the others were faring. Mickey and Destiny must be feeling pretty bad too. Mickey's charity match had been marred by the arrests and he now had a huge hole in the finances of his kids' project. Mind you, thought Sally, in the world of football it shouldn't take long to make up the shortfall. Looking back, Sally realised that even Destiny had worked out more than she had. Destiny knew that not only was Stephane not a chauffeur but that he was also Russian.

Diana, too, was in a position to recover pretty quickly.

She felt most terrible about Jackie. Not only had she been lied to and for a while been physically held captive by Stanislav, he had frightened her so much that after Sally left her cowering behind the banisters that morning, Jackie had packed her bags and gone straight to the airport. Jackie was so scared of Stanislav coming after her that she had altogether given up the idea of going to the party she thought would be useful to her career and headed home. It was there, at the airport, while standing in a queue to check in, that Jackie had phoned the *gendarmes* and reported everything she'd seen. Her information was the last part of the puzzle for the police. They arrived at the airport to take her into protective custody while they swooped. They already had men at the football stadium, as usual on match days. Jean-Philippe had gone with another officer to point Stanislav out, in case he chose to mingle with the crowd. Sally was also told that the police stayed with Jean-Philippe so that he could not fore-warn her.

The train pulled to a stop. A few people got out.

Sally took a deep breath. The police had told her that they had known all week about a gang of four Russians operating in the Nice–Cannes region. Two men and a woman holed up somewhere near Nice; another man had moved over to work from Marseille. Some boy, who had passed on the initial tip-off, had been killed and dumped off the rocks just outside Nice old port ten days ago.

Sally shuddered. She wondered if Stanislav himself had taken part in the murder.

After Jackie had given the police the address in Vence, it didn't take long for them to piece everything together and pick up Stephane and Cecile. Then they went to the football stadium and arrested Stanislav himself.

Another train stop and the crush became bearable. Sally leaned on a stair rail. He had been so plausible.

Or was it simply that she had been so gullible?

How easy it was to pose as a millionaire. What did it cost to print a business card? About five pounds. Three impressive addresses, two in faraway places. All fake. The Paris and St Petersburg addresses existed on a map, so you could look them up on Google, but they had nothing whatsoever to do with Stanislav. He had had the cards made up specifically to take people in during his two weeks in Cannes. And all the time, while her heart was stupidly fluttering, Stanislav was up in the rented villa in Vence with his two partners in crime, Stephane and Cecile, organising the short operation of bringing in drugs across the Mediterranean: picking them up, dispersing them and then laundering the money in a place where no one worried too much where money came from, as long as they got it.

How had she fallen for all that romantic nonsense? She was a grown woman with grown-up children.

She thought of Marianne and Tom and their mad *amours*. As their mother, she might have lectured them in the past, but it turned out she herself was just as foolish and trusting. How could she ever again think herself in a position to give them advice when she had just been taken in by the biggest confidence trickster of them all?

Many people got out of the train at Nice, and Sally found herself a seat for the rest of the journey. Now she was surrounded only by Chinese tourists heading for Monte Carlo and the casino.

She sighed and gazed out at the diamond-studded black-silk throw of sea. All along the shore, amber-coloured lights glowed against the navy-blue sky.

Sally thanked God it was night-time, so that, when she arrived in Bellevue-Sur-Mer, she could walk with her head down, and no one would notice her pass out of the station and move along the dark alleyways leading up to her house.

Theresa was content working in the kitchen alone. Cathy had crawled down to the cellar again after a tongue-lashing from William. But, as Theresa had pointed out, it was not the girl's fault. She didn't know anything about the medallions.

Theresa was preparing desserts for Jean-Philippe, Tom and his lady friend. The old gent was munching through his starter swiftly so then she would begin frying up the fish for his main course.

To Theresa's amusement, Destiny and Mickey had asked whether they could have something simple like egg, chips and beans. William, who had been so against the idea of the café by the station, with its greasy-spoon image, had come in pressing her to indulge them: 'They're famous, Theresa. If we please them, we please the world.'

'A minute ago you didn't know who they were.'

'The critic woman is scribbling away since they came in. It's our chance.'

'Fried eggs are a doddle, and for chips they can have the *panisse* ones, like everyone else. But we have no baked beans, William. Do you want to send Benjamin up to the Huit-à-8?'

William's eyes had flared and his mouth tightened. 'Improvise!'

'How many empty tables left?'

'Five tables for four and the one Sally reserved for herself. I have to say when I see her she will be getting a rocket from me. A no-show? And she's supposed to be my friend.'

'Our friend.'

'Apparently all these others, the footballer and the boat-man, knew she was going to be here and came in specifically to talk to her. So what does Sally do? Stand us *all* up!'

William pivoted on the spot. He had intended to go back into the dining room but had seen something in there and turned now to address Theresa.

'*Zut alors!*' he cried. 'A second celebrity. It's that nutty woman from the TV show about women in the war. And she's with a *gendarme*. In uniform, if you please.'

William wheeled again, and headed in their direction.

Theresa did enjoy cooking, and due to the sluggish arrival of guests the service tonight had not been too difficult. Much as she loved the kitchen, however, she missed the chitchat, the hustle and bustle of the public side of things out there in the dining room.

It was tantalising, hearing the odd snippet of conversation, and, whenever the door opened, she might catch a glimpse of a diner as they made their way towards the washroom.

She longed to go out and walk among the tables. But that was rather naff, wasn't it? Whenever did you see a chef in the dining room, unless it was Gordon Ramsay or Marco Pierre White or someone of that ilk?

Theresa heard the rattle of the door and another gaggle of people coming in. Was that Imogen's voice, talking with some man? She could definitely hear children's high-pitched tones.

Carol swung in with a barely touched plate of apple pie, and another scribbled order.

'The ruddy big-tits woman has changed her mind *again*. She thought apple pie was the same thing as *tarte tatin*. She wants a different dessert.'

'What does she want this time?' asked Theresa.

'Ice cream.'

'No problem.' Theresa opened the freezer door and took out a couple of scoops of her home-made ice cream. 'Let me bring it to her. Please.'

'William won't like it if you come through.'

'Is Imogen here?'

'Yes. And your grandchildren. Chloe is very excited to see Destiny MacDonald.'

Theresa poured a few drips of raspberry *jus* on to the ice-cream bowl, and stuck a fan wafer in the top. 'Come on. Let's go.'

Carol shrugged. 'William won't be happy.'

The sight that greeted them took them both by surprise. The three children were grabbing on to the legs of the moustached old-gentleman tourist, while Tom's lady friend was bent over and appeared to be bashing him over the head with her notebook.

The old gentleman grabbed the woman's head and shoved it down into his dessert.

'Good God!' said Theresa. 'That man! It's my ex-husband!'

The woman pulled herself up into a standing position and turned to face Theresa.

'You?' she shrieked, taking a step in Theresa's direction.

Theresa meanwhile took a step back. 'Annunziata?'

'Theresa!'

'Peter!'

'Brandad! Brandma!'

'Daddy! Mummy! Annunziata!'

The other guests sat staring in amazement as the Simmonds family recognised and recoiled from one another.

Tom got to his feet and hollered, 'Signora Simmonds, what is going on?'

Theresa looked round at Tom, but it was Annunziata who yelled: 'Mind your own business!'

Then both Annunziata and Theresa turned and advanced on Peter Simmonds, their mutual ex-husband.

Now it was Imogen who stood up and started to shout.

'Annunziata! I had no idea you would be here. Why would you be here? You're in Italy.'

'I was advised to come here by my idiot of a design assistant, Tom Connor. I was due to write an article about this pathetic little town, with its manky hotel and this excuse for a restaurant. That is, if it's any of *your* business.' Annunziata brought herself up to her full height and gave Imogen the once-over. 'I see, Imogen, that you remain as irritating as you were when you were a child, only now you share the interfering tendencies of your cow of a mother.'

Tom put his face in his hands.

'No! Signora Simmonds!'

Annunziata swung round, pointed at Tom and said, 'You're fired!'

Meanwhile Theresa turned to Peter.

'What the hell are you doing here? Go away, Peter. Leave me alone.'

'It's my fault,' yelled Imogen. 'I invited Daddy here because . . .'

'I know why you did it!' screamed Annunziata. 'That idiot ex-assistant of mine told you I'd be here in this poxy place and you wanted to lumber him on me again. But those days are over, Imogen, since the moment I caught him sleeping with the skivvy.'

'No, no, no!' shouted Imogen. 'That's not it at all.'

'Enough!' Tom marched across the dining-room floor. 'I am nobody's idiot.'

William grabbed at him. 'You can't leave us now.'

'I'm going to find out what's kept my mother,' said Tom. 'She is never late like this.'

Destiny, Mickey, Jackie and Jean-Philippe rose to speak but were silenced by Peter, who moved in on wife number two, shouting: 'I wouldn't ever get back with you, Annunziata. Not if you were the last woman on earth.'

'Aha! I get it!' Theresa had been staring at Imogen. Finally the penny dropped and she rejoined the fray. 'Now I see why you invited your father here. You needed to get him out of *your* house, so you thought you'd dump him on *me*, hoping that he could live in *mine*.'

'Sorry, Mummy.' Imogen shrugged. 'It was an idea . . .' Her voice fizzled out.

William took charge. 'Can we have some calm here, please? Theresa, take your family squabble outside. There are people trying to eat.'

He swept his arm around, indicating the other tables where Jackie, Destiny, Mickey and Jean-Philippe were watching, open-mouthed.

'What? Outside for the paparazzi?' Carol stood arms spread, barring the exit. 'And get the whole thing photographed and filmed. That is *not* the sort of front page we're after, sweetie.'

Peter picked up a bread roll from Jackie's table, and flung it at Annunziata. Annunziata seized the melting ice cream from Theresa's hand and brought it down on Peter's head.

'Don't they say that no publicity is bad publicity?' said Benjamin weakly, as the door behind him opened.

'What a load of total bollocks,' replied William.

'I say! What a turn-up!' said Jackie to her *gendarme* friend. 'Do things like this happen often here in *la belle France?*'

'*Les anglais sont fou!*' he replied. 'What they say? Mad cooooos!'

Diana Sparks stood alone at the welcome desk.

She took in the scene. Three children tearing at Annunziata's clothing, while in turn she bashed Peter, who threw rolls towards Theresa, who scowled at Imogen, who was sobbing, while all the other diners sat like spectators in the Colosseum, enjoying the rowdy show.

'Who do I have to shag round here,' she shouted above the din, 'to get a table for two?'

The room fell silent.

376

No one moved.

All eyes were on Diana Sparks. But then they re-focused to look at the woman who had followed her into the restaurant and who now stood behind her.

Resplendent in a red floor-length gown was none other than the multi-Oscar-winning American film star, Marina Martel.

31

I N THE TIME IT took Tom to persuade Sally to join him for dinner, a lot had gone on at La Mosaïque.

Annunziata and Peter left together, leaving the dining room in relative peace.

Jackie's *gendarme* had put on his cap and gone through to the back to speak privately with William and Theresa and let them know that any money Stanislav had put in their account had been withdrawn by the police. After that, duty done, he had taken off his cap and jacket and rejoined Jackie for dinner. 'My guardian angel,' she said to Destiny, at the adjacent table. 'He took me from the airport to the police HQ so that I could spill the beans on the Russkie rotter. And now he's off duty, we're on a date.'

Theresa, William and Carol shuffled over to the table where Zoe sat, alone, tucking into her battered fish and *panisse* chips.

'We're sorry if we tried to shake you off,' said William.

'It was all such a panic,' added Carol. 'Nothing personal.'

Zoe looked up through reptilian eyes.

William pulled Zoe's cheque out of his pocket. 'Can we . . . ?'

'You can do whatever you like,' said Zoe. 'But I only wanted to join up so I could have a share of the Chagall. Now what would be the point?'

William held up the cheque. 'Shall I tear it up?'

Zoe pursed her lips, a difficult job. 'No. Go on. Count me in. I like the idea of owning a restaurant. But I'll want the odd freebie. This grub is pretty delicious.'

Jackie, the *gendarme*, Destiny and Mickey leaned over the gap between their tables to discuss what each of their involvement with Stanislav Serafim had cost them.

'It was me who grassed him up,' said Jackie with some pride. 'He tried to kill me this morning, you know. Up at some villa near Vence. But luckily I had learned many escape techniques while rehearsing for *Skirts Fly Over Suffolk*.'

'Like kneeing him in the knackers?' asked Destiny, miming out a karate attack. 'Take that, Stanislav Serapig!'

Having already had three coffees, Jean-Philippe remained alone at his corner table, picking at a plate of *petits fours*. At Stanislav's name he looked up.

'*Vous aussi?*' he said to Destiny. 'My English not too good. But Stanislav . . . bad crook.'

'Bad crook is putting it kindly,' said Mickey. 'He's what we in England call a conniving twisted lying bastard.'

Imogen, now contrite at having been the cause of the catastrophic reunion that had all but wrecked her mother's opening night, sat solemnly in another corner, surrounded by three very quiet little girls.

Diana explained to William that, like many others, she had left the Brits in Film party early, after the police arrived to tell a number of guests that their finances had been breached by Stanislav's fake promises. The atmosphere had become far too gloomy. Marina Martel had heard the news and told Diana how Stanislav had taken her to lunch rather showily at Le Negresco. But his smooth ways had instantly put her hackles up, and she had, thankfully, eschewed his offer. While Marina and Diana exchanged their stories they decided to escape together, to get out of town and go eat. Marina asked her driver to bring them to Bellevue-Sur-Mer.

Her bodyguards were waiting outside, she told William. If he could perhaps offer them a table . . . ?

In the kitchen Theresa had gone into a robotic state, too busy now to rewind the dramatic and unpleasant scenes between herself, her ex-husband and her ex-nanny. She would definitely have words later with her daughter, but meanwhile . . . there were diners to be served.

Cathy, who had come up to join them from the cellar, was the only one who seemed unfazed by the recent commotion. She whirled round the kitchen like a dervish, grabbing plates, taking ingredients from the fridge and larder, helping to fry fish and *panisse*, and plating up. She snatched the orders from Carol's hands and whizzed back to Theresa with them, then seized fully prepared plates and laid them on the pass. She was a woman transformed.

As he steered his mother in through the front door of La Mosaïque, Tom put his arm around her. Most of the photographers had packed up and gone home to bed – they had their shot for tomorrow's gossip column. 'Hollywood star shines at local restaurant opening.'

Tom had told her about the scenes in the restaurant, which had marred the early part of the evening.

'Honestly, Mum,' he said. 'How the hell was I to know my new boss was the woman who had run off with Theresa's husband? What a small world, eh?'

Sally listened to Tom talking about Theresa's ordeal, and realised that, however foolish she had been over Stanislav, she was not the sole focus of everyone's attention.

Tom was right. It really was a small world and life was short. Late in life, both she and Theresa had been humiliated over love.

She stepped quietly over the threshold into the restaurant.

'You took your time,' said William, by way of a greeting. 'Where's the ruddy Russian? He did us in, you know.'

'From what I gather,' said Sally, taking her seat at a corner table, 'he did everyone in. Now let's forget him.'

She held her menu up to hide her face while she made her choice.

Then Carol came over to take her order.

'That boyfriend of yours suckered us,' she said.

32

THERESA'S WORK FOR THE night was coming to an end. Apart from Sally's dishes, all the main courses had gone out and the desserts on tonight's menu only required plating.

'May I go out and say hello to my mama now?' asked Cathy, her eyes like an eager puppy-dog.

Theresa waved her off.

When Cathy was gone, Theresa flopped down on a stool and wiped her brow. She was knackered. Was this what she had signed up for?

Imogen had imagined she had come to Bellevue-Sur-Mer to relax her remaining days away with her feet up, preferably in slippers. But Theresa liked to be busy. Maybe not quite this busy, but ... Even though she was doing a job she loved, something else was lacking.

She thought about it for a few seconds and realised what that thing was.

'How are you doing?' Sally stood at the door to the kitchen. 'Tom told me about what happened here earlier.'

'Looking back, we'll all have a good laugh about it, I'm sure, Sally.' Theresa shrugged. 'I hear you also were rather let down.'

Sally smiled and closed the door behind her. 'We're a pair of old fools, aren't we?'

'Less of the old,' said Theresa, patting the stool beside her, inviting Sally to sit.

'Look, Theresa, I know I was evasive about it all from the start, but what would you say if I wanted to be part of this? Would you be put out if I offered to help you in the kitchen?'

Theresa leaned back against the cool white wall.

'Do you know, Sally, I've been thinking all night long what a lonely life this job might turn out to be. Having a friend in here cooking with me sounds like a wonderful idea.'

'Are you serious?' said Sally, sitting next to Theresa. 'I cannot think of anything that would be more rewarding, and more fun.'

The kitchen door burst open and Cathy rushed in. 'I was telling Mummy and her friend about that horrible man. Can I show them the Lion thing?'

Theresa nodded and Cathy grabbed the lime-green bag that Vito had so angrily flung to the floor. She ran back to the dining room with it.

'She's a sweet kid, really,' said Theresa. 'But a bit of a klutz. She's good as an assistant, when she's actually in the room, but it would be nice to share the work with a true pal.'

'What's going on now?' asked Sally.

They could hear sounds of another small commotion coming from the dining room. Together they moved to the door to take a peek.

Diana was standing up, holding the piece of mosaic, with William, Benjamin and Carol gathered round her table.

'Theresa!' called William. 'Quickly!'

Theresa took Sally by the arm. 'Come on. Let's have a squint at what's up.'

Diana was speaking earnestly, while, at her side, Marina Martel's eyes popped. They were holding the mosaic medallion between them.

'When it fell on the hard floor the copper band broke off,' said William, his face slightly flushed with excitement. 'But just look what's underneath!'

Theresa peered down at the greyish side of the medallion, as Zoe rose from her table and crept forward to join them.

'It looks like a signature, carved into the wet cement,' said Theresa.

'What does it say?' asked Sally, screwing up her eyes.

'That's not anything *like* the name Marc Chagall,' said Zoe with an enormous sigh.

'That's because it says Picasso.'

'Picasso?'

'Picasso!'

'Picasso!!!'

'Thank you, God,' Zoe crossed herself, 'for letting me buy in, just in time.'

'Excuse me?' Throughout all this excitement over the mosaic medallion, Marina Martel had been staring at Sally. She spoke in a deep Texan drawl. 'Aren't you Sally Doyle?'

Sally nodded.

'I cannot tell you how thrilled I am to meet you.'

'Meet *me*?' said Sally.

'Yeah. I thought I saw you at my movie première. That was you, wasn't it?'

Sally thought back to the night in the Cinema Lumière, when Ted had made his unwelcome appearance and she thought that she and Marina Martel had briefly caught eyes.

'I was there,' said Sally. 'At the side, near the front.'

'I knew it was you! I used to watch you every Saturday, when my pa was stationed over in the UK – Greenham Common. I loved the funny faces you pulled in the skits, and . . . all the gloop.'

'*Sccerrrunch!*' said Sally.

'*Sccerrrunch!* Yes. That was it.' Marina Martel looked at Sally as though she was the fan and Sally the movie star. 'It was because of you I became an actress.' She touched Sally's arm. 'Look, sweetie, I'm going to start rolling on a new movie I'm directing. We're shooting hereabouts, and there's a little role in the script, and you would be just dandy in the part. Would you care to join us?'

Sally looked around at her friends' eager faces.

In the corner Jean-Philippe was standing beside Tom. Both men were grinning; to her side Destiny and Jackie looked up with wide eyes; and, close enough to hug, stood William, Benjamin, Carol and Theresa, all hanging on Sally's reply.

Sally thought of golden opportunities and how they panned out, about how often promised gold turned to lead. And, for all the funny stories and earnest trials, the adulation and the applause, Sally knew she was no longer cut out for the world of drama.

Sally knew where she would prefer to be.

'Miss Martel, I could not be more flattered that you thought of me,' said Sally. 'But do you know what I just signed up for a new job.'

She faced Theresa.

'Can I start my apprenticeship now?'

'If you're sure.' Theresa held out her hand. 'Let's go, kid.'

Theresa and Sally shook.

Theresa looked around the dining room and burst out laughing.

'Everyone got their desserts?'

ÎLES FLOTTANTES with CRÈME ANGLAISE

Îles flottantes
3 egg whites
100g caster sugar
milk, for poaching

Whip the egg whites to stiff peaks, gradually stir in the sugar and whisk till smooth and glossy. To poach the individual meringues, carefully drop tablespoons of the egg white/sugar mixture in a frying pan of warm simmering milk for 30 seconds, then turn and give them another 30 seconds. Drain and leave on a baking tray until the custard is prepared

Crème Anglaise
250ml milk
250ml single cream
1 vanilla pod, halved and scraped
5 egg yolks
120g caster sugar
toasted flaked almonds

Infuse milk and cream with the vanilla pod in a small saucepan and bring to the boil. Remove from heat. In a separate bowl, mix the egg yolks with the caster sugar. Remove the vanilla pod from the milk/cream mix, then slowly whisk the cream mixture into the yolks. Return the custard to the pan on a low heat for a few minutes, stirring continuously, until the mixture is thick enough to coat the back of a wooden spoon.

Sieve into a clean bowl then serve on wide plates. Place the meringue 'islands' on top and decorate with the almonds.

33

AFTER THE SHAKY START, La Mosaïque became a winner. It was popular with tourists and locals alike. People liked the quirky atmosphere and the badinage between the team who ran the place, and said so (in glowing terms) on all the appropriate websites.

By the end of the season they were turning a profit and had also, thanks to Zoe's cheque, bought the building and all its contents.

Costanzo's Uncle Vito had since been picked up, arrested and imprisoned on separate charges by Italian police.

The Chagall medallion passed into the ownership of Costanzo, who, out of the profits from its sale, now runs a business along the coast, just over the Italian border, hiring out sea-bikes and kayaks.

Stanislav and his gang are in prison in France, awaiting extradition to various other countries around Europe, where the police have similar stories, and further charges to press.

Destiny and Mickey continue to lead a charmed and charming life. They send the occasional postcard from glamorous spots around the world addressed to Sally and all the staff at La Mosaïque.

Both Jackie's and Diana's projects found new, genuine funding and are in pre-production. They both hope that the films they make will get on the list for a future festival at Cannes.

Cathy works most nights at La Mosaïque. But she's heading back to England once her mother's current film contract comes to an end.

Zoe still regularly pops off to the hairdresser's only to reappear with a new set of lips and a very shiny-smooth forehead.

William and Benjamin happily divide their time between squabbling and making up, while Carol is now renting a stunning studio apartment with a ravishing view of the sea. She slinks about town in her chic suits, with matching gloves and handbags, and few people ever notice the deep voice or Adam's apple.

Sally's son Tom has a small shop in Rue Droite in the Old Town of Nice, where he sells enough paintings to make a small but sufficient living, while his sister Marianne is working in the City in London, with little time for poets or trips to the South of France.

Imogen is back in London, now that her father has moved out, and Theresa's grandchildren are doing very well in school, excelling in French. Theresa wishes she could learn as fast.

Now that they have settled permanently in Darling Point, Sydney, everyone has all but forgotten Sian and Ted. They occupy a very grand apartment overlooking the harbour and the Opera House. 'Just as good as Bellevue-Sur-Mer – in fact better!' Sian wrote to Sally on the back of a recent postcard. (She can't help herself, thought Sally.)

Sally is enjoying her time working at La Mosaïque. On her nights off she goes for the occasional dinner or to the cinema with Jean-Philippe. There is nothing romantic between them. She is content to enjoy his company, their shared remembrance of being duped by a charismatic conman and the odd trip out to sea together.

Theresa is very happy to hear that her ex-husband has got back together with the busty former nanny, Annunziata. She is only too glad to be out of all that stuff.

She rises each morning with a purpose and the knowledge that she is surrounded by friends.

She still manages the occasional morning slumped in an armchair with a coffee and the morning paper, though, all in all, she prefers knowing that her days may be busy, but they will not be dull. She is sure that, in moving to Bellevue-Sur-Mer, she made the best decision of her life.

The Picasso mosaic is in Paris, waiting for its date to come up in the auction house's sale calendar.

Acknowledgements

Thank you to:

Charles, Raymond, Daniel, Gilbert and all our friends
at Le Safari
All my friends at La Civette
Daniel, Gianni and Fabrizio at Jardins du Capitole
Fidelis Morgan – superior five-star travel agent
My favourite Gardienne – Lina
Nerys and Patrick
The organisers of the Cannes Film Festival
Madame Jacqueline Harroch and Dominique and
Gaëlle at Le 8 Couture, Nice
Manager at Terminus Nord
OGC, Nice
Manager at Auberge Saint-Antoine
The kind staff at Le Negresco
Kiaran MacDonald, managing director, and the staff
at the Savoy, London
Angus
Constance Vanuxeem

ALSO AVAILABLE BY CELIA IMRIE

NOT QUITE NICE

A *SUNDAY TIMES* BESTSELLER

Theresa is desperate for a change. Forced into early retirement, tired of baby-sitting her bossy daughter's obnoxious children, she sells her house and moves to a picture-perfect town, just outside Nice. Once the hideaway of artists and writers, Bellevue-Sur-Mer is now home to the odd movie star and, as Theresa discovers, a close-knit set of expats. Settling to the gentle rhythm of the seaside, Theresa embraces her new-found friendships and freedom. But life is never as simple as it seems, and when skeletons fall out of several closets, Theresa starts to wonder if life on the French Riviera is quite as nice as it first appeared…

'A very witty novel by a very witty woman'
JULIAN FELLOWES

'A shaft of early summer sunshine, a funny, spirited read'
WENDY HOLDEN, DAILY MAIL

'A hugely enjoyable romp of a novel with eccentric characters, a delightful background and a savoury tang of crime'
KATIE FFORDE